Finding Fare

Faith, Family, Friends & Horses
Book 3

Linda Amick Algire

2021
Ava Lorren,
Enjoy the story!
Linda Algire

Fawn Song Books

York, South Carolina

Cover Artwork & Design Kayleen MacDonald
Book Layout © 2017 Book Design Templates
Copyediting by Espoir Editing

Finding Fare/ Linda Amick Algire—1st ed.

ISBN 978-1-7337884-8-9 (Hard Cover Edition)
ISBN 978-1-7337884-7-2 (Paperback Edition)
ISBN 978-1-7337884-6-5 (Kindle eBook)

Library of Congress Control Number: 2020910935

Printed in the United States of America

For **Ralph and Joyce Napotnik**
Maple Spring Morgan Farm

In honor of their mission to save the endangered Lambert
Morgan horses, and in tribute to their very own Fare—
Quietude Fare Thee Well.

I would like to thank my test readers
Adrian Algire, Anna Newman, and **Stacy Peters**
—their honest comments and insights always make my
stories better.

Also by Linda Amick Algire

Trusting Truth
Faith, Family, Friends & Horses in Appleridge, Book 2

Gathering Goodness
Faith, Family, Friends & Horses in Appleridge, Book 1

Thank You God for Everything—Especially Horses

My Horse Flicka
Short Story, Horse Tales for the Soul, Vol. 1

Welcome to Appleridge!

Find a comfy chair, kick off your boots, grab a glass of cold ice tea, and get cozy!

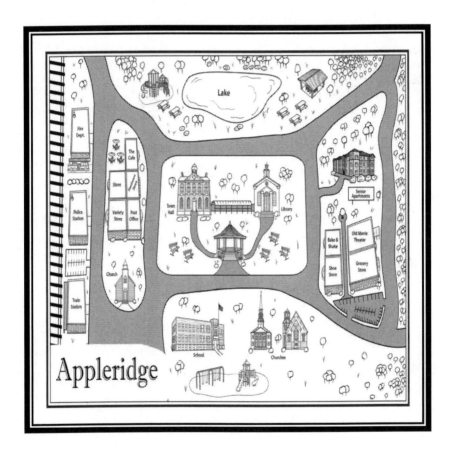

May the grace of the Lord Jesus Christ, and the love of God,
and the fellowship of the Holy Spirit be with you all.
2 Corinthians 13:14 NIV

Be kind and compassionate to one another, forgiving each
other, just as in Christ God forgave you.

Ephesians 4:32 NIV

Cast of Characters

In Alphabetical Order

Lainie Anderson—Lainie, aka Elaine, has recently reunited with her mother, Constance, after years of estrangement. She runs a small business, Lessons with Lainie, teaching horsemanship.

Kerry Casin—Heart and soul of Save a Morgan Rescue along with Deb Thompkins.

Charles Gantzler—Also known as Charlie, an active senior citizen. He loves root beer, horses, and his granddaughter, Jennie McKenzie—not necessarily in that order!

Sam Garrett—High school friend of Belinda Peterson, Jennie McKenzie, and Jeremy James. Sam is a hard-working talented farrier, and boards his Quarter Horse, Sadie, at Jennie's barn.

Jeremy James— Jeremy is *in love* with Jennie, although she teased Jeremy in high school, calling him the boy with two first names. He is currently attending seminary in Columbus, Ohio and serves as a mission trip leader.

Edward and Ellen McKenzie—Jennie's parents. Jennie's dad is retired and makes chairs and benches for fun.

Jennie McKenzie—Jennie works for the *Farm & Family Country Chronicle*, known locally as the CC. She has a horse named Mint Julep, and also boards horses at her farm. Jennie is *in love* with Jeremy James.

Wilson Mark—Wilson is Jennie's boss. He owns the *Farm & Family Country Chronicle*.

Elizabeth Miller—Elizabeth is a young Amish widow, mother to Charlie, Micah, and baby Mary Ann.

Charlie Miller—Charlie *rides like the wind*. He dreams of following in his father's footsteps raising Morgan horses.

Cassy Morton—Cassy boards her horse, Treasure Trove, at Lainie's barn while she attends college in Richburg, Ohio. Cassy loves to jump Treasure; the higher the better.

Dr. Adrian Peterson—Adrian is a local veterinarian and the father of Belinda (Jennie's best friend) and Megan. He leased his barn and acreage to Lainie to *get out of the horse business.* He and his wife, Susan, live on the farm in their restored farm house.

Belinda Peterson—Belinda is Jennie's best friend and currently a veterinary student at the University of Florida. She and Sam are a couple.

Megan Peterson—After a failed internship with a horse trainer with attitude, she rescued a young horse, Starlight, and returned to Appleridge to finish her senior year of high school.

Barton Shaw—Barton, sometimes simply called Bart, manages the family grocery, Mark's Market, in Engleton, Ohio.

Margaret Shaw—Margaret lives in Engleton, Ohio and is the mother of Trina and Barton.

Trina Shaw—Trina owns a small boarding barn, Loving Life Farm, in Appleridge, Ohio. Her story is just waiting to be told.

Amos and Agnes Stoltz—An older Amish couple, parents of Elizabeth Miller, and grandparents of Charlie, Micah, and baby Mary Ann Miller.

Marcy Streeter—When she isn't working long shifts as an RN at Appleridge Community Hospital, Marcy hitches her ponies, Riley and Stuffin, to a marathon carriage and competes in combined driving events.

Deb Thompkins—Heart and soul of Save a Morgan Rescue along with Kerry Casin

Mrs. Williams—Sweet older widow and Charlie Gantzler's *lady friend.*

Cast of Characters—Animals

Horses

Mint Julep—Jennie's childhood horse, sold to Megan while Jennie attended college, returned to Jennie when she finished college. Julep is a bay American Quarter Horse mare.

Melody May—A chocolate chestnut Morgan mare introduced in this story.

My Fare Thee Well—A Lambert Morgan gelding. This is Fare's story.

Oscar—A bay Lambert Morgan gelding introduced in this story.

Riley and Stuffin—Marcy's Welsh ponies. Riley is an ornery bay gelding, and Stuffin is a sweet gray mare. Marcy drives them in competitions as a pair.

Sadie—Sam's palomino Quarter Horse cross. Sam waited his entire life for a horse of his own.

Shadow Me—Lainie Anderson's rescued Quarter Horse and love of her life.

Starlight—A chestnut Quarter Horse mare Megan rescued from the Double J program. She is young but willing.

Treasure Trove—A Dutch Warmblood, liver chestnut color, owned by Cassy Morton.

Cat

Beauty—A black cat that owns Jennie.

Dog

Moose—A large, shaggy black dog owned by Mrs. Williams. Likes to cause a bit of trouble and loves belly rubs.

Chapter One

"I don't see anything that looks like a Morgan horse going through the sale. Let's take a peek at the horses behind the barn."

Kerry thought this was the worst job ever. She hated looking at the horses behind the big barn—horses sold in back door deals to meat buyers. How many times would her heart break, seeing the horses squeezed into pens, waiting for their nasty trip to slaughter?

Deb nodded. "At least the horses actually going through the sale have a chance to end up in a good home. These guys back here never have a chance." She shook her head. "It never gets any easier."

As volunteers for Save a Morgan Rescue, Kerry Casin and Deb Thomkins visited the sale looking for horses in danger. They would do whatever they could to get a horse to safety quickly, and with very limited funds they weren't always successful. They couldn't save them all, but they tried to save a few.

The various rescues worked together; some, like the Morgan rescue, focused on a particular breed of horse. The kill buyers liked working with the rescue groups—not out of compassion, but out of greed. It was easy money selling to a rescue, knowing those horse lovers would move heaven and earth to raise the funds. If they couldn't raise the money, too bad. The kill buyers could still turn a profit by throwing the horse on the next load leaving for the slaughter plant. It didn't make any difference to them. Money was money.

"Kerry, look." Deb stopped and grabbed Kerry's arm. "That's got to be a Morgan. The skinny chestnut with the really light mane and tail."

"Let's talk to the dealer. We've gotten horses from him before. His name is Mack. He'll talk."

"Hello, ladies. Which one can I send home with you today? I bet it's that little chestnut. I think I have some papers on him, too. Well, at least I did. Might of thrown them in the trash. It's not like he'll need them where he's going." He snorted and held out his hand. Neither Kerry nor Deb offered their hands in return. They didn't respond to Mack's sick humor. Instead, they focused on the gelding. This was business—a business they hated.

"He's a Morgan?" Kerry was pretty sure he was.
"Yup, pure blooded. I can let you have him for a little over my cost. Let's say $750 and he's yours. He's a *little worse for the wear*, as my grandma liked to say. If he had a few more pounds on him, I'd get more money."

Kerry wondered if Mack's grandma would think he was a *little worse for the wear* for doing what he was doing. She reached for the papers he offered. Maybe they could contact a few of the names listed. Sometimes a former owner would donate funds.

"How much time do we have?" Their bank account was gasping. Deb would need to make a few calls begging for donations and also get a campaign running on social media as soon as possible.

"Well, I can give you until 9:00 tonight." The dealer grinned, revealing tobacco-stained teeth.

"That's not much time. Can you give us a day or maybe two?" Kerry hated pleading but she'd do it for the horse.

"Naw, sorry. There's a truck leaving tonight." Mack didn't look very sorry.

"Could you at least get him out of this pen?" The pen was crowded with scared horses. Deb didn't want the little guy to get kicked or injured.

The horse turned his head and gazed with soft brown eyes at the girls. It was as if he was saying, "I know you're trying to help me."

"Are you interested? If not, he'll be just fine where he is."

"We're interested. We just need to get the money together." Kerry somehow kept her tone friendly. She should get an academy award. What a sleaze! She wanted to give old Mack a piece of her mind but first they had a horse to save.

"Show me the money and we'll talk. And, ladies, you only have seven hours so I would hurry if I was you." Mack turned and chuckled as he walked back to the barn.

Kerry turned to look at Deb who was already on her phone.

Chapter Two

*L*ife was sometimes like a train. Just when you think life is chugging along smoothly, you hit a bad stretch of track, and it becomes rough for a little while.

Trina Shaw figured her life was about to change. She just didn't know how much. Today, waiting for a horse; praying for his safety, it felt like a bad stretch of track.

Trina paced the barn aisle waiting—every few seconds walking to the door, looking down the long drive. *What's that? A truck?* She sighed. It was a truck, but it wasn't pulling a horse trailer. Then she smiled. The candy apple red truck belonged to her friend, Lainie Anderson, and Lainie wasn't alone. Jennie McKenzie and Marcy Streeter climbed out of the truck along with Lainie.

"Are you excited?" Lainie reached Trina first and gave her a hug. "I hope you don't mind." She glanced at Marcy and Jennie. "I called the gang after I read your text."

Trina nodded her approval and brushed a tear. "I don't know what to think. What if he's in bad shape? What if he's suffered and lost all trust in people? What if I can't help him?"

"Whoa, Trina!" Marcy placed her hand gently on Trina's arm. "You'll just do the best you can, and he'll live the rest of his life, however long, with dignity and love."

Jennie nodded. "And we'll help. Have you heard anything from the rescue?"

"They pulled him from the slaughter pen and were able to get him to a friend's farm for the night. The rescue has a good reputation with the local vet. He came out early this morning to issue the necessary health papers so they could bring him across state lines. I haven't gotten a call or text this morning."

"That's good news. I'm excited for you—and him. I want to hear the whole story!" Lainie motioned toward the bench in the barn aisle. "Come on! A good story will help pass the time while we wait."

Jennie walked to Lainie's truck and pulled out a small cooler. "And I have some cold tea and a few snacks."

Trina found two folding camp chairs and the four friends sat—two on the bench, two in chairs—drinking, eating, watching, listening. At least her friends were eating. Trina wasn't interested in food, but she could talk.

"I got a call late yesterday afternoon from Save a Morgan Rescue. They wanted to know if I was Trina Shaw and if I remembered a small chestnut Morgan with a white mane and tail."

"And you did!" Her three friends encouraged.

"His name is My Fare Thee Well—I called him Fare." She smiled at a memory. "Sometimes I called him The Trickster. He was a pretty smart pony and was always getting into something—or out of something." Trina smiled. "I wonder if he's still so ornery?"

"Wait, I'm confused, I've seen a lot of Morgan horses at carriage driving competitions and I don't think chestnut with a white mane and tail is all that common for a Morgan." Marcy competed with her two Welsh ponies named Riley and Stuffin.

"No, I guess it isn't, except for a family of Morgan horses called Lamberts. They trace back to a Morgan sire named, Daniel Lambert. I didn't think too much about it as a kid. I just loved him. I'm going to dig a little deeper into his history now."

"You called him a pony? Is it because of his size?" Lainie placed her empty plastic cup on the cement barn floor.

"He's a horse by breed, but when measured, he doesn't quite make it to horse size, so he would fall into the pony classification. Even so, he was always a sturdy fellow." Trina sat back in her chair, thinking about what to say next. "I didn't sell him because I outgrew him. He was sold when I left for college."

"Boy, do I know that scenario." Jennie remembered the day she sold her horse, Julep, before moving to Chicago to begin college.

"And now you have Julep back and Trina will have Fare back. So exciting!" Lainie was happy and excited for both of her friends. "Go on, Trina, tell us the rest of the story."

"Somehow Fare ended up at a sale in Pennsylvania. The rescue found him in a pen of horses waiting for a trip to Canada—for slaughter. They didn't have the funds to get him out, so they started fundraising. They saw my name, as a former owner, on his papers, and tracked me down through the registry. They wanted to know if I would donate, and if possible, give him a home. If they raised the money, they still needed a place to keep him safe. Of course, I said, yes! I sent his entire bail via PayPal. They got him out of the pen with only minutes to spare last night."

"Was it much?" Jennie leaned forward in her chair. "Do you need us to chip in?"

"No, thanks. The price per pound, according to the kill buyers, is high right now, but I would have mortgaged the farm to save Fare."

"And you trust this rescue?" Marcy was a bit skeptical.

"I've donated to this group many times. They do good work. I just hate how those kill buyers are making money selling horses for slaughter. What kind of person does that for a living?"

Marcy wasn't convinced yet. "I thought they closed all the horse slaughter plants."

"Yes, in the United States, so now they haul horses to Canada or Mexico where it's legal."

"I can't believe his registration papers were with him at the sale. What a lucky break for him." Lainie found that interesting.

"I think someone cared about him and thought he would get a better home if buyers knew he was a registered Morgan. I'm surprised he didn't go through the sale, though. I suppose, if he's in bad shape, he wouldn't have much of a chance of finding a good home." Trina was preparing for the worse possible scenario.

Jennie worked at the Farm & Family Country Chronicle, and as a writer, she smelled a possible story. "I've heard kill buyers travel around to the sales looking for cheap horses. They make a promise to the family selling the horse—telling them the horse will have a good home and be loved by children. It's all a lie."

"Anyone selling a horse for under $800, or advertises it free to a good home, should be very careful. The kill buyers look for horses selling for less than what they'll get from the slaughter plant, and tell lies to make a profit." Trina shuddered. "And my poor Fare ended up in a kill pen." She swallowed. "I'm afraid he's not doing very well."

"Did the rescue say anything about his condition?" Jennie wondered if they should have Dr. Peterson prepared for a farm visit.

"They said he is really skinny, has a dull coat, and his feet need attention. It looks like he needs a lot of love and care." Trina hated thinking about Fare in such bad shape.

"Sometimes people try to save money or lose interest and forget they still need to take care of a horse. It's sad." Marcy saw the worry on Trina's face and wanted to offer a bit of encouragement. "TLC does do wonders. Riley and Stuffin are the proof. They came to me underweight because the family who loved them lost interest, and basically didn't want to spend money on their care and cut corners."

"You're right. I've already called Dr. Peterson to come out tomorrow morning to give him a good going over. I'm keeping him away from the other horses until I know he isn't carrying anything harmful. I have to keep my boarders' horses safe." Trina took good care of the five horses on her farm, belonging to five different owners, and she loved them all—horses and humans.

"I'm sure all your boarders will be here tonight to meet Fare." Jennie smiled.

"It all happened so fast, I'm not sure if they know. It doesn't seem like time is moving fast right now, though. I sure wish he would get here." She glanced at her phone. "Oh wait, I have a text. They're about thirty minutes out."

"Where are you putting him?" Lainie looked around.

"In the paddock beside the barn. He'll have a little cover under the roof overhang but won't be able to touch noses with any of the other horses. I'll keep them in the pasture on the other side. I'll ask Dr. Peterson how long he should be in quarantine. Who knows what he could have picked up at the sale—or before?"

Trina got up to pace again. She was excited. She was afraid. And she was very thankful her friends were waiting with her.

Jennie wished Jeremy, her boyfriend and a good friend to Trina, Lainie, and Marcy, was with them. She thought this was a good time for a prayer and he prayed beautiful prayers. Maybe she could say something? She took a deep breath. "Hey, guys, I sort of think this would be a good time for a prayer. Where is Jeremy when you need him?" They all laughed. They all loved Jeremy and his prayers. Jennie glanced around the group as they stood and took one another's hands.

"Father, we thank you for this day. We thank you for giving Trina the chance to help her much-loved Fare. Please give her guidance as she takes care of Fare. Help him to arrive safely and heal both emotionally and physically. In your name we pray, Amen."

"That was nice, Jennie, thanks." Trina went to the same church as Jennie and Lainie. Marcy didn't attend a church, but she believed in the power of prayer.

All four heard an engine and looked down the drive and grinned—a truck pulling a horse trailer. Fare was here!

.

DEB THOMPKINS AND KERRY CASIN climbed out of the older model truck and stretched. They were exhausted from the stress of getting the horse safe and away from the sale barn last night, and then getting up at dawn to meet the vet and then haul Fare to his new home. This rescue work wasn't for the faint of heart—in many ways.

Trina walked quickly to the truck. "Hi, I'm Trina. We talked last night." She motioned for her friends. "And these are my good friends, Marcy, Jennie, and Lainie."

"I'm Kerry and this is Deb. We have your boy. He's a sweetie, that's for sure. I'm so happy we found you. I don't think we would have raised enough money in time."

Trina hesitated before asking, "How is he?"

"Like we talked about last night, very thin. Life wasn't treating him well."

Lainie spoke up. "Until now."

Kerry smiled. "Yes, until now. Let's get him off the trailer."

Deb was already opening the back door and lowering the ramp. Kerry opened the side door and reached in to untie the gelding.

Trina heard a soft nicker and peeked in the door. She would know those eyes anywhere. "Oh, Fare." She couldn't stop the tears if she tried, so she didn't try.

Fare backed slowly down the trailer ramp and stood quietly. He was a dirty, skinny mess. "Oh, Fare." Trina sobbed again as she placed her head next to his and heard another nicker. He lifted his head and sniffed her face.

"I think he remembers you." Jennie was sure he did.

"Let's get him in the paddock so he can move around. I talked to Dr. Peterson and he said to give him hay and water but nothing else yet."

Trina led him into the paddock and took off the rope halter. Fare stood quietly by her side; eyes focused on the pile of hay.

"Go ahead, boy; it's all for you." Trina walked over to the hay and Fare followed.

The group stood at the fence and watched as Fare lowered his head to eat. He seemed content. No one said anything for a few minutes. They just watched the horse as he ate, all the while, watching them.

Trina motioned for the group to follow her. "As much as I want to stand here and stare at Fare, let's give him some time alone to relax and eat." She looked at Kerry and Deb. "You've had a long trip. Let's go up to the house. Are you hungry?"

"Thanks. I would love something cold to drink and to use your bathroom. But we won't stay. If we leave soon, we could get home before dark." Kerry sounded as tired as she looked.

"I have an extra room and you're welcome to spend the night." Trina thought the ladies looked too tired to get back in the truck for the drive home.

Kerry looked at Deb. "Do you need to be home?"

"No, but I need to be home fairly early tomorrow."

"Are you sure? You don't really know us." Kerry hoped Trina was sure. She was exhausted.

"I'm very sure, and besides, even though I've never met you in person, I've read your blog posts and website for years."

"Ok, then, we would love to stay tonight and leave early tomorrow. If it's ok, I will probably shower and go to bed." Kerry looked at Deb.

"It's been a long couple of days." Deb added.

"I've got a few things for an impromptu early supper. Why don't you shower and get comfortable while I get things ready? It won't take long and then you can get to bed early. What about you guys? Can you stay for supper?" Trina looked at her friends.

"I need to go home and feed the horses first and then I could come back for a bite to eat. What do you want me to bring?" Jennie knew she could stop at the store on the way home.

"Anything easy that will go with hotdogs on the grill."

"Thanks for the invite but I'm teaching a few lessons tonight." Lainie's new business, called Lessons with Lainie, was a huge success. She looked forward to teaching all her students and their horses.

"I'll go home with Jennie to help feed and visit with my ponies, then I'll come back. Jennie and I will figure out what to bring." Marcy had a few ideas; especially if they stopped at the store.

Marcy kept her ponies at Jennie's farm, along with Jennie's mare, Julep, and Sam's horse, Sadie. Sam Garrett was a long-time friend of Jennie's. Sam also happened to be one of the best farriers in their area. When she moved to Appleridge and found Jennie's barn, she also found an entire group of new friends— friends that also seemed like family. She loved her new friends.

Marcy was older than the others—she didn't feel older. *Perhaps, driving my ponies in competitions and working as an RN at the local hospital keeps me young. Well, maybe not young, but definitely in pretty good shape.*

Chapter Three

ennie leaned back in her rolling chair at the Chronicle's office, thinking about Trina's new horse. What a story. Actually, two stories—the history of Lambert Morgan horses and the horse slaughter issue. She typed a few notes before the thoughts flew out of her head. The Chronicle's readership may have varying opinions about horse slaughter. She would make it informative, without voicing a particular point of view. Actually, shouldn't all journalists do the same on every issue? She thought so, anyway. She would also write a few more *Dear Equestrian* letters—entertaining letters written by horses to their humans. Her boss, Mr. Mark, loved the first few letters added to the Chronicle.

So many ideas, so little time, and speaking of time, it was time for her to shut down her computer and make the journey home to Appleridge. She had two hungry horses, two hungry ponies, and one hungry cat to feed.

"Good night, Sherilynn." Jennie moved toward the office door. "I have interviews in the morning and then I'll work from home in the afternoon."

"Night, Jennie, I'll see you on Monday. Enjoy your weekend. Any plans?" Sherilynn Adams ran the Chronicle's office from what Jennie called her command station—a U-shaped desk in front. She was a whiz at everything needed to get each issue of the *Farm & Family Country Chronicle*, affectionately called the CC, out to their readers each month.

"Jeremy will be back in town tonight. I think we'll have pizza and watch a movie at my house. He's usually exhausted when he gets back from a mission trip and has a ton of stinky laundry." Jennie held her nose as she laughed.

Doing laundry at Jennie's house gave them time to spend together, and it also helped keep his mom's house *show ready*. If you could call the mess still being cleared *show ready*. After the loss of his mom, Jeremy and his sister, Sarah, put the house on the market, although he still lived there. Jennie didn't know what he would do when the house sold—probably rent a small apartment. He even talked about renting a room from their friend, Sam. Sam rented a small house in town with two bedrooms and offered one to his friend on a short-term basis.

Jennie knew Jeremy would never ask to stay with her. Although marriage didn't appear to be in the near future, they were waiting before living together. Most people thought that was a very old-fashioned idea in today's world. Maybe it was old-fashioned, but Jeremy and Jennie didn't follow what *the world* thought—or expected.

JENNIE SMILED as she pulled into her farm drive. Jeremy's small SUV was parked near the house. Parking her older but serviceable Silverado, named Blue Boy, Jennie made a dash from the truck and into Jeremy's arms.

"Hey, how's my girl?" Jeremy held her close

"I'm good. Missed you."

"I missed you, too. I hope you don't mind; I started a load of laundry while I waited."

Jennie laughed. "Nope, it's good to get it done before it stinks up the house."

"Are you saying I stink?" Jeremy caught the spirit of Jennie's tease.

"Not you, but your laundry is sometimes quite revealing." Jennie linked her arm through Jeremy's.

"Do you want pizza tonight or should we go to the Café? My treat." Jeremy loved to treat Jennie.

"Hmmm, that's a tough decision. Are you tired? If you are, we can just eat here. I have a frozen pizza." Jennie hoped Jeremy wasn't too tired to go out.

"No, I'm good. Let's go to the Café." Jeremy wasn't very excited about frozen pizza and he was starved from his drive home from the mountains.

"And then to Trina's farm after we eat."

"Trina's farm? Is something going on out there?" Jeremy loved Trina's farm, especially when Trina cooked; she was a great cook.

"I know what you're thinking. You wish we were eating there, too!" Jennie could read Jeremy's thoughts most of the time. "Come on, I'm hungry. I'll tell you all about it while we eat, and I want to hear all about your trip."

JEREMY AND JENNIE talked nonstop on their drive to the Café and as they waited for their meals. But when their food arrived, eating took over.

Jeremy eyed the last few fries remaining on Jennie's plate. "Are you going to eat those?"

"No, I'm full. That was a great cheeseburger. How was yours?" Jennie pushed her plate toward the middle of the table.

"Good as usual. Hey, did you have onions on your burger?" Jeremy loved to tease Jennie about her love affair with onions.

"Yes, Jeremy James." She paused but didn't add what he expected her to say. Instead she said, "Don't worry, they were sweet onions and not very strong." Jennie laughed, then added, "And, yes, I still think of you as *the boy with two first names.*"

Jennie always teased Jeremy about his name when they were younger, and although she still loved to tease Jeremy about many things, she didn't tease him about his name anymore. After all, maybe someday she would be Jennie James.

"Ok, thanks for the warning." Jeremy laughed. "I guess I did open the door and gave you the perfect opportunity to bring that up. Especially after my comment about your love affair with onions."

"I was just waiting for the opportunity. I'm sure you missed my teasing."

"Well, maybe a little. I missed you." Jeremy reached across the table for Jennie's hand. "Now that you've heard all about the challenges of my mission trip, what's going on at Trina's?"

"It's a great story. Trina got a call from a horse rescue. They pulled a little Morgan from the kill pen at a horse auction and found her name on his papers. It was actually a miracle that his papers came with him, as that doesn't usually happen. They were trying to raise money to pay his bail or he was going to be shipped to Canada on the slaughter truck that night."

"Wow! And she helped raise the money?" Jeremy knew there was more to the story.

"She paid his entire bail and for his transport to Appleridge. They brought him to her yesterday. He was the pony she owned as a teenager. His name is My Fare Thee Well and he's what they call a Lambert Morgan—old foundation Morgan bloodlines. He's in pretty bad shape but she's optimistic that TLC will be the cure. Dr. Peterson planned to be at the farm today to check him over."

"And you're dying to see the horse again and talk to Trina." It was more of a statement than a question from Jeremy.

"Do you want to go?" Jennie hoped so. She was pretty sure the answer would be yes.

"You know I do. I've always wondered why Trina owned a farm and boarded horses but didn't own a horse."

"Me, too. I guess she was waiting for that special horse to show up." Jennie thought maybe they didn't know Trina's whole story.

"Trina is a pretty private person. We don't really know what brought her to Appleridge. Boarding horses doesn't pay that well. Do you know if she has another job?" Jeremy accepted people for who they were but sometimes it was nice to know their history. He wasn't nosey; he found the details interesting.

"I've never asked. She may have some sort of work she does from home. Shame on me for never asking. A friend should want to know more about another friend."

"I think it's better to wait until a friend offers to share." Jeremy stood and picked up the check. "I'll just take this to the register and we'll drive out to check on Trina and her miracle pony."

TRINA'S FARM was only a few miles outside of Appleridge, Ohio. The smaller farms were just outside the town limits and the larger spreads were further out.

"Whoa! Look at all the cars and trucks. I think Trina's having a party." Jeremy stopped his SUV to scan the parking situation. "I hope we were invited."

Jennie laughed. "I think it is probably an impromptu party and we're welcome."

They squeezed into an empty spot near the practice arena and walked to the barn. Trina ran over to greet them.

"Come on and join the fun. Jeremy! You're home!" Trina hugged Jeremy and Jennie at the same time. Come meet Fare."

"What did Dr. Peterson say?" Jennie knew Doctor Peterson would be very thorough with his exam, and if there were any concerns, very informative.

"He didn't find anything alarming. We wormed him, and Sam came out first thing this afternoon to work on his feet. His coat has a little bit of rain rot. Dr. Peterson gave me something to use for treatment. He took blood for some lab tests. All in all, Dr. Peterson thinks TLC is the best medicine."

As they talked, they made their way over to Fare's small paddock. A large group of friends were in a row, leaning on the paddock fence, admiring Fare.

"Well, My Fare Thee Well, you seem to have a large fan club." Jeremy greeted several people he knew from town, as he looked at the Morgan. "What a handsome gelding. You can see his good conformation in spite of his condition."

"Thanks, Jeremy, he is handsome. And he was so quiet while Dr. Peterson examined him and gave him a few vaccinations. We don't have any records. We don't know what he's had or hasn't had. We gave him the basics today. It was a lot for his first day and he was a trooper."

Fare walked over to be loved on by his adoring public and looking hopeful for a treat. Trina presented him with a peppermint from her pocket.

"What are your plans for him?" Teresa, a boarder at the farm, asked.

"Fare can do just about anything. Well, at least he did when he was younger. He's older now, so we'll have to see." Trina ran her hand down Fare's neck. "But he doesn't have to do anything. Just being here for the rest of his days is enough. Right, boy?"

Fare seemed to understand. He nuzzled Trina's hand. Possibly just looking for another treat, or possibly, to tell her he agreed.

Jennie barely constrained herself from asking Trina a thousand questions; tonight wasn't the time. "Trina, I've done a bit of research. I have two interviews tomorrow and then I could stop out later in the afternoon and share what I've learned. Would that be ok?"

"Sure, I can't wait to hear what you found." Trina couldn't quite settle down long enough to concentrate and do any research of her own.

"Did Kerry and Deb leave early today?" Jennie couldn't resist asking at least one question.

"They did. And promised to keep in touch. They care so much about every horse they rescue. I'm so thankful for what they do.

19

Hey, friends, I may hit you up for a small donation. I want to send the rescue some funds to help with their mission."

Jeremy took off his ball cap. "Let's pass the hat right now before any of us leaves. Any amount, even a dollar or two, will give Trina something to send."

Trina's friends pulled out wallets and purses, and the cap made its way back to Jeremy overflowing with green. Trina burst into tears. All these people were her new friends, people she met since moving to Appleridge, and they really cared about her.

"Thanks so much. Thank you, thank you, so much. Ok, now I'm babbling—and blubbering."

Somewhere down the line the applause started. "We love you, Trina!" was shouted from someone on her right. Fare tossed his head and pranced around the paddock. He agreed.

Chapter Four

ennie grabbed her purse and raced for her truck. She loved mornings in the barn and today was starting out to be a particularly beautiful day—so she lingered—a bit too long. Her long brown braid swung across her back as she raced. She didn't have time to dry her hair. She squeezed out as much water possible with a towel, braided it, and hoped for the best. Hopefully, the braid wouldn't leave a wet spot on the back of her shirt.

Her first stop was at a small farm to talk with the owners of a new business. They recently joined a program called Community Supported Agriculture (CSA). While researching CSAs in preparation for her interview, Jennie learned that farmers pre-sold shares in what they planted. The spring CSA buy-in for this farm was $160. Each person buying a share would receive a basket of produce every week in May and June. According to their website, the spring baskets would include asparagus, spinach, kale, rhubarb, strawberries, turnip greens, cabbage, and radishes. Jennie loved vegetables and found the program interesting. This farm even grew morels and made cheese.

She was more interested in the summer share. The cost was $180 to receive baskets in July and August. The summer baskets promised sweet corn, tomatoes, peas, green beans, broccoli, cucumbers, melons, blueberries, and cherries—yum! Fall wasn't listed yet, but she imagined a few pumpkins sitting on her steps and red apples to enjoy.

Jennie left the interview with a tiny jar of strawberry jam and a sample of cheese. Her job certainly had a few perks. She loved the enthusiasm of the young couple starting their cottage industry and vowed to give them a really nice write-up in the CC. Jennie supposed there were quite a few CC readers growing their own vegetables, but, some, like her, may prefer to purchase healthy, locally grown produce instead of working in a garden. Jennie loved being outdoors—in the barn or on a horse—not so much in the garden.

Her next stop was at an apple orchard boasting hard ciders— The Appleridge Cidery. Maybe she would get a few samples there, too!

The new owners of the orchard and cidery were an older retired couple. And, yes, they were eager for Jennie to try one of their hard ciders. It was too early for apples, but she promised to return. The cidery was only open on Fridays and Saturdays during the summer to sell apple cider vinegar and a few different hard ciders. In the fall, depending on the apple harvest, they would be open Monday thru Saturday, and sell several varieties of apples, apple donuts, fried apple pies, wassail, fresh cider, and of course, vinegar and hard cider. Yes, she would definitely make a return trip to the cidery. She would also save her article on the cidery for later, maybe July or August—just before they geared up for their busiest season. The couple explained they would close after Christmas and spend the winter in Florida, coming back in the spring to work in the orchard. Jennie thought they had a nice retirement plan—nice for them and nice for the Appleridge community, as well.

What a busy morning. Fun!

JENNIE DIDN'T NOTICE anyone at the barn as she parked. She walked over to see Fare, contentedly munching a pile of timothy and alfalfa hay. "Hey, buddy, how are you this morning?"

Fare seemed relaxed. He stopped eating and walked over to the paddock fence, studying her with his brown eyes. "You certainly are a sweet and friendly fellow."

"Hey, Jennie. I thought I heard someone drive up." Trina leaned a stall fork against the barn wall.

"Do you have a few minutes? I have some research to share."

"Sure, let's grab two chairs and sit out here with Fare. Hey, do you want something to drink?"

"Yeah, that sounds good. I've had a great morning of sampling goodies at all my stops. Why stop now?" Jennie followed Trina into the tack room and reached for the cold can she pulled from a small fridge.

"It's a great day to be out and about. Winter seemed exceptionally long and cold this year." Trina lead the way to the paddock with one folded chair in its bag slung over her shoulder; Jennie grabbed the other.

"I know. This was my first winter being back in the barn on cold mornings. I have to say, though, Chicago was pretty frigid." Jennie spent her college years in Chicago commuting around the city.

"I'm sure it was. I've been there visiting in January. There's something about the wind blowing off Lake Michigan that can

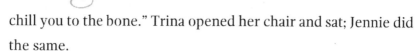

chill you to the bone." Trina opened her chair and sat; Jennie did the same.

"I'm ready. Thanks so much for doing the research. I haven't been able to sit down long enough to read much of anything."

"You're welcome. It's all very interesting, and if it's ok with you, I may do a little article on Fare. It seems he may be quite a treasure in the Morgan horse world. More of a treasure if he were still a breeding stallion, but still, he's unique."

"Now I'm really intrigued—spill it, friend." Trina popped the lid on her can.

"Ok. As you already know, the Morgan horses called Lambert Morgans are from a line of horses descended from a stallion, of some renown, Daniel Lambert. Daniel Lambert, the horse, was born in 1859 and known for his beauty and athleticism. He was a chestnut color with a very blond, almost white, mane and tail. I think they called it flaxen." Jennie glanced at her notes before continuing.

"Daniel Lambert was known for his speed and for passing all his best qualities down through his progeny. He was a direct descendant of the very first Morgan named Figure, born in 1789."

"Yes, being a Morgan horse lover, I know all about Figure. I also know he was called 'that Morgan horse,' after his owner, Justin Morgan. There's an ancient Disney movie, *Justin Morgan had a Horse*. I think I have it on VHS." Trina laughed. "I wish I could get it on DVD because I haven't had a VHS tape player since I was a kid when we had one at home."

"Mom and Dad had a VHS player." Jennie remembered sitting on a stool facing the corner after her mom caught her shoving a cookie into the tape player. She didn't share that little bit of trivia with Trina.

"You probably know a lot more about Morgan horses than me. Let me know if I just need to move on." Jennie scanned her notes as she took a sip from her can.

"Here's where I found it interesting. Back in the 1930s, the Morgan Horse Association allowed several Saddlebred horses into the registry. I guess they wanted to add more height and leg action to the breed; not sure." Jennie looked up to see if she was sharing something Trina already knew."

"There does seem to be a lot of Morgan horses that look and move like a Saddlebred at some of the Morgan shows. I've always loved the ones that look more like Fare—smaller, stockier— just good, solid citizens." Trina gazed fondly at her boy.

"Apparently, there were quite a few people who agreed with you and those traditional Morgan lovers protested. They didn't want the Morgan horse to change. Shortly after, the registry stopped allowing the Saddlebred outcrosses; however, if a horse carries the lineage of one of the Saddlebred horses prior to 1930, they are still considered full-blooded Morgan horses." Jennie took a breath. "And included in the registry."

Trina added, "And those bloodlines are very desirable and found in most Morgan horses shown today, especially in the park and classic pleasure classes at Morgan shows."

"Saddlebreds are very athletic. I guess that makes sense." Jennie paused.

"But there are those who still like the foundation-looking Morgan like Fare. I know you have more. Please continue."

"Ok—on a mission to protect and preserve the original Morgan bloodlines, several groups formed to protect, what they call clean-blooded or foundation Morgan horse families. These horses have no Saddlebred outcrosses in their pedigree. That includes the Lambert family, the Lippitt family, and there are others."

"Wow! Hey there, Mr. Fare, I've always known you were pretty special. Now I know, you are a clean-blooded descendant of Figure, the original Morgan, like in the movie I loved." Trina laughed. "I've never been interested in researching my own genealogy. You know, I love learning about Fare's relatives."

"Me, too! I love looking at horse pedigrees. Mint Julep is a descendant of Man O' War—way back in her pedigree. I've always thought that was pretty cool. When I was in high school, we were given an assignment to trace a family, so I traced Julep's horse relatives. Fortunately, my teacher rewarded my *thinking outside the box* and gave my project an A."

"That's funny." Fare's sweet hay breath caressed Trina's face as she sat by the fence. "Thanks for doing the research."

"Wait, I have a little more." Jennie waited to make sure Trina was interested.

"Great! Go on!"

"Foundation Morgan horses are on the Livestock Conservation list as endangered. I didn't research all of the foundation families, and there are several, but I do know there are only about 300 Lambert Morgan horses in the entire world, with only a couple of farms trying to breed Lamberts exclusively."

"How sad." Trina thought for a moment. "I'd like to visit those farms."

"Me, too. I'll try to get more information." Jennie swallowed the last sip of her diet Coke. "When I visited the Livestock Conservancy website, I was surprised at how many horse breeds are on the endangered list, as well as other livestock. I could do an entire series of articles."

"I think your readers would find it very interesting. Wouldn't those who read the Country Chronicle be very interested in protecting and preserving heritage breeds—and heritage flowers and vegetables?"

Fare nickered. *Those human sure can talk. Where's the treats?*

Trina laughed. "It's easy to read his mind. He thinks—too much talk; too little attention."

"Hey, buddy, if you're like most of us, you'll need to watch the sweets." As Jennie spoke, she dug a peppermint out of her pocket and looked at Trina for permission.

With a nod from Trina, Jennie unwrapped the peppermint. Fare heard the crinkle of the wrapper, pricked up his ears, and waited in anticipation.

"He's so careful when he takes a treat from my hand." Jennie stoked Fare's neck over the top of the fence.

"Yeah, and I think I'll need to cut back on the treats a little. I don't want to create a monster."

"Good luck with that! Marcy always puts treats in a little bucket for her ponies. She never feeds them by hand. I suppose Riley could easily turn into a treat monster." Jennie loved both Riley and Stuffin.

"That's actually a good idea. I've done that with little kids." When Trina looked at Jennie's surprised expression, she continued. "No, silly, I don't make kids get their treats from a bucket. I give them a bucket to use when they feed a treat to a horse. I don't want those precious little fingers to get bitten."

"I do that with Jeremy's nephew, Daniel. Sometimes horses can't tell a little finger from a little carrot." Jennie looked at her phone for the time. "Hey, I need to go." She walked over to give Trina a hug. "I'm so happy for you and Fare. I can't wait to see how he blossoms with your care."

"Thanks. I'm started to feel more normal again. The last two days have been exciting, but I wouldn't mind a little less excitement."

"I'm sure your boarders have a million questions."

"They do. But I don't have a million answers." Trina didn't like a lot of questions, especially personal questions.

"Change the conversation by asking your own question. Most people will answer and forget the original question they asked."

"I'll have to remember to try that idea." Trina walked Jennie out to her truck.

"Take care—see ya later!" Jennie couldn't wait to get home and get some ideas on paper—she was a great written list maker. She had two notebooks full of lists—one for her work and one for her farm. Today was a very good day for gathering information and inspiration.

TRINA WATCHED Jennie's truck disappear before returning the chairs to the tack room. Her barn bench beckoned. She sat down, lowered her head, and began to pray.

Father, I'm in awe of you. Thank you for bringing Fare home. It's like a piece of my heart has been returned. I get the feeling there is more to this story and that makes me nervous. Please take this worry. You are forever faithful, and I'll trust you want only good things for me. And, Father, please lead me in the right direction. You know what I'm talking about. You know everything. Amen.

Trina was truthful when she told her friends Fare was sold at the time she left for college. She didn't share she was estranged from her family and the reason why. Her brother, Barton, who she usually called Bart, got mixed up with drugs, and her father went into debt hiring lawyers and paying for his therapy. Later that summer, her dad died in a robbery, and her brother sold Fare to, supposedly, pay for the funeral. After college, Trina never went home. Her brother managed the small grocery store their father started. He felt it *his duty* to keep her out of what he called *his business.* When her mom supported her brother's idea, she vowed to never forgive their actions. She forced herself to visit her mom on Mother's Day and her mom's birthday. Conversation was always painful—they danced around the real story. She avoided her brother and always visited while he was working. Bart seemed to take good care of her mom. That was good. In her mind, her mom seemed fine without her—more reason to stay away.

Father, it's me again. I know you teach about forgiveness. I don't hate my brother but I'm not sure I've forgiven him—for what he did to Fare and for running me out of both his and Mom's lives. Mom and Bart never gave me a choice. That hurts. I've moved to a different town but I'm not sure if I've moved on. Father, please help me move on. Amen.

Trina felt a little better after her quiet time in prayer. *Is Fare's return a sign I need to reconcile with Bart and Mom?* When Trina moved to Appleridge, she began a new life, and named the farm,

Loving Life Farm. So far, it was a good life with good friends. *What would my friends think if they knew my whole ugly story?*

AS JENNIE DROVE HOME, she thought about how much she didn't know about her friend's life before she moved to Appleridge. Shame on her. She spent the entire time this afternoon doing most of the talking. Trina was interested in the information, but Jennie also believed, a good friend, or a good reporter, doesn't do most of the talking. Her next visit with Trina would be different. Jennie just didn't know how different.

Chapter Five

At work in her home office, something still bothered Jennie about Trina, but what? Worry? That's it! She seemed worried. *She's probably still worried about Fare.* Without thinking, Jennie typed *Trina Shaw* into the search engine of her computer. Nothing. No, wait a minute, a Trina Shaw was listed in an obituary for a Mark Shaw.

Mark Shaw of Engleton, Ohio, died from a shooting at his business, Mark's Market. He is survived by his wife, Margaret, his daughter, Trina Marie, and his son, Barton. Services are scheduled for Monday at Briarwood Baptist Church in Engleton.

A shooting? Jennie's fingers flew over the keyboard. *There has to be a news report—there it is!*

Engleton police responded to a 911 call at Mark's Market. Store owner, Mark Shaw, was found deceased in the freezer from a gunshot wound. His son, Barton, went to the closed store searching for his father, after he failed to arrive home, and found the deceased. An Engleton police investigation determined Mr. Shaw was shot during an apparent robbery and then dragged to the freezer. Further investigation is pending. There were no employees in the store at the time of the shooting.

Oh my! What a tragic story! Poor Trina. I need to help her—somehow.

How could she help unless Trina was ready to share the story with her friends?

Maybe in time she'll trust me enough to share. I don't want her to know I did a search on the internet. It feels like I've invaded her privacy in a way, and if I share this with Lainie or Marcy, would it be considered gossip?

She would ask Jeremy for advice, although Jeremy thought she occasionally stuck her nose into business where her nose didn't need to be sniffing. *Maybe I'll think about this for a while— and pray for guidance and pray for my friend.*

BARTON SHAW SIPPED his coffee. Good coffee, early-in-the-morning coffee, before-the-rest-of-the-world-began-their-day coffee, was one of life's pleasures. He needed to be at the store before dawn—they had a truck to unload—and he always made sure he worked alongside his crew.

On truck unloading day, he stopped at the local bakery for fresh donuts. The bakery wasn't open yet, but the owners were good friends and opened the door when he tapped on the window. Since they also baked for Mark's Market, he would save them a delivery and fetch the trays of baked goods.

At the store, he pulled a jug of orange juice and a carton of milk from the store cooler—one of the perks of owning a grocery store. His crew appreciated the gesture. Good help wasn't hard to find and keep—if you treated them well.

He hadn't treated his sister well and that truth haunted him. He thought of Trina quite a bit, especially since his mom ached for her daughter. Family should take care of one another; family was forever. Too bad he didn't recognize that simple truth a few years ago. It was time to get his family back together and he was working on a plan.

I did what I had to do at the time it needed done. That's what he had been telling himself for years but now he wasn't so sure.

It was better to keep Trina away and safe. Dad's death wasn't random. I don't have any proof, but when I ran from my drug dealer, it was an invitation to hurt my family.

Mark Shaw's death was ruled a murder, and after no leads turned up a suspect, the case was shelved. It wasn't closed for Barton. Each and every day he asked God to take away his pain, to give him strength to live his miserable life, and to make amends with his sister. He loved his mom and sister and it was time to show how much.

TRINA GLANCED at her phone; she didn't recognize the number. Usually she didn't answer a call from an unknown number. Today, she felt a gentle nudge to answer the call.

"Trina, is that you? This is Barton." Silence. A long silence. He waited.

"Yes, it's me." More silence. "Is Mom ok?" Trina couldn't get her voice to sound normal.

"Mom's good; she misses you. She's been thinking about you a lot lately—we both have."

"I've been thinking about you, too, and praying." Trina's heart beat a little faster than normal. *Calm down, it will be ok; this is good.*

"I was wrong." There he said it. "I thought I was doing what was best. I was wrong. I've wanted to talk to you and tell you why I did what I did."

Trina sighed. "It hurt, Bart; it still hurts."

"I know, Sis, I'm sorry. You're in Appleridge now? Mom said you bought a farm, board horses, and bale hay. I'm happy for you—you know."

"I don't know what to say, Bart, thank you for calling, but what is left to say?" Trina didn't think she was ready to have this conversation.

"There's a lot. A lot you don't know. Mom doesn't even know." Barton swallowed to clear the words sticking in his throat. "Can I come see you? You know, to talk? Then I'll leave you alone."

Trina didn't want to talk to Bart or have him visit her farm. He didn't know about finding Fare. She didn't want him to know. "Not now. I'm not ready."

Barton ran his fingers through his hair. "I understand. When you're ready, could you call? I just want you to know how sorry I am—for everything. For breaking up our family, for everything I did, for losing Dad."

Was that sincerity? She thought so. Her heart softened a little. "I will, Bart, and I'll come visit Mom more often."

"Good. And, Trina, thanks."

"Don't thank me yet." Trina pressed off before Bart could respond. What a strange week. First Fare shows up and now Bart.

God, I see your hand all over this and I'll somehow find the faith to believe this is good, so I'll say thank you right now—in faith.

MARCY FINISHED her long shift at the hospital and slowly found her way outside and into her truck. Sighing, she put the truck in gear and backed out of the parking space. She took a left turn out of the parking lot and headed toward Jennie's farm to visit her ponies. She was too tired for more than a quick visit. Tomorrow started three days off work—pony time! As she approached the road to Trina's Farm, she felt a nudge to check on Trina and the little Morgan. *Fare, that's his name, Fare.*

Trina heard the truck and put down the grooming brush. Fare nickered as she walked away.

"I'll be right back, buddy. I just need to see who's here."

"Hi, Marcy, what brings you out this way?" Trina greeted her friend with a hug.

"No reason except I wanted to check on you and Fare. How's he doing?"

"Come see for yourself." Trina motioned for Marcy to follow her into the barn where Fare stood in the aisle, patiently waiting for his spa session to continue.

"Wow, it looks like TLC is working already." Marcy saw a big difference. There was a light in Fare's eyes that wasn't there before. "He sure cleans up nice. I didn't realize his mane and tail were so white."

"He's had a bath, although he prefers to be dirty. I don't mind dirt, but I want any dirt on him to be my dirt and not that nasty sale barn dirt."

Marcy agreed. "Have you ever been to a horse sale? I don't think I would be able to handle it well, especially the low-end sales. It's sad to think about."

"I went once and once was enough. I really admire Kerry and Deb for going week after week."

Marcy thought it was time for a happier subject. "Do you know if Fare has ever been hooked to a cart or carriage?"

"I had a little cart and a little sleigh, and took the neighborhood kids for rides."

"I didn't know you have driving experience. You'll have to come out and drive the ponies. It would be a good way to brush up on what you already know." Marcy was always ready to help anyone interested in driving a pony or horse.

"I don't have the experience you have, and I've never driven a pair, but, yes, maybe you could help me find a cart or carriage to fit this boy—when he gets healthier." Trina pictured herself driving with Marcy—what fun!

"It's a plan. We'll start with long-lines, following him on the ground, without a vehicle attached, and see what he remembers. It would be a great way to condition him."

"It really would—and it wouldn't hurt me, either." Trina grinned. "I'll be working as hard as Fare as I walk behind him holding the reins." Trina was petite but thought she could be more fit.

Neither friend said anything as they gazed at Fare. Trina pictured him as he was when he was younger and more fit. Marcy pictured him fit and in competition. It would be fun to compete at shows with a friend.

Fare gazed at the friends and then nickered. A low, soft nicker. Then he cocked a hind leg and relaxed for a little nap. This could take a while.

"Marcy, do you have a few minutes?"

"Sure. I'm going to visit my ponies but I'm not doing much with them tonight."

"Let me take Fare out to his paddock and then we'll talk."

Fare opened his eyes when he felt Trina stroke his neck. Together, they walked quietly to the paddock.

Marcy found a seat on the barn bench. It seemed like she was just sitting in that seat as they waited for Fare to arrive. Was it only a few days ago?

Trina returned and sat down beside Marcy.

"I love having you, Lainie, and Jennie as my friends. We don't see one another very often but we're always ready to help one another when needed." Trina sighed.

"We should meet occasionally for dinner and talk. Don't you think?" Marcy knew her schedule would present a challenge. She also thought good friends were worth the effort.

"That's a good idea. I'm usually free in the evenings, well, at least most evenings. Lainie comes to the farm to teach a few of my boarders two nights a week. Hey, maybe we should meet here?"

"No, because then you'll feel obligated to cook. You're a great cook but wouldn't it become a chore after a while?"

Trina didn't think cooking for friends was ever a chore, especially when she lived alone and only cooked for herself most of the time. "Maybe going out to a restaurant would be fun. We could always come back here for dessert."

"You win! We'll come back here for a piece of your award-winning pie."

Marcy said nothing; quietly she waited. She was sure her friend had something to share.

"I love all of you. I need to share something about my life, and I don't know, but I feel like you would understand what I'm going through the most. Maybe because we're older than Jennie and Lainie. I don't know." Trina glanced at Marcy and was encouraged.

"I'm older that's for sure—I'm the senior of the group. You're close to their age, but wiser—in a way." Marcy sensed this conversation was serious and wanted her friend to relax. A little bit of humor usually helped. "Well, that didn't sound nice!" She laughed.

"I don't know about being wise but I feel like I can trust you. You don't gossip and you're a good listener."

"I would be honored to listen. I promise to keep anything you share confidential." She silently vowed to be both a good listener and a trusted friend.

Trina took a deep breath. "Finding Fare has caused me to revisit my past. It's not something I've shared much—actually I've never shared this with anyone. Fare was sold at the time I went to college, but it wasn't my choice. He was sold to pay for my father's funeral. Dad was shot during a robbery in the family grocery store and was found in the store freezer."

Marcy scooted over and reached for Trina's hand.

"My brother took charge. He sold Fare without my permission. We didn't talk. I guess my brother did what he thought he had to do. It was only my mom, Bart, and me left to deal with Dad's murder, and instead of sharing our grief, he took over, pushed me away, and Mom said nothing. Bart took over the store, he threw some money my way, said he wanted me out of his business."

"I can understand how finding Fare brought this all back. Have you visited your mom since?"

"I've been back, usually on Mother's Day and a few times on Mom's birthday. Mom always seems uncomfortable and I've assumed Bart is angry. I haven't spent a holiday or my birthday with my family for years. It's like I don't have a family. You, Lainie, and Jennie are more family than Mom and Bart. I can't tell you how much it meant to me to have you three here the morning I waited for Fare to arrive."

"Do you think there is any hope for reconciliation?" Marcy was divorced and knew how hard she fought bitterness. "I know it's hard not to be bitter. I survived a nasty divorce before I moved back to Appleridge. You guys have helped me find peace and friendship. We're going to help you, too, Trina."

"Thanks. I miss Mom. I've been angry, thinking she chose Bart over me. Now I think maybe she didn't have a choice—at least not at the time. I know she grieved terribly for Dad. If Dad and Mom hadn't spent so much money helping Bart with his drug addiction, there would have been money for Dad's funeral. I had money saved and planned on moving Fare to a barn close to school. You know, just like Cassy having Treasure here while she's in college."

Trina looked at the confusion on Marcy's face and knew she needed to explain. "Bart got mixed up in drugs, he never went to class, flunked out of college, and almost went to prison. As far as I can tell, he's clean now. He takes care of Mom and the store is doing well."

"Is Bart the first born? He's how old now?"

"Yes, my older brother, he's thirty-two. He was twenty-two when Dad was murdered and he's never married."

"And your family's been estranged for what, ten years or so?" Marcy did the math. She knew Trina was maybe twenty-eight or twenty-nine.

"A long time. I've been alone a long time. I finished school, worked a little, but didn't know what I wanted to do, so I went to graduate school. I worked and saved money. I didn't go to church or have any hobbies. Then I found the farm. It was in foreclosure so I got a great price. I do website and IT work from home, started boarding horses, met their owners, found my church, met Jennie, you, and Lainie, and now I'm not alone."

"No, you aren't alone. And you know what? I was alone and I don't feel so alone anymore, either."

Both Marcy and Trina sat further back on the bench and relaxed. Neither spoke for a while. It wasn't necessary. Marcy decided to allow Trina to break the silence—when she was ready.

"My brother called this morning. He apologized. He actually apologized. He sounded sincere. He wants to come to the farm and talk. He says he has a lot to share. I told him I wasn't ready for him to visit. I promised to visit Mom. He said she misses me. I got the feeling he wanted to say more but preferred to talk face to face."

"How did it feel to talk to him?"

"It was good. I was sitting here talking to God right before Bart called. I suppose I experienced a miracle of sorts. I didn't feel afraid—or angry."

"Would you like me to go with you when you visit your mom?" Marcy thought maybe it would help Trina to have a friend along. She could always excuse herself if it seemed like

Trina wanted private time with her mom. Marcy wouldn't mind meeting Bart. She was a good judge of a person's motives. She wanted to make sure her friend wasn't hurt again.

"That would be nice. Maybe it would help Mom be more comfortable. She never seems to know what to say to me."

"Maybe we could pick her up and bring her here? You could show her the farm, she could meet your friends, and see you have a nice life. We could have a little cook-out in her honor. You know us, we have no trouble keeping a conversation going." Marcy could just imagine. Trina's mom wouldn't need to worry about adding anything to the conversation—she wouldn't get the chance.

"You have a smile on your face. You're thinking about my mom being loved on by all my friends. That puts a smile on my face, also."

"And it's good to see that smile." Marcy stood up. "I need to get going. Why don't you think about bringing your mom here for a little visit? Maybe for a weekend. Test the waters. Then maybe you'll know if you're ready to invite Bart."

"I will. And Marcy."

"Yes."

"Thanks for listening."

"My pleasure. Thanks for trusting me with your story."

Trina stood at the barn door and watched her friend drive away. It felt good to share her story. Well, not that the story was good, but sharing and receiving encouragement felt really good. She wanted to reunite with her family. She really did. Bart's apology seemed genuine.

Father, I know many families have been hurt by drug addiction. Drugs stole Bart's life. That makes me sad. It makes me sad to think he carries the pain of remorse, too. I've often thought Dad was shot by a drug addict looking for cash. Does that cause Bart pain—knowing his drug abuse brought pain and sadness to Mom and Dad? I feel bad for my brother. I admit, I'm still angry. His poor choices hurt us all. I'll need your help. I'll always need your help. I wonder if Bart knows you. Is that what I'm to share—my faith, my trust in you, and the joy you bring into my life? And, God, thank you. I think you're using Fare to bring my family back together. We've lost a lot of time, but we still have forever.

Chapter Six

Jeremy arrived at Jennie's house with his laptop computer under his arm, ready to catch up on a few administrative tasks, and her kitchen table made a great office. He loved his work out in the mission field. Of course, he didn't enjoy writing case studies, the endless reports, or playing catch-up with classes after missing two weeks of school. Taking a total of three mission trips during his first full-time semester of seminary was a huge challenge. He was a good organizer, enjoyed motivating the volunteers, and sharing devotions in the evening. He could imagine himself leading mission trips as his ministry—his calling. The need was great, both in the states and abroad. People in great need appreciated the help.

He stretched. Maybe he could peek in at Jennie in her home office and convince her to take a little break. His nephew, Daniel, had a pee wee basketball game tonight. They could grab a hotdog at the school concession stand and maybe have ice cream.

"Hey, that doesn't look like you're working very hard." Jennie walked into the kitchen, opened the fridge, and grabbed a jar of ice tea. "Want some?"

"Yeah, that would be nice. Hey, are you ready for a break? Daniel has a game tonight." Jeremy walked over to get his tea and leaned against the counter.

"I love watching the little guy play—or sit the bench." She laughed because Daniel never seemed to mind if he sat on the sidelines. There was always another kid sitting on the bench and they played their own little games.

"I'm hungry. Do you want to grab something here or catch a hotdog at the game?"

"Hotdog at the game. And Jeremy James, just so you know, I'm adding lots of onions along with my mustard and relish."

"I figured. I'll bring the breath mints—mint flavored." He then preceded to use his Star Wars voice—"Obi Wan, breath mints are my only hope; save me from the evil onions."

"Very funny." She thought he was funny most of the time. "It's a bit early but I think I'll feed the horses before we leave. I'm not sure if Marcy and Sam are stopping out tonight. I'll leave a note just in case they do stop."

Jeremy went to find the barn boots he kept in the basement as Jennie shoved her feet into the old boots she kicked off at the back door.

"Do you ever think about getting a horse? I know a nice place where you could board a horse."

"I do sometimes. I'd like to get one to drive. I could see me driving and you hanging off the back of the marathon carriage as we raced through obstacles like Marcy."

"Maybe I'll drive and you'll hang," Jennie teased.

"We'll take turns. Hey, there's Marcy now."

Marcy parked her diesel truck beside the barn and pulled a backpack from the passenger seat. She still needed to change out of her work scrubs.

"Hi, Marcy, we were going to feed the horses early before going to Daniel's game. Are you driving Riley and Stuffin tonight?" Jennie didn't think so but wanted to ask.

"No, not tonight. It's been a hard day. I'm off the next three days so I'm thinking about taking them to the state park and driving the trails tomorrow. Do you have time to go along, Jeremy?"

"It's Saturday, no class, I'd love to go!" He looked at Jennie. "Did we have plans?"

"Well—no—I guess not." Jennie didn't try to hide her disappointment.

Jeremy noticed. "Marcy, are you going in the morning?"

"Yes, is that ok? I thought we could load and leave here around 9:00 or so." Marcy glanced at Jennie. "Then you'll have the rest of the day to do something else." *Maybe I should invite Jennie, too, but I don't think it's fair to ask the ponies to pull three people in the carriage on unpaved trails.*

"I'll see you then. We'll get these critters taken care of and then we're off to Daniel's game." Jeremy waited for Jennie to say something before starting the barn chores.

Jennie didn't answer. She quickly walked to the feed room, scolding herself. *Grow up! We don't have morning plans or any plans for the weekend, and besides, I'll do a quick cleanup of the house and get a few outside chores done while Jeremy is with Marcy.*

Jeremy could almost hear Jennie's thoughts by watching her face. She was giving herself an attitude check. He loved that about her.

JENNIE WAS QUIET on their way to Daniel's game. On one hand, she loved her friends loving Jeremy. On the other,

sometimes that meant she was forced to share Jeremy. Maybe forced was too strong of a word. *Stop it, don't be so selfish.*

Sometimes when you know you're being unreasonable, it's still hard not to have bad feelings. At least that's what Jennie thought.

Daniel spotted his Uncle Jeremy and Jennie as they climbed the bleachers steps and found a seat. "Hey, Uncle Jeremy, hey Jennie."

They waved and Jeremy motioned for Daniel to pay attention to the game. "Wow, he's on the court. I'm glad we came to watch him play. I think it's the last game of the season."

"Look at that grin. He's pretty proud of himself." Jennie gave Daniel a thumbs up.

Sarah waved from the end of the second row. "There's Sarah! Let's move and sit with her." Jennie was already up and on the move. Jeremy followed.

"Jennie, it's good to see you." They hugged. "And you, too, brother. I haven't seen you since you got home. How was the trip?"

"Good; exhausting, but so good. I can't wait until the next trip. We're going back to the same area." He glanced at Jennie. "But I missed all of you."

Sarah punched his arm. "Good cover, clever boy."

"Yes, I'm good and now I'm going to get my clever self down to the concession stand and buy my date and my sis a hotdog."

"Nothing for me, I promised Daniel we would take something home for his dad; he should be home from work by then, and we'll eat together."

"One for me, please—mustard, relish, and EXTRA onions."

"I know, I know." Jeremy searched his pocket and pulled out the breath mints. "I'm armed and ready."

"How do you put up with him?!" Sarah shook her head, but she couldn't stop the corners of her mouth from revealing how she really felt.

"Oh, it's a challenge." Jennie played along.

DANIEL PLAYED the entire game and he was thrilled. He was more thrilled about the ice cream cones the players were given to celebrate their win.

Jennie shivered. Maybe ice cream wasn't the best idea. She would opt for a hot chocolate instead. Today was a good, and what she called, sweatshirt weather day. Spring had barely sprung. It would turn cold again.

"I THINK TOMORROW is supposed to be another nice day. Have fun with Marcy. I know how much you like driving the ponies." After a nice night and a full stomach, Jennie was feeling a little more generous.

"Do you want to do something tomorrow night? Something special?"

"I don't have anything in mind. We can watch a movie at my house. Just relax."

"Sound good. Do you need anything done at the farm? I'll have time tomorrow afternoon."

Jeremy needed to clean up his mom's yard—he could do that Sunday afternoon. He was trying to keep it looking nice since the house was on the market.

"I know you haven't been at your mom's house for two weeks. Why don't you do what you need to do there and then come over when you're done?" Jennie was starting to feel pretty silly about her earlier mood, especially when she had nothing planned, anyway. *I don't want to be one of those jealous, annoying girls. Maybe Jeremy didn't notice.*

He noticed. And he also noticed Jennie's efforts to change her attitude. *Good job, sweet Jennie.*

BARTON PLACED his phone on the desk in the small back room office of Mark's Market. It really wasn't much of an office, but at least it had four walls and a door. The door was only closed when he needed to speak to an employee in private. Thankfully, that wasn't often. Barton liked to think working alongside his employees enhanced boss and employee relationships, and if they had a concern, they usually felt comfortable speaking to him as they worked.

Today, he closed the office door to make a personal call. A call to another possible lead, as he continued his mission of tracking his sister's horse, Fare. Maybe, just maybe, if he found Fare, Trina would forgive him. Barton prayed today's call would lead him one more step in the right direction. When he came up with the idea, he told himself it was a real long shot given the years that had passed. He worked hard, followed every lead, losing count of all the people he called, following dead-end trails, and car trips to nowhere. Finally, he was getting close; he could feel it.

Barton ended the call and leaned back in his squeaking chair. Wow, Fare was still alive, and recently sold at a horse sale to a man looking for a nice pony for his children. Barton replayed the conversation in his head, trying to remember what else the woman shared. He pulled a writing pad from the drawer and started writing a few quick notes.

Their children were grown so they took Fare to a sale. A man approached them as they unloaded Fare at the auction and offered to buy Fare before he went through the sale. He was looking for a nice pony for his children, and suggested they make a deal to avoid paying the sale commission. She didn't think that was probably very honest, but she needed to sell him quickly. She needed the money. They agreed on a price, which was lower than what the horse was worth, but she was happy to sell him to a good home. The man didn't give her a bill of sale and she didn't think to ask for his last name or address, but she thought his first name was Jack.

Bart tore the page from his notepad, folded it, and placed it in his back pocket. It looked like he would be taking a trip to the sale next week. Maybe he could get a name and address for this man possibly named Jack. He hated to think about taking a horse from children. Maybe enough money would convince the parents to sell before they became too attached.

Chapter Seven

*T*rina glanced at her phone and answered quickly when she saw Kerry's name on the screen.

"Hi, Kerry, are you checking on Fare?"

"Yes, but I also wanted to talk to you about something else."

"Fare is doing really well. He's already gained some weight and his eyes seem more alive."

"That's great. I'm so happy for Fare, and you, Trina." In Kerry's mind, bringing Fare home to Trina was one of the best deliveries they have ever made and worth every mile.

"What I wanted to talk to you about was a call we received this morning. A young Amish woman has lost her husband recently. She has three children and needs to make a few changes. She is keeping the farm, because it's been in her husband's family for years, but several families are leasing most of the land. Her husband loved Morgan horses, especially the old-style type, and he has some nice stock. She is keeping one for her personal driving horse, one for her 14-year-old son, and maybe another, but she needs to rehome a couple more. She's been encouraged to take them to the sale. She wants to find good homes. She's attached to all of them."

"I don't think I can take on two more horses, Kerry. I'll ask around and see if I can find anyone interested."

"I thought about your friends. I know one of them drives. This pair of horses is trained to both drive and ride." Kerry wanted to place the horses in good homes. "She has them reasonably priced and said she would prefer them to be rehomed together."

"Did you say they were old style Morgan horses, like Fare?" Trina knew Jeremy and Jennie were very interested in Fare. Maybe they would be interested in looking and possibly buying a horse.

"I believe they may be either from the Lambert or Lippitt family of old-style Morgan horses. I drove over to see them and they are very nice—a gelding and a mare. I think they hitch them together as a driving pair."

"My friend, Marcy, drives two Welsh ponies, a gelding and a mare, so I know it isn't unusual." Trina paused. "Marcy competes at combined driving events. She probably knows quite a few people interested in driving horses. Can they be separated?"

"Yes, I think that's fine, if needed. Her husband loved all of his horses and they seem very well-trained. She could probably get a lot more than she's asking. She said the home is more important than money—even though she needs the money." Kerry sighed. "It's always better when we can place horses instead of finding them in the kill pen. I really want to help her. Please share with your friends."

"I will. Thanks for calling, Kerry. I'll keep in touch." Trina hung up the phone and walked over to Fare's pen. He looked at her with his kind eyes that spoke to Trina's heart. "Don't worry, Fare, I'll help them; somehow I'll help them."

TRINA FELT A STRONG URGE to drive to Jennie's farm early on Saturday. Pulling into the drive, she spotted Marcy's truck. Perfect!

"Hey, there's Trina. I wonder what she's doing out and about so early today?" Jennie waved as Trina parked her truck.

Marcy stopped grooming Riley. "Hi, Trina. What are you up to today?"

"I couldn't wait to talk to all of you. I got a call from the Morgan rescue last night. They have a team of Morgan horses to rehome."

"Oh, no, don't tell me there are more horses in the kill pen." Jennie hated to think of any horse in that situation.

"No, they are at an Amish farm. Their owner passed away and his young widow needs to rehome some of his horses. She is going to keep her driving horse, her son's horse, and I think a pony for the younger kids, but she has two nice driving horses that need homes. She says she won't take them to the sale, at least not right now. She loves them both."

Marcy put down her grooming brush. "When could we look at them?"

"I know you have a lot of friends in the combined driving world. Do you have a possible home?" Trina hoped so.

"Well, yes, and I'm looking at him—at them." She turned to look at Jeremy and then at Jennie.

"Me?" But Jeremy was already on the same page. "Do you think I'm ready?"

"It depends on their training and experience. I don't consider you green. You or Jennie are experienced enough to take this next step. Maybe we could delay our trip to the state park and go look at them today. Where are they, Trina?"

"I'm not sure but I think they're in the Sugar Creek Amish community. Let me call Kerry, but first, are you really interested?"

Jeremy looked at Jennie who happened to be smiling. "Are we ready, Jennie?"

"I'm ready for a driving horse." She took a deep breath to get calm. "How much does she want for them?"

"We didn't talk price. Kerry thought she was more interested in placing them in a good home than making money, although she could certainly use the money. She has several children. Do you want me to call Kerry?"

They all nodded.

Trina's fingers found the last call on her phone and hit Send.

"Hi, Trina, I didn't expect to hear from you so quickly."

"My friends are very interested in looking at the horses. I forgot to ask, where are they located?"

"Not too far from you, in Sugar Creek. When do they want to go?"

"Today, if possible. If not, maybe next weekend?" Trina mentally reviewed her calendar.

Kerry hesitated. "I'm not sure if I can get in touch with Elizabeth so quickly. She uses the neighborhood phone shack down the road. She doesn't have a phone in the house. Maybe we'll get lucky and someone will check the phone shack for messages."

"Thanks, Kerry. We'll keep this afternoon open—just in case."

Trina hung up and walked to her friends. "She's going to try to get in touch with Elizabeth, the young Amish woman. It'll probably not be today."

"Yeah, it's not like she'll send a text." Jennie knew some Amish used phones for their businesses but cell phones and texting probably weren't used as much.

"Jeremy and I were going to take the ponies to drive in the state park this morning." Marcy looked at Jeremy. "Maybe we should drive here, instead. Just in case?"

"Are you going with us to look at the horses? I would feel a lot better if we had your eyes on them before we made a decision." Jeremy trusted Marcy's knowledge and experience.

"I wouldn't miss it! I can always take Riley and Stuffin to the park tomorrow. I'm pretty sure we won't be doing any visiting in Amish country on a Sunday."

Jennie spoke up, "Probably not. I feel really bad for Elizabeth—losing her husband and now selling some horses."

"Kerry said her family is nearby and the Amish community will help her farm the land. It's sad, though." Trina thought about how the Amish families helped one another in time of crisis but her own family fell apart during their crisis.

"Grandpa used to know several Amish families in Sugar Creek. I wonder if he would like to ride along to look at the horses? I promised to take him to the grocery store this morning. Maybe I should give him a call. We could go to the store now—just in case we end up on a field trip this afternoon."

Jennie called her grandpa. Yes, he could go to the store early. And, yes, he wanted to ride along to Sugar Creek.

EVERYONE MADE tentative plans to meet up again later. Jennie and Grandpa went grocery shopping, Trina went back to her farm, and Marcy and Jeremy drove the ponies on the pasture trails.

It was almost noon by the time Kerry called. "Elizabeth said this afternoon would be fine."

"There will be five of us; do you think that will be ok?" Trina didn't know too much about the Amish community but wanted to be respectful.

"I think so. I'll leave another message. I don't know how often they check for messages. Maybe since they're trying to sell a few horses they're checking more often."

JENNIE PARKED in an empty space beside Grandpa's apartment. "Do you want to come on out to the farm after we unload your groceries? I bought some lunch meat, cheese, and buns so we could have sandwiches for lunch and then we'll wait for Trina to call about making a trip to Sugar Creek. Marcy and Jeremy are probably finished driving the ponies by now."

"Yup, that sounds good. Let's get these bags inside. I'm getting hungry after all that food shopping." Grandpa climbed out of Jennie's truck. He was still pretty limber for his age.

JEREMY GROOMED Riley as Marcy groomed Stuffin. "They were great today and you weren't too bad yourself." Marcy leaned over and asked Stuffin to pick up her foot for cleaning. "You seem to be a natural handling the lines. You're ready. Buying an already trained driving horse, especially one that has been driven on the road, is a great opportunity. That is, as long as they haven't had too much time being driven on pavement. Some of the Amish horses suffer leg injuries caused by their feet pounding the pavement."

"Will you be able to look at their feet and legs and determine if they have any issues?" Although Jeremy thought he would see swelling and stiffness, he was sure Marcy had a better eye for that sort of thing.

"We'll give them a good look. We'll also be able to tell how they've been cared for just by looking at their overall condition—weight, coat, eyes."

"I'm sure, just like any place, there are good Amish horse people, and not so good, but Kerry thought this Amish family cared for their horses as something more than just transportation."

Marcy nodded in agreement. "Yes, I've seen good, and I've seen poor—same as anywhere, I guess."

They turned Riley and Stuffin out into the pasture just as Jennie walked into the paddock looking for them.

"Kerry called. We can look at the horses this afternoon. I left Grandpa sitting on the back porch happily eating a sandwich. Are you hungry?"

"Yes, starved!" Jeremy was almost always hungry. "I'll help Marcy roll the carriage into her trailer and we'll come up to the house."

Marcy garaged her marathon carriage in her horse trailer. It was easy to roll up the back ramp and it kept the carriage clean. Jennie's barn wasn't big enough to park the carriage in the aisle.

"You know, if you buy a driving horse, you'll also need to look for a vehicle. Maybe we should ask if they have harness for sale?" Marcy closed the trailer door after Jeremy lifted the ramp.

"Yeah, and where are we going to keep a carriage? Jennie won't want to clutter up her barn. We may need to build a little carriage barn." Jeremy laughed. "I think I just heard my checking account wheeze!"

"Horses seem to do harm to most checking accounts but they're worth every penny." Marcy motioned toward the house. "Let's get some food so we can hit the road."

JENNIE WATCHED THE CLOCK. "I hate to rush lunch, but we're picking Trina up in thirty minutes, and since there are five of us, I called my dad and asked if we could take his Enclave. It seats seven tight and six fairly comfortable." Jennie started picking up plates.

"And your dad said yes? Wow, I'm impressed!" Jeremy teased, as he hung onto his plate with one hand, grabbing a handful of chips with the other.

"He said yes, but only if you drive. I'm a great driver; I'm not sure why he said you needed to drive." Jennie didn't really mind, but she thought it was strange.

Grandpa spoke up. "Ed is from the old school and considers it respectful for men to drive."

"You can't hide that grin, Grandpa. You're teasing." Jennie thought so, anyway.

Marcy jumped into the conversation. "Maybe not. I don't know your dad very well, but I can see him thinking a man should drive." Marcy nodded to Grandpa. "Either that or he really thinks Jeremy is the better driver." Marcy couldn't resist.

The four of them climbed into Jeremy's small SUV to pick up the Enclave. Grandpa and Jeremy in front, the ladies in back.

"Your chauffer only had time for one sandwich. I think we should think about eating an early dinner." Jeremy was still hungry. Sadly, he thought eating in the Enclave wouldn't be an option.

Jennie pulled a bag of Red Vines licorice from her bag. "I've got a treat and I think it will be fine to eat them in Dad's car."

"That's my girl." Jeremy glanced over at Grandpa who was wearing a huge smile.

IT ONLY TOOK a few minutes to switch vehicles. Jeremy left his SUV keys with Ed, just in case he needed to go anywhere. "I know it isn't as nice as yours, but it's reliable."

Jennie's dad laughed, shook Jeremy's hand, all the while thinking—*my two oldest daughters married good men and if Jennie ends up with Jeremy, I'll be three for three. That's a lot to be thankful for.*

"HEY, THERE'S LAINIE waiting with Trina. I wonder if she wants to go with us?" Jennie waved at both friends.

Lainie wanted to go. "Is there room for me?" Lainie hoped so. "I can sit way in back."

Trina piped up. "I can sit in back with Lainie."

Relieved that her friends wanted the back seat, Jennie climbed out of the car to make room for Lainie and Trina to squeeze into the rear seat. "Thanks, guys, I sometimes get a little car sick in the back." The second seat was as far back as she was willing to sit.

Marcy added, "I'm calling seniority—literally!"

WITH THE SUV fully loaded and ready to *hit the road*, Jeremy hesitated before moving the gear shift into drive. "Mr. Gantzler, would you like to say a little trip prayer?"

"I certainly would."

"Heavenly Father, thank you for this time together. Please keep us safe. Please be with Elizabeth and her family. And, Father, finding a good restaurant would be most appreciated." Six voices saying Amen, agreed with the prayer.

Jennie loved her grandpa's honest and to-the-point prayers. He never wasted words or tried to get all fancy with God.

Once on the highway, Jeremy glanced in the rearview mirror. "Where are those Red Vines?"

"Coming right up to the front seat, sir." Jennie pulled the large package out of her bag. "If everyone wants some, we can each take five pieces on the first round. There are forty-five pieces in the bag.

Grandpa chuckled. "I'll think my dentures and I will take a pass on the licorice."

"Sorry, Gramps. I wasn't thinking." Jennie hoped she never had dentures and would need to give up her favorite road trip snack.

The licorice made it from front seat to back and conversation paused while the crew chewed.

"Mr. Gantzler, Jennie mentioned you knew some of the Sugar Creek Amish families. I bet there's a story there somewhere." Marcy was sitting behind Grandpa, so she peered around the seat as she spoke.

"Yup. I haven't been there for a while, though. I used to haul the horses to an Amish farrier in Sugar Creek. Jennie, you went with me a few times."

"I think I remember a few trips. That was before we found a good farrier in Appleridge, right?"

Grandpa didn't answer; he was already in story mode. "One time, I saw a crew out in the hay field picking up freshly baled hay. The wagon and baler were pulled by four draft horses."

"Was it a two-and-two hitch or four across?" Marcy was intrigued.

"Four across. They pulled the baler with a wagon attached."

Grandpa cleared his throat. "I could see the sky getting dark in the west and knew they needed to get that hay in the barn before the storm hit. I asked the farrier if he could work on my horses while they were tied in the aisle, so I could go out and help with the hay. He, in turn, asked me if I minded if he went out and helped, along with me, before the storm hit."

Lainie leaned forward. "Did you get the hay in the barn?"

"Yes, barely. I think we felt the first drops just as we unloaded the last few bales. By then, it was lunch time. They brought me over to a big table, set up on the side porch, and filled with enough food to feed an army. I call it lunch but it was really a huge meal."

"Jeremy took his eyes briefly off the road to glance at Grandpa. "And I bet it was good, too!"

"Yes, it was."

Grandpa sat quietly, thinking—remembering. "I went back a few more times. They usually found something for me to do and they thought it was quite a joke having this Englisher help with chores. I enjoyed the visits."

"Englisher?" Marcy asked.

Lainie spoke up. "I was raised around several Amish communities in Pennsylvania and Englisher is what they call everyone not Amish."

The licorice bag was passed one more time, conversation covered a multitude of subjects, and soon they entered Sugar Creek.

"According to the GPS, we go through town and continue straight for a couple of miles." Jeremy held his phone to the side and Jennie reached forward. "Go ahead and turn up the sound. I'll need directions from here."

After a few more miles, Jeremy steered the SUV onto an immaculate farm, with a white house surrounded by an array of brightly colored flowers, a huge white barn, and a clothesline full of clothes—black trousers, and brightly colored shirts.

"Look at the little fenced-in garden." Trina thought the entire place was lovely. "Oh, look!" She pointed to a couple of tables covered with quilts. Several women hurried out of the house carrying plates of cookies and pitchers of what looked like lemonade. "I hope we aren't interrupting anything."

"Knowing Amish hospitality, I think those are for us," Grandpa reassured.

JEREMY PARKED behind a grape arbor, away from the house, and secluded from the road. He wanted to respect their way of life. All six climbed out of the SUV, stretched, and waited as an older Amish gentleman, a young woman, and a young teenage boy approached.

"Why Charlie Gantzler, it's good to see you again." The man held out his hand.

"Amos Stoltz, it's been a long time." Grandpa reached for Amos's hand and they shook.

"This is my daughter, Elizabeth, and her oldest son, Charlie."

"Ahh, a much younger Charlie." Grandpa held his hand out to the boy who stepped forward.

"Let me make our introductions. This is my granddaughter, Jennie. Her friends, Jeremy, Trina, Marcy, and Lainie." As he said each of their names, they stepped forward and greeted Amos, Elizabeth, and young Charlie.

"And we're all horse lovers." Jennie added with a smile, looking at Elizabeth.

Jennie thought Elizabeth seemed shy. Of course, maybe she was just allowing her father to take the lead, out of respect.

"Did one of you recently get a horse from the Save a Morgan Rescue?" Elizabeth looked at her father before she asked the question.

"That was me. They saved a horse I had years ago. I'm thrilled to get him back again." Trina started to pull out her phone to show a picture before she remembered they didn't take pictures—or use cell phones—so casually. Instead, she put her hands in her jeans pockets and smiled.

"Marcy, here, is really good with driving horses, and now Jennie and Jeremy would like to have a driving horse. So here we are." It seemed like both Grandpa and Amos were taking the lead which was fine with everyone else.

"Let's walk out to the barn. Isaiah loved his Morgan horses. I don't think you'll find a nicer pair anywhere." Amos and

Grandpa started walking. Charlie looked at his mom, and when she nodded, he ran to catch up with the two old friends.

Jeremy looked at Elizabeth. "We're so very sorry for your loss, Elizabeth." Jennie, Lainie, and Trina nodded in agreement.

"Thank you. Shall we go on out to the barn?" Elizabeth glanced back at the house, where a toddler and a boy about seven played. An older woman nodded and looked at the children. It appeared to be a *don't worry, I'll keep an eye on them* silent conversation.

The horses waited in a small paddock on the side of the barn. Jeremy immediately walked to the bay gelding and stroked his neck. Jennie walked to the chocolate chestnut mare and stroked her neck.

"Were you interested in one or both?" Amos tried to hide a smile.

Well, sir. I thought one." Jeremy laughed. "I can see the plan may have changed. Do they both drive?"

"Yes, single and together as a pair. Charlie rides both; however, I would say they are green broke at best."

"Grandpa Amos, should I get the harness?" Young Charlie was ready to get beyond talking.

"Yes, go ahead. Do you want to drive them single first?"

Marcy stepped up. "Yes, please."

WHAT AN AFTERNOON. They drove each horse hitched to a small road cart, then Amos brought out a farm wagon and hitched them as a pair. They all climbed into the wagon for a tour of the farm and several other farms down the road. Marcy drove first and then nodded for Jeremy to take the reins. Jennie drove the mare as single earlier but declined driving the team as they pulled the wagon. She didn't think she was ready to drive a pair of horses.

When they returned to the barn. Marcy and Jeremy helped Amos unhitch the horses and groomed them as they stood tied in the aisle. As she groomed, Marcy ran her hands down their legs, feeling for heat or puffiness. She was giving them a good going over.

"Are they both registered?" Jennie wanted to know a bit more. "Do you know their history?"

Elizabeth pulled a folder containing registration papers out of a small trunk in the barn aisle. "Yes, my husband only bought and bred good bloodlines. He loved raising and training Morgan horses. He planned to eventually make it his full-time job." She swallowed; wetness gathered in the corner of her eyes. That plan would never happen now. She handed the folder to Jennie.

Jennie read the first paper. "His registered name is Win an Oscar."

Elizabeth smiled, "Yes, when he first arrived, we sometimes called him Oscar the Grouch."

"That's funny. He doesn't seem very grouchy." Jennie glanced at Oscar who was enjoying his grooming session.

"No, not anymore. Charlie knows more than I do about the bloodlines. Charlie, come on over a minute, son."

"We don't call Oscar grouchy anymore, do we?"

"No, he's not grouchy. He puts his ears back sometimes when he isn't sure about something. It doesn't mean anything."

"And Melody May. She seems like a sweet mare." Jennie was already in love.

"She is sweet. We could never get a foal from her, though."

"But she's a great driving horse, right, Mom?"

"Yes, she certainly is. It's been a very difficult decision to sell her and Oscar."

Jennie thought it would be a good idea to get Charlie talking about his horse—the one he chose to keep. "Is that your horse in the pasture, Charlie?" She pointed to a beautiful bright chestnut with a flaxen mane and tail. "It looks like Trina's horse, Fare. He's a Lambert Morgan."

Amos heard Jennie's comment about a Lambert Morgan, and seeing that Jeremy and Marcy were quite capable of taking care of Oscar and Melody May, walked over to join the conversation.

"Yes, I believe Charlie's horse is a Lambert Morgan, as is Oscar and Elizabeth's horse. You'll have to check the bloodlines to be sure. Melody May is a Lippitt. Isaiah wanted to raise horses with both Lambert and Lippitt bloodlines, and maybe cross the two."

"I'm still learning about the different foundation families, Mr. Stoltz." Trina looked at Jennie. "Jennie did a bit of research on Lamberts, because my horse, Fare, is from the Lambert family. It's all very interesting—confusing, but interesting."

"Mr. Stoltz, do you want us to turn Oscar and Melody May back out into the paddock?" Jeremy was ready to do business.

"Yes. And then let's walk up to the house. My wife prepared refreshments."

Jeremy could hardly stop himself from rushing ahead and grabbing a fistful of sugar cookies. It was times like this when he wished he was still a small boy. Well, to be truthful, brief times. He liked all the advantages of being an adult.

When everyone had a small plate of cookies and a glass of lemonade, they sat down at the second quilt-covered table.

"This quilt is so beautiful, are you sure we should be eating here?" Lainie hoped she didn't spill her lemonade.

"Yes, please sit. This is an old quilt." An older woman, probably Amos's wife, smiled. "We have plenty."

Jennie noticed that the Amish seemed to enjoy a bit of humor and wondered why more people didn't find the little bits of humor in life.

"These cookies really hit the spot. Thank you, Mrs. Stoltz." Grandpa couldn't remember her first name. She quickly supplied it.

"Now, Charlie, call me Agnes. You're an old friend."

"Agnes, yes, a very old friend, and feeling older when I'm traveling with these young people."

"And your wife? Her name is Fern?"

"You certainly have a good memory. Fern passed away a few years ago and she is missed."

"I'm very sorry. She was a very warm lady. I enjoyed speaking with her about gardens." Agnes remembered her fondly.

"She loved talking about her gardens." Grandpa wanted to put Agnes at ease. He didn't mind talking about the love of his life.

The group sat in silence for a few minutes, each enjoying the snack and perhaps a fond memory.

Grandpa cleared his throat and looked at Jennie and Jeremy. "Do you need a day or two to discuss the horses?" He noticed Jeremy, Jennie, and Marcy all stayed at the barn a few minutes longer than the rest of them—deep in discussion.

Jennie nodded at Jeremy to speak on their behalf. "We were originally thinking about only one horse." He hesitated. "I like Oscar and Jennie has fallen in love with Melody May. I guess we need to discuss a package deal." He didn't really expect a package deal—it was just a figure of speech.

Amos nodded at Elizabeth to answer. "I think they would find a good home with you both." She named a price much lower than expected.

"Do you have harness to sell?" Marcy thought they may want to sell the pair harness. She knew they wouldn't have a suitable vehicle to sell. Amish buggies weren't used outside of the Amish community.

"The harness we used on them today is for sale." Elizabeth knew how important it was to fit the harness to the horse and wanted both Oscar and Melody to have a well-fitted harness.

Jeremy sat up and named a price for both horses and their harness. It was a fair price and one Elizabeth didn't expect.

"A sound well-trained driving horse, with a well-fitted harness, is worth their weight in gold. I can't give you gold, but we'll certainly offer a fair price." Jennie nodded in agreement as Jeremy talked.

"Thank you. I accept your price on one condition."

"And that condition is?" Jennie said softly, then held her breath.

"On the condition Mr. Gantzler and all of you come visit again. We want to know how Oscar and Melody May like their new home."

Smiles around the group confirmed the deal.

Trina pulled Jennie away from the group. "Do you think we could use their bathroom before we leave?"

"I think so; they seem very friendly and comfortable having us here. It could be an outhouse and not a bathroom." Jennie thought they had indoor plumbing, although she did notice a little outhouse on the edge of the garden. Maybe that was for emergencies.

"Elizabeth, may we use your bathroom before we leave?" Jennie didn't know who lived at the farm, but she thought it was Elizabeth. Or maybe the entire family.

"Yes, of course."

Before Elizabeth could lead them to the house, Amos pointed to the outhouse. "It's over there."

Only the crinkles around his sparkling eyes revealed his joke.

Glancing at Trina's wide eyes, Elizabeth quickly added using the Amish word for dad, "Now, Daed, you know that is just for decoration. Follow me ladies, we've had indoor plumbing for a while now."

THE COOKIES WERE GREAT, but they still needed a meal. Sitting around a large table at the Der Dutchman restaurant, the group enjoyed a hearty supper.

Lainie leaned back in her chair. "I can't believe I ate all that food after eating about a dozen cookies. I wanted to hide some of those bar cookies in my pocket for later. They were so good!"

"And I can't believe we're getting two horses. I only have five stalls. We have four horses on the farm and two more make six. We didn't do our math." Jennie didn't like math, anyway.

"Julep runs the farm. She doesn't need a stall. She can eat in the aisle and roam around while the others eat in their stalls." Another thought popped into Jeremy's head quickly. "Besides, Marcy and I were discussing vehicle storage. We'll need to build a small carriage house or add to the barn."

"And where am I going to get the funds for such a project, Mr. Jeremy James?" Jennie couldn't imagine budgeting for a barn addition.

"My full name means I better think quick." Jeremy could tell he really wasn't in trouble but pretended he was.

"And?"

"Don't worry, I'll think of something. I'll need to sleep on it."

Grandpa chuckled. "First we'll need to get those horses to their new home."

"Marcy, can I hire your rig?" Jeremy hadn't actually discussed it with Marcy yet.

"I'm off work on Monday. If we don't go then, my next day off isn't until Saturday. I can't believe I got two Saturdays off work in a row but somehow I did." She didn't share her secret. Marcy agreed to trade with someone who needed another Saturday off in a few weeks.

"I probably shouldn't miss class on Monday, especially since I've already missed several weeks. I guess we'll go Saturday. Jennie?"

"I may be able to go Monday. I'll ask Mr. Mark. He may consider the trip a research trip if I write an article. Anyway, I have a few hours coming to me and Mr. Mark always says, whenever I need to work extra hours, I should take a few hours off, and it'll *all come out in the wash.* I think this is one of those *all come out in the wash* times."

"I wonder how Oscar and Melody will walk onto the trailer? It's not like Amish horses travel in horse trailers much." Lainie didn't think so, anyway. "I could go with you on Monday just in case we need to spend some time with trailer-loading lessons. I just need to be back at my barn by three for lessons."

"Let's plan on going early on Monday." Marcy was glad Lainie offered to go. Lainie was the best when it came to teaching horses to be confident in a horse trailer.

When Lainie and her horse, Shadow, were hit by a teenage driver texting through a stop sign, Shadow was trapped in the trailer until the firemen used the jaws of life to open the door. Fortunately, her injuries were minor and Lainie patiently helped Shadow become confident walking into a horse trailer again. It would be good to have Lainie along on the trip—just in case.

"What a great day. Trina, I'll drop you and Lainie off first. Then, Mr. Gantzler." Jeremy still had trouble calling Jennie's grandpa anything but Mr. Gantzler.

Grandpa woke up from his little nap in the front seat when he heard his name. "Jeremy, I think it's time you start calling me Charlie or Grandpa. You pick."

"I like Charlie, if that's ok."

"Perfectly fine." He turned his head to look at Jennie. "I'm still Grandpa to you, Jennie girl."

"I wouldn't have it any other way, Gramps." Jennie grinned.

"That will do, as well. This Gramps is tired. It was a big but enjoyable day. I'll need to turn on the TV and fall asleep in my recliner soon."

Grandpa usually fell asleep waiting on the evening news, and tonight he wouldn't keep his eyes open much past nine—if that long.

WITH ONLY JENNIE and Marcy remaining in the Enclave, Jeremy pulled into a gas station to fill up Ed's tank.

Jennie dug into her purse. "Jeremy, let me get that or at least help."

Jeremy took the twenty and ten she held in her hand. He knew Jennie well, and since he paid for dinner, he respected her offer to pay for filling the tank. Sometimes it was important, and in fact appropriate, to graciously accept help when it was offered.

"WHEW, WHAT A DAY." Marcy climbed out of Jeremy's small SUV and stretched. "I'm going to help you feed the horses, put the ponies' harness in my horse trailer for tomorrow, and then go home. I think I'm as tired as Grandpa Charlie."

"Me, too." Jennie looked at Jeremy. "Are you staying for a little while?"

"Just a little because I'll be back bright and early for church." Jeremy and Jennie liked the early service. They enjoyed the worship band and casual service. Jennie's parents preferred the traditional Lutheran liturgy at the eleven o'clock service.

"I forgot to ask Lainie and Trina if they were going to church." Jennie looked at Marcy. "And you know you're always welcome to come with us."

"Thanks. I'm still not feeling called to attend church, but I do enjoy the prayers you share. Trina is going with me to the park to drive the ponies. Did you know she used to drive Fare? Anyway, I know she's planning on church. She's going to pack a sandwich for the trail and change her clothes here."

"I guess that answers my question." Jennie filled the individual feed buckets. As she talked, Jeremy went to the pasture to get the horses, and they were now waiting patiently, or in Riley's case impatiently, for their supper.

"Here you go. Enjoy." Jennie fed Julep and Sadie, as Marcy fed Riley and Stuffin. "We'll need to make room for Oscar and Melody May."

Marcy sat on her tack trunk in front of Riley's stall. "I bet Megan and Cassy will be over as soon as they hear we have two new horses on the farm." She laughed. "If you want to find out how green they are under saddle, just put Megan and Cassy on their backs. Those girls can really ride!"

"That's not a bad idea. Young Charlie said he rode them both. I don't think they'll be more than the girls can handle." Jeremy sat down on the bench beside Jennie.

Jennie chuckled. "You called him Young Charlie just like Grandpa?"

"Too many Charlies gets confusing. I guess we won't see him enough to get confused, though. I just thought it was funny."

Jennie went back to the subject of her young friends, Megan and Cassy. "Just for the record, I think you're correct about Megan and Cassy. They'll want to ride both Oscar and Melody."

Megan Peterson and Cassy Morton kept their horses at Lainie's barn which she leased from the Peterson family. Both enjoyed being a part of Lainie's performance team—Megan on her young horse named Starlight, and Cassy on her horse, named

Treasure. Megan was finishing her senior year at Appleridge High School, and Cassy her freshman year at Richburg College. When the girls met at the end of last summer, they quickly became good friends, both had boundless energy, and both were fearless in the saddle.

"Even though, Belinda and I had a lot of fun growing up, I don't think we were ever as bold as those two girls on the back of a horse." Belinda Peterson, Megan's older sister, and now a vet student at the University of Florida, was Jennie's best friend all through high school, through college, and now as young adults. "I'm glad they have so much fun together. I miss their energy around the place."

Both Megan and Cassy boarded their horses at Jennie's barn until Lainie moved to Appleridge and started her business, Lessons with Lainie.

"Just think, if they were still here, there wouldn't be room for Oscar and Melody." Jeremy reminded Jennie.

"So true, and Sam wouldn't have moved Sadie to my barn. Changes always seem to work out for the best." Jennie usually remained positive in most situations. She missed both girls, although the Peterson barn wasn't far, and she enjoyed having Sam, Marcy, and of course, Jeremy, around the place.

"I'm ready to get home, hit the shower, and snuggle in bed reading my book. It's been fun. I'll see you tomorrow. Probably sometime after you get home from church and before I leave to drive the ponies."

Jennie and Jeremy stood up for their goodbye hug from Marcy.

"Thanks for your help today, and for the help I'm sure Jennie and I will need in the future."

"Anytime, friends, anytime."

Chapter Eight

Trina hung on tight as Marcy expertly handled the reins. Riley and Stuffin flew down the trail at a fast trot. The marathon carriage was built for off-road adventures and this trail was a rough ride.

Slowing to a walk, Marcy glanced over her shoulder at Trina standing on the back step. "It's going to be fun shopping for a cart or carriage for you, and Jennie and Jeremy. What do you want for Fare?"

"I think a nice road cart would be fine. I can't imagine him flying along the trail at his age, although I do like this carriage."

"They aren't cheap. Sometimes you can find a good buy on a used carriage. How old is Fare, anyway?"

"He's nineteen this year. Not ancient but not young. I would like to drive him again, maybe compete in a few fun shows, but probably not in a combined driving event."

"Morgan horses are hearty; you may be surprised. Competing at Training Level wouldn't be too demanding." Marcy added, "Riley is eighteen and Stuffin is sixteen, but I think the three of us together have a few more good years."

"I'm surprised. They look and act much younger. That certainly is a testament to the huge difference good care and thoughtful training makes for a horse. Poor Fare, I don't know what he's been through, but I'll do my best to make a difference."

"You already are making a difference. He looks great." Marcy made it a habit to stop out at Trina's place every couple of days. Their friendship blossomed. "Have you thought any more about having your mom visit?"

"I'm glad you brought that up. She's coming in two weeks. Any chance you'll have some days off?"

"I'll check my schedule, but I should. If not, I'll try to trade for at least one day off."

"Thanks. I'm a little nervous. She's my mom and I'm nervous. How crazy is that?"

"It's not crazy. Maybe you're more excited than nervous." Marcy knew this was a huge step for her friend.

"You may be right, but say a prayer for me, anyway."

"Sure thing. Let's head back to the trailer. It's time to get these wonder kids home." Marcy sure loved her ponies.

DRIVING BACK TO SUGAR CREEK early on Monday morning proved to be a quick and easy trip for Jennie, Lainie, Marcy, and Trina. They stopped for breakfast at a Bob Evans restaurant and arrived at the Miller farm by nine in the morning. Amos and Charlie greeted them and motioned for Marcy to swing the truck and trailer through the yard to turn around. Marcy was glad she didn't need to back the trailer out of the drive or navigate in a small place; however, she could do it if needed.

Jennie held the check Jeremy had written. He paid for both Oscar and Melody.

"We made the check out to Elizabeth. Is that correct? Is she here today?"

Amos stepped forward. "She's here. She asked me to apologize. She's decided to stay in the house to avoid saying goodbye to the horses again. She said her goodbyes last night."

Jennie noticed Charlie looked a little sad. "We'll take really good care of them both; I promise." Amos put his arm around the youngster's shoulders and gave him a little squeeze.

Lainie led Oscar into the trailer, then Melody May, while Jennie stood at the ramp to fasten the rear bars. Both Oscar and Melody May stood quietly as they lifted the ramp to close the trailer. Marcy hung the harness in her trailer dressing room as Jennie and Lainie worked with the horses. It all only took a few minutes.

"That was smooth." Jennie turned to look at Amos and Charlie. "They've learned to trust, and we'll never violate that trust."

"Miss Jennie, do all of you always travel together? Do you live together?" Charlie didn't think they were sisters. He was confused.

"We're very good friends." Jennie didn't understand Charlie's confusion.

"Oh, I thought you were sisters, but you don't look alike."

Trina laughed because with her dark skin, she was the one that obviously couldn't be a sister. "No, I guess we don't look alike but I consider these girls my sisters."

Charlie smiled. "I think you look like sisters, now. You all smile the same."

Amos chuckled. "Smiles are good, Charlie." Amos was glad to see both Charlie's smile and being comfortable holding a conversation. After his father passed away, the boy had been very withdrawn.

"We better get Oscar and Melody to their new home." Marcy thought they shouldn't linger.

"We'll keep in touch, I promise." Jennie wanted to hug both Amos and Charlie but she knew the Amish probably didn't hug people they didn't know well.

"YOU KNOW, WE ARE LIKE SISTERS." Trina commented from the back seat of Marcy's diesel truck. "And, just so you know, I'm enjoying our time together."

Lainie piped in, "Me, too! I don't have any siblings."

"I have one brother but no sisters." Marcy added.

"I guess I'm the only one with sisters—two. But I have room for the three of you—my horse-crazy sisters." Jennie didn't want to be left out.

"We need a name." Marcy looked a Jennie. "You're good at thinking up names."

"Hmmm, how about calling ourselves The Four Evers, like forever friends, only spell it like the number four—Four Evers?"

Trina thought for a moment. "I don't think we should limit our friends. We may want to add new friends to our group."

"I think Trina's right. If we get a chance to add friends, we should. You can never have too many good friends. I'll keep thinking." Jennie pondered a name. Horses brought them together. Maybe horses would lead them to a name—and more friends, too?"

Lainie was quiet—thinking. "I've known you guys for a while, and I thought we were friends. It wasn't until Fare came that we've really seemed to have bonded. Is it just me or do you think our friendship changed after we spent the morning together waiting for Fare?"

"Yeah, I think so. Our friendship seems to have taken on a new life just about then." Marcy kept her eyes on the road as she talked.

"I just looked up the word *fare* on my phone. One of the definitions for *fare* is *to get along, to succeed,*" Trina shared.

"That's perfect! We want to have great experiences as we travel through life and help one another succeed." Jennie's mind was busily trying to come up with a great name.

"I know finding Fare has certainly changed my life—and for the better. I've only shared this with Marcy but my family has been estranged since my dad was murdered." Trina couldn't believe she was sharing her tightly held secret.

"Your dad was murdered! I'm so sorry, Trina." Lainie wasn't close to her father, who divorced her mom and now had a new family, but she couldn't imagine him being murdered.

"Thanks. He owned a grocery store and they think it was an after-hours robbery. The police said he was shot before the killers dragged him into the freezer. That's where my brother, Bart, found him." Trina went on to tell her friends about Bart's drug use, how he sold Fare behind her back, and then kicked her out of the family business. "Mom didn't hold Bart responsible and that made me angry. Now, I think her grief was responsible. She couldn't handle losing Dad and shut down. Bart called recently. He apologized and wants to come see me. He says we have a lot to talk about."

"You don't owe your brother the time of day." This story made Lainie angry. She didn't want Trina to get hurt again. "You owe him nothing."

"I know, but his apology felt very sincere. I told him I wasn't ready for him to visit but I'm ready to mend my relationship with Mom. I invited her to spend a week on the farm. I'm picking her up tomorrow. I'm planning a gathering on Saturday and my Fare Friends are invited."

"Hey, I like that; we're the Fare Friends." Marcy knew how hard it must have been for Trina to share, and wanted to help lighten the mood a little. Besides, she liked the name.

"I like it, too. Jeremy and I would love to come over on Saturday. Just let us know what we can bring."

"Thanks, Jennie. I'll also invite my boarders and maybe a few friends from church, but I'll count on my Fare Friends for the most help."

Marcy expertly pull the truck and trailer into Jennie's farm drive. "Well, Fare Friends, let's get these beauties off the trailer so they can meet their new friends. I'm sure Julep and Riley will accept them—eventually." Julep was the lead mare at the farm and Riley her sidekick. It would be an interesting introduction. And it was.

Jennie put Oscar and Melody in a pasture adjoining the field where Sadie, Julep, Riley, and Stuffin were grazing. There was a lot of snorting and running along the fence before they settled down and started grazing again. Every once in a while, one of the horses would lift their head, whinny, and start running again. It was fun to watch.

"I see mostly play going on and not too much to be concerned about." Jennie observed.

"They'll all be together in one big herd soon." Marcy leaned on the gate. "I think Julep will retain her leader status."

"I think so. I don't think Riley will drop in the pecking order, either. Oscar and Melody don't seem to have a desire to take over the herd. At least not from their side of the fence. We'll introduce them slowly, just to be sure, though." Jennie was always aware of the herd dynamics.

"I think six is probably the limit for your farm," Lainie added.

"I agree—limit for my pastures, my checking account, and my time." Jennie laughed. "Fare has sure brought a lot of changes to all of us!"

AFTER LAINIE AND TRINA left the farm, Jennie helped Marcy clean out her horse trailer, groomed Julep, did a few barn chores, and checked on Oscar and Melody every fifteen minutes. She rode along with Marcy as she drove the ponies in the pasture. She was busy—doing everything but her work for the CC. Sometimes it was just too hard to work from home when you really wanted to stay in the barn.

She decided to go inside and work for a few hours after Marcy said goodbye. She knew Jeremy would drive directly to the farm after his classes.

A truck pulled into the drive, a little too fast, horn tooting. *And there they are. That didn't take very long.*

"Jennie, we want to see your new horses." Cassy shouted from the passenger side as she leaned over Megan sitting in the driver's seat.

Jennie laughed and waited for Megan to park.

"It's good to see you. You haven't been out for a while."

Megan hugged Jennie. "I know; Lainie keeps us busy."

A second hug from Cassy. "We miss you!"

"I miss you, too, but I know you're having a great time on the performance team. I can't wait to see your debut in a few weeks. Are you ready?"

"I think so. Starlight isn't as experienced as the rest of the horses, so we aren't asking her to do as much. I think she likes it." Megan was proud of her young mare.

"I'm sure Treasure is the old pro of the group." Jennie looked at Cassy.

"She's learning some new things—we both are. Lainie's an awesome teacher. We're learning a lot about connecting with our horses and working as a team."

Cassy jogged ahead. "You're taking too long."

Jennie and Megan hurried to catch up.

"Oh, Jennie, they're beautiful. And they both drive?" Cassy stroked Oscar's neck as he nuzzled her hand.

"Mostly drive. They're pretty green under saddle."

Cassy and Megan looked at each other.

"I know, I know, you want to put a few rides on them." Jennie laughed. "Let me work with them from the ground for a few days and I'll let you know when I think that's a good idea."

"You only have five stalls and now you have six horses." Cassy moved her hand pretending she was counting. "And you also know, Lainie is looking for a school master for some of her young students."

Jennie knew Cassy was leading the conversation somewhere but she wasn't sure where.

"So." Cassy looked at Megan.

Megan took the hint and continued for Cassy. "So maybe Julep could come over to Lainie's and be a teacher until Lainie finds a horse?"

Jennie's first instinct was to declare, "Definitely not!" But she said nothing. She couldn't give up Julep, especially after just getting her back home this year. However, she also knew Julep enjoyed the attention of little girls. She didn't want to be stingy, but she wasn't quite ready to share, either.

"I'm not sure if I'm ready for that idea. I promise to keep an open mind."

"An open mind about what? Hey, girls." Jeremy walked into the barn and grabbed both Cassy and Megan in a three-person hug before reaching for Jennie's arm and pulling her into the group.

"We just thought maybe Julep could help Lainie out for a while," Cassy shared.

Megan tag teamed. "She needs a good teacher for the little kids."

Jeremy glanced at Jennie. "I'm not so sure Julep will ever leave Jennie's farm again."

Jennie nodded and smiled. She wanted Jeremy to see she wasn't upset.

Jeremy changed the subject. "What do you think of our new friends?"

"We love them!" Cassy answered.

"And we want to ride them!" Megan jumped in.

"You're hired!" Jeremy put two thumbs up.

THE GIRLS LEFT and took a high level of energy with them. The barn was quiet. Jeremy motioned for Jennie to sit on the bench in the barn aisle.

"I guess we should talk about the horses, buying a cart or carriage, how much I need to pay for board—you know, business stuff."

"Thank you for buying Melody. I can give you half now and pay you the other half over time—if that's agreeable? Or maybe trade out board to pay for Melody?" Jennie waited for Jeremy's answer.

"That's good. Or, maybe she'll be an engagement present," he teased. "I don't think you're the type for a large diamond ring."

"No—I'm not the type for a large diamond engagement ring or even a small one. I love the ring you already gave me." She glanced at the ring, with three small blue stones, on her hand—a ring that belonged to Jeremy's mom. It wasn't an engagement ring—it was a commitment ring until they were ready to be engaged. "Wait! What are you saying?" Jennie held her breath.

"I'm saying I would love to give you Melody, instead of a ring."

"Does that mean we are now officially engaged?" Jennie wasn't sure if that's what it meant or not.

"This isn't exactly what I planned. I guess I didn't have a plan." Jeremy got down on one knee on the barn floor. "Jennie McKenzie, will you marry me?"

"Jeremy James." She swallowed a little lump in her throat. "Yes, I will marry you."

"Then please accept Melody as your engagement horse." Jeremy got up and they kissed.

"Well, this was a surprise, very unique, and will certainly make a great story to tell our children some day."

"Are you ready to set a date? Or do you want to wait until I know what I'm doing the rest of my life to support my wife?"

Jennie sighed. "That's a good question. I think we need some time to figure out a few things." They were still holding hands. "Let's wait to announce our engagement until we're ready to set a date."

"I agree. By the way, what kind of wedding do we want?" Jeremy would give Jennie anything she wanted.

"Small, intimate, country, maybe at the church with the reception here at the farm." Jennie wasn't really the type of girl to dream of a future wedding, but since she was asked, she had a few ideas.

"I like that idea."

Jennie sighed, Jeremy grinned, and in the pasture, the horses grazed. All creatures were content on the farm.

Several miles away, in a pasture, grazing on Trina's farm, an older Morgan horse lifted his head and sniffed the air. He blew out a breath and stood quietly looking in the distance, then lowered his head to graze. Content.

Chapter Nine

The following Monday, Trina pulled into her mom's drive, parked the truck, and sat.

Father, here I am. Is Mom as nervous as I am? Be with us, please. I love Mom and I believe she loves me. Please help us be a family again. Thank you.

The front door of her childhood home opened as Trina closed her truck door. She cradled her purse and walked to the house she'd rarely entered after college. Ten years. She could count on one hand how many times she crossed its threshold in ten years. Trina heard a voice in her head. *Leave the pain behind, move forward, always move forward. I am with you.*

"Hi, sweetie." Margaret stood in the open doorway. "Come on in. I'm ready but maybe you could help me with my suitcase?"

"Hi, Mom. Sure, I'll help." Trina spotted the wheeled suitcase leaning against the wingback chair in the living room. She glanced around. The room looked nice. She recognized some familiar furniture and also noticed a few new pieces. She could see into the dining room and it also looked very clean and nice. Her mom was always a good housekeeper but Trina guessed someone was helping with maintenance. The house looked freshly painted.

"The house looks very nice. Did you paint recently?"

"Barton and some of the young employees at the store did. He has his own place now, but he helps with whatever I need, and he likes to hire some of the employees that could use a little extra cash. He rewards hard work." Margaret hesitated. She realized Trina may not want to hear anything more about her brother.

"That's good to hear." Trina could tell her mom was trying to be careful about what she said. That made her sad. *Mom shouldn't be afraid to talk to me. Father, help please!*

"I'm happy you have Bart to help and I'm happy to hear he takes good care of his employees—just like Dad."

Margaret's eyes lit up. "Yes. Your father was very respected and loved. That's why he never sold out to a large grocery chain and why Barton won't, either. It's taken a while, but Barton has found his direction and purpose."

"I'm happy; I really am. Are you ready to meet my friends? And another little, or maybe I should say big, surprise?" Trina lifted the suitcase. "Judging by the weight of this suitcase, you're ready!" She laughed. Margaret thought it was so very nice to hear her daughter laugh. Hearing Trina laugh was an answered prayer.

"OH, TRINA YOUR PLACE is so beautiful." Margaret took in the long curvy tree-lined drive, the pastures, the barn, and finally the house. "Oh my, a log home!"

"I fell in love with this place the first time I saw it. The house is small, more like a cabin, but it's perfect for me. I actually think I bought the property for the barn, though."

"I'm sure you did." Margaret looked at her daughter. "You board five horses for their owners. Did you ever get another horse, honey?"

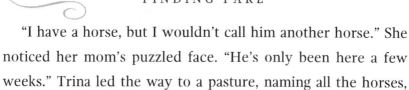

"I have a horse, but I wouldn't call him another horse." She noticed her mom's puzzled face. "He's only been here a few weeks." Trina led the way to a pasture, naming all the horses, except one.

"That one over there. What's his name? He reminds me of Fare." As soon as Margaret said the name, she felt sad. She quickly glanced at Trina, but Trina didn't look sad; she looked— happy.

Fare heard his name, nickered, and walked over to the fence. "Oh, my."

"It's Fare. Mom, please don't cry." She put her arms around her mom's small frame—smaller than she remembered.

Margaret reached over the fence to touch the horse now standing very quiet. "Oh, my."

Fare turned his head and studied Margaret. *Don't worry. I'm here. I'm fine.*

"Let's get your suitcase and I'll tell you the whole story over lunch. I made a spinach quiche. I know how much you love quiche."

"Oh, my." Margaret stepped back away from the fence, still gazing at Fare. Fare returned her gaze with soft brown eyes.

"He looks good, Trina. He certainly is a sight for sore eyes." What she didn't say—he certainly is a sight for a sore heart, too.

"LUNCH WAS DELICIOUS. Thanks, sweetie." Margaret placed her paper napkin beside her plate. "Let me help you clean up."

"No, please sit and relax. It's just a few things." Trina reached for the plates.

"I still can't believe Fare is in your pasture. That makes me so happy." Margaret hesitated. "I know it will make your brother happy, too."

Trina remained facing the sink, her back to her mom. *Father, give me healing words.*

"I've forgiven Bart. I'm not sure how much you know; you were grieving so terribly for Dad. Bart sold Fare without my permission."

"I didn't know at the time. He told me a few years later—one day when he found me crying. I'm so sorry. I should have helped you through the loss of your father. Instead I dug a hole and hid from life." Margaret brushed a tear with her fingers.

Trina turned to face Margaret. "I know. I'm ok. I've let go of a lot of anger. My friends have helped. I've got good friends, Mom. You'll meet them Saturday night. And..." Trina wanted to share her faith but didn't know quite what to say.

"And?" Margaret wiped a tear from her cheek.

"Please don't cry. I'm happy. I've found a great church. A church that has taught me so much about forgiveness, love, and the importance of family."

"Honey, we always went to church."

"I know." Trina didn't know how to explain; somehow, she missed some very important teaching about love and forgiveness. "I guess I wasn't ready to hear the messages I needed to hear."

"Sometimes you just need to be ready." Margaret smiled. "I can't wait to go to this church and meet your good friends. I'm glad you found both—good friends and a good church family."

"We'll do it all, Mom! We'll make up for lost years. I'm so glad you're here."

Chapter Ten

ear Equestrian,

Thank you for taking good care of us, and please, care for us for as long as possible. The world isn't a kind place for an unwanted horse. We suppose it isn't a very kind place for any unwanted person or animal.

We promise to do our very best to understand what you ask. Please be patient. Sometimes we have been taught the wrong answers. But you, Dear Equestrian, could help us find all the right answers. If you're willing. If you're patient.

Like you, as we age, we'll have health problems, and get old. We may become unable to do much at all, but we never want to become unlovable. Dear Equestrian, please love us forever—if possible.

Sometimes life becomes hard for you, too, and when that happens, and you may not be able to take care of us anymore, please find a good home. Please care for us the best way you can until the very end.

Looking forward to a long life together,

Your Horse

JENNIE WORKED on her articles and her Dear Equestrian letters until late into the night. She had a million thoughts and ideas running through her head and knew she wouldn't sleep, anyway. When she finally climbed the stairs to her bedroom, morning and work were just a blink away. It seemed as if the alarm on her phone played its cheery wakeup music only minutes after her head hit the pillow.

She opened her eyes, looking at the time, hoping she could steal a few more minutes of sleep. Her cat, Beauty, had other ideas. Beauty sat on her chest kneading the quilt and purring loudly.

"Ok, Beauty, I'm up. Well, I'm awake and I'll try to get up."

Only the thought of four horses and two ponies waiting for their hay helped her roll to a sitting position and scan the floor, searching for her barn clothes. They were on the floor next to the closet, neatly folded. It seemed to Jennie like she changed her clothes several times every day—barn clothes, work clothes, casual-trip-to-the-store clothes. She tried to wear each several times, if possible, to save on laundry.

She pulled on her jeans, grabbed a shirt, then glanced at her phone's weather app before adding a hoodie sweatshirt. Brrr! It was a little chilly this morning, although the bright sunrise promised a beautiful day.

The horses were lined up at the gate, waiting to come in for breakfast. Jennie brought Melody and Oscar in first, then opened the gate for the other four. She put a small rope around Julep's neck and asked her to stay in the aisle while Sadie and the ponies found their usual places. Julep looked at her stall, now holding Melody, and then looked at Jennie.

"You're going to eat out here in the aisle, sweetie." To sweeten the deal, Jennie pulled a horse cookie from her pocket. Julep enjoyed the treat and then followed Jennie to the feed room and watched her prepare a bucket for each horse. Jennie put Julep's bucket in the aisle first, and then carried the other buckets to the stalls.

This certainly did complicate her morning routine a little. Maybe she really would need to add onto her barn so each horse had a private place to eat. Fortunately, Julep didn't seem to mind eating her breakfast in the aisle instead of in a stall. Horses learned routines quickly. Each day would become easier.

Jennie loaded her little garden wagon with hay and pulled it out to the pastures, making hay piles for each horse and one extra. Julep, now finished with her breakfast bucket, followed. "Good girl, Julep."

She returned to the barn and opened the stalls for Sadie, Riley, and Stuffin to follow Julep to their pasture. Then she opened the stall doors for Melody and Oscar to follow her to their little pasture. She didn't know if they would follow her like the other horses; however, she thought they would follow the promise of hay. And they did.

She gathered and rinsed six feed buckets, swept the barn aisle, checked the water tanks, filling one, and after checking all gates and the feed room door, returned to the house for a quick shower. Looking at the time, she decided she may need to add about fifteen minutes to her schedule each morning. She vowed to get to bed at a decent hour in the future.

Two new horses—Jeremy had his own horse and she had an engagement horse. She couldn't wait to get home from work and spend some quality time with her engagement horse.

ACROSS FIELDS AND SEVERAL SMALL WOODS, about three miles as the crow flies, Fare waited patiently by the pasture gate for his own breakfast. He sighed. He was content. He nickered a low nicker when he saw Trina on her front porch.

Trina, sipping a cup of coffee, looked for Fare and a sigh escaped. She would never get tired of seeing him every morning. He had a home for the rest of his life. She drank in his calmness and felt peace. How, she didn't know. She turned when she heard the door softly close behind her.

"May I join you? I found the coffee." Margaret shuffled outside, still in her robe and slippers.

"Are you warm enough?"

"Hey, who's the mom anyway?" Margaret teased.

"You are and I'm loving having you here." Trina put her coffee mug on a small table and walked over to give her mom a hug.

"I'm enjoying my time, too, and I can't believe how fast the days are flying by. What do we need to do for Saturday's gathering?"

"Not much. My friends like casual gatherings with good food, and since I learned how to cook from you, they love my food. They'll be happy with whatever we make. We'll make a list and go to the store today if you're game." Trina sat down on a porch rocker.

"I'm game." Margaret found her own rocker and they sat in silence for a few minutes, sipping coffee and rocking.

"What's on the menu?" Margaret looked at her daughter.

"I thought we could make a nice pot of chili and I would talk you into making some of your special cornbread. I've never been able to quite master the technique for crispy-on-the-outside and soft-on-the-inside cornbread."

"Do you have a nice cast iron skillet?" Margaret asked.

"I do. I use it often but not for cornbread. I'm going to keep the appetizers simple. Maybe cheese, crackers, and a little relish tray. I'm making a pie. They love my pie, but they'll love your crust even more. I don't make pie crust as flaky and light as you do."

"It sounds fun. We'll have a nice baking day. When do you want me to be ready to leave for the store?"

"Oh, no rush. I still need to feed horses and do a few barn chores. If I don't get too dirty, I'll clean up but won't shower again. I want to take you to the Café for lunch. We'll leave around noon. Is that ok?"

"Sounds perfect. I'll finish my coffee, grab a piece of leftover quiche for breakfast, and get my shower out of the way. It's so relaxing here, I hope you don't mind if I'm a bit lazy." Margaret sighed with contentment.

"I don't mind. I love my little place and I'm happy you feel comfortable here. I hope you come back and stay many more times." Trina got up from her rocker. "I'm just going to put my cup in the kitchen and get on out to the barn. You enjoy as much coffee and rocking as you want." She leaned over and gave her mom a kiss on the cheek as her mom patted her arm.

"I love you, sweetie."

"I love you, too, Mom." Those words warmed Margaret more than the coffee.

MARCY SEARCHED several internet sites for cart and carriage ads as she drank her morning cup. She was anxious to help both Jeremy and Jennie drive their new horses. Neither Melody

nor Oscar were large horses, at barely 14.2 hands, but her po-nies' carriage was definitely too small. She didn't have to work at the hospital and planned a lazy day running errands and spending the afternoon with her ponies. And she would print out a few nice ads and leave the information at the barn for Jen-nie to find later. She loved the look of the two new Morgan horses. They were a nice-looking pair; very responsive when she held their lines in her hands on the trial drive. Yup, they needed to find a vehicle as soon as possible. Marcy never let much grass grow under her feet, as Jennie's grandpa liked to say.

CHARLIE GANTZLER SAT with his buddies at the local bak-ery, the Bake & Shake, enjoying their morning coffee, muffins, and conversation. His thoughts turned to Jennie's new horses. Well, actually, Jennie and Jeremy's new horses. Jennie called earlier in the week to tell him they were at the farm. He was anxious to see how they settled into their new home. He would give Jennie a call tonight and set up a time for her fetch him for a trip to the farm. Of his three granddaughters, Jennie was the only one who loved horses. He guessed it was either in your blood or not. Some may even call it an addiction. He liked to think of horses as a very precious gift from a very loving God. But, then, so were granddaughters, whether they loved horses or not.

JEREMY SAT IN CLASS, trying to concentrate. Instead of the lecture, he was thinking about Jennie and the horses. He would be spending quite a few evenings at Jennie's barn and that was certainly fine with him. He just hoped his studies didn't suffer. He had a future wife to support. That thought made him sit up a bit straighter and focus on the speaker.

MELODY AND OSCAR MUNCHED grass next to the larger pasture where Julep, Sadie, Riley, and Stuffin grazed. They were content. They missed grooming sessions with the little human, Charlie, but this new place seemed alright. They had plenty of hay, grass, clean water, and the humans were gentle with their touch.

FARE NICKERED as Trina walked to his pasture. He waited patiently for her to lead each horse into their stall for breakfast until she returned for him. He was a patient soul. Some things are worth waiting for, and coming home to Trina was worth the long, painful journey of the last ten years—although he didn't know what a year meant. Horses live in the moment, so Fare didn't dwell in the past. He only looked forward to a kind stroke along his neck and breakfast. Humans could learn a few lessons from horses.

Dear Equestrian,

Don't worry too much about our care. Give us plenty of hay, clean fresh water, and soothing grooming sessions, and we'll be fine. We like to have a job, so let's go for a ride, take a walk in the woods, or perform for a crowd. We want to please. We just need to understand what you ask, and if we don't understand, make sure you slow down and help us learn.

I think humans like to understand what they are asked, too, and I'm sure they like plenty of food and water to help them work.

So, Dear Equestrian, take a deep breath and relax. We'll learn to trust. It's our most precious gift to offer. When we trust, there isn't much we won't be able to accomplish together. And don't forget, let's have some fun!

I want to be a willing partner,

Your Horse

Chapter Eleven

A loud crash woke Elizabeth suddenly. *Lightening hit somewhere near.* She waited a few minutes, listening for the children. No sounds. No crying. She rolled over and closed her eyes, willing herself to sleep. She was so tired. She drifted off.

She sat up quickly. Her heart racing. Panic filled her chest. *What are those sounds? Smoke? Is that smoke?* She bolted from her bed, ready to grab the children. An orange glow filled her window. The barn!

"Charlie, Charlie!" Elizabeth grabbed her heavy shawl and rushed to check the children's rooms. Charlie wasn't in his bed. Micah, seven-year-old, was in bed, wide awake. The baby, asleep in her crib.

"Mama, I'm scared."

"I know. Can you please stay in your bed and watch your sister? Promise me, Micah; you'll be safe in the house."

"Yes, mama, I promise." Micah clung to his quilt. Tears running down his face.

Elizabeth kissed her small son on the forehead, gave him a quick reassuring hug, and ran downstairs, only stopping to grab a pair of boots.

Oh, please, Father, protect Charlie and send help. Glancing at the barn, Elizabeth knew it was gone. *Please, God, not my Charlie.* She heard horses screaming. She felt sick.

"Charlie! Charlie!"

"I'm over here, Mama. I can't get them...I can't get them. I can't get Star and Stormy."

Elizabeth ran toward the voice, sobbing. She found Charlie on the ground about thirty feet from the barn. "Get up, Charlie; we need to move; you're too close." She grabbed his arm and pulled, breathing hard.

Charlie slowly stood up. "The pony is out. I can't get Star and Stormy. Oh, Mama, mama, I couldn't find them."

"Elizabeth! Charlie!"

A pair of strong arms wrapped themselves around both Elizabeth and Charlie—gently guiding them away from the barn. The only sounds heard were timbers crashing as the barn collapsed, destroying another part of their lives, and the sobs of a young boy over the loss of his horse.

In the distance, sirens. Too late for the barn.

Elizabeth closed her eyes. *Thank you, God; thank you for keeping Charlie safe.* She turned her soot-streaked face toward her father. Her strong arms of safety.

"I'll go talk to the firemen. They'll make sure the fire is out and the property safe." He guided his daughter to the front porch where Agnes waited with Micah and the baby.

"Charlie, you come with me." His grandson needed to be with him. *How much more will this young family endure?*

The Amish community would rebuild the barn. Nothing would bring back the horses. An Amish family needed horses for transportation, but for Charlie and Elizabeth, the loss was much greater. Elizabeth's buggy horse, Star, and Charlie's gelding, Stormy, were the last horses raised and trained by Isaiah, before he passed away. To lose so much in such a short time was heartbreaking. Amos shook his head and placed his arm around Charlie's shoulders. They would rely on their faith as they took another step on a journey they never wanted to take.

JENNY'S PHONE SANG a little tune. Driving home from work, she glanced at the screen but didn't pick it up. Whoever it was could leave a message. Once home, she waited until she changed into her barn chore clothes and sat on a stool in the kitchen before checking voicemail.

"Jennie, hi, this is Kerry. Trina gave me your number. The Miller barn was hit by lightning last night and burned to the ground. They lost the two Morgan horses. The pony survived. I just thought you and Jeremy would want to know. Elizabeth and the children are fine, grieving for many reasons, but not injured."

Oh my! Poor Charlie. Poor Elizabeth. Jennie sunk to her knees. *Father, be with our friends. Comfort them. So much loss.*

She couldn't continue with words, but she remained on her knees, head bowed. God would hear her unspoken prayer. She debated about calling Jeremy. He planned to eat with her at the farm tonight. She would wait and tell him in person.

She jumped as her phone sang again. The song was too happy; stupid phone. She answered; it was Trina.

"Hey, I heard."

"I hope it was ok to give Kerry your number."

"Sure. I can't imagine so much sadness for Elizabeth and Charlie." Jennie hesitated. "Should I call them?" She thought she should call. What should she say?

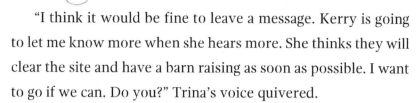

"I think it would be fine to leave a message. Kerry is going to let me know more when she hears more. She thinks they will clear the site and have a barn raising as soon as possible. I want to go if we can. Do you?" Trina's voice quivered.

"Yes, I want to go and so would Jeremy and probably Marcy." Jennie thought for a moment. "I guess they don't have insurance so they won't need to wait on an adjuster to get started with cleaning up the site."

"No, I think the Amish are self-insured."

"How did Kerry and Deb get so connected to the Amish community? They don't live near Sugar Creek, do they?" Jennie thought it was probably because of their horse rescue. Maybe there was more to the story. "Because of the horses?"

"Well, yes, the horses. Once the Amish community found out about Save a Morgan, several families started calling Kerry and Deb before taking their horses to the sale. They don't keep horses around that can't earn their keep. Horses have jobs in their world."

Jennie didn't understand. "I think horses like having a purpose, but I also think we owe them a nice retirement after they serve us faithfully."

Trina shrugged her shoulders, but Jennie couldn't see the gesture. All she heard was a moment of silence. "I don't disagree, but we live in a different world. Even so, I think some Amish do care and that's why they call the rescue for help. Maybe we think a bit differently about some things. I'm not sure. Some of us look into a horse's eyes and see their soul."

"The same with any creature—dog, cat, or the little bird sitting on my porch railing right now as we talk."

They both sighed.

"Jeremy's coming over tonight for supper. I'll wait until then to tell him about the Millers' barn and the horses. Do you want to come over tonight? Marcy will be here. I'll order pizza." Jennie wanted to gather her friends close.

"Mom's here."

"Bring your mom. We want to meet her."

"Ok, we'll be there about six. Is that good?"

"Yes, perfect."

Jennie called Marcy and asked her to pick up the pizza she was about to order and pay for over the phone.

"Oh, my, so much tragedy for that young family. My heart hurts."

"Mine, too."

"You order the pizza and I'll pick it up. I was planning to be at the barn around six."

"Perfect, that's when Trina and her mom are coming. I don't know why, but I wanted to be with friends tonight. Lainie's teaching lessons but she may stop by later."

"See you soon."

After Marcy hung up, Jennie sent a text to Sam. Although he usually worked late shoeing and trimming horses' feet, several evenings a week he stopped by to love on his horse, Sadie. If he stopped by tonight, Jennie wanted Sam to feel welcome to join them for pizza.

JENNIE KEPT HER BROOM BUSY in the barn aisle. She swept Julep's hay into a neat pile and stroked the mare's neck before hanging her broom on its wall hook. Julep seemed to enjoy having the run of the barn. The other horses were content munching their supper hay in their stalls. She would keep them in the barn. Marcy, Jeremy, and Sam would probably want to groom or spend some time with their equine friends later. Jennie glanced in Melody May's stall. She had settled into her new home well, although tonight she followed Jennie's every move. Oscar seemed a bit unsettled. Horses have amazing abilities to sense emotion in humans. Perhaps they felt Jennie's sadness, or sensed the tragedy and loss of their former pasture pals.

She turned to look toward the house when she heard a car. Jeremy parked near the back porch of the house and waved— indicating he saw her in the barn.

Jennie ran to the car.

"What's wrong?" Jeremy saw the worry she couldn't outrun.

"It's the Miller farm. Lightning hit the barn. They lost Elizabeth's buggy horse and Charlie's horse. Charlie's dog is ok. He was with him in the house when it happened. He woke up Charlie. Charlie tried to save the horses. Elizabeth found him sprawled outside the barn." The words spilled out of Jennie but Jeremy caught most of them.

"Ok, slow down. Are Elizabeth and Charlie ok?"

"Yes."

"They lost the horses?"

"Yes, and the barn. Kerry thinks they will rebuild the barn quickly, but..."

"But they lost the horses and they can't be replaced." Jeremy looked at Jennie and she read something on his face she didn't want to read.

Jeremy grabbed her hand to lead her into the barn. Together they sat on their favorite bench. "Those horses are special because they were raised and trained by Isaiah."

"Yes." Jennie swallowed trying to breath calmly. "I know what you're thinking." She wouldn't cry. Not, yet.

"Oscar and Melody." Jeremy brushed a tear from Jennie's cheek.

"We love Oscar and Melody."

"We do, but so do Charlie and Elizabeth."

Jennie didn't want to talk about Oscar and Melody. "Marcy and Trina are coming over for pizza. I wanted to gather friends when I heard the news. I wanted to talk about how we could help Elizabeth."

"That's good. There's probably many ways to help but..." Jeremy hesitated.

"But we know what we need to do." Her heart was breaking for the Amish family. She hoped she wasn't being selfish—her heart was breaking for her and Jeremy, too.

Jeremy pulled her close. Heart beating against heart. Jennie was crying.

"Hey, it'll be ok."

"I'm sad." *It sure is hard to do the right thing. Why did Jeremy always want to do the right thing?* She wanted to be selfish.

They remained embraced until they heard a diesel engine. Straightening, they stood as Marcy walked into the barn.

"Hey, you two; didn't mean to interrupt."

Jennie took out a tissue and wiped her face as Jeremy answered, "We were just talking about the fire and Elizabeth's loss. It's a lot to imagine. We were talking about how to help."

Marcy motioned to her truck. "Let's get the pizza out of my truck first. House party or barn party?"

"It's a nice night. How about a barn party? I'll pull the chairs out of the tack room." Jennie glanced at Melody again, sniffed, and walked to the tack room.

"I know Jennie is upset about the fire. She's taking it really hard." Marcy studied Jeremy's face as they walked.

Jeremy opened the passenger door of Marcy's truck as Trina pulled into the drive. "Yes. We'll explain; there's more."

Marcy nodded.

Trina jumped out of her truck and then helped Margaret navigate the big step to the ground. Together they walked to the barn.

"Mom, these are my friends, Jennie, Jeremy, and Marcy. This is Jennie's farm. She and Jeremy are an *item* and Marcy keeps her two ponies here."

"Nice to meet you, Jennie; you have a beautiful place and look at these lovely horses."

"Thank you, Mrs. Shaw; I hope you like pizza in the barn. Nothing fancy but the plates are clean."

"I love pizza and a party in the barn. It reminds me of old times when..." Margaret covered her face with both hands.

"It's ok, Mom, my friends know the whole story about Fare." Trina gently moved Margaret's hands away from her face. "Hey, I'm hungry. Wow, that's a lot of pizza!"

"You know my girl. Leftovers are good. She'll live on cold leftover pizza for days." Jeremy looked for affirmation from his friends.

"Boo-hoo, poor Jeremy; that means you'll be eating cold pizza, too." Trina couldn't resist. These were really good friends. Her mom didn't need to be afraid of saying the wrong thing.

"Oh, no, not me. I'll leave it all to Jennie. I'm generous like that!"

Jennie waved her hands. "Hey, guys, I'm right here. I can hear you." Her voice revealed she really wasn't upset.

Everyone laughed with her.

Marcy returned to her truck to grab the jug of cold tea. She didn't know why they were laughing, but laughing was good. "I couldn't remember what type of pop everyone drank so tea was easy."

"Tea or water are always right," Trina confirmed.

Jennie added, "If anyone wants a root beer, I have that in the barn fridge. We can raid Grandpa's stash."

They arranged the pizza, tea, a roll of paper towels, paper plates, and cups on the small folding table Jennie stored in the tack room for impromptu barn parties. Then, Marcy, Jennie, and Trina looked expectedly at Jeremy. Mrs. Shaw followed the crowd.

"Ah, you want me to say grace before we eat?" Four nods and five sets of clasped hands readied as Jeremy began.

"Father, thank you for this time together eating pizza with friends. Please be with Elizabeth Miller and her family, especially Charlie, as they cope with the loss of their barn and their cherished horses. Father, we thank you that in this time of tragedy, the family is safe and no other buildings were lost. Guide us tonight as we come together to find how we can best help them. In your name we pray."

Five voices joined together, "Amen."

The barn was quiet except for horses munching hay as the friends grabbed pizza and poured tea. Julep wandered over to check out the table.

"Go on, Julep." Jennie shooed Julep away from the pizza and walked her back to her own supper of hay.

Trina wiped her mouth with a paper towel. "I can't believe what happened. It's such a tragedy for the Miller family and so soon after the loss of Isaiah Miller. Kerry said the Amish community has already surrounded Elizabeth and the kids with help. They'll clear the debris, although I don't think there was much left."

"Were any other buildings destroyed? She had a little chicken coop and another shed fairly close." Marcy thought the little farm was picture perfect when they visited.

"No, I think they saved the other buildings and the house was far enough away to escape damage. I think they did some cleaning because of the smoke, though." I'll call Kerry for an update. She stays in touch with Elizabeth."

"Ask Kerry what we can do to help. I'm sure they'll have a barn raising." Jeremy wondered if they would allow an Englisher–him being nonAmish—to work on the crew.

"I would love to help. Do they need anything?" Jennie held her breath, because she knew what they needed.

"I'll ask Kerry." Trina sensed Jeremy was ready to share something.

"Jennie and I haven't actually worked this out, yet..." He glanced at Jennie who nodded. "We're going to offer to return Oscar and Melody."

"No!" Marcy reacted without thinking. "Sorry, but you'll never find two nicer horses already trained to drive. Have they asked for them to be returned?"

Jennie stood up. As she approached Melody's stall, the mare took two steps forward and hung her head over the stall door to nuzzle Jennie's arm.

Marcy didn't understand. "Jennie?"

"We love Oscar and Melody." Jennie stroked Melody's neck. "They were bred and trained by Isaiah and we think Charlie and Elizabeth need them right now."

Marcy shook her head. "Ok, I guess I understand. It feels right, but, yet, so wrong for you guys."

Trina added, "Why does doing the right thing always hurt so much?" She didn't expect an answer.

Mrs. Shaw followed the conversation, remaining silent. *Trina has certainly found good-hearted friends in Appleridge. These friends are the type of friends to help Trina with her own struggles.*

"Do you want me to call Kerry to see if she can set up a time for you to visit Elizabeth?"

"Thanks for the offer, Trina. I have Kerry's number saved on my phone. I'll call. Actually, I may call Elizabeth, instead, and leave a message at their phone shack." Jennie hoped they could go this weekend because Jeremy was leaving for another mission trip on Monday.

"I'm leaving on Monday for Appalachia. Marcy, if Elizabeth chooses to have Oscar and Melody returned..."

"Yes, I'll haul them to Sugar Creek. But Jeremy, she doesn't have a barn. She probably won't want them right away."

"I think her father lives down the road. Not sure. We'll work it out." Jeremy reached for Jennie's hand.

TWO LARGE PIZZAS and one hour later, the party dispersed. Jennie tied Julep in the aisle so she wouldn't get into trouble while Marcy groomed her ponies.

"I'm glad you met my friends tonight, Mom. You met Lainie at my place, so now you know just about everyone coming to the party Saturday.

"And I look forward to seeing all of you again soon." Mrs. Shaw smiled as she took her daughter's arm for the walk to the truck.

Jeremy and Jennie folded the chairs and table.

"Hey, I'm only going to groom Riley and Stuffin tonight. I have tomorrow off. I'll spend more time then. I took Saturday off because of Trina's gathering. We could make that trip to Sugar Creek Saturday morning and get back in time for the party."

"Thanks. I guess that depends on when we talk to Elizabeth." Jennie mentally checked her schedule. "I'd rather Elizabeth take them sooner rather than later. Each day I get more attached."

Jeremy added, "Me, too." Then silently, *I'll miss them, too.*

"I LIKE YOUR friends, sweetie. They seem very caring. It's nice to have caring and kind friends."

"Yeah, it is. I've enjoyed getting to know them. We go to the same church, although Jennie and I didn't realize the horse connection until she came to my farm to interview Lainie. I told you all about how we met Lainie, right?"

"You did. And she reconnected with her mother. Just like us." Margaret smiled at her daughter. "I've enjoyed our time together."

"I've missed you, Mom. I'm so sorry for staying away. I didn't mean to blame you."

"No more than I've blamed myself."

"In the past. That's all in the past." Trina kept her eyes on the road. She could read her mom's mind and was waiting for the next words.

"Your brother has changed. He's a kind and caring man and boss. I won't apologize for Barton, but I know he wants to apologize to you—when you're ready."

"It's hard. I've spent so many years being angry. I'm tired of being angry. It's not fun anymore."

Margaret laughed. "Sorry, I didn't mean to laugh. Did I detect a bit of humor in your voice?"

"A bit. It's hard to be angry when Fare is right there." She stopped the truck in the middle of the drive and pointed. "My barn wasn't struck by lightning, I have good friends, and my mom is sitting right here beside me." Trina meant every word.

"Yes, let's be thankful for what we have. You just never know."

"I think I'm ready to talk to Bart. I need to talk to Bart about Fare. Fare's been a good teacher—a healer. After everything that must have happened to him, he's still the sweet, trusting pony I remember. I think he should probably hate people instead."

Fare moseyed over to the fence and nickered.

Trina opened the door and walked to the fence, searching for a horse treat almost always found in the pocket of every coat she wore. Margaret followed.

"When you're ready, just give Barton a call. I promise he's not the brother you remember. Drugs stole his life and hurt us all. He didn't kill your father, but his addiction brought a lot of pain into our family. He'll always carry that burden and we'll always wear the scars. But..."

"It's hard to forget."

"You'll never forget. Forgiveness is different than forgetting. Forgiveness requires grace."

"Grace. Hmmm, you mean like how none of us deserves grace and Jesus doesn't make us earn grace—it's offered freely and we're forgiven?"

"Yes, just like."

"Mom, when did you become so smart?" Trina teased.

"I don't know if I'm smart, but I do know Barton is a kind and generous boss to the employees at the market. He's loved by his customers. The market is thriving. He's doing his best to be a better person. When you're ready, please talk to Barton."

Trina rubbed a hand down Fare's sleek neck. "I will, Mom. Soon."

Chapter Twelve

art parked his truck in the pasture parking lot. Horse trailers and horses indicated he was in the right place. He could hear an auctioneer's chant. He couldn't understand a word being said, but he followed the sound, stopping at the small sales office. No information there. Only a huffy comment, "We can't help you track any back-door deal."

Grabbing a styrofoam cup of coffee from the vendor parked near the office, Bart walked to the auction barn entrance and scanned the crowd. He needed to make friends with a few sale regulars and ask questions. The group of old guys clustered around the side door near the sale ring were a good possibility. Tossing his cup in the trash barrel, he decided to take the quickest route around the building instead of walking through the rows of rickety folding chairs.

Casually walking to the group, he nodded. "I'm trying to track a horse that went through this sale a couple of weeks ago and wondered if any of you know someone named Jack? He bought a small Morgan with a white mane and tail for his children." Bart hesitated and then continued, "I tried the sales office, but the horse didn't actually go through the sale."

The man to Bart's right, leaning forward with his hands balanced on the back of a chair, straightened and spit out a wad of chew. Bart heard a few chuckles from the others. "Jack, you say.

Are you sure his name isn't Mack? That's who does all the back-door deals around here."

"The woman I talked to didn't get a bill of sale, she thought his name was Jack, but I suppose it could have been Mack." Bart glanced at the other men. They didn't say anything. Several walked away shaking their heads. He thought one mumbled, "Not another one."

"I'm Barton Shaw. I guess I've wandered into a can of worms."

"You guessed right. Not your fault, young man. I'm sorry to say it probably was Mack and he ain't got children. He's a kill buyer. He tells a good story, gets people to sell their horse thinking they found a good home, but all its gonna get is a one-way trip to the meat market. Horse meat is a good business for some who don't care much for horses."

Barton felt sick. "Oh, man, I hate to hear that. Is that legal?"

"Sure; not here, though. They haul the horses to Canada."

Bart clenched his fists. He wasn't a fighting man, but he sure would like to punch this Mack guy right in his lying face. "Is Mack here today?"

"I don't reckon you'll find your horse 'cause he loads the trailer and heads out to Canada the night of the sale. 'Course if that horse happened to be a Morgan, like you said, and those rescue gals were at the sale, it's possible they bailed him and old Mack made an even larger profit. You could check with them."

"Thanks for your help. I didn't get your name." Bart waited.

"And you're not gonna get it. Good luck. I hope you find your horse but I wouldn't hold my breath if I was you."

Bart didn't hold his breath. Instead, he let out a huge groan. *Fare? Come on, God; why lead me this far and now this? I know this whole mess is my fault. I want to make it right, God, please!*

Somehow, he was able to ask. "Do you happen to know where this Mack guy is?"

Go around back. You'll spot a big stock trailer near a few pens with too many horses squeezed in for my taste. That'll be him."

It was easy to spot the old trailer. If the sales office wasn't happy about the back-door deals, why didn't they put a stop to it? This Mack guy was in plain view. Maybe they had some sort of back-door deal happening with the back-door deal. Anything for a buck. This was a messy world. Messy used to be his world. The things he used to do—his addiction still tainted his life—and now this.

Stop it! Go talk to this Mack guy. Bart straightened his shoulders and marched to the trailer, he was ready to bribe the jerk, if needed. Money obviously talked.

"Hey, I'm looking for a small Morgan horse with a white mane and tail. He was sold at the sale a few weeks ago, but didn't go through the auction. Do you remember a horse like that?" Bart decided not to mention the *for my children lie.* That would get him nothing except sealed lips.

"Yeah, I remember. He was a skinny thing. Not much meat on those bones."

"Do—do you remember where he went?" Bart felt sick. He braced for the answer he didn't want to hear.

"Why I believe I did good on that one. I can't be real sure but he might of gone to those Morgan rescue gals. They are my very best customers." He sneered. "Yup, those gals work real hard to come up with the cash to save a horse."

"Is there any way you can check?" Bart already knew that was a silly question. What fraud actually kept records?

"Nope, sorry pal." He spit. "You go check with those gals 'cause I'm not sure. He may have been on my last load north. If he was, don't worry, he's not feeling any pain now." He turned and added over his shoulder. "Now you get on out of here, boy. I've got a business to run."

Bart watched Mack swagger away as if he owned the world. "Business? Don't you mean dirty business?" Bart didn't talk loud enough for Mack to hear. He wasn't as stupid as he looked but right now he was looking pretty stupid.

JENNIE LEFT A MESSAGE for Elizabeth on the phone shack answering machine—it sure sounded like an old-fashioned answering machine and not voicemail. Surprisingly, Charlie returned the call while she was in the barn. "His mom would love for them to visit Thursday evening. Come for supper at six."

JENNIE WORKED FROM HOME on Thursday so she would be ready to leave by four o'clock for supper in Sugar Creek. Jeremy didn't have class and spent most of the day sorting a mess at his mom's place. He and his sister, Sarah, were slowly clearing out the house. It was on the market, but so far, no bites. The house was mostly empty. Currently, they were still sorting an accumulation of items in the attic, basement, and large garage, deciding which items to trash, sell, or give away. *Stuffed to the rafters* would describe the property at its worse. Perhaps, they were a little premature listing it with a realtor.

He couldn't resist a quick call to Jennie. "Hey, favorite girl. Are you having a good day?"

"I am. It's nice and quiet; I'm getting a lot done. I've only wandered out to the barn two or three times." Jennie laughed. It was a beautiful spring day. Too nice to work inside. Still, she was officially on the clock. Instead of taking coffee breaks, she took horse breaks.

"I'll pick you up around four if that's ok."

"Yes, perfect. I'll be ready. Oh, and Grandpa wants to come with us. Could you pick him up on your way?"

"Certainly. It will be nice to have him along. He'll be a real help. He always knows what to say."

"That's what I thought, too." Jennie pressed End. *Oh no! I'm getting just like Grandpa. He never says goodbye, either. I bet Jeremy will have a field day teasing me about not saying goodbye. He may not do it in front of Grandpa, and he may forget. Nope, he won't forget.*

Jennie stared at her phone and decided to leave another message for Elizabeth, knowing the Amish wouldn't have a problem with a set of extra knees under the table. Just the same, it was only polite to warn Elizabeth about Grandpa joining them for supper.

After leaving another phone shack message, she decided to call Jeremy back and ask him a question she forgot to ask earlier.

"Well, hello, favorite fiancée. Did you call just to say goodbye?"

"I can hear you laughing! Goodbye and also—well—I wanted to know and can't ask you in front of Grandpa—if Melody is returned to the Miller's—well—"

Jeremy heard the hesitation. "Yes, we are still engaged, we will find a wonderful way to celebrate, and don't you ever be embarrassed to ask me anything."

Jennie sighed. "I guess I was a little embarrassed. I know our engagement isn't just about a horse or a gift—I'm—" It wasn't often that Jennie found herself without words. Why was she having trouble sharing what was really in her heart?

"I know this is hard—hard to do something that feels so right and so wrong at the same time. Besides, giving you an engagement horse instead of a ring does make a pretty awesome story to tell our kids some day."

Jennie swallowed, "It's a great story; however, we may need to write another engagement story."

"Maybe. Or at least another chapter. There will always be another chapter, I promise. And, now, say goodbye so I can get a shower and pick up our passenger."

"Goodbye." Jennie smiled.

Chapter Thirteen

Jeremy pulled his small SUV onto the Miller farm and parked near what used to be the barn.

"They've done a good job clearing away the debris. They may be planning on building on the same spot." Grandpa seemed to be talking to himself.

"I'm sure that was quite a job. The barn was huge." Jeremy reached for the door handle but waited to open the car door.

Jennie added from the back seat. "Many hands probably worked together to get the job done. I like how they left the old stone foundation. I wonder how they'll use it to build a new barn."

"I see Amos waving from the porch. Let's go on up. We don't want to be late for what I'm sure will be a grand supper." Grandpa was out of the car before he finished talking.

"Welcome, welcome." Amos shook Grandpa's hand. "Come on in."

The Appleridge guests hesitated for a moment before wiping their feet on a rag rug. Noticing Amos in his stocking feet, Jennie kicked off her shoes.

"Oh, my, don't worry about your shoes. Come on in." Elizabeth motioned for them to hang their jackets on the hooks by the door.

"I'll keep my shoes off; it's what I do at my house." Jennie wanted to walk over and give Elizabeth a hug. She didn't know if a hug would be welcome, so she smiled instead. "Is there anything I can do to help with supper?"

"No, Mom and I have everything ready."

Jennie turned to smile at Agnes standing near the sink. She opened the bag she carried. "I brought the kids a little after-supper treat."

Charlie and Micah edged closer to peek into Jennie's bag. It wasn't much but Jennie thought maybe the children would enjoy an assortment of candy. Judging by the gleam in their eyes, she was right.

"We're ready to eat now and we'll save the treats until after you clean your plates." The young Amish mother motioned for the men and Charlie to sit on one side of the large table and Jennie, Agnes, and Micah on the other. The baby sat in what looked like an antique high chair banging a spoon on a gummy cracker. Elizabeth didn't sit until after the silent prayer and the bowls of steaming foods were being passed.

"This looks delicious." Jeremy passed bowls of green beans, mashed potatoes, gravy, roast beef, and biscuits, as he eyed the cherry pie on the kitchen counter.

Jennie spied the pie, too, and decided to make sure she left a bit of room in her stomach. She loved pie.

Eating took the place of talking for a few minutes. They would take Grandpa's lead to know when it was time to share their thoughts about the horses.

Grandpa cleared his throat. "I haven't had a meal like this in a long time. Thank you. It really hits the spot." There were quite a few heads bobbing up and down around the table.

"You are most welcome." Agnes tipped her head.

Jeremy spoke quietly. "Yes, thank you. And, please know, we are so very sorry for your recent tragedy."

"Thank you all. I praise God my children were not injured and the house was spared. There is always so much to be grateful for, yes?" Elizabeth stood to gather the empty plates. Jennie stood to help.

"Oh, please sit, you are a guest."

"And I hope a friend." Jennie hoped she hadn't offended Elizabeth by assuming a friendship that wasn't welcome.

Elizabeth handed Jennie an empty bowl. "Yes, a friend, so put this bowl on the counter so you can come back for more." She laughed. "I'll find a place for leftovers after we eat pie. Does everyone want pie?"

A chorus of "yes" filled the cozy kitchen.

The sweet dessert warmed the conversation. Grandpa looked at Jeremy. Jeremy nodded back.

Jeremy looked at Elizabeth. "Jennie and I know the horses you lost were very special for many reasons—" His eyes found young Charlie before continuing, "We know that Isaiah raised and trained both."

Elizabeth wasn't sure what Jeremy was going to say, but she sensed that he needed her response before continuing. "Yes, Isaiah and Charlie enjoyed nice time together working with Star and Stormy. Star was my trusty buggy horse and Charlie raised Stormy himself." A few tears gathered in the corner of her eyes. She lifted her chin and continued. "It's always a loss to lose such special horses."

Jeremy waited for Jennie to take over. Praying over this decision brought her peace and the right words. "We love Oscar and Melody. We know they're special horses because they were bred, trained, and loved by Isaiah. Jeremy and I want to return them to you because they belong with you."

Elizabeth stood with her hands clasped in front of her apron, head down. One hand reached up to wipe a tear sneaking down her cheek.

Jennie looked at young Charlie. The poor kid looked like he wanted to cry, but at fourteen, and trying to be the man of the house, he fought tears.

Grandpa added, "It's what is right. Please accept this gesture of friendship out of respect for your loss."

Elizabeth remained silent with head bowed; shoulders shaking. Agnes got up and wrapped her arms around her daughter. "What a beautiful gift. God wants us to receive when beautiful gifts are offered—yes, daughter?"

"Yes. We will accept one for Charlie. I have a new buggy horse. Well, not so new. I drove and loved on Aggie when I was first married and now Dad has given her to me again."

Amos found this to be a perfect opportunity to add to the conversation. "Yes, Aggie is a fine older mare and one Elizabeth trusts."

"Aggie? Isn't that a nickname for Agnes?" Grandpa looked at Agnes who was wearing a grin.

"Yes, and Amos always thought that was a good joke, too. She is a nice Lippitt Morgan mare, and Melody's mum, I believe."

Amos spoke up. "Affectionately named after my Agnes because she is such a sweet mare. Isaiah found her in a bad situation as a yearling and worked his magic."

Elizabeth shook her head. "Yes, trained by Isaiah. He called her Aggie before he knew Mom would be his mother-in-law. Melody was her first, and I believe, her only filly."

"I'm pretty sure Isaiah knew Elizabeth would be family before he found Agnes." Amos chuckled. "But we won't tell that story." He looked at his daughter. He wanted her to remember precious moments.

Jeremy loved how this family loved one another. He loved how they leaned on one another in times of great tragedy. And he especially loved their fun humor. Bowing his head, he said a silent prayer.

Father, these new friends are such perfect examples of your great love. Please continue to hold them close. Thank you for bringing them into our lives.

"Jeremy?" Jennie reached for his hand, giving him a look that said, *what should we do now?*

Jeremy spoke to Elizabeth, looking at young Charlie. "Elizabeth, you'll choose one, then? And we'll keep the other and promise to care for whichever one it is—always."

"Charlie, you choose." Elizabeth walked over and laid her hand on her son's shoulder for encouragement.

Young Charlie's voice cracked as he started to speak. "Grandad, do you think we should split them up? They've been together a long time."

"They'll be fine. Have they settled in well at your place, Jennie?"

"Yes, they are now comfortably in our herd. They don't seem to be distraught when we do something with one and not the other. Of course, there are four other horses at the farm—three mares and one gelding."

Charlie stood up, deep in thought. "I would be tempted to ask for Melody if I knew she could get in foal and carry on my father's breeding program. Since that hasn't been possible, I choose Oscar. Dad and I trained Oscar together; I didn't want to sell him."

"Good decision, young man. And I'm sure Jennie and Jeremy would love to have you visit the farm to see Melody whenever you want." Grandpa Gantzler looked at Jennie.

"Yes, please visit. If your mother agrees, we'll pick you up for a day or two." She looked at Elizabeth, suddenly afraid she overstepped. She should have spoken to Elizabeth in private before making the offer. Jennie quickly added, "The entire family is invited."

"Thank you. Charlie may visit. It would make a nice day to see our new friends at their home and visit Melody and the other horses."

"And the ponies, too!" Micah shouted and then hid behind his mom's apron.

"Yes, Micah, I can guarantee Miss Marcy would love to show you her ponies." Jennie picked up the candy bag. "Now, do these kids get a treat?"

Elizabeth motioned for Micah to take the bag. "Yes, they deserve a treat. Thank you for thinking of them and thank you for this very kind offer." Elizabeth's words were simple, but her eyes said so much more. *Thank you for bringing joy back into my son's life.*

Jeremy couldn't leave without asking, "Will there be a barn raising soon?"

Amos answered, "Yes, in a few weeks, and if you know how to swing a hammer, we welcome your help."

Grandpa laughed, "Watch out Jeremy! Amos is a whiz at getting people to work."

"Just leave a message and I'll be here—if I'm not in Appalachia on a mission team." He saw Amos's puzzled look and continued, "I'm attending seminary and serving on several mission trips this spring. I'm trying to find God's plan for my life."

"Ahh, God's plan is something we desire but is sometimes hard to know. Ja?" Jennie noticed that Amos spoke with a German accent but was usually careful not to use Amish words around his English friends. The ja instead of yes must have been a slip just now.

"Yes, I'm praying. I suppose I'll know more when it's time. Patience is hard."

"Speaking of patience, I bet Charlie here is eager to know when Oscar will return." Jennie's grandpa knew the youngster was anxious to have Oscar back home. "I suppose that will happen after the barn raising?"

Amos looked at his eldest grandson and answered, "He can come home anytime. My farm is near and he will stay with us. We are keeping Aggie there so Charlie has been riding his bike back and forth."

Micah tugged on his brother's arm pulling his face closer and whispered. Charlie straightened. "Micah wants you to know, his pony is at our Grandpa's farm and his name is

Freckles because he has a white blaze with little spots that look like Freckles."

Micah nodded with a big grin. Baby Mary Ann sat with sticky jelly hands and face and banged on her highchair.

THE CAR WAS QUIET on the drive home to Appleridge. All three occupants were lost in their private but similar thoughts. They would keep Melody. Jennie would have an engagement horse. Jeremy had a horse to drive. All the horses would fit in the barn. Charlie would have a horse bred and trained by his father. They were invited to the barn raising and couldn't wait to see their Amish friends again. Out of the ashes, faith, hope, and love reigned this day.

IT WAS ALMOST TEN-THIRTY when they entered the city limits of Appleridge. First stop was Grandpa's senior apartment. Jeremy escorted Charlie to his door.

"You'll find your path, young man. God has an amazing future planned for you—and Jennie. I think there is more to that story, and if I'm correct, I'm happy for you both."

"Thank you, Charlie. Yes, Jennie and I are planning a future together. We're waiting for me to find my direction in life before making an official announcement. What tipped you off?"

"You put her happiness before your own. I happen to know how much you wanted to keep Oscar, but you were genuinely happy for Jennie, because she'll have Melody. I really like you, young man."

"That means a lot—to us both." He shook Grandpa's hand. "Hey, thanks for going with us. I know it helped having you with us."

"You're welcome. Thanks for the invite to accompany you tonight. Now I'm going on in to watch the news and fall asleep in my recliner before I go to bed." Grandpa chuckled as he unlocked his door.

"WHAT ARE ALL THOSE LIGHTS doing on in the barn? Oh, wait, I know all those trucks. It looks like our friends are having a party without us."

"Ok if I park by the porch and we walk to the barn?" Jeremy figured a little exercise wouldn't hurt, especially after tonight's huge supper.

As soon as they walked through the barn door, they were pummeled with questions.

"Did they want Oscar and Melody? Were they surprised you offered? Are they going to be ok? Will they build a new barn? Was supper good?"

Jennie and Jeremy's heads swung back and forth, trying to track which friend was asking what question. Wow, was everyone here? Marcy, Trina, Margaret Shaw, Lainie, Megan, Cassy, and Sam—yes, all here.

"Whoa! One at a time, please!" Jeremy held put both hands on top his head laughing. "You answer." He looked at Jennie.

"Elizabeth was very touched by our gesture. At first, I didn't think she was going to accept, but her mom reminded her about the goodness of accepting gifts, and I think she realized the joy it would bring to her son, Charlie. She agreed to one horse because her dad has already given her a mare she loved before she was married. The mare is a trusty older driving horse. She asked Charlie to choose and he chose Oscar because he helped Isaiah train Oscar. Charlie asked his grandfather if he thought it would be fine to separate Oscar and Melody and he said yes. Did I cover everything?" She looked at Jeremy.

He nodded. "Good job!"

"You'll keep Melody for driving?" Lainie asked. "Is she also started under saddle?"

Jeremy answered this time, "Yes to driving, not sure about much saddle training." He looked at Megan and Cassy. "These two young ladies have already volunteered to put a few rides on her back."

Lainie laughed. "I'm sure they did."

"I think Charlie has been on Melody and she was fine. She doesn't know much about communication yet. Oh, yeah, Charlie is going to visit the farm soon. I hope you'll all get to meet him."

Cassy looked at Lainie. "Maybe he would be interested in watching our jump team practice."

Megan added, "Great idea!"

Lainie motioned to her truck. "Ok, you two, time to go. It's late, you have classes tomorrow, and I'm teaching adult lessons bright and early. And I'm tired."

"I'm tired, too. I'm glad you're keeping one of the horses." Marcy picked up her grooming bag. "I understand why you felt it was right to offer them to Elizabeth, though." She turned for a walk to the tack room.

"Well, Mom and I need to leave, too. We've had a busy day and I need to throw one more flake of hay to each horse." She hugged Jennie and then Jeremy. Margaret smiled, not sure if she should offer a hug. Jeremy walked over to settle that question with a hug of his own.

"Goodnight, everyone. Thanks for waiting here for us to return. See you Saturday!" Jennie noticed that Sam hung back—waiting for the others to walk to their vehicles.

"Hey, Sam." Jeremy waited.

"I'm glad you're keeping the mare. I admit, my first thought was why make the offer? You paid for both fair and square. I didn't know the whole story until tonight. I just wanted to say, in this terribly unkind and selfish world, it's nice to have friends like you both." Sam's face reddened. He wasn't comfortable sharing his private thoughts.

"Thanks." Jennie squeezed his arm. She thought about going for a hug—for a brief moment. "It wasn't easy, but it was the right thing to do."

Jeremy and Sam did the handshake, backslap, buddy sort of thing.

"Hey, will we see you at Trina's party Saturday night? Oh, wait, we have official business Saturday morning." Jennie looked at her phone calendar. It was handy having their farrier boarding his horse at her barn—always convenient for trimming or shoeing appointments.

"Yup, I'm working here, then going to Lainie's barn, then calling it a day and spending some time with my horse for a change. I told Trina I wouldn't make it. I promised my brother I would lend him a hand. He wants to pick up supplies for a project he's working on and he needs my truck." Sam paused. That was more than he would usually share. "Hey, do you want me to work on Oscar before he leaves? I could squeeze him in tomorrow night."

Jeremy shook his head. "No need. I was going to ask you take off his road shoes, but since he's going back to the Millers, he'll need them on.'"

"Just know you're welcome to use my horse trailer any-time."

"Thanks, Sam. I don't have a gooseneck hitch on my truck, though—just a bumper pull hitch." Jennie glanced at Blue Boy parked near the house. "It may be a good investment to install a gooseneck hitch, but I don't know; my boy is getting old. I need to start saving for a newer truck.

"Sorry I can't lend my truck. That would put me out of busi-ness for the day."

"It sure would. No, it's ok. Will you be ok trimming Julep and the ponies without us here?" Jennie thought so; she trusted Sam.

"Yup, I'll tie them in the aisle."

"Would you take Melody's road shoes off and give her a lit-tle trim?" Jennie looked at Jeremy for confirmation.

Jeremy added, "Melody won't need road shoes here.'"

"No, I guess she won't." Sam agreed. "If you compete with her, you may want to do at least front shoes later."

"Ok, guys, I'm ready to walk to the house, climb into my pjs, and snuggle with Beauty." She looked at Sam and Jeremy to see if they took the hint. They could talk shoes and horses all night.

Sam only smiled, tipped his cap, and chuckled as he walked to his truck. Jeremy waited for Jennie to check on the horses in the pasture, do a final check of the barn, and turn out the lights. The security light on a pole between the house and the barn was plenty of light to guide their path to the house.

"I'll close the gate. Sleep tight and don't let the bed bugs bite."

Jennie added, "And if they do, I'll hit them with a shoe and they'll go away, half past two." She waited for her goodnight kiss and wasn't disappointed.

Chapter Fourteen

Barton scanned the store. Both checkouts were operating, there were no lines; no sales reps needed his attention at the moment. Perfect. He Googled Save a Morgan Rescue on his phone and made the call. Several rings, then he heard a message to leave a message.

"Oh, um, hello, my name is Barton Shaw. I'm looking for a little Morgan horse. I was told he was possibly sold at the auction a few weeks ago in a back-door deal. He's chestnut with a white mane and tail. I'm praying, somehow, he was rescued by your group. It's very important." He gave both his cell number and the store number. "Thanks." Then he recited both numbers again.

Sitting in his little office, he smelled the cartons of dish soap, canned goods, and cleaning products. He loved this store—Mark's Market. The independent grocery store was an important part of the community. Many of his customers couldn't drive to another town to pick up groceries. Most people had either forgotten his past or were new to the community and never heard about his years of addiction, or how his father was killed. They didn't see the scars he wore, safely hidden. Bart didn't need to look in a mirror to see them; he felt them on his heart.

His present life was not like his past. He took care of his mom, helped friends, ran an honest business, and he was happy.

Yes, he was happy—most of the time. Only one thing could make his life better; to be forgiven and loved by his sister. He missed Trina. They had been more than siblings. They were good friends. As the older brother, Barton looked out for his sister as they grew up. Even when he was at his worst, Trina never gave up on him—until he sold Fare. After that, Trina disappeared from his life.

God, I'm not sure what to ask, except I pray Fare is fine and I can return him to Trina; then maybe, just maybe, our family will be complete and happy again. I know you've forgiven me, but Trina hasn't. I pray her life has been happy and full, and thank you for bringing Mom and Trina together this week. Thank you for giving me your grace when I deserved nothing. Just thank you. Amen.

IT WAS KERRY'S TURN to carry the rescue's cell phone. Save a Morgan Rescue didn't have a permanent location. They ran the rescue from Kerry's kitchen table. They had a small list of foster homes that helped out when needed. They sure could rescue a lot more if they had the money and a place of their own.

Kerry listened to Bart's long message, then called Deb. "I don't want to give him much information until I talk to Trina. They have the same last name, though. I think he's talking about Fare. What do you think?"

"I think, go ahead and call him, but, I agree, we need to talk to Trina before sharing any info with him. How did he sound?"

"He sounded desperate. Worried. Like he cared." Kerry was a pretty good judge of people. "Even so, we need to protect Trina's privacy. You never know."

Deb agreed. "Maybe tell him Fare is safe. It seems heartless to allow him to think Fare suffered a sad end."

BART UNCLIPPED HIS PHONE from his belt. He saw the display and recognized the number. He said a silent *Please let this be good news* prayer and answered the call.

"This is Barton Shaw."

"Mr. Shaw, this is Kerry Casin from Save a Morgan."

"Thanks for returning my call." He waited.

"I listened to your message. Could you please share more information?"

Bart shared his story. The entire personal, sad story. "I did something terrible. This was my sister's horse. Our father was killed, I was a recovering addict, still not at my best, and I sold Fare without my sister's permission. Her name is Trina Shaw. Fare is a little chestnut Morgan with a white mane and tail. He would be about eighteen or twenty, I think. I've been following leads for about eight months and finally traced him to the sale a few weeks ago. Please tell me I'm not too late." Bart took a deep breath. "His registered name is My Fare Thee Well."

"No, Mr. Shaw, you aren't too late."

Thank you, thank you. "Please call me Bart." His voice was full of hope.

"He didn't go on the kill truck to Canada. We got him out of the kill pen with only an hour to spare. He has a new home and we know it's a very good home. I'm sure your sister will be thrilled to hear he's fine." Kerry happened to know she was very thrilled.

"That's good news; real good news. Do you think his new home—well—would they listen to my story and maybe think about selling him to my sister? I would pay any fees or expenses they may have incurred." Bart knew he was pleading, but he didn't care. Being prideful wasn't something he valued any-more.

"It's not for me, it's for Trina. Well, maybe it is for me, too; I want to make my sister happy. What I did was terrible and we've been estranged for ten years and..."

Kerry interrupted. "Barton, wait, I understand. I'll talk to the owner and will explain everything. Give me a few days and I'll get back to you, ok?"

"Yes, thank you." He shouldn't feel disappointed because Fare was safe. But Fare wasn't with Trina. Now he would never be able to show Trina how much he loved her and how sorry he was for what he did to both her and Fare.

Kerry pressed End on her phone and sighed. "You heard?"

"Yeah, I could hear most of it. So sad for the family. We're going to share everything with Trina, right?"

"I think that would be the best and then we'll let Trina de-cide if she wants to contact her brother." Kerry thought for a moment. "I'm not sure Trina will be happy when I tell her eve-rything her brother shared. This seems like personal family business."

"I'm not sure, either. She seems like a very private person. But, Kerry, you always know what to say."

"Gee, thanks, I think, friend."

Deb just smiled. "I've got your back."

MARCY MET JEREMY AND JENNIE at the farm bright and early Saturday morning, after picking up Jennie's grandpa. Grandpa Gantzler sat in the passenger's seat as Marcy hitched up her trailer.

Jennie walked over to the truck and motioned for Grandpa to roll down his window. "Hey, Grandpa. Do you need anything before we leave?"

"I'm fine. I think I'll just sit here and wait for you to load Oscar."

By the time Jennie walked back to the barn, Jeremy had a halter on Oscar and was leading him toward the trailer. The gelding walked into the trailer like a champ. He didn't call for Melody and Melody seemed content grazing side by side with Sadie, Julep, Riley, and Stuffin.

"Well, that makes it a little bit easier," Jennie observed. "It would break my heart if separating them caused either Oscar or Melody any distress."

Marcy added quickly, "But let's not press our luck!" She closed the trailer doors and walked to the driver's side of her truck, ready to go. "Will someone check my lights?"

Jeremy walked to the back of the trailer as Jennie climbed into the back seat behind Grandpa.

"It's like he knows, Grandpa."

"I think horses are very intuitive; they just know these things. Oscar knows Melody will be fine and he knows he's going home to young Charlie." Grandpa was also very intuitive.

"Check; lights and turn signals are working." Jeremy climbed into the second seat beside Jennie. "Let's hit the road.

We need to return a horse to a young man and get home in time for a party."

"That sure puts a nice spin on the day," Jennie shared.

"Well, why not?"

"I know you really wanted to keep Oscar, and I'm keeping Melody, and it all doesn't seem fair."

"Fair? Fair is taking Oscar to Charlie. And, besides, we're sharing Melody. Oh wait, don't you share well, Jennie girl?"

"Jennie girl? Now you sound like Grandpa." She peeked around the seat to see if her Grandpa heard. He did, and was grinning.

"Yes, I'll share. Thanks! She's a very special present."

Marcy grinned. She thought maybe there was more to this conversation. She couldn't resist jumping in. "Why is Melody a very special present? I sense you two are up to something."

"Hmmm, maybe." Jennie didn't mind filling Marcy and Grandpa in on their plans. They both knew how to keep a secret. She glanced at Jeremy. She would let him decide.

"Did you know that my favorite girl, here, doesn't particularly like diamonds but she loves horses?"

"Yeah, I can see that but...oh, wait! Are you saying what I think?" Marcy attempted to look at them.

"Keep your eyes on the road! We have precious cargo we need to deliver."

Marcy knew Jeremy was kidding when she saw his grin in her rearview mirror.

"Yes, Melody is my engagement present. And I happen to think she's a diamond. I just can't wear her on my hand." Jennie didn't want to be left out of the fun. "Grandpa, we haven't told

Mom and Dad or my sisters, yet. We aren't setting a date or anything right now."

He nodded.

"I'm so happy for you both! If I wasn't driving, I'd show you how happy." She did reach over the seat searching for Jennie or Jeremy's hand.

"Thanks." Jennie found her hand and gave it a brief squeeze.

"Why don't you want to share your news?" Marcy asked while keeping her eyes on the road.

"I'm trying to figure out God's plan for my life. All I know for now is it includes Jennie."

Jennie smiled at Jeremy. "We decided to wait to announce our engagement until we can actually set a date for the wedding. When we're ready, it'll be small wedding, maybe at the farm."

"Oh, Jennie, I can see you coming down a grassy path, instead of an aisle, riding on the back of my carriage. I'll have Riley and Stuffin braided with ribbons, and..."

"Whoa, that sounds good, very good, but we aren't planning a wedding yet. Jeremy leaves on another mission trip on Monday, and then he has another one a month after. We can't make many plans yet."

"But do you want to be married this year?" Marcy was ready, even if they weren't.

Jeremy answered this time. "We're not sure. With everything that has happened, we haven't had time to really talk about our future."

"Sorry. No pressure. Thanks for trusting me with your news. I won't share because it's your news to share."

Jeremy leaned forward to follow the conversation.

"But, really, can't we plan a little?" Marcy added, "Just for fun. You know, to put a nice spin on the day?"

"Why Miss Marcy, are you throwing my words back at me?"

"Only a little. Well?"

"I think that's a deep subject; in more ways than one."

Jennie knew Jeremy was playing with Marcy so she just sat with a silly grin on her face and listened. She noticed Grandpa was sitting with a silly grin on his face, too.

THE TRIP TO SUGAR CREEK seemed shorter this time. Pulling into the Miller farm drive, Marcy positioned the trailer so she could circle around on a small part of the yard. "I'm not sure if they want Oscar here, or they want us to unload him down the road at the Stoltz farm."

"Sorry, I didn't ask. Here they are now." Jennie waved at Elizabeth as she walked down the porch steps carrying the baby.

"Did you have a good trip? Charlie is so very excited!" Elizabeth nodded toward the road. Here he comes. He's been at Dad's taking care of the pony and Aggie."

Marcy spoke up, "Do you want me to take Oscar to the other farm?"

"No, Charlie can walk him down when he's ready. Or ride him. You never know about Charlie."

Jeremy met Charlie as he jogged up the drive. "Hey, young man. We have a special delivery. Are you ready?"

Charlie grinned. "Yes, sir!"

Together they opened the back doors and latched them open. Marcy reached in the side door, untied Oscar, and threw the lead rope over his back. Charlie tugged on Oscar's tail and asked him to back down the ramp and out of the trailer.

Oscar stopped and looked around the farm and nickered.

"He knows he's home, Mama, but he doesn't know what to think about the missing barn." Charlie led Oscar over to the scorched earth. "They're gone, Oscar. Star and Stormy are gone."

Charlie continued to talk in a soothing voice to his horse. "But I'll take you to the pony and Aggie. You'll remember them. I'll never let you go again. I promise."

Jennie felt a little stab of guilt for buying Oscar and taking him away. Even if it did help Elizabeth.

Elizabeth must have read her thoughts. "Just think, if you wouldn't have picked up Melody and Oscar, we would have lost them in the fire, also. God's ways are truly a mystery. I think he sent them to you for safe keeping."

"Thank you for Melody." Jennie's voice quivered. "I hope you know our offer to return them both was sincere. I hope you didn't let us keep Melody because you felt bad about taking them both. I hope..."

"I know you are sincere. I really do have a nice mare. Aggie is my girl. Thank you! Thank you for the joy and hope you have given to my son. I know Melody belongs with you and Jeremy." She walked over to give Jennie a one-armed hug, trying not to squish the baby, held in her other arm. The baby giggled. She thought squeezing was fun.

"Charlie is fine. Come on up to the house. I have a check for you, Jeremy, and I baked cookies and brewed a jug of tea." She looked at Jeremy, knowing he had a sweet spot for cookies.

"I'm in," agreed Marcy. She took Grandpa's arm to assist his walk.

"You don't have to ask me twice." Jeremy ushered Jennie and Elizabeth up the path to the house.

Chapter Fifteen

*T*rina heard her phone. With her hands in dish water, she didn't answer. "You know, Mom, I'm glad we decided to keep our group small instead of having a big party. You already know everyone coming for chili tonight."

Margaret stood at the stove browning hamburger and ground sausage in a large pot. "And I love them all. I love your boarders and church friends, too, but Marcy, Jennie, Jeremy, and Lainie are my favorites—if I'm allowed to have favorites." Margaret laughed.

"You're allowed. I guess I'm a bit guilty, also. Lainie, Jennie, Marcy, and I have gotten to be very good friends, especially after Fare arrived."

"And you all seem to love Jeremy."

"We do, but not as much as Jennie!" Trina wanted to make that perfectly clear.

"Oh, I love him, too, but, yes, not as much as Jennie." Margaret turned back to the stove. "I'll just add the peppers, onion, and the seasonings and get the chili simmering before I take my shower. The cornbread is ready for the oven. I think we're pretty much set." She looked at her daughter.

"I think so. I'm caught up with the dirty dishes, so the kitchen looks presentable. While the chili simmers, I'll feed the horses and then be ready to hop in the shower after you." Trina smiled at her mom. "You know, it's been a lot of fun having you here. Can I keep you?"

"Oh, my, thanks, honey, but I need to go home. I don't want to wear out my welcome."

"Never, Mom."

"I'll come back. It's so nice here. Don't you need to get back to work?"

"Yeah, I'll need to catch up on some website work I've promised several clients. I've done a bit this week, so I'm fine. Besides, you're more than capable of entertaining yourself while I work."

"Now that I know what a nice library Appleridge has, I'll make sure to have plenty of books to read for entertainment. I have one more I need to finish before I leave Monday."

"If you don't get a chance to finish it, we can always try to renew it online, and I'll pick it up on my next visit. I don't plan on letting much time pass between visits."

"I agree, let's not allow much time between visits, sweetie." Margaret turned back to her chili masterpiece and gave it a good stir. "Ok, it's on simmer and I'm going to get myself ready."

"Take your time, Mom." Trina sat at the kitchen table sipping a glass of ice tea. She was content.

She picked up her phone, remembering the call she missed. *Kerry? I sure hope they don't have another horse to rehome.*

She retrieved Kerry's message. *Hi, Trina, when you get a chance, please call. It's not an emergency but I do need to run something by you soon.*

Trina walked to the back door to pull on her barn boots. She had horses to feed and supper to finish before her friends arrived. She'd return the call later.

TRINA HUGGED Jennie and Jeremy as they walked through the door. "Lainie's down at the barn talking to a couple of her students. She just finished a lesson. Marcy's been held up at the hospital."

"The hospital?" Jennie asked.

"Yes, apparently the emergency department was swamped and they called Marcy in for a few hours. She hopes to leave by seven at the latest.

"Hello, Mrs. Shaw. Good to see you again." Jeremy put the cookie container on the table so he could offer a hug—a hug she eagerly accepted.

"What did you bring?" Trina opened the container lid a crack. "I smell peanut butter. Your peanut butter cookies are the best. Thanks, Jennie."

"You're very welcome. I wish I could have stolen a container of Elizabeth's snicker doodles today. I did get her recipe; I'll make them soon."

"That's right, you took Oscar to Sugar Creek." Trina motioned for everyone to grab a place to sit. It always seemed like visitors congregated in her kitchen. It was her favorite room. She carried a tray of cheese, crackers, salami, olives, and pickles to the table as an appetizer.

Jeremy glanced at Margaret before sitting.

"I'm fine, you sit; I'm on chili duty." Margaret waved a big wooden spoon.

"We did." Jeremy joined Jennie at the table before continuing. "Grandpa Charlie went with us. We had a nice visit with Elizabeth, the kids, Amos, and Agnes. Oscar seemed fine. Young Charlie jumped on him bareback and rode him down the road to his grandpa's farm."

Jennie added, "And Melody didn't fuss when we loaded Oscar in the trailer. That would have broken my heart."

Margaret replaced the lid on the chili pot. "It was a very kind thing that you both did."

"We thought it was the right thing, and after watching Charlie with Oscar, we know it was the right thing." Jennie reached for a cracker. "You wouldn't think I'd be hungry after all the cookies I ate. We only grabbed a hot dog at the Bake & Shake for quick lunch. That's my story and I'm sticking to it!"

"I couldn't believe your grandpa turned down an all-the-way dog today." Jeremy filled a small plate with goodies.

"He seemed tired from the trip. I need to remember he's getting older and is slowing down a little." Jennie didn't like thinking about her grandpa slowing down. She noticed he was also more quiet than usual.

"Oh, I know that *slowing down* feeling." Margaret laughed. "I've sure had a great time this week but it's been more active than my normal week."

"Did I poop you out, Mom?" Trina's voice revealed humor more than concern.

"Just a little. I've had fun."

"It's early to bed for you, then." Trina couldn't help teasing.

"Who's going to bed early?" Lainie walked into the conversation. "Yeah!" She spied the snacks. "I'm starved." She grabbed a couple of crackers and two slices of cheese. "What have I missed?"

Jeremy handed her a plate and did a quick recap. "Trina wore Margaret out this week and thinks she needs to go to bed early. We took Oscar to Sugar Creek this morning. Jennie's grandpa went with us and was so tired he turned down a hotdog lunch at the Bake & Shake." He paused. "I think that covers it except for everything we said about you."

"I know you're kidding. I'm not worried. You would only say good things about me."

"Yes, ma'am, only good things." Jeremy got up so Lainie could take his seat near the snacks and he moved, along with his filled plate, to an empty bar stool beside Trina.

"Lainie, do you know if Cassy and Megan are coming tonight?" Trina asked.

"I don't think so. Something is up with those two. There's been a lot of whispering, Megan seems upset with Cassy, and Cassy has missed several team practices."

Jennie spoke up, "Do you think Cassy is getting swamped at school? The first year of college can be a real wake-up call."

"I'm not sure. All I know is something isn't quite right. I talked to Megan when Cassy wasn't at practice on Wednesday. She didn't want to share much. She said something about a boyfriend who doesn't want Cassy to spend time with her horse friends or her horse."

"Why not?" Trina was curious.

"Megan says he's a jerk and thinks the world revolves around him." Lainie shook her head, then continued. "Sorry, Jeremy, but no guy is ever worth giving up a horse."

"I happen to agree. No decent guy would ask, and not just a horse, but anything else the other person loves."

"I'm going to try to talk to Cassy as soon as I get a chance. There isn't much private time during practice, and she's been rushing away after practice. She used to stick around and follow Megan up to her house." Lainie was determined to help.

"Maybe Megan will share her concerns with her sister." Megan's sister, Belinda, was Jennie's best friend. In spite of the distance, they still spoke at least once a week. "I may bring it up the next time I call Belinda."

"I'm going to guess that will be tomorrow at the latest." Jeremy teased. He knew Jennie always wanted to make sure her friends were ok, and she especially felt protective of Cassy, since her parents lived in another state.

When Cassy Morton arrived to begin her freshman year at Richburg College, she brought her horse, Treasure, along and boarded her at Jennie's farm. Cassy moved to Lainie's barn to be more involved with the performance team, but only after Jennie promised Joan and Tom Morton that she would continue to look out for their daughter. Tom and Joan trusted Jennie and kept in touch. They also approved of Lainie.

"Well, Cassy can't get off course. She made a deal with her parents. She can keep Treasure at school as long as she maintains her grades. This demanding boyfriend situation needs to be watched. I promised her parents I would be a good friend, and..."

"I'm just teasing. Of course, the situation needs to be watched," Jeremy assured.

"Especially since it seems to be hurting Cassy and Megan's friendship," Lainie added. "It just isn't the same. That's been bothering me more than the missed practices."

Margaret listened as the friends talked. "I only met the girls briefly when Trina took me over to see your barn and watch practice on Wednesday, but I overheard something that makes more sense now."

"What, Mom?" Trina knew her mom wasn't a gossip. She wouldn't share what she overheard unless she felt it was important.

"Well, I overheard Cassy on the phone, apologizing for being at the barn, and it seemed like she was pleading. I remember thinking it seemed odd. Why should she apologize to anyone for being at practice? Then I heard her say, 'Please give me another chance. I promise I'll be around when you want me, and I won't have any horse smells on me again' or something like that."

"That certainly is cause for concern." Jennie was getting angry. "That's an old story. The story of a very domineering boyfriend and the story never ends well. It steals a young woman's confidence when they're belittled for what they enjoy."

Trina looked at her friend with concern. "Are you speaking from experience?"

"It happened to me in college. Fortunately, two very good friends, who were also my roommates, saw what was happening and did an intervention of sorts." Jennie looked at Jeremy.

"Sorry, I've never told you any of this. I guess because it never came up. I was one of the lucky ones; only my pride was hurt."

"For many young girls, it can be more than their pride hurt." Marcy added from the doorway to the living room.

"Marcy, I didn't see you. Come on in." Trina motioned for Marcy to join the group.

"I heard most of the conversation. I gather you're concerned about one of our very talented friends. Megan or Cassy?"

"Cassy. Megan has shared a little with me, and I'm not really sure what to do. I'll talk to Cassy in private and see if I can get a feel for what's happening. It may not be as serious as we think." Lainie explained.

"Better to find out if we can." Jennie spoke and five other heads nodded. "I'll find a way to share my experience. Sometimes it helps to talk to someone who's had the same experience."

"Mom, let's put your cornbread in the oven and we'll eat. I don't think we should wait on Megan and Cassy. It's getting late and we've picked over the appetizer tray pretty good."

AS EVERYONE PICKED up their now-empty chili bowls and carried them to the kitchen sink, Trina announced, "Cherry pie! Did everyone save room for a piece of cherry pie with vanilla ice cream?"

"I didn't save room, but if you give me a little time, I'll be ready. The chili was awesome, and I don't think I've ever had such tasty cornbread before. My compliments to the cooks." Jeremy complimented both Trina and Margaret.

"It was delicious. I've never been a big fan of cornbread. Now I know, I've never had really good cornbread." Marcy added, "Baked in a skillet, crispy on the outside, and moist on the inside."

Margaret laughed. "Thanks. Cornbread is an art form."

"And you've nailed it." Jeremy patted Margaret's shoulder as he walked by. "And your daughter is the best pie baker I know. I assume she learned from you?"

"Mom made the pie tonight. Her crust melts in your mouth. You're in for a treat."

JENNIE GROANED. "Just roll me to the car. Thanks, Trina. And Margaret, it was so very nice seeing you again. I know we'll see you often. If you want to make supper for all of us again, when you come back, that would be fine."

Margaret laughed. "Yes, I'll be back as often as Trina wants me around." She was kidding but also sincere. "Goodnight, all. I'm going to get ready for bed and try to finish my library book."

"She'll be back, I promise." Trina waited for everyone to grab their things, and she walked them to the porch as Margaret retreated to Trina's small extra room.

"Thanks for coming. Keep me in the loop about Cassy. I feel like we need to help, although I'm not sure what we should do."

Lainie added, "I don't want to make her feel like she needs to defend her actions. That will only push her further away— the wrong direction."

"I agree. I'm going to pray on this because I feel called to share my experience and I'm not sure how to start that conversation." Jennie looked at Jeremy. "Actually, why don't we pray now? Jeremy?"

The five friends held hands on Trina's front porch.

"Jennie, you start." Jeremy encouraged.

She hesitated. *Father, please give me the words.*

"Father, we love you and thank you for your goodness. We thank you for our friendships. We ask that you watch over Cassy and Megan and heal their friendship. Please protect Cassy from any situation that isn't your will. And also, be with the young man that is, perhaps, forcing his will on Cassy. Heal his desire to dominate and to hurt our friend or anyone. Help him to seek your will and find the goodness in being humble and caring." Jennie paused, thinking Jeremy would continue, but he simply squeezed her hand, so she continued, "In your name we pray, your will be done. Amen."

"Thank you, that was nice." Marcy didn't attend church but she believed in the power of prayer. Moving to Appleridge and meeting Jeremy and Jennie opened a whole new world of prayer for her.

"Well, I'm going home, I'm tired from our early morning trip to Sugar Creek and then an unexpected and very busy shift at the hospital. I'm scheduled for tomorrow morning, but I'll be out to the farm to see my kids late in the afternoon."

"Thanks for taking us to Sugar Creek. I'm sorry you were called in to work. That's a long day." Jennie was tired and she hadn't worked a shift in the emergency department of a hospital.

"Just so you know, this invitation to supper was a nice way to end my long day." Marcy yawned. "Oh, my! Enough talking.

Bye." She jogged down the porch steps, her last jog of the day, and jumped in her truck before Jeremy and Jennie reached the bottom step.

Once in the SUV, Jeremy reached over and took Jennie's hand. "That was a nice prayer."

Jennie sighed. "I'm still not comfortable praying in a group but my heart just took over."

"I think that's the way it should always be—let your heart take over."

JENNIE DIDN'T SAY much as they drove to her farm.

"Jennie, do you want to talk about it? It's ok if you don't, but would it help?"

"Talk about what?" Jennie pretended she didn't know what he meant.

"About your scary boyfriend experience. I'm sure it was very scary. I'm so thankful you had Kate and Kyiko as room-mates."

"You remember their names."

"I know they were, and still are, very special friends."

"I want you to get to know them, too." Jennie thought it was very likely he would—at a future wedding.

"So, what happened? If you want to share." Jeremy parked the SUV at the farm but sat quietly.

"I met this guy after one of our dance workshops. He was in the audience and approached me in the lobby. He said he loved the way I danced. You already know, I wasn't a dance major, but I took as many dance classes as I could schedule."

Jeremy nodded.

"I saw him several more times. Always near the dance theater. He seemed nice. He asked me out and I declined. I didn't know anything about him."

Jeremy nodded. "That was wise."

"He was also a student at Columbia College. I ran into him a few times at the main building and also at a local party. Kate and Kyiko were with me and I introduced them."

"Did they like him?"

"At first? I'm not sure." She looked at Jeremy. "I thought he was nice. He was a theater major. I went to several of his performances. He was a pretty good actor. I guess you could say we were sort of dating. When I started to trust him, I let him pick me up at my apartment. Several times he met me at the deli where I worked."

"Was that ok?"

"Yes, except Mrs. Samuelson didn't seem to care for him. I thought maybe she was being protective. She cared for all her employees as if we were her children."

"I've heard you talk about her and I know you were closer than just employer and employee."

Jennie laughed. "She was my surrogate mom."

Jeremy thought he would like to meet Mrs. Samuelson. "She cared about you. Did it worry you that she didn't like this guy?"

"No, not really. We were having fun. He seemed very interested in what I liked—at first. Then he started to make fun of what I liked. It was strange. I thought it was my imagination until he asked me to miss dance class several times, saying it was a waste of my time."

"A waste of your time? I thought he said he loved the way you danced."

"He did, but after we started dating a bit, he said I was wasting my time since I wasn't a dance major and wasn't actually going to do anything that involved dance. I actually skipped class a few times when he asked."

"I'm sure you missed going to class. Do you miss dance now?"

"Not too much now that I have horses again. Both dancing and horses are good stress relievers. When I can budget the expense, I may sign up for an adult dance class. There's a studio opening up right here in Appleridge. Lainie's thinking about teaming up with the instructor and offering a combo class for equestrians."

Jeremy steered the conversation back to Jennie missing her dance classes. "So, after you missed a few classes, what happened?"

"I felt bad when I missed. And to make it worse, when I skipped class, we never did anything special except watch him in his class, or in his rehearsal, or sit around at his friends' apartments. It felt like such a waste."

"So, when did it take a bad turn?"

"I think we dated maybe two months before I decided he wasn't the guy for me. We still talked and I answered his calls and texts, but I refused to miss class when he asked. I stopped watching his rehearsals or going out with his friends. I tried to explain. I had my own classes, rehearsals, and work, so I couldn't sit and watch him. He would pout and call me selfish.

"I started to avoid him; he would get angry and yell at me like I was a disobedient child. After he yelled, he would be really sweet—for a few days—then I would feel stupid and mean. I would apologize and meet him for lunch or at school."

"Ok, so he was following a classic pattern. Gain trust, make demands, make the person feel guilty." Jeremy didn't know if it was really a classic pattern; however, it seemed like a pattern to undermine someone's confidence.

"Does he have a name? Or is saying his name uncomfortable?" Jeremy thought maybe it would help to send the bad feelings away if Jennie said his name.

"His name was—Kevin. Actually, it probably still is his name." A soft snicker escaped.

Jeremy loved hearing that little touch of humor. A laugh could chase away a few demons. "Yeah, it probably still is his name—if he didn't party himself into an early grave."

"That's possible. He and the other theater majors partied quite a bit. They bar hopped and sometime held huge parties in their apartments."

"And that is totally not you." Jeremy knew Jennie wasn't comfortable in large groups of people she didn't know. He also suspected some not-so-nice things were happening at those parties.

"No, it wasn't me. I went to one and never went back. I wasn't thinking of us as a couple anymore, but I didn't want to hurt his feelings."

Jeremy knew the story wasn't finished. "So, what happened?

"One night I went to dinner with Kyiko and Kate. After dinner, we stopped at a local bistro to listen to a band we liked. He saw us there and threw a fit; ranting about how I thought I was too good to go out with him and his friends. He called me Miss Goody Dance Shoes, prude, and accused me of lying about why I couldn't go out with him.

"I actually felt guilty and tried to justify being with Kate and Kyiko. When that didn't work, I tried to apologize for everything else until my good friends ushered me out of the bar. I know, unbelievable. I thought I had more sense."

"You did and you do have good sense." Jeremy confirmed.

"I guess in this instance, I didn't, until—"

"Until what?"

"Until I noticed he was following me—everywhere."

"Following you?" Jeremy realized he was hearing old news, but he still felt a strong urge to protect Jennie. He took her hand.

"He followed me to class; both at the main building and to the dance center. He followed me to work and stood outside the deli. He even followed me to church. When I noticed, he would just laugh and pretend it was a coincidence. It wasn't; it started to feel a little creepy."

"Did you ask for help?"

"I did. I talked to my school counselor and she filed a report. He was given a warning and was threatened with being expelled if he didn't leave me alone. She also spoke to the Director of the Dance Department and asked them to watch for him at the dance center. It was scary for a while. Kate and Kyiko wouldn't let me go anywhere alone for weeks. I started carrying mace and a whistle when I walked to work or commuted to school.

Jeremy knew Kevin was an abuser and they never give up easily. "He stole your sense of self-worth. They call people like him a narcissist. They use aggression to control. They think they're more important than anyone or anything. They have a deep need for attention."

"And they make people feel guilty; and when you feel guilty, you can't think straight." Jennie added, "and they steal your life."

"I'm so thankful your friends had your back."

Jennie nodded. "And now I have Cassy's back."

Chapter Sixteen

rina leaned on the fence and looked into Fare's brown eyes. Such kind eyes. Listening eyes.

"I miss Mom, Fare. I've caught up on a lot of my work, but this week seemed long without Mom in the kitchen. Even our trips to the grocery store were fun shopping together. I wonder if she would consider moving in with me. She seemed to like the little bedroom. It's small but cozy." *No, it would be best to allow Mom to have her independence for as long as possible. When and if she needs help, then it will be the time to ask Mom to move here.*

Fare nudged her arm. He agreed. He always seemed to read Trina's thoughts. Fare was doing really well. After gaining a bit of weight, he looked great. Trina decided to follow a sudden impulse. She jogged to the barn and grabbed Fare's rope halter and lead rope. Fare was still waiting by the fence when she returned. Trina climbed up on the fence and swung her legs over. Fare brought his face toward her knees and she put on his halter. She clipped on the rope and then swung the other end across his neck to tie, making reins. He swung his body near the fence, offering his back, and she climbed on.

The other horses looked up but didn't approach. Good. She hadn't ridden for a while—a long while. She felt Fare relax, she relaxed. He felt good. Ears forward, walking with rhythm, they walked around the entire pasture, following the fence line. She asked for a slow trot. "Good boy, Fare."

Trotting to the fence in front of the barn, Trina asked him to move sideways to the fence and she climbed off.

"You haven't forgotten anything." Fare searched her pocket. "Including where I keep the goodies." Trina laughed as she found a treat for Fare.

"Time to eat. You get to come in first today, boy." She led her horse into the barn and into his stall where she already had a nice flake of hay waiting. "I think I may need to shop for a saddle. But for now, we'll just keep moseying about."

As the horses ate, Trina swept the aisle. She decided to leave them in for an hour to finish their hay while she did a few more chores. She wasn't quite ready to return to the house where more work waited. She looked at Fare and became motivated. *I need to finish a few projects and send out invoices.* After all, she had a dependent to support and he was worth every penny.

CASSY JUMPED as she felt someone tug her long blond hair. She turned and found herself staring into a broad male chest. Stepping back, she attempted to reclaim her personal space. Why did Cal always get so close—too close? "Hey, how was practice?"

"Perfect. You didn't come watch." Cal leaned on Cassy's car. "You going somewhere? I thought we were doing something tonight."

"I'm riding tonight." Cassy didn't say more. She didn't look at Cal.

"Oh, I see how it is." Cal didn't move away from the car as she opened the door.

"Why? What did you want to do tonight?" Cassy was interested.

"Oh, just hanging around with friends, or maybe you could help me study. I didn't have time, you know, with practice and all." Call smiled and reached for her hand. "You're so beautiful. Maybe I just want to look at you."

Cassy was flattered but not as flattered as the first time Cal used that line on her to get his way.

"I need to go to the barn. I'll try to watch your game tomorrow. It's home, right?"

"Try? You'll try? I'm the leading scorer on the basketball team." Cal said those words like they made him the most important man on the squad.

Cassy didn't really like basketball, but she wanted to pacify Cal. He was so popular and being with him made her feel chosen and special. She knew there was a long line of girls just waiting to take her place. "I'll be there."

Cal finally stepped away from Cassy's car. She glanced in her rearview mirror as she drove away. Cal didn't look happy. Maybe she should turn around. No, Megan would storm over to Richburg, hold her hostage in her dorm room, and demand to know why she missed practice again—and she wasn't ready to share.

JENNIE SHUT DOWN her computer at the Country Chronicle office. Sherilynn approached her desk.

"I'm leaving; don't stay too long. It's the weekend!"

Jennie looked up. "Don't worry, I'm ready to call it a day." Jennie opened her desk drawer to grab her purse and lifted her sweater from the back of her chair.

"Have you heard from Jeremy?" Sherilynn didn't mean to be nosey. She thought Jeremy's mission trips were interesting. It was something she always wanted to do, but somehow, never had the confidence.

Jennie smiled at her friend and co-worker. "I did last night. He couldn't talk long; he was exhausted. They work hard."

"It's hard work saving souls." Sherilynn wasn't trying to be funny. "Because saving souls means a lot of hard work showing you care. If you don't show how much you care, your words mean nothing."

Jennie simply said, "Yes."

"What are they doing this time?" Sherilynn knew that every team took on a large project to help the community.

"They're building a library. It's a vacant cabin that will, hopefully, with a bit of work, become a library with lots of activities."

Sherilynn locked the office door and then turned to face Jennie. "Wow."

They walked down the stairs together, pausing at the bottom to peek into the ladies clothing store windows.

Jennie sighed. "They have beautiful things."

"They do; very nice clothes. I've gotten a few things on sale and the quality is worth a few extra pennies." Sherilynn didn't make a huge salary at the CC, but she could pinch a penny. That was something she and Jennie had in common.

"I agree. Sometimes it's worth a few extra dollars to get something that's not only beautiful but well-made."

Sherilynn laughed. "I'm preaching to the choir! I forgot your mom is a beautiful seamstress."

"She is, and I'm still wearing things that she made for me when I was in high school."

"Now you're just bragging."

Jennie turned away from the window to look at Sherilynn. The comment hurt.

"Silly! I'm just teasing because you can STILL wear the clothes you wore in high school." Sherilynn's smile chased any hurt away.

She looked at the very petite office manager. "I bet you can say the same thing."

"Actually, no; I was much heavier in high school."

Jennie couldn't imagine Sherilynn as much heavier. "Well, you look great now."

They reached their cars—Sherilynn's car and Jennie's older truck.

"Have a good weekend! The calendar is finished. I want to give it one more review on Monday. Are you finished with your articles?" Sherilynn wasn't exactly checking up on Jennie but this month's deadline was on Tuesday.

Everyone at the CC wore several hats. Sherilynn was office manager, webmaster, and kept the calendar interesting and current for CC readers. Jennie wrote articles and was responsible for the CC's layout each month. It was a small staff that also included the owner, Wilson Mark, and retired banker and part-time ad man, Charles Troyer.

"I'm finished, but like you, I'll give everything another look on Monday. The layout is almost set. Charles sent all his ads. I'm going to tweak a few to fit the page. I suppose something could happen over the weekend to change things, but I really don't think so.

Jennie loved working on the CC. She never ran out of ideas for interesting articles. She thought her article on Community-Supported Agriculture turned out especially well, after interviewing several farm owners and snapping a couple of nice pictures. Mr. Mark always approved several color photos each month and this month's farm photos were particularly colorful.

ON THE DRIVE home to Appleridge, Jennie pondered last Saturday's conversation concerning Cassy. Cassy had been at the top of her prayer list all week. She always included all her friends and Cassy held the largest piece of her heart this week.

It was Friday. Jennie made a quick decision to stop at Lainie's barn before going home. She knew the performance team practiced on Fridays. Maybe she could catch Cassy and Megan at the farm. Hopefully, Cassy wouldn't skip practice again tonight.

MEGAN MOTIONED for Cassy to follow her and Starlight as they walked around the arena for a cool down. "Wow! Was that a hard practice or what?"

"It was really fun." Cassy reached down to stroke Treasure's neck. "What a great jumping pattern."

"That's easy for you to say. You and Treasure looked perfect. Even if you—" Megan didn't finish.

"Even if what?" Cassy asked. She knew where their conversation was heading.

"Well, you haven't been at practice much and I've missed you." Megan stopped Starlight and waited for Cassy to reach her side before continuing. "Did you bring clothes? Are you staying over tonight?"

"I have clothes in the car but maybe I should get back to school tonight." Cassy thought she could catch up with Cal and make amends. "I've got a lot going on at school." The words sounded lame, even to Cassy.

"You usually stay over on Friday and then we spend the entire day riding and helping Lainie teach on Saturday. At least we used to, anyway. It's been a while." Megan hated to beg. She missed her friend.

Cassy didn't say anything, trying to sort all of the thoughts tumbling around inside her head.

Megan pressed harder. "And Jennie wants us to come over and ride Melody tomorrow. She's anxious to see someone on her back."

"Well, maybe. Let's take care of the horses and then I'll let you know."

After putting Treasure in her stall to eat a flake of hay, Cassy sneaked outside and around the corner of the barn to make a call.

No answer. Either Cal couldn't hear his phone or he was ignoring her. Cassy started checking social media. It seemed Cal was having a good time tonight—without her. She rushed back into the barn. She needed to get back to Richburg before Cal found a girl who would stick around on a Friday night.

"I gotta go; sorry."

"What! Really?" Megan decided to fight for her friend because something just wasn't right.

Jennie walked into the barn in time to catch the exchange. Megan's voice wasn't hard to hear.

Lainie jogged down the stairs from her barn apartment. "What's going on?" She noticed Jennie standing in the barn aisle. "Oh, hi."

"Um, hi. I just hoped to catch, you know, your practice, to see, well, I heard good things—" Jennie couldn't seem to speak a coherent sentence.

Lainie motioned for them all to find a seat. She sat on a small stool, Megan and Jennie sat on the aisle bench, and Cassy remained standing with her arms folded.

"I really need to go." Cassy fidgeted.

"Why?" Lainie looked at her friend and student. "Why do you need to go?"

"I have to meet someone." Cassy retorted.

"Who?" Lainie wasn't going to let her off the hook. She wanted an answer. "Are you ok? Is anyone bothering you at school?"

"I'm fine." Cassy stared out the barn door.

"Cassy, you don't owe me an explanation. I care about you—we all do. Something is happening to you. Maybe it isn't our business, but when you care for someone, you make them your business." Lainie was determined to get an answer to what was bothering Cassy.

"When I arrived in Appleridge, and a few bad experiences followed me, my new friends made it their business to help. I'm really thankful they cared." She was thankful—thankful enough to risk making Cassy angry.

Jennie found her voice. "We want the best for you. We care. People who care always want the best for their friends."

Megan sat, unusually quiet, and waited for her turn to speak. "When you find a good friend, you know when they need help, and then you risk everything to help. I'm here to risk everything."

"I don't need help. I just need to go." Cassy really didn't want to go. *This is so silly, if I don't want to go, why do I feel a need to go?*

"But do you want to go?" Jennie asked softly.

Cassy didn't answer.

Jennie knew it was time to share her experience. "Have you ever read the book or watched the movie, Safe Haven?"

Everyone nodded, including Cassy, as she plopped down on her tack box across the aisle.

Megan spoke up. "I loved that movie but the first part is intense, especially when she plans her escape."

Lainie added, "I could never figure out how a relationship or marriage could turn into such a nightmare." She paused. "Oh."

Jennie nodded at Lainie. "Right. If you remember the story, Katie has to flee her husband who is keeping her as a prisoner. She plans a pretty creative escape. It's hard to understand how you can have a relationship with someone, marry them, and then have them totally control your life to the point of making you a prisoner. Trust me. It happens more than you may think."

"Especially when your husband is a police officer, like in the movie, and he somehow adds her to a wanted list or something like that." Megan couldn't remember all the details.

"Yes. How does that happen?" Jennie waited but no one answered. "It almost happened to me."

Megan sucked in a breath. "Really?"

"Really." Jennie shared the same story she shared with Jeremy after the chili supper. "I really thought Kevin loved me. At first, he made me feel special. I believed every nice thing he said. Then when he said things that didn't make me feel so special anymore, I still believed what he said. He became angry if I didn't do everything he wanted, and I thought it was my fault."

Cassy wiped away a few tears sneaking down her cheek, and said quietly, "What happened?"

"I had two really good friends who sat me down and said a few things I didn't want to hear." Jennie smiled at Cassy. "And you have more than two friends right here who really care."

No one said anything for a few minutes. Jennie broke the silence. "I was lucky. I didn't need to plan a dangerous escape like Katie in the movie. When Kevin followed me, I reported him to the school and after that he gave up."

Cassy asked, "How did you know? About me, I mean?"

Megan was the first to answer. "I started to lose my best friend."

Lainie added, "When someone truly cares about you, they care about everything that makes you happy. That includes your friends. When they try to separate you from your friends, and in this case, your horse and the performance team, we knew something was wrong."

167

Jennie declared, "No good man would ever dare to separate a woman from her horse!"

Megan pumped her fist in the air. "That's right!"

Everyone laughed. The air became lighter.

"Megan, I'm staying tonight. What's for dinner?"

Everyone looked at Cassy. Relieved. Except for Lainie. She was ready to charge into battle. "Do you need help? Do we need to speak to someone at school? Mom isn't teaching at the college yet; even so, I can ask her for help if needed."

Lainie's mom, Constance Anderson, recently resigned from her partnership in a Philadelphia law firm to live near her daughter and teach a few courses at Richburg College, starting summer semester.

"No, I'm fine. I don't think I'll need to plan an escape. I'm not fully vested but I was heading in that direction."

"Did you want to head in that direction?" Megan was curious. She couldn't understand how her feisty friend could get pulled into that sort of situation.

"No, not really, but Cal, that's his name, Cal is a basketball star and well-known. I guess it just felt good to be with someone so popular. At least at first. He made me feel really beautiful."

"You are beautiful." Megan still couldn't understand why her smart, beautiful friend would need a guy to help her feel beautiful.

"It's hard to explain. My friends didn't understand, either," Jennie answered. "But when I told my story to Jeremy, he understood. He said it's a classic pattern; make someone feel really good to gain trust, then when you have their trust, use that trust for control and make demands. When a person feels uncomfortable or wants to distance themself from the relationship, they say and do things to make them feel guilty."

Megan shook her head. "But why do they want to hurt someone they love—or like?"

"There isn't any love involved—or even much like. It's all about power and feeding their ego. They don't really care," Jennie explained.

"I just don't see why anyone would peg you or Cassy as an easy mark." Megan shook her head.

"I don't think we were exactly marked as *easy*." Jennie didn't think so, anyway.

Lainie knew the answer. "Oh, not easy, but you both are very caring and kind. They used kindness against you. They knew you wouldn't want to be unkind and that gave them both a lot of opportunity."

Cassy left her seat on the tack box and stood closer to her friends.

"I get it." Megan stood up. "But we still want to be kind, right?"

"Yeah, kind, but sadly, there's a need to also be careful. If something makes you feel uncomfortable, that's a pretty good sign something isn't right. I bet you were starting to feel uncomfortable." Jennie put her arm around Cassy.

"I did today." Cassy walked over to Treasure's stall. "My girl has finished her hay and wants back out in the pasture. And I wouldn't mind a peek into Mrs. Peterson's cookie jar before Dr. Peterson gets home.

"Good idea! Dad is the ultimate cookie monster. Let's go!"

JENNIE AND LAINIE WATCHED their young friends walk up the lane to the Peterson farmhouse.

"Whew, I'm tired!" Jennie was emotionally exhausted.

"Too tired to share a pizza?" Lainie was more hungry than tired.

"Hmmm, I think I could be persuaded. I need to go home, change clothes, and feed horses. Do you think our Fare Friends would want to join us?"

"Maybe. You go on home and do what you need to do. Maybe Marcy will be there. If not, send her a text. I'll text Trina. Then we'll make a plan."

"I looked up the meaning of Fare Thee Well again. It means you wish someone the best. It also means to the most degree. I like that—wishing my friends the best to the most degree." Jennie really liked the sentiment.

"We'll have to share that with our friends, especially Cassy and Megan. It sure goes along with our talk."

"It really does." Jennie added, "Fare Thee Well, my friend. See you soon."

Chapter Seventeen

erry motioned for Deb to come over to the table. They were doing Save a Morgan Rescue business at Kerry's kitchen table. Deb had a small little farm and could foster a couple of horses at a time, as could Kerry, but Save a Morgan was definitely a kitchen-table business.

"We held our head up above water this month. Rescued four horses and two have been placed. We are both fostering a horse, and we have two remaining at other fosters. Those two will be hard to place." Kerry tapped the keys of her laptop computer.

Deb pulled a chair near Kerry to see the computer screen and sat down. "I'm ok with my foster for a while. He's really nice. Doing well and will make someone a wonderful horse."

"Mine, too." Kerry switched screens. "Here's our donation totals for the year. Not great, but if we're careful, we'll get by."

Deb sat back in her chair—thinking. "Once we place the horses we have, we can each take one of the two horses that will be hard to place. We don't want to take advantage of our temporary foster homes."

"I agree. I spoke to both this week, and so far, they're fine. Actually, the one seems to be attached to that older brood mare we rescued last month."

"Hey, did Trina call back, yet?" Deb didn't think so, but she wasn't sure.

"No, and that's odd." Kerry looked at the time. "I'll call again."

TRINA SEARCHED her pockets for her phone and found it in the front pocket of her hoodie, under a wad of paper towels, and a few horse treats. She glanced at the display. Kerry. "Kerry, I'm so sorry. I totally forgot to return your call." Trina apologized.

"It's ok, Trina. Deb and I thought it was strange not to hear from you. I guess I did say it wasn't an emergency."

Trina could hear the smile in Kerry's voice and relaxed.

"My Mom was here visiting when you called."

Kerry thought about what that would mean. "That sounds fun. Did you have a good time?" She really was curious, especially after her conversation with Barton. Maybe Trina was no longer estranged from her family.

"We did. Mom and I had a wonderful week and she couldn't believe I have Fare. It made her cry. But you don't want to know all about that—what's up?"

Kerry hesitated. She wasn't quite sure what to say next. "I don't know how to say this exactly. I think I do know about all that—your estrangement from your family and—"

Trina gasped. She didn't know where this conversation was leading but it felt like it wasn't going in a good direction. She didn't wait for Kerry to finish. "What? How? I mean, does this involve Fare?" She suddenly felt defensive. "It shouldn't involve Fare, or the rescue, or you."

"I'm so sorry." Kerry quickly added, "I'm not doing a very good job here. Let me start over."

Trina waited.

"We received a call from your brother, Barton." Kerry heard Trina suck in a breath but continued quickly. "He's been looking for Fare—for years. He finally tracked him to the lady who took him to the sale. She told him about a nice man at the sale who was looking for a good horse for his children and how she sold him in a private deal."

"Oh." It was all Trina could manage to squeak.

"Obviously, we've heard that story before, but it was new for Barton. He asked for the man's name. The lady didn't have a name or a bill of sale. Barton decided to visit the sale barn and talked to a few people which led him to the kill buyer."

Kerry took a breath and continued. "The kill buyer gave him a hard time before eventually mentioning our rescue. Now this buyer knew darn well we had Fare, but he preferred to play his usual sick game."

"And Bart called the rescue?"

"He did. He shared the whole story. I'm sorry. You probably didn't want the whole story shared. He was so desperate, begging me to tell him Fare was with us, so I did. I told him Fare was in a good home, but I couldn't reveal where he was out of respect for the adopter's privacy. He said he understood. That's when he shared the whole story. He wanted us to know why he was desperate to bring Fare home to you."

"I don't know what to say. I'm, I'm—" Trina started to cry.

Kerry wiped a tear from her own face. "I know. This must be a lot to take in."

"Yeah. First Fare comes home, then I have a nice week with my Mom who I've missed so much, and now I find out Bart has been searching for Fare and actually traced him to you. Oh my."

"Yeah." Kerry wasn't sure how to continue so she simply asked, "What do you want me to do? What should I tell your brother?"

"I'm not sure. No, wait. Don't tell him anything."

"I have to tell him something. Should I tell him the new home is a great home and they wish to keep Fare and remain anonymous?" Kerry would do as asked even if she felt bad for Barton.

"That would be good." Trina answered.

"I have to admit, I feel bad for Barton." Kerry sensed she didn't have an invitation to get involved and fix this family's brokenness.

"Don't feel bad. I'm going to tell Bart. I'm not sure how, yet, but I won't leave him hanging. He'll know Fare is fine and with me."

"Good." Kerry said a silent prayer that Barton would also be forgiven by his sister. "Will you contact him soon? I hate to leave him hanging."

"I will; I promise."

"Thanks. Give Fare our love."

"Thanks. Please tell Deb hello for me."

"I will. I'm still waiting to hear back about Elizabeth's barn raising. I'll either call or send a text when I get more info."

"Great. Bye." Trina sat staring at the wall. Her brother searched for Fare—for years. *Mom never said anything. I wonder if she knew.*

KERRY PLACED her phone on the table. "Could you follow the conversation?"

"Most of it. You did good. It was touch and go for a while." Deb was glad it was Kerry who made the call and not her.

"Is this in our pay grade?" Kerry asked.

"Pay? Who's getting a paycheck around here? Are you holding out on me?" Deb knew the answer. They were good friends, working hard, for no pay—unless you call saving horses good pay. And they did.

TRINA JUMPED when her phone rang again. Another call? *I haven't recovered from the last one, yet.*

"Hi, Lainie." She used her best *I'm fine* voice.

"Are you ok?" Lainie thought her friend's voice sounded strange.

"I'm ok, but I had the most, well, the most interesting call."

Lainie jumped in, "I want to hear all about it. I'm calling to invite you to Jennie's for an impromptu pizza party. Can you share with everyone?"

"Everyone?"

"Yes, the Fare Friends; me, Jennie, and Marcy." Lainie added, "Jeremy is out on his mission trip, Sam won't be at the barn tonight. Cassy and Megan won't be there, and I'll fill everyone in about them. That's how this party started." She quickly added, "If you need to talk to me alone, I'm available."

"No, I'll share with everyone. I need input from all my good friends."

"Good. Do you want me to pick you up?" Trina's barn was a little out of the way for Lainie but she didn't mind. "I have pizza pick-up duty."

"I don't want to keep you from pizza pick-up duty. You go on. I'll get there once I let the horses back out to pasture for the night."

"See you soon! Bye." Lainie was already walking toward her truck.

JENNIE finished her barn chores as Marcy groomed Riley. "I'm going to go on up to the house. It's a little chilly. I think we should gather in the kitchen tonight."

"I've almost finished with Mr. Riley, aka Mr. Piggy. Stuffin isn't too dirty. I'll just do a quick dusting and be up in a few minutes."

Jennie hung up her broom. "Let's leave them in stalls to finish their hay. I'll come back later to take them out to the pasture."

Marcy nodded in agreement.

WALKING TO the house, Jennie hummed a simple tune, ending with a sigh. She loved this old house. Oh, the memories—good memories made here.

She kicked off her boots at the door, sending them flying, something that drove Jeremy crazy. Tonight, he wasn't here to retrieve them and sit them neatly on the mat beside his own boots. She missed him.

Father, I miss Jeremy. Hold him close. Help him to find your will. Please keep him safe, and guide people to him so he may serve you. Amen.

She washed her hands in the tiny bathroom under the stairs and set out plates and cups. There wasn't a need to change into clean clothes. They were all horse girls and wouldn't mind horse-scented clothes and a few wisps of hay in their hair or hidden in pockets.

"Meow."

"Well, hello, sweetie." Jennie's cat, Beauty, wrapped her body around Jennie's leg. "I missed you." Jennie reached down and rubbed behind Beauty's ears and on top her head for a minute. Beauty wasn't an it's-ok-to-pick-me-up type of feline; however, she did love attention.

JENNIE'S GANG arrived—laughing, hugging, all talking at once.

"Yay! You tracked down Trina," Jennie cheered.

"It wasn't too hard. Just look in the barn." Lainie laughed.

Trina joined the comradery. "I really was in the barn when you called."

"Jennie found me in the barn, too." Marcy added, "I'm starved; let's eat, and then talk."

Marcy carried the pizza to the table in the little kitchen extension while her friends picked up plates, napkins, cups, and a jug of tea.

"I just love this little eating nook." Lainie settled into her chair.

"That's what Grandma always called it. She called it her breakfast nook. We ate every meal here—not just breakfast. She didn't use the dining room."

Trina poured the tea. "How did everyone fit?"

"She set up card tables and they extended out into the kitchen." Jennie remembered. "That's where I sat. The kids always sat at the card tables. She shoved them all together like one big long table. We didn't feel left out; all the cousins liked being together."

"Well, if she was as nice as your grandpa, I would have loved to have known her." Marcy loved Mr. Gantzler; he was her good driving-the-ponies pal.

"Oh, she was. She was the perfect grandma; she cooked, baked, made lots of Kool-Aid, and never seemed to lose her patience—even though we sure tested that theory."

"Who wants to say a prayer before we start chowing down on this pizza?" Trina looked at Jennie.

"I miss Jeremy!" Jennie did miss him and not only because he was their go-to prayer person.

Lainie spoke up. "I'll let Jennie off the hook. I'll pray and do my best. You know I'm new at this sort of thing."

They bowed their heads as Lainie began to pray.

"Father, thank you for this time with friends. Help us to always be good friends who love and trust one another. Thank you for pizza! Amen."

"I love it; good job!" Jennie leaned over toward Lainie and they touched elbows.

"Yum, no one makes pizza like the Pizza Pie," Trina managed to say as she chewed. She held her hand up to hide her mouth as she realized what she was doing: talking with food in her mouth. "Sorry."

"You're among friends," Lainie added, hiding her own mouth.

They decided to eat first, talk later. It didn't take too long to finish.

"Anyone still hungry? I have some chips and I think dip." Jennie got up to check her pantry supplies. "And for the weight conscious, I have—nothing. Sorry."

They were getting good at talking and eating. "After all this pizza, it's a little late to worry about calories. Bring on those chips!" Marcy used her napkin to hide her mouth.

"So." Lainie decided to start the conversation. "Jennie and I talked to Cassy and Megan tonight. It went well. We were right. Cassy was getting a bit of pressure from a boy—a very popular boy." She looked at Jennie and waited for her to add her thoughts.

"Fortunately, she wasn't too heavily invested in the relationship. I think she was relieved to know this sort of thing happens—I mean—happened to me, too."

Marcy refilled her cup. "So, you think she's going to be ok? Did she need help?"

Lainie answered, "She says she'll be fine and didn't think this Cal guy would pursue the issue. I guess he's sort of a big man on campus and has lots of opportunities. Cassy didn't know why he singled her out from all the other girls."

"Too bad we couldn't put him on a beware list." Marcy hated the thought of other young girls being pushed and controlled.

"I know. Not everyone has a mentor to look out for them. I'm glad Cassy and Megan have us." Lainie really didn't care for bullies. Her thoughts were based on her own personal experiences. "I'm going to make sure I watch over all my students."

"That's a huge commitment but I know you'll do your best." Trina believed in Lainie. Now it was her turn to share.

"I have something to share. I could use some good friend advice." She paused. Her three friends sat quietly waiting.

"You know about how I lost Fare and how I've been estranged from my family."

"But now you and your mom are together again." Jennie liked to look for the positive.

"Yes, and that's been a real blessing."

"Go on, Trina, sorry to interrupt."

"You also know how Save a Morgan found Fare in the kill pen." They all nodded. "Kerry, from Save a Morgan, called. She said my brother called the rescue. He's been searching for Fare." Trina's voice quivered. "For a few years, he's been searching, because he thinks that if he finds Fare, and brings him home to me, I'll forgive him." She wiped her face. "Sorry guys."

"Don't be sorry." Jennie handed Trina a paper towel. "It's a wonderfully sad story."

"I know." She wiped her face with the paper towel. "Bart traced him to the lady who took him to the sale. Then he went to the sale and found the kill buyer. I guess the kill buyer made Bart think Fare went to Canada on the slaughter truck before he hinted that *those rescue gals* may have gotten him.

Lainie hit the table with the palm of her hand. "What a jerk!"

"What do you expect from a man who makes his money telling people he has a great home for a horse and then sends them to slaughter? Jerk is probably being too kind." Marcy's thoughts weren't very kind at the moment.

Lainie agreed. "Go on, Trina, I'm sorry."

"Bart called Kerry. She was able to assure him that Fare was alive and in a good home. That seemed to help, but he's desperate to bring Fare home to me. He poured out the whole story to Kerry."

"The whole story?" Jennie whispered. She knew this was difficult for her very private friend.

"Yeah, the whole sad story. Kerry said she felt really bad for him. He begged her to help get Fare home to me. Kerry said he's convinced that's the only way I'll ever think about forgiving him."

"Do you think your mom knew Bart was looking for Fare?" Jennie didn't think so but had to ask.

"I wouldn't be surprised if she knows now. If Bart actually traced Fare to the rescue, he probably needed to share the news with Mom."

Marcy asked, "What are you going to do?"

"I don't know; I'm open to suggestions. I don't want to ask Mom to keep the secret. That wouldn't be fair. I don't want all this to make Mom feel uncomfortable around me again. She loves Bart and me equally."

Jennie thought the best answer was to always show love. "Do you miss your brother?"

"I do miss him, and since my week with Mom, I miss him more."

"Do you forgive him?" Jennie wanted to be clear. "I don't mean to make light of what he did. It was wrong. Mean. That won't go away. But forgiveness can happen, especially if he's repentant."

Lainie and Marcy sat and listened, allowing Jennie to lead the conversation.

"I do forgive him. I forgave him a while back, but knowing what I know now, I also feel that he loves me, and I didn't feel that before."

"Searching for Fare and finding him is a testament to how much he cares and wants to make you happy."

"Mom said he's really good to her and to his employees. It seems he's trying to make amends for his past. I think he suffers knowing he's been the cause of so much unhappiness. I don't want to make him suffer. I never want to be the cause of anyone's suffering."

Marcy spoke up, "I think you have your answer. Now you just need to figure out how to make it happen."

Trina looked at her friends. "Any suggestions?"

"Would it make you more comfortable to be with friends when you approach Bart or would you prefer to speak to him alone?" Knowing her friend, Marcy thought she already knew the answer.

"With friends." Trina answered. "But in a very personal way. Does that make sense?"

"You shared the story about how your mom spotted what she thought was a horse that looked like Fare, and how she cried when she realized it really was Fare." Marcy remembered because she was touched by the story.

Trina nodded. "I didn't know how to tell her but Fare seemed to know. He nickered and walked to the fence."

Marcy continued, "What if you invited Margaret and Bart to the farm and he would just happen to see Fare? Sometimes it's hard finding the right words to share. What is that saying? A picture is worth a thousand words?"

"And you guys would be there to meet my brother?" Trina was starting to warm up to the idea.

"We could, hmmm, we could turn it into a celebration." Lainie added, "A very touching and sweet celebration."

AS THE LAST piece of pizza was eaten, the dishes carried to the sink, with four friends hugging their goodbyes, Jennie heard her pocket make a noise. Her phone. She pulled it out to glance at the display. It was Mrs. Williams. Her grandpa's widowed lady friend.

"Just a moment, I need to see why Mrs. Williams is calling. She wouldn't call just to talk."

"Hello."

"Jennie, Jennie, you have to help!"

"Mrs. Williams, I'm here, what's happened?" Jennie motioned for her friends to wait.

"I was talking to Charlie and then nothing. I think he dropped the phone. It keeps ringing busy. I can't get your Mom and Dad to answer." She started to cry.

"Please don't cry. Marcy is here with me and we'll go now. Don't worry. I'll call you as soon as I can. Ok?"

She cried, "Hurry!"

Marcy grabbed her purse. "Your grandpa?"

"Yes! He was talking to Mrs. Williams and she said it sounded like he dropped the phone."

"Let's go!" Jennie looked at Trina and Lainie.

"We're coming with you!" Both said in unison.

They piled into Marcy's truck for the short drive into Appleridge.

"Should I phone for an ambulance?" She looked at Marcy.

"We'll be there in minutes. Let's wait." She prayed that wouldn't prove to be the wrong answer.

Jennie called her mom's phone. No answer. Then her dad's phone. No answer.

At the Appleridge Senior Apartments, they parked on the street and ran into the small complex of one-floor buildings. As she ran, Jennie searched for the key to Grandpa's apartment, buried in her purse, on a ring of seldom used keys.

"Here! This is his apartment." She inserted the key. "Grandpa, Grandpa!"

Pushing open the door, they rushed inside. Grandpa was on the floor in front of his favorite recliner. Marcy fell to her knees feeling for a pulse, looking into his eyes.

He mumbled.

"Is your Grandpa diabetic?"

"Yes, recently diagnosed Type II." She sunk to her knees beside the older man she loved, praying. "He's been really tired lately."

"Look in the refrigerator for orange juice. Anything. Quick." She motioned for Trina to grab a small pillow from the sofa. "Lainie, please call 911."

Jennie returned with a small glass of orange juice. Marcy lifted Grandpa's head and encouraged him to take a sip. He continued to mumble, tasted the orange juice, and then took a small swallow.

The Appleridge Senior Apartments were uptown only a few blocks from the fire station. In minutes they heard the siren. Lainie was outside waiting to direct the EMTs to Grandpa's door.

"Marcy. What do we have?" The EMT crew knew Marcy, one of their favorite emergency nurses.

"I think we have a low blood sugar incident. The patient has been recently diagnosed with diabetes. He's been able to drink a bit of orange juice.

"I'm here, I'm here." Grandpa's words were only slightly slurred.

"Mr. Gantzler, it's Mark, your friendly EMT." Mark didn't think the situation was life threatening and decided to reduce the stress level in the small room. "How are you feeling now?"

"Better. A bit better." Grandpa swallowed, took another sip of orange juice, then looked around the room. "Am I having a party?"

"Yes, young man. It appears you're having a party." Mark patted Grandpa's hand. "Why don't we move this party to the hospital and let one of our nice doctors check you out?"

"Oh, I don't think—"

"Grandpa, you scared us. Something happened and you passed out while talking to Mrs. Williams. You scared her, too." Jennie voice was firm.

Grandpa attempted to sit up. "Ok, easy partner, go slowly now." Mark motioned to his partner to bring the gurney. "We'll even throw in a nice carnival ride for free."

"Young man, I don't think any of this will be free." Grandpa chuckled. Jennie was relieved to hear a weak chuckle.

"We'll go with you. I'm sure Marcy will see you get VIP treatment." Jennie was pretty sure an ambulance ride would be enough for Grandpa to get VIP treatment; of course, having Marcy along wouldn't hurt.

Grandpa looked around the room. It appeared to be six against one. Not good odds. Not good odds at all. "Jennie, please call Lizzie and tell her I'm fine. Tell her I'll call when I can. And, Jennie."

"Yes." She waited.

"Tell her thank you."

"I will. Now you go with Mark and we'll meet you at the hospital. I'll leave a message for Mom."

"You tell her not to go rushing up to the hospital this late at night. I'm fine."

"Yeah, sure, like she'll listen to me. You're stubborn, Mom is stubborn, I'm stubborn. Hmmm, I'm seeing a little pattern here. The Granddaughter apple and Mother apple doesn't fall far from the Grandfather apple tree here in good old Appleridge."

"I concede your point, Jennie girl."

Hearing Grandpa say "Jennie girl" was good. He must be feeling better.

On the way to the hospital, Jennie called Mrs. Williams. "He's fine. It appears he had a low blood sugar incident."

"Oh, my."

"It was good that you called for help. He told me to tell you thank you and he'll call you as soon as he can."

"Did he go to the hospital?" Mrs. Williams voice quivered. She was relieved, but so very tired.

"He's on his way there now. Marcy doesn't think they'll keep him. He'll get a good check-up, though."

"That's good. Thank you for calling."

"You are so very welcome. And Mrs. Williams—."

"Yes, dear."

"Thank You! Please get some rest and give Moose some nice belly scratches."

Jennie thought she heard Mrs. Williams laugh as she hung up the phone. Her large dog, Moose, was well-known for his antics around town and also for rolling over any chance he got, begging for a few belly rubs.

TRINA THOUGHT about last night's emergency. She was thankful Mr. Gantzler was going to be fine. Life is so precious and so temporary. She wouldn't delay any longer. It was time to call Bart. First, she needed to talk to her mom.

"Well, hello, dear. It's good to hear from you." Margaret loved hearing from her daughter. Currently, almost on a daily basis. They still had a lot of catching up to do.

"Hi, Mom. I'm not sure if you know anything about what I'm going to share, but if you do, it's ok, I understand."

Margaret didn't quite follow what Trina was trying to say. At least not at first.

"I got a call from Save a Morgan Rescue."

Then Margaret knew. "Yes, Bart—I wasn't sure—"

"It's ok, Mom. I know you didn't know any of this when you were here."

"No, not when I was visiting. Bart shared a bit with me later. I didn't know how much I should say to you about him or to him about you. I didn't tell him you have Fare. I feel really bad about that, though. I'm sure he'll wonder why I didn't say anything."

"I'm not trying to put you in the middle, Mom. I don't want Bart to be left hanging, either. I promised Kerry, from the rescue, I would talk to Bart and tell him I have Fare. But I'm not going to actually tell him."

"You're not?" Margaret didn't understand.

"No, I'm going to let him see Fare when he visits; you know, like you did."

"Oh, my, yes, that was quite a surprise." Margaret remembered the huge lump in her throat when she mentioned the horse looked like Fare and then found out it actually was Fare. She wondered how Bart would react. "You're going to invite Barton for a visit?"

"I am. I'm going to also invite you and my friends. I'm having a little gathering. Do you think he'll come? It's next Saturday."

"I think he'll love to visit your farm and meet your friends. Are you are going to tell him he'll meet your friends?" Margaret thought it would be enough of a surprise to see Fare.

"I'll tell him. I don't want to spring too much on him at one time. I thought maybe he would feel more comfortable with a group, or am I just being a chicken?"

"No, honey, I think that will be nice. Your friends will bring just the right feeling to the gathering. I like them. Are you going to call him?"

"Yup, just as soon as I hang up. Oh, wait, could you give me his cell number? I don't want to call the store."

Margaret joyfully shared Barton's number, then eagerly hung up. Her daughter was making the miracle call—an answered prayer. *Thank you, Jesus!*

Chapter Eighteen

*T*rina dialed Bart's number, heart thumping as she waited. He answered on the third ring.

"Hi, Bart, it's Trina." Trina didn't think he would recognize her number.

"It's so good to hear from you. Mom had a wonderful time during her week with you."

"I loved having her. We had a great time."

All very polite. Then silence. Then both spoke at once.

"Trina—"

"Bart—"

"You go first." Bart wanted to jump in and tell his sister how sorry he was. Maybe she still wasn't ready. He was anxious to hear why she called.

"I'm calling to invite you to a picnic on the farm. On Saturday. I'm also inviting several friends."

"Mom told me about your friends; she loved them. I'm happy for you, and I would love to come on Saturday." Bart didn't want to ruin the moment, so he decided to just follow Trina's lead. "I'm bringing Mom. Correct?"

"Yes, please. I'm going to ask her if she wants to spend a night or two. I'll bring her home."

"Do you want me to bring anything?" He chuckled. "Other than Mom, I mean. As you know, Mark's Market has some nice things." Bart was trying to be funny but suddenly wished he hadn't mentioned the store.

Trina laughed. "No, nothing other than Mom unless I forget something and ask you to raid the store at the last moment."

Bart was relieved. *I made my sister laugh.*

"I am counting on you to man the grill and I'm sure Jeremy will help. We're having cheeseburgers. Do you still like to grill?"

"I sure do, and I still love cheeseburgers." Bart was enjoying the conversation.

"Good. See you soon."

"Trina, wait." Bart wanted to tell her about Fare.

Trina answered quickly. "We'll get a chance to talk Saturday."

Bart realized he was being subtly told to wait. "I'm looking forward to seeing you and meeting your friends. Thanks, Squirt." *I hope Trina remembers our game.*

She remembered. "It will be good to see you, too, Bart Fart." She quickly hung up.

Oh, the memories!

JENNIE HURRIED home after work on Thursday. What a week. Another issue of the *Farm and Family Country Chronicle* was a wrap and in the stores or out for delivery. Grandpa was recovered, if not a bit cranky. She quickly learned he didn't like being reminded about eating healthy and regular meals.

She wouldn't go into the office tomorrow. Instead, she had several interviews scheduled and would work the rest of the day from home. Jeremy would also be home tomorrow—yay!

Trina's party to introduce Bart was Saturday. Jennie wondered if Trina was nervous. Maybe she should call her friend. No. Better yet, she would swing by the farm before going home.

"HEY, TRINA, you have company. I think it's Jennie." Teresa, one of her long-time boarders called to Trina.

"Thanks!" Trina leaned her stall fork against the wall and wiped her hands on her jeans before walking to the other end of the barn aisle.

"What's up?" Trina hugged Jennie.

"Hi, Teresa! How's your pony?" Jennie couldn't remember Teresa's horse's name, which was very unusual. Usually, she remembered horses' names before human names. Oh, wait. It's Misty. How could she forget a small white and brown horse named Misty? "I think I heard something about you and Misty doing really well on the last Hunter's Pace."

"We did. It was a great ride. I'm proud of my girl." Teresa beamed. "When will we see you out on the rides?"

"Soon, I hope. I'll let Jeremy ride Melody and I'll ride my trusty-true-blue, Julep." Jennie thought that would be a very good plan.

"First, I need to find a nice used horse trailer. Something Blue Boy can pull." She motioned to her truck.

"I'll keep my eyes open." Teresa was looking for her own horse trailer. She was a frequent visitor to the horse trailer online ads. "What are you looking for? A two-horse bumper pull?

"Yes, nothing too big. Something just nice for local trips." Jennie sat down on the barn bench. She liked that bench and seemed to find herself a frequent visitor resting on it while in Trina's barn.

"Trina, I need to go. Do you want me to leave Misty in her stall?" Teresa closed the stall door.

"Yes, please. I'll be getting the rest of our herd in for dinner soon. Go ahead and throw her a flake of hay, if you don't mind."

Teresa didn't mind. She loved seeing Misty happily munching a nice flake of hay when she said goodbye for the night.

TRINA WAITED until Teresa climbed into her truck and was half-way down the farm lane before looking at Jennie with a questioning look.

"How's your grandpa?"

"He's going to be fine. They adjusted some of his medication and he's supposed to watch his diet."

"I've been diagnosed with pre-diabetes. Your grandpa's episode was a good reminder for me, also. I haven't been watching my diet very well lately."

"I guess I should, too. Adult onset diabetes runs in our family. Hey, I didn't want to talk about diets; I came to see what I could do for your gathering on Saturday. What should I bring? Are you excited? Nervous?"

"Yes, I'm excited and nervous." Trina added, "But don't worry, we'll have good food. Good food doesn't necessarily mean unhealthy. Everything in moderation is my motto."

"I like that motto. You're so right."

"I'm going to keep it simple. We're having picnic food. Cheeseburgers on the grill, because if I remember correctly,

Bart loves to grill. I'm going to buy fresh baked buns from the Bake & Shake."

"Want me to make a couple of salads? How about a tossed salad and a pea salad? The tossed salad for all those people who hate peas." Jennie laughed because while she loved pea salad, Jeremy hated peas, and many other vegetables, for that matter.

"Yes, both sound good. Marcy is bringing a charcuterie board."

"What's a charcuterie board?"

"It's a fancy name for a relish tray that includes all sorts of little things—cheese, olives, fruit, meat, nuts—I'm sure Marcy will be very creative."

Yum! Sounds good—and pretty. How did you learn about charcuterie boards? Did I say that right?"

"Oh, do I know something our local wordsmith didn't know?" Trina teased. "It's *shar-KOOT-ter-ee.*"

"I've never heard the word." Jennie vowed to use the word soon; maybe the next time she went to Mom and Dad's house for a family night.

"I just finished a website for a client who happens to have a catering business."

"Now I know another new thing. I've never known what you do besides run the boarding barn. I suspected it was some sort of home-based tech business. I noticed you moved your computer to the corner of the kitchen while your mom was visiting."

Trina laughed. "You are a very good snoopy reporter. I needed to do a bit of work while Mom was here and she had the extra room that was also my office. I liked working in the kitchen. I like being able to see the horses in their pastures. I'm making that corner my new office nook. By the way, I like that word, too—nook."

"That word I understand, as you know, and I like the little corner in your kitchen. It's a perfect fit."

"I'm going to turn my former office into a cozy bedroom for Mom. I want her to visit more often. She fussed a bit when she thought she was disrupting my work."

Jennie hugged her friend. "I'm so happy for you and Margaret. And soon, very soon, you'll have a brother again. It's going to be great!"

Trina decided to change the subject before she got all emotional. "Mom is baking her world-famous cherry pie, of course. Lainie is bringing chips and dip. She doesn't have much of a kitchen in her little haven above the barn." Trina referred to Lainie's small but cozy apartment above the barn she leased from the Peterson family.

"Sounds like a great menu. I can't wait to meet Bart. I know it's going to be a very special gathering."

"You sound like Megan with all your *greats*!" Trina and friends loved to tease Megan about using the word *great* to describe just about everything.

ELIZABETH POURED her parents a mug of coffee and filled her favorite blue plate with sugar cookies. Micah reached for a cookie before she set it on the table, but a firm look from his mother stopped his hand mid-grab.

He politely put his hands in his lap and waited for his grandparents to each take a cookie.

Charlie made a *you got caught* snickering noise, resulting in his own firm look from Elizabeth.

"The Elders have decided the barn raising will be held one week from today." Amos Stoltz looked at his daughter. "I shared your desire to have a smaller barn for the horses and also a separate barn for hay storage. They agreed it was a good plan."

Elizabeth nodded, although as head of her household, she wanted to be involved in the barn discussion. She knew, being a woman, it wasn't the Amish way. But, still. "Thanks, Daed."

"I shared your drawing. Is there anything else you would like to add, or change?"

She felt fortunate to have Daed as her representative. He was a good man and understood her need to be involved.

"Charlie drew the barn plan. I think it's exactly what we need."

Charlie looked at his mom, seeking permission to speak. Elizabeth nodded. "I want to train horses."

Amos carefully sipped the steaming coffee. "And you'll do a fine job."

"Me, too!" Micah didn't want to be left out of the conversation.

Grandpa chuckled. "And you'll do a fine job, if you watch Charlie and learn."

Mary Ann banged a spoon on her highchair.

"Daed, did you ask permission for our Appleridge friends to be at the barn raising?"

"I did. The Bishop gave his blessing. He didn't say anything at first, but when I saw him stroke his beard, I knew he was thinking. I told him about Jeremy and Jennie returning Oscar and also about their offer to return Melody. And, he remembers Mr. Gantzler fondly."

"I'm so pleased." She looked at her son. "Charlie, you have permission to call Jennie from the phone shack."

Amos raised his eyebrows. "You're not getting too comfortable using the phone shack, are you, Charlie?"

"No, sir. I will need to check it sometimes when I go into the horse training business; right, Grandpa?"

Amos looked at his wife, Agnes. "What do you say, Grandmother?" He tried to hide a smile.

"I say our Charlie will be very wise and very careful." She patted her young grandson's hand then used her other hand to pat Micah's shoulder. "As will our Micah."

Yes, thought Elizabeth. *I am very fortunate to have such loving parents. Very fortunate, indeed.*

ELIZABETH WALKED to the phone shack to leave a message for Deb Thompkins and Kerry from the Save a Morgan Rescue. They were invited to the barn raising along with her Appleridge friends.

She shifted Mary Ann to her other arm. "Baby, you are getting heavy. Too many cookies."

Mary Ann giggled.

I am also getting too comfortable using the phone shack. I will need to set a better example for Charlie. Which is exactly why she was walking to the shack before Charlie and Micah returned home from the schoolhouse.

Elizabeth dialed Deb's number written on a small scrap of paper.

"Hello."

"Hi, Deb. This is Elizabeth Miller. I just wanted to let you and Kerry know the barn raising is next week."

"How wonderful! I'm happy for you, Elizabeth. Do you want me to call Trina or Jennie?"

"Charlie has Jennie's number and he will call. But thank you."

"I'm not sure if Kerry and I will be able to attend. We both have jobs, besides running the rescue, and we've missed a bit of work lately."

"I understand." Elizabeth did understand. She didn't know them well, but she thought they worked hard. "If you are able, just show up. Don't worry about letting me know in advance. There will be plenty of food."

"Thank you. It would certainly be something to see."

"Yes, it is. The Bishop gave permission for our English friends, but not a crowd."

It was Deb's turn to say, "I understand. We don't want to invade your community on this very special day."

ELIZABETH LEFT the phone shack, carrying the baby, switching arms occasionally, thinking. She missed Isaiah. He was a good husband and her best friend. Their time together was too short. But in spite of her loss, she was thankful for her parents and her community; they cared, she wasn't alone, her children were healthy and happy. She would spoil them just as much as Mom and Dad spoiled her, and she would teach them to respect and treasure their Amish heritage.

She stopped at the end of her gravel drive to survey the farm—the white house with two porches, the little chicken coop, her husband's heritage, his dream.

"Isaiah, I'm doing my best. We'll have a barn again soon. I miss having the horses here. I'm sure you know we have Oscar again. Melody is fine. I like Jennie and Jeremy. They'll give her a good home. I miss you." Her voice quivered. "I'll always love you."

The baby searched her Mom's face. Listening.

"Dah, dah." She pointed to the ground and wiggled her little legs.

Elizabeth put Mary Ann down and held her tiny hand as they walked to the house. Mary Ann stopped to pick a dandelion. She wouldn't remember Isaiah. She was too little to remember. The Amish life didn't allow photographs. Elizabeth vowed to talk about Isaiah often. She wanted her children to remember their good father. He loved them dearly. Just like God; God the good father.

Yes, their faith will keep them strong and my love will keep Isaiah alive in their hearts.

Chapter Nineteen

*T*rina glanced out the front window again. And again. *Where is everyone? They're supposed to arrive before Bart. That's the plan. Everything's ready. Well, the grill isn't lit yet. I'll give Bart that honor.*

She found her phone on the kitchen counter. No calls, no texts. Looking at the time, she realized it would probably be another forty minutes before anyone arrive. *Settle down, it's still early. They'll be here soon.* She decided to walk down to the barn and visit with the few boarders, enjoying their horses.

"Hi, Trina, we wondered where you were keeping yourself." Teresa brushed Misty's long tail.

As Trina walked down the aisle, she noticed another boarder, Sharon, grooming her roan horse, Nosey. She laughed thinking Nosey was an appropriate barn name for the gelding. He was always getting his nose into a bit of trouble. His registered name was In Good Time.

"Did you ladies have a good ride?"

Teresa answered. "We did. We played with obstacles in the arena and then walked around the hay field a few times."

Sharon stopped grooming Nosey to talk. "I love how you keep that wide path mowed around the hay field. It's a nice place to ride. Tomorrow we're going to trot around and then maybe eventually be able to canter!"

"What fun. I'm glad it's a good place to ride. I may get Fare out there soon. I rode him around the pasture bareback and he was a real gentleman.

"Fare is a gentleman. A kind soul." Sharon loved the older horse.

"Thanks. You should have seen him in his prime. He had a bit of energy; my older self doesn't miss that much energy!" Trina didn't.

Teresa laughed before sharing, "I bet some of that energy is back. He was looking quite spry in the pasture today as we rode by."

"I think you have company again." Teresa motioned. "At least I hear a truck. I seem to be your friendly barn lookout these days."

Trina walked to the barn door. She didn't recognize the truck. It didn't belong to Jeremy, Jennie, Lainie, or Marcy. *Oh no! Is Bart early?*

"Um, I'll see you guys later." Trina watched the gray Silverado truck park in the grass beside the arena. It WAS Bart. *Oh no! He's parking right in front of Fare's pasture.*

Bart slowly opened his truck door, climbed out, stretched, waved at Trina, then walked to the other side to help Margaret. He didn't seem to be looking at the horses.

Trina took a deep breath and walked to the truck.

"Hi, Bart." She walked to Margaret but looked at Bart.

Bart released Margaret's arm and gathered Trina into a hug. He didn't know if it was the right thing to do, or if it would be welcome, but it felt right.

Trina stiffened. Then she relaxed and hugged him back. They stood like that for a long time. Maybe an entire minute.

When her brother finally released his hold, she stepped back to look at his face. He looked the same. Older, of course, but good—healthy.

"You look good, brother." Trina positioned herself so when Bart looked at her, he wasn't also facing the pasture.

"You look good, too, Squirt."

She laughed. "Just so you know, you started it, and now calling you Bart Fart is a fair game."

"Kids, behave." Margaret's voice held laughter and not discipline.

"This place is beautiful. I love the tree-lined drive. I felt like I was driving onto a grand estate." Bart surveyed the property. His eyes landing on several horses grazing side by side.

"Are those your horses? No, wait." He looked at his mom. "Mom mentioned you board horses."

"I do. Two of my boarders are in the barn now." Perfect, now she could move their conversation into the barn and away from Fare.

"But do you have a horse?" Bart continued to stare at the pasture.

"I didn't, but now I do, he hasn't been here very long."

Bart cleared his throat. "I was going to wait for a better time—I can't—I'm so sorry. I searched and searched and found him. I found Fare."

Trina didn't dare glance at her mom. "You found him?"

"Well, almost. I know he's been rescued and I was told he has a very good home. I shared our story." He noticed Trina's troubled expression. "I'm sorry. I needed them to know how important it is for Fare to come home to you." Bart waited for a reaction. Nothing. "They promised to contact Fare's new home. I haven't heard anything yet. I'm trying. I'm trying to bring Fare home to you." Bart brushed his hand across his cheek and down to his chin and whispered, "I tried."

As Bart talked, he continued to stare at the horse with the white mane and tail.

Trina thought it was odd that Fare hadn't wandered over to the fence. He was usually the first horse to greet people. Strange. He remained with his back to the fence, not grazing, head low.

Trina suddenly realized Bart had stopped talking and was waiting for her to respond.

"I don't know what to say." She didn't. She spent the entire week rehearsing this conversation in her head and now she couldn't think of a thing to say.

"I'm sorry. I'm sorry for taking Fare away and I'm sorry I can't bring him back. I'm sorry for hurting you, sis. I'm sorry for not being a good person. I'm sorry for everything."

She could see the remorse in her brother's eyes. He wanted forgiveness. Her forgiveness. *Why was this so hard? Why can't I say the words?* Instead, she said a silent prayer. *Father, forgive me. Help me to forgive Bart—and to forgive myself. Myself? God, what?*

Trina suddenly realized the problem. She couldn't forgive herself for being bitter. Her years of bitterness hurt both her mom and Bart.

Bart waited. Margaret waited. Their eyes pleaded. Fare nickered. It was the nicker that caused Trina to be brave—and honest. Horses live in the moment. They didn't live in the past.

"I've forgiven you. I did a long time ago. Now I need to ask for your forgiveness." She looked at her mom. "And for your forgiveness."

"But you haven't done anything wrong." Bart suddenly felt the need to lean against the wooden fence for support. "I'm the one who caused all the trouble. Me! Not you."

"You did. But I'm the one who chose to make our family suffer for your mistake long after you turned your life around. I've missed you both and—" Tears. Darn those tears drowning her words just when she finally knew what to say.

Bart moved away from the fence and put strong arms around his sister. It was time to step up and hold his family. It was time to be strong in his faith, and when someone asks for forgiveness, you don't argue about who was right and who was wrong. You simply forgive.

"I forgive you." He whispered into her hair as she hugged him. He freed one arm to pull his mom into their hug.

They stood together for a few minutes. No one speaking. Everyone holding tight. Bart heard a low nicker and realized a horse was standing next to the fence with his muzzle over the top rail, now breathing into his ear.

"I think I need to see what this fellow is saying." Bart dropped his arms as Trina and Margaret stepped away.

"This is my horse. He hasn't been here long, but I've known him for a very long time. He forgives you and wants you to know he's fine." Trina watched her brother's face travel through several phases—curiosity, bewilderment, then slowly realization.

"Fare?" Bart whispered. He stroked the horse's neck. "Fare?"

Fare nickered again and nuzzled Bart's hair. Bart turned and looked at his sister. "It's Fare!"

She laughed. "Yes, I know."

"You're the good home?" He wiped a little wetness from the corner of his eye. "Fare, your home!"

Fare moved away from the fence and trotted in a little circle, tossing his head, and adding a little buck before stopping in front of his family again.

Margaret finally spoke. "Well, I'm sure glad that's taken care of, and I bet Kerry and Deb will be, too! Its hard work being in the middle of such a huge secret."

"Mom, you knew?"

"I had a little surprise, or maybe I should say a big surprise, the last time I was here. It was Trina's story to share when she was ready. Then you told me about searching for Fare, and that was your story to share when you were ready. Oh, my, what a week!"

"Finding Fare has helped me to see a few things differently. I forgave you when I found Fare. Life is too short to hold grudges. He doesn't. When I heard about how you searched and searched for Fare, I realized how much you love me."

"I do love you." Bart ran his fingers through Fare's long mane. "Thanks for the help, boy."

JEREMY PARKED his car next to the gray truck.

"Oh no. Trina wanted us here before Bart arrived. It looks like he's already here." Jennie fretted.

"I think our timing is perfect. Look at the smiles."

As Jennie climbed out of the car, Jeremy reached in the back seat, pulled out the pea salad, and handed it to Jennie. "Here, you carry the peas; I'll get the tossed salad."

"You hate peas so much you can't even carry them," Jennie teased.

"I may accidentally drop the bowl in the manure pile."

"Jeremy James, don't you dare!"

They were still laughing when they approached the Shaw family.

TRINA MOTIONED with a welcoming smile for her friends to come over to the fence. Jennie noticed she was hanging onto her brother's arm.

"Bart, I'd like you to meet my good friends Jeremy James and Jennie McKenzie."

"It's so nice to meet you both." Bart reached out to shake Jeremy's hand as Jeremy balanced the large bowl of salad in the crook of one arm.

"It's nice to meet you, too." Jennie added, "It's good to see you again, Mrs. Shaw."

"Remember, call me Margaret; Mrs. Shaw is too formal."

"I'll try." Jennie found it difficult, but she would try.

"Let's go on up to the house. I'm sure Lainie and Marcy will be here soon. What time is it?"

Trina thought it couldn't be very late. How can years of pain be healed in just a few minutes? She knew the answer. *Thank you, Jesus.*

TERESA AND SHARON walked to their vehicles as Trina and others walked toward the house. It seemed like a good time to say goodbye, after waiting in the barn, afraid to invade what seemed like a very emotional family moment.

Teresa called, "We're leaving now. I turned Misty back out to pasture."

"I turned Nosey out, too. Bye, Trina."

Trina wanted to introduce her boarders, who were also her friends, to her brother, but too much was happening all at once. She decided to simply wave. "Thanks!" She would call them both later and explain.

JUST AS THEY REACHED the front porch of the small log home, Trina spotted Lainie's truck followed by Marcy in her diesel truck. You could always hear Marcy coming.

"Hey, hey, the gang's all here," Trina sang.

They waited on the porch.

Lainie and Marcy walked together. Whispering.

"Hey, everyone." Lainie was the first to speak.

Marcy remained silent as she scrutinized Bart.

"Ok, let's get these introductions out of the way so I can put Bart to work." Trina took the lead.

"We can introduce ourselves. I'm Lainie. I met Trina when I taught a horsemanship clinic here at the farm."

"It's good to meet you, Lainie."

"I'm Marcy. I have two ponies I keep at Jennie's farm, and I met your sister because of these friends." Marcy smiled at her friends and then back at Bart. "And it's good to see you again, Margaret."

"It's good to see you again, and finally someone willing to call me by my first name. See, it isn't so hard!" Margaret beamed.

"Not for me because I'm older than these youngsters." Marcy figured she was somewhere between Margaret and her young friends in age.

"Come on in, everyone. Bart, the grill is on the back deck. Maybe you can talk Jeremy into helping."

"I'm on it. Show me the way." He looked at Jeremy.

"I guess we're being tasked with the *guy thing.*" Jeremy put the salad on the kitchen bar and led the way to the deck.

"Wait, before you go, do you want a glass of tea, or a pop, or anything?" Trina put on her hostess hat, figuratively speaking.

Bart thought a nice cold beer would taste good. Trying to be on his best behavior, he didn't ask for one. He sure didn't want to embarrass his sister in front of her friends.

Jeremy looked at Bart and then grinned. "I don't suppose you have any beer?"

Bart nodded in agreement.

"I do. I still have a couple of bottles from our chili supper." She looked at her brother. "It's your favorite, or used to be, anyway. Glass or bottle?"

"Bottle for me." Jeremy spoke first.

"Me, too." So far, Bart really liked Jeremy. He seemed so down-to-earth.

The brown bottle brought back a memory for Jennie. "The old-time horsemen used to give beer to their horses."

"I heard that." Lainie remembered something about beer for horses. "Wasn't it for digestion issues or something?"

"I think so. Belinda told me hops is being researched as a possible treatment for equine metabolic conditions. Or something like that. I'll have to ask her for more information the next time we talk."

"Belinda is Jennie's best friend—for years, right?" Trina didn't want her brother left out of the conversation.

"We were in the church nursery together as infants and rarely separated until college. Belinda's significant friend, Sam, boards his horse, Sadie, at my farm." She added for Bart, who looked puzzled, "Belinda is a veterinary student at the University of Florida."

"And for years they picked on sweet little me!" Jeremy pretending to wipe tears with a sad face.

"Oh, poor baby. Don't you have a job to do? I'm hungry." Marcy shooed Jeremy and Bart outside. "I think the grill is waiting for you on the deck, boys."

"See what I put up with? I'm so glad you're here. Sam works too much and leaves me to fend for myself." Jeremy opened the back door.

"I've got your back, friend." Bart picked up the platter of hamburgers.

THE GIRLS waited until Jeremy and Bart were outside before starting the inquisition. Questions came from every direction.

"What happened?" "When did Bart notice Fare?" "Was he happy to see Fare?" "Does he like the farm?"

"Hold on. One at a time, please." Trina looked at her mom. "You tell it, Mom. I'd like to hear it from your point of view."

Margaret pulled out a kitchen chair and sat down. "I could tell Trina was nervous. I already knew Barton was anxious from listening to him talk on the drive here." She reached for the cold glass of tea Trina brought to the table and took a sip. "Thanks, honey."

"So sorry we put you right smack in the middle of our secrets." Trina motioned to the ice tea pitcher. Marcy nodded yes, Lainie and Jennie helped themselves to a soft drink.

"It was interesting. I prayed a few prayers this week." She cleared her throat, remembering the scene and how her prayers were answered so beautifully.

"We parked and Bart stared at the horses. Trina kept trying to move his attention from the pasture to everything else."

"Oh, you noticed."

"I did. I swear I was holding my breath the whole time. Fare didn't come to the fence and he kept his back to us."

"I know! He's always the first one to greet visitors, but not today. It was almost like he knew what part he was playing in this scene." Trina glowed.

"Bart started to apologize—well, for everything. Trina didn't answer at first and I thought, oh no!"

"I was praying for words. I spent the whole week practicing what I was going to say, and when I needed the words, none came."

"And then my daughter told her brother he was forgiven and she asked us to forgive her." Margaret felt a tear slide down her wrinkled cheek. "I remember thinking, why did she ask us to forgive her?"

"That wasn't my plan, but while I was praying for words, that's what I heard. I needed to ask forgiveness for my desire to make Bart pay for his mistakes over and over again and for staying away from my family."

"Wow. What a powerful message." Jennie wished Jeremy was in the kitchen to hear this testimony. She would be sure to fill him in later.

"Go ahead and finish, dear," Margaret encouraged her daughter.

"While we were all hugging and crying, Fare walked over to the fence and breathed in Bart's ear."

Lainie was amazed. "What a smart horse! Did Bart recognize him?"

"He did, but it took a minute or two. You could almost watch the different thoughts racing through his head. It was very cool."

Marcy pulled out a chair to join Margaret at the table. "That's a great story. I'm so happy for all three of you. No, wait, all four of you. We can't forget Fare."

Trina thought a moment. "No, we can't forget Fare. It appears none of us has ever forgotten Fare."

Chapter Twenty

Kerry ended the call and leaned back in her chair. What a wonderful happy ending to Fare's story! No, it wasn't an ending. It was a wonderful new beginning for Trina's whole family. She couldn't wait to share the news with Deb.

She would share Trina's good news first, and then the rescue's bad news. They were very low on funds and wouldn't be able to rescue any more horses until the horses currently in foster care found forever homes.

Kerry tried not feel discouraged, but it was hard. So many wonderful horses just waiting to be loved.

As Kerry sat pondering the fate of waiting horses, she heard a truck pull into her drive and stood up to peek out her kitchen window. Deb. Perfect.

"You are NOT GOING TO BELIEVE THIS!" Deb bounced into the house.

"What?" Kerry's heart thumped. She told herself to calm down. It must be good news. Deb is happy.

"I stopped to check our post office box and—look!" Deb thrust an opened envelope into Kerry's hands.

Kerry pulled out a piece of paper and a check. A bank check for one thousand dollars.

They both started jumping up and down with Kerry shouting, "Oh, my! Oh, my!"

"I was getting ready to tell you we couldn't rescue any more horses and now this. Wait! Who sent this?"

"Read the note!" Deb pranced around the kitchen.

"In thankfulness for the rescue of My Fare Thee Well." She looked at the check. It was a cashier's check and didn't reveal the sender. "It must be from Trina or maybe her brother?"

Kerry thought for a moment. "I think maybe her brother. Remember he offered to pay Fare's expenses if we could bring him home to Trina."

"And we did! We brought him home to Trina." Deb stopped bouncing. "But we didn't really have any expenses except our time and fuel. Trina paid for his bail."

"Should we call him?" Kerry asked.

"Maybe."

"Wait! Let's just soak this in for now."

Deb added, "And make a trip to the bank to resuscitate our account!"

"Good idea!"

JENNIE FINISHED grooming Julep and led the mare into her stall to finish her supper hay. It was a nice quiet evening in her barn. Unusually quiet. Sam was working, Marcy was still at the hospital, and Jeremy was attending a required lecture at school.

She unlatched Melody's stall door. "Your turn, pretty girl."

Melody nickered and lowered her head into the halter Jennie held open. She led the little mare into the barn aisle and got to work, first squirting detangler into her hands, and then combing her hands through Melody's long, thick mane and tail.

Jennie found a bit of music on her phone and turned on the little barn bluetooth speaker. The horses always seemed to enjoy the music. Jennie ran her hands over the horse, checking for bumps, cuts, or anything unusual. The sweet mare nuzzled her arm.

"You'll get a little treat when I'm done. I promise."

Walking around Melody, Jennie cleaned each hoof. Melody offered each foot before Jennie could ask. "Thank you. What a good girl!"

Jennie wondered if this mare just happened to have a gentle, cooperative nature or if it was the result of Isaiah and Charlie's influence and training. It was probably the result of a great start by Isaiah, because while Oscar was more extroverted, he was also very respectful, trusting, and cooperative.

I miss Oscar.

In the short time he was at Fawn Song Farm, the gelding wormed his way into her heart. Even so, she would never regret the decision to return him to the Miller farm. She would never forget the joy on Charlie's face as Oscar backed down the ramp of the horse trailer and nickered.

"Ok, sweetie, back you go to eat your hay." Jennie lead Melody into her stall and closed the door. She hung the halter on a hook, talking to the horses. "Finish your hay while I sweep the aisle, and then you five can go back to the pasture to spend the night." Melody waited patiently for Jennie to find a horse cookie in her jean pocket.

She swept bay and chestnut hair into a pile and brushed more of the fuzz from her sweatshirt. She pulled long hair out of the mane and tail brush and carried it out of the barn, hanging some on a bush, some on a tree branch, and stuffed a few strands in a corner of the fence. The birds loved using mane and tail hair for their nests. She often found horsehair nests in the yard following a storm. Several were saved and on her bookshelf. The color of hair told her which horse donated the building material—Julep and Riley's were the nests with black hair, Sadie was the blond, Stuffin was the gray. She thought maybe Melody would donate some pretty chocolate chestnut hair this year.

SNUG IN soft sweats, following her long soak in the tub, Jennie hunted for her phone. One message.

"Hello. This is Elizabeth Miller. We are having the barn raising on Tuesday. Our bishop has given his blessing for you and Jeremy, and your friends to attend—the friends who traveled with you to meet the horses. We will have plenty of food. I hope to see you. Goodbye."

Short and sweet message. I can't wait to tell all my friends. She chuckled. *The friends who traveled with me to meet the horses.* She knew it was a special invite, since Elizabeth mentioned the bishop's approval. *The Amish certainly live in a different world.*

MR. MARK leaned back in his chair at the Chronicle office. "I like it." Music to Jennie's ears.

The Chronicle staff gathered around the table, planning next month's issue. The small staff included Wilson Mark, the owner; Charles Troyer, advertising manager; Sherilynn Adams, office manager and webmaster in training; and, of course, Jennie. They all wore several hats at this small publication.

"I won't be able to include the Amish in any of the photos." Jennie wanted to make that perfectly clear.

"I understand. I think most people are aware of the Amish beliefs concerning pictures as a graven image."

"I will try to get a few nice shots without people. Maybe an unhitched Amish buggy or a quilt draped over a railing, you know, something like that."

"How exciting that you were invited to the barn raising." Sherilynn knew the Amish were very private people.

"I'm going to try to include how we met the Miller family in the article and the barn fire leading to the barn raising. I want it to be more like a story. Their Bishop has agreed to my writing their story; however, he has reserved the right to read it before publication."

Charles spoke up, "That seems only fair. I'm not sure you know: I have Amish relatives."

Of course, Jennie thought. "I should have known. Troyer is a common Amish surname."

"My grandfather left the Amish because he wanted to be a doctor. He wasn't shunned. He left before being baptized into the church. There were restrictions he followed to honor his family."

"Do you have time to talk later? I need a better understanding of the Amish culture." Jennie thought talking to Charles would be extremely helpful.

"Yes. I spent a bit of time with my Amish cousins growing up."

Mr. Mark cleared his throat and looked at his notes. "I think that covers everything. Let's eat!"

They waited for Mr. Mark to say a short prayer and then all adjourned to a small counter holding a lunch of sandwiches and chips. The CC always provided lunch on staff meeting days. A nice perk. They moved notebooks aside to sit and eat at the conference table. What they called the conference table was actually an old but attractive wooden farm table. A small refrigerator held water and soft drinks at one end of the counter and a microwave sat on the other end.

The farm table was a new addition to the office after Mr. Mark found it at an estate auction. Jennie liked the new table. It was sturdy and perfect for both assembling projects and eating lunch. The office consisted of one large room with the table in the middle, Jennie's desk in back of the room near a window, and Sherilynn's U-shaped *command station* in position to welcome visitors as soon as they stepped through the door. Mr. Mark and Charles each had a small private office. They had a small supply closet and a bathroom about the same size as the closet. Small but efficient.

Mr. Mark looked at Sherilynn who was the best office manager he had ever hired and asked, "Is Trish coming in today?"

"Yes. She's feeling better. She hated to miss work and classes. I've sure missed her."

Trish, a Richburg College Junior, worked several afternoons a week, giving Sherilynn some uninterrupted time away from the phone.

"Good to hear she's feeling better and you'll have some help today."

He then looked at Jennie. "And you'll be at the barn raising on Tuesday? Are you still working from home most Fridays?"

"Yes, sir. I try to go out on interviews on Monday or Friday." Jennie wondered where Mr. Mark was leading the conversation. He usually didn't pay attention to the office staff schedule. He just trusted them to do their jobs.

"Charles, what's your schedule like next week?" Charles worked part-time and most of his time was on the road drumming up advertising. He rarely worked in the office.

"I'll be out and about. I usually stop in one day a week to check my desk. Why?"

All three looked at Mr. Mark and waited.

"Well, then, that's all for today. We'll meet again next Wednesday." Mr. Mark gathered his lunch things and threw away the trash. He paused. Said nothing. Then picked up his notebook and retreated into his office.

Charles, Jennie, and Sherilynn remained seated. No one said anything but their eyes said plenty. Mr. Mark's behavior was strange. He certainly had the right to know his staff's schedule, although it seemed strange. He never asked before.

Charles stood up and cleared his throat. "Well, I'm heading out. I'll see you ladies next week." He gathered his sandwich wrapper and cup, tossing them into the trash bin.

Jennie and Sherilynn said in unison, "Bye." Both remained seated as Charles grabbed his jacket from his office and quickly left the building.

Sherilynn slowly gathered her trash as she rose from her seat. Jennie followed. Together they cleaned the counter before Sherilynn broke the silence.

"That was a bit strange, don't you think?"

"Yeah, a bit," Jennie agreed.

"Maybe Mr. Mark is worried about something."

"He did seem worried," Jennie agreed again.

"I need to get busy." Sherilynn thought it a good idea to change the subject. Especially since the subject of their conversation sat in his office only a few yards away. The door was closed but the walls were thin.

Jennie caught the hint. "Me, too." She walked to her desk and sat down, scanning her computer and notebooks, trying to focus on the article she started writing before lunch.

There you go again getting worried about nothing. Mr. Mark was just making conversation. Don't read anything more into it; you have work to do. It took several minutes before her fingers started to tap the keyboard.

BEFORE STARTING HIS CAR and pulling onto the highway for the trip home to Appleridge, Jeremy sent a quick text.

Leaving C U soon.

Jennie waited for her computer to shut down as she answered. *Be safe.*

Supper?

Yes?

Café? I'll treat.

Yum!

Yay, Jeremy was taking her to dinner. She looked at the time. It would take him an hour to get home, just enough time for her to leave Richburg and stop at the grocery. Probably not enough time to feed the horses. Jeremy wouldn't mind helping. He enjoyed getting to know Melody.

Jennie started Blue Boy and waved to Sherilynn as she pulled out of her parking spot. Mr. Mark remained in his office the entire afternoon, opening his door only when Sherilynn knocked and announced their departure.

In twenty-five minutes, Jennie pulled into the grocery parking lot with a mental list of needed items—milk, swiss cheese, wheat crackers, diet Coke—she was trying to quit the pop habit. She made a quick decision to call Grandpa.

"Grandpa, it's me. I'm at the store. Do you need anything?"

"I wouldn't mind a carton of root beer. I took my daily walk and picked up a few things today; couldn't carry a carton of root beer."

"Ok; anything else?" Jennie didn't argue but she would definitely ask Grandpa if root beer was good for a diabetic.

"No, that's all. Don't get those cans. Get the brown bottles." End.

Grandpa never ended a phone conversation with goodbye and it was too late to teach an old dog new tricks. *Not that I would call Grandpa an old dog.*

She wheeled her cart down the pop aisle. *Darn, now I can't say no, especially when it's a buy one, get one sale.*

Walking back to her truck, Jennie waved at Marcy who rolled down her truck window. "Are you coming out to the farm tonight?" Jennie shouted over the diesel engine still running.

Marcy held up her finger in a *wait* message, pulled into a parking spot, and shut off the truck. She rolled her window up before opening the door.

"I am—first I need to pick up a few things and change into barn clothes." Marcy still wore her hospital scrubs.

"Did you get my message about the barn raising?"

"I did. I'm on the schedule to work, and so far, I haven't been able to find anyone willing to trade days."

"We didn't get much notice," Jennie commiserated. "I'm going to write a story for the Chronicle so I'm calling it a work-day."

"I hate to miss it. I'll keep trying." Marcy didn't hold much hope and the hospital was too short staffed to call in sick. "Is anyone else going?"

"Jeremy is going and so is Trina. Lainie is teaching and doesn't want to cancel lessons."

"What about Grandpa Charlie? Is he feeling well enough to go?"

"I'm not sure. I'm stopping by his apartment in a few minutes. I have a root beer delivery." Everyone at the farm was quite aware of Charlie Gantzler's weakness for an ice-cold bottle of root beer.

Jennie finished putting her grocery bags in the truck as Marcy claimed her now-empty grocery cart. "Then you better not keep him waiting. I'll see you later."

JENNIE CARRIED the carton of root beer with her left hand as she knocked on Grandpa's apartment door with the right.

"Come on in; it's open."

"Your wish is my command," Jennie teased as she carried the carton into the kitchen.

Grandpa followed. "Put two bottles in the fridge and the rest in the pantry."

Jennie did as she was told and then asked, "Feeling better?"

"Yup, things seem to be good. I'm watching my diet."

Jennie gave him a skeptical look.

"Now don't you lecture me about the root beer, Jennie girl. I'm being careful. I'm not going to drink that diet root beer. Those chemicals are worse than a bit of real sugar." Grandpa only drank root beer with real sugar, none of that corn syrup for him.

"If you say so." Jennie didn't want to argue.

"I do say so." Grandpa's firm answer ended any further discussion.

Jennie figured anyone at Grandpa's age should be able to have at least one vice, within reason. He didn't smoke, didn't partake of alcohol, and took no medications except Metformin for his recently diagnosed diabetes.

"I gave up my nightly bowl of ice cream. That's probably what sent me over the edge. Well, that and a few cookies."

"Ok, I get it. Did you also give up cookies?"

"Mostly." He hesitated. "Unless Lizzie happens to bake."

"Does Mrs. Williams bake often?"

"She's cutting back. Her cholesterol's been running high. I think she's just trying to make me feel better."

"How so?" Jennie followed her grandpa into the living room as they talked.

"She's trying to make sure I don't get too many sweets and pretends she shouldn't have cookies." He lowered himself into his favorite recliner. "I tell you, Jennie girl, growing old is not for the weak."

"I thought it was, 'growing old is not for the faint of heart,'" Jennie teased.

"Same thing, young lady, same thing."

"Have you decided to go to the barn raising?" Jennie, with her reputation as the organizer, wanted to get their day planned.

"I'd like to go and I'd like to bring Lizzie. Do we have room?"

Jennie nodded. "I think so. Lainie can't go and Marcy will probably have to work unless she finds someone to take her hours."

She knew the invitation was for the *friends who visited the horses*, even so, she wasn't going to tell her grandpa he couldn't bring Mrs. Williams.

"We'll leave early and probably stay late."

"Lizzie and I will be fine, young lady."

Oh, my, with more than one *young lady* comment in this conversation, Jennie thought she was on shaky ground.

"Yes, sir." Jennie tried to hide her smile. Grandpa wasn't fooled.

"Just as soon as you decide a time, let me know, and we'll be ready."

"I will." She walked over to kiss her grandpa on the forehead. "I better get home to feed five hungry horses. What are you eating for supper tonight?" Jennie couldn't resist asking.

"I'm having my Meals on Wheels lunch from today. I didn't eat it."

"You didn't eat lunch?"

"I had a chili dog at the Bake & Shake following my walk."

"Grandpa, I'm not so sure chili dogs—"

Grandpa interrupted. "May I remind you, young lady, I'm old enough to choose what I eat."

Uh-oh, a third *young lady*. Yikes! "Yes, you are." Jennie made a quick escape.

JEREMY LAUGHED when Jennie shared the story of the three *young lady* comments during her visit with Grandpa. He thought it was hilarious.

"It's not that funny." Jennie declared.

"Yes, it is."

"Why?"

"It's funny because of the way you told the story. Your voice changed when you mimicked your grandpa. You sounded just like him."

"Oh." Jennie felt a bit better. "But his diet isn't funny."

"No, but he'll be fine. No one likes being told what to eat."

"I guess not." She thought for a moment. "When someone comments on what I eat, it makes me more determined to do what I want."

"You are your grandpa's granddaughter." He started laughing again.

"Jeremy James, what are you saying?"

"Oh, nothing. Let's eat; I'm hungry." Jeremy turned toward the door.

"I haven't fed the horses yet. Marcy's at the barn. It shouldn't take long."

Jeremy chuckled again as they walked to the barn.

"Now what?" Jennie didn't try to hide her annoyance. Was he laughing at her?

"I was just thinking about driving to Sugar Creek with both Grandpa and Mrs. Williams in the car. It should be very interesting."

Jennie laughed with him. "It will. I'll need to behave myself."

"We all will—*young lady!*"

MARCY FED Riley and Stuffin while Jeremy fed Sadie and Melody. Jennie fed Julep. It didn't take long.

Jennie brushed hay from her jeans. "If they're done before you leave, would you mind turning them out?"

"Got it. I'm not going to do much tonight except groom Riley and Stuffin in their stalls while they eat. It's been a long day."

"Sorry you can't go to the barn raising." Jeremy knew Marcy was disappointed.

"I haven't given up yet." She opened Riley's stall door. "Hey, buddy."

"Would you like to go to dinner with us?" Jennie asked.

"No, you guys go on. I have a nice piece of quiche waiting for me at home." Marcy didn't want to intrude.

Jeremy berated himself for not asking Marcy first. "You sure? 'Cause your ponies don't look too terribly dirty tonight."

"I'm sure. But thanks."

Marcy hummed as she started grooming Riley. She considered Jennie and Jeremy good friends, and she enjoyed their company, but they never seemed to get much time alone, and besides, she really did feel like a nice piece of spinach quiche tonight.

TRINA SAT DOWN on the barn bench, thinking about Elizabeth Miller's invitation to the barn raising. Jennie's message indicated only the friends who visited the farm were invited but Bart wanted to attend. What should she do? Maybe talk to Kerry or Deb? They knew the Miller family and could ask Elizabeth about inviting Bart. No, Elizabeth called Jennie to invite the Appleridge gang. She didn't want to step on Jennie's toes. *Jennie's not like that—but maybe—we all get our feelings hurt easily. I'll talk to Jennie first.*

JENNIE AND JEREMY waited for their check at the Café.

"That was a good cheeseburger, as always." Jeremy placed his crumbled paper napkin on the now- empty plate.

"It looked good." After her *you need to eat better* conversation with Grandpa, Jennie decided to order a salad, instead of her usual cheeseburger.

"How was your salad?"

"It was good. But I really wanted a sandwich. I'm trying to be healthy."

"You were very good. You even drank water instead of pop," Jeremy noticed.

"Yeah, but I wanted a diet Coke—badly."

"It may have been what you wanted but you didn't have one. Good for you."

"How do you do it?" Jennie asked.

"Do what?"

"How do you eat cheeseburgers and french fries and never seem to gain an ounce?"

"I don't eat them all the time. Just when we go out." Jeremy defended his choice.

"Sorry, now I'm monitoring your diet." Jennie caught Jeremy's tone.

"It does put one on the defense, doesn't it?" Jeremy reached for her hand across the table. "But you're forgiven. Hey, do you want to share a piece of pie?"

"Jeremy!" She pretended outrage. "You're a very bad influence."

"I try my best." He picked up the meal check that the waitress placed on the table.

"Anything else, folks?"

"No, that's it, thanks." Jeremy calculated the tip and placed it on the table. "I'll just go pay the check."

As Jeremy walked to the cashier, Jennie looked at her phone. She missed a call from Trina. She started to call and then decided to send a text instead.

Sorry to miss your call. Just finished eating at the Café. Should we stop by the farm?

Jennie always wrote her texts with proper punctuation.

Ping. *Yes, come on out.*

Jennie met Jeremy at the door. "Do you mind a quick detour to Trina's place?"

"Maybe she has pie."

"Jeremy!"

He laughed an evil laugh as they walked to the car.

TRINA HEARD the car as she walked to the house. Turning around, she walked back to the barn to greet her friends.

"Hey, guys. Thanks for stopping. How was the Café?"

"I had a perfect cheeseburger as usual." Jeremy didn't feel one bit bad about enjoying his meal.

Trina looked at Jennie. "I had a salad. It was, well, a salad."

Trina commiserated. "I know what you mean. Come on up to the house. It's getting a bit nippy out here." She led the way to her cozy home and held open the door. "I may have a bit of pie left from the other night. Jeremy?"

Jeremy didn't attempt to hide his Cheshire cat-like smile. "Sounds good."

"Jennie?"

"No, thanks, but if you have a diet Coke, I'll take that." She didn't look at Jeremy.

"I do. And if you don't mind, I'm making a sandwich. I haven't eaten supper yet."

They talked as Jeremy enjoyed pie—smacking his lips. Trina made a turkey and swiss cheese sandwich. Jennie waited for Trina to share the real reason for her call.

"I'm excited about the barn raising. I have a little problem, though. Bart wants to go along, and I know Elizabeth only invited those of us who came on the day we went to see the horses." Trina took a little bite of her sandwich.

"Grandpa wants to bring Mrs. Williams and I told him, yes. Lainie can't go and possibly not Marcy, either."

"Bart and I could drive a second car—or in his case, a truck." Trina didn't think Bart would mind driving. "I could call and leave a message for Elizabeth."

"Go ahead and call. Tell her we aren't bringing more people, just different people." Jennie didn't think Elizabeth would mind. "Tell her it's your brother and Grandpa's lady friend."

Jeremy paused his pie eating. "Why don't you call and leave a message now?"

Jennie looked at Trina who added, "Please, you call, especially since she left the message with you."

Jennie picked up her phone.

"Elizabeth, this is Jennie McKenzie. There will be six of us attending the barn raising; me, Jeremy, Grandpa, his lady friend, Trina, and Trina's brother. Grandpa's friend and Trina's brother, Bart, did not visit the farm with us but they are friends and family. Please let me know if this isn't acceptable. See you soon!"

"I think it will be fine. She probably didn't give a detailed list to her bishop." Jeremy scraped his plate with his fork to capture every crumb. "If Marcy finds someone to work for her, it will still be fine."

Trina was excited about the trip. "Bart says he's bringing work gloves and tools just in case he gets invited to help."

"I'm bringing my tools, too. Elizabeth indicated we could help." Jeremy hope so. "They'll probably find something we can do, but I hope it doesn't require climbing across the rafters."

"Do you and Bart want to follow us?" Jennie couldn't take off her organizer hat.

"Yes. Do you want to stop for breakfast on the way? I think there's a Cracker Barrel not too far from our exit." Trina loved a hearty breakfast. "Are you making anything to share at lunch?"

"I'm making something; not sure what yet. Elizabeth said there will be plenty of food, but I don't want to show up empty handed."

"I suppose you're making your pea salad," Jeremy teased.

"I'll make it just for you." Jennie couldn't resist. "It's a popular Amish recipe."

"In that case, maybe I'll climb those rafters!"

Chapter Twenty-One

YAHOO! Cassy shouted as her horse, Treasure, flew around the jump course.

Lainie watched from her seat on the top board of the fence—cheering. The rest of the team gathered at the end of the arena, on their horses, waiting for their turns to ride the course.

After the last jump, Cassy released the reins and pumped both arms over her head. Treasure felt Cassy's body asking her to slow to a trot and then a walk.

"Awesome! That's how it's done!" Lainie complimented Cassy. She looked at the group nervously waiting. "Cassy just set a high bar, but don't worry; do your best and have fun."

One by one they went. A few horses balked, a few hit a jump with their back hooves, knocking down a rail, a few cantered the course with no faults, but none flew as fast as Treasure and Cassy. There was one more rider to go. Megan.

"Megan, go slow. Starlight is young and she's still learning." Lainie never wanted to overwhelm a young horse.

"Remember, I'm just as green at jumping as Starlight," Megan answered.

"I do remember. I also remember you're a great rider," Lainie encouraged.

Megan took several cleansing breaths and sat deep in the saddle. She asked her mare to trot in a circle, then asked

Starlight for a slow canter as she headed toward the first jump. Starlight pricked her ears forward and jumped the first jump smoothly.

"Good girl," Megan whispered.

They finished the course with only one hesitation. Starlight wasn't too sure about the jump made from bales of straw.

Her friends cheered. "Great job, Megan and Starlight!"

Lainie hopped off the fence. "I'm proud of you all!" She walked into the middle of the arena. "Next week, we're going to start practicing our drill pattern. I've been listening to music and will pick something that fits."

Cassy rode over to Megan and reached out for a fist bump.

Lainie noticed several mothers waiting, somewhat impatiently, for the practice to end. "Ok, that's it for today. Make sure you cool down your horses before loading them into the trailers. If you need any help, I'm here."

Lainie didn't think anyone would need help. The girls trailered in for lessons every week; some several times a week; they were trailering pros. She walked over to where a few mothers and fathers gathered near the barn.

"Did you see the group jump the course? They make me proud!"

Lainie enjoyed the responses. "My daughter loves coming to practice." "My daughter has gotten a lot more confident with her horse." "My daughters talk about jumping all the time. I think they jump their horses in their dreams." "My daughter loves her pony, and you made that happen by helping her become confident. She's having fun." "I love the way you never pressure the girls or horses."

Lainie enjoyed hearing the enthusiasm of the parents as it matched the enthusiasm of her riders.

"Thank you all. Thank you for hauling your kids and their horses here several times a week. I know being a horse parent isn't easy."

Lainie knew the level of dedication it required to buy and keep horses, to outfit riders, and to haul horses to practice and events.

"Thank you for not pressuring your children to chase ribbons." Lainie added, "You're giving them a great gift to simply allow them to enjoy their time with their horses and riding with friends."

One mom spoke up, "But we may enter them in a drill team competition at some point, right? Healthy competition is good."

Lainie smiled and nodded before answering. "Yes, healthy competition is good. Healthy competition with good horsemanship is even better. Agreed?"

All agreed.

Lainie turned to watch her riders as they prepared their horses for the trip home. It was a nice group and she vowed to keep it that way. Her goal for Lessons with Lainie and the performance team was to build solid horsemanship skills between young adults and their horses.

Competition is fun. Goals are motivating. Winning is awesome. Good horsemanship and friendship must never be sacrificed. This is what Lainie valued and would always teach.

Waving at the last trailer as it pulled out of the parking lot, Lainie turned to look for Megan and Cassy in the barn aisle grooming their horses.

"Great riding today, ladies." Lainie greeted her best students and team leaders.

"That was so much fun!" Cassy was still beaming over her and Treasure's success on the jump course.

"It was!" Megan did a little dance in the aisle. Her helmet was off and her short haircut messy and cute.

"Megan, looking at your cute haircut makes me what to chop off my hair." Lainie didn't remember ever having short hair.

"I got tired of long hair. This is so easy." Megan used her fingers as a comb. "I don't worry about helmet hair."

Cassy sported long hair. "I guess I'll stick with my long hair for now." She pulled out her scrunchie, smoothed her hair, and recaptured it into a new ponytail. "It works."

"What are you two up to tonight?" Lainie didn't know about them but she was ready for a nice shower.

"We're going up to the house to eat. Hey, come with us. Mom always has plenty." Megan knew her mom wouldn't mind if Lainie joined them for supper.

"Thanks, I'm ready for a shower and a good book. I may call Trina to see what she's doing tonight. You girls have fun. Will I see you tomorrow?"

"I'm staying over and we're going to ride the trails at the state park tomorrow." Cassy hesitated. "Unless you need us to help with anything."

"I'm teaching at Trina's barn tomorrow morning and I have only a couple of private lessons here in the afternoon." Lainie thought a moment. "Hey, don't you both have school tomorrow?"

"It's a teacher's conference day for me and Cassy's class was cancelled." Megan started to dance again, moving and wiggling in delight.

"Yup, my professor has the flu, or something, so she sent an email cancelling class."

"We have a free day!" They cheered in unison.

"Well, then, have a good time. Be safe."

Lainie turned to climb the steps to her cozy barn apartment, then stopped. "Why don't we go ahead and feed the horses?"

"We'll do it." Megan looked at Cassy for confirmation.

"Yup, we'll do it and then turn all three out," Cassy agreed.

"Thanks!" Lainie gave each girl a quick hug. "See you tomorrow. I may be at Trina's before you get here. If I am, I'll see you when you return."

"TIME TO FIGURE out this mystery." Deb picked up her phone. Kerry nodded in agreement.

"Trina. Hi. Do you have a minute?"

Trina sat down on her bench. She sure did love this much-used bench when she needed to take a load off her tired legs. "Perfect timing, Deb. I just finished weed eating the fence lines, the horses are happily munching their hay, and I don't mind sitting down right now."

Deb laughed. "Good. I have Kerry here with me and I'm going to put the phone on speaker."

"Ok, what's up?" Trina talked as she walked to the barn fridge and grabbed a bottle of water. Opening the water, she took a long drink as she listened.

"We received a surprise in the mail. A very big and much-needed surprise."

Trina waited, not knowing what this had to do with her.

"It was a very large check—a check for $1,000." Deb's voice went up an octave when she said $1,000.

"I'm sure it was needed." Trina was more puzzled than excited.

"It was a bank check with a note that said, 'In thankfulness for the rescue of My Fare Thee Well.'" Deb waited for Trina to react but heard nothing.

Kerry spoke first. "Trina, are you there? We think it was from Barton. Well, unless it was from you."

Trina didn't know what to say. "It wasn't me. I wish I could send a large donation."

"Actually, you did because you paid for Fare's bail when we didn't have the funds. Do you think Barton sent the check?"

"Yes, I think maybe Bart. I suppose it could have been Mom, but I don't think so." She didn't know much about their finances.

"We're going to call him and ask." It was now Deb talking.

"If he sent it, I'm proud of him." Trina's voice quivered. "What a wonderful thing to do to honor Fare."

Kerry's turn. "It truly was and is very much appreciated. We'll let you go. Give Fare some nice scratches for us."

"I will. Bye." Trina ended the call.

Bart, what an incredible thing to do. It was so very nice to be proud of her brother again. Just like before.

"HEY, TRINA. What are you doing tonight?"

Trina didn't look at her phone before answering but she recognized Lainie's voice. "Hi, I was just thinking about you."

"Do you want to go to the Café for dinner? For some reason, I feel like a night out on the town."

Trina couldn't help but laugh. "Out on the town? That must mean you're getting dessert with your meal tonight."

"Yup, going wild." Lainie suddenly thought about an ice cream sundae from the Bake & Shake.

"I could be persuaded. I need a shower. I just fed the horses and I mowed today." Trina could hardly stand to smell herself.

"Me, too. You wouldn't want to eat with me if I didn't shower."

Trina looked at the time. "Meet you in about an hour?"

Lainie thought it would work. "That's good. Should I pick you up?"

"No, I'll pick you up. It's on my way."

"Great! See you soon." Lainie was hungry—for both food and friendship.

TRINA PULLED INTO the gravel lot next to Lainie's barn. Lainie appeared before she could honk her horn.

"Thanks for calling. I didn't feel like eating a peanut butter and jelly sandwich again tonight. That's about all I have right now." Trina waited for Lainie to fasten her seatbelt. "I really need to go grocery shopping."

"That's about all I have, too. Hey, do you want to stop at the store after dinner? Not to do a big shopping—maybe pick up a few things."

"Good idea." Trina pulled onto the county road leading to Appleridge. "How was practice tonight?"

"Good. Really good. You should have seen Cassy on Treasure. Megan and Starlight were amazing, too; they all were."

"Did Cassy seem ok?" Trina turned off the radio.

"She seemed just like the Cassy we know and love." Lainie glanced over at her friend. "She worried me for a while. I worry about all the kids at my barn and they aren't even my kids."

Trina chuckled. "I suppose there is a bit more worry attached when teaching kids with horses. You want to keep them safe, yet still have fun."

"Yeah, like teaching sky diving." Lainie snickered. "You better pay attention to details when teaching sky diving."

"That's about as dangerous as teaching a teen to drive a car. Bart taught me to drive. That's probably what drove him to drugs." Trina meant her comment to be funny. It wasn't. She wished she could swallow every word.

Lainie looked at her friend and saw the pain. "It's ok. I know you are just trying to put a lighter spin on a very bad memory."

Trina parked and sat quietly. Lainie waited. "Let's get a table. I have something to share about Bart." Trina looked at her friend's concerned face and added, "Don't worry; it's good, very good."

THE SUPPER HOUR had passed and the crowd was light. The friends seated themselves at a vacant booth in front of a window.

"Hey, Miss Lainie." The young waitress, Angie, greeted the diners. "Hey, Miss Trina."

"Angie, when did you start working here?" Lainie smiled at the young girl.

"This is my first week. I promised my mom I would start paying for what she calls my *habit*." Angie laughed.

"Good for you and I can't think of any better habit for you to have." Laine leaned back against the back of her seat. She looked at Trina and added, "Angie just joined the performance team. She has this really cute pony named Elfie."

Trina asked, "Does Elfie jump?"

"Yup, the small jumps. We're not ready for much over a foot or so."

"They make a great team." Lainie complimented her student. "You must have rushed to get home after practice and make it here in time for work."

"I wasn't supposed to be here tonight." She shrugged. "Someone called in sick and here I am. They just need a little extra help prepping for tomorrow." She looked around and then whispered, "Don't tell anyone—I didn't have time to shower, I just did a quick clean up."

"We won't tell, and you don't smell." Trina pretended to sniff the air.

"Thanks! Are you ready to order?" Angie quickly got back to business.

Lainie looked at her menu. "A sweet tea to drink, no lemon please, and I'm going to have a cheeseburger all the way. Trina, how about splitting an order of onion rings?"

"Perfect. And I'll also have a cheeseburger to go along with my half order of onion rings. I would like mustard, onion, and pickles on my burger. I'll take ice tea, also, unsweet with lemon."

"You got it." Angie stowed her tablet in her front apron pocket and gathered the menus. "I'll be right back with your drinks."

"Good kid." Lainie watched the teen pour the tea. "Horses raise good kids."

"I agree. Horses keep teens too busy to get into trouble. Not to mention teaching lessons on dedication and hard work." Trina smiled as Angie placed the full glasses on the table.

"Miss Trina, I heard the story about your horse and how you lost him and then how you found him. Very cool."

"Yes, it's very cool," Trina agreed. "Come out sometime and meet Fare."

"I will. Thanks." She turned to get another order.

"I was thinking—" Lainie hesitated. "I was thinking about asking if we could use your arena occasionally. It's much larger than mine."

Trina didn't hesitate. "Of course. I was thinking about doing a little fundraiser for the rescue and asking your team to perform."

"Wow, our first gig!" Lainie was eager. "When?"

"I'm not sure. There's been a new development." Trina went on to share the news about Bart's donation. "I was going to ask Bart to help me raise money; he beat me to the punch."

"I'm sure he'll still want to help." Lainie thought so, anyway.

"We're going to the barn raising on Tuesday. I'll guess I should talk to him before we get there. He'll be embarrassed if I say anything about the check in front of everyone."

Lainie reached for the plate Angie delivered. "Yum!"

"TRINA, WHAT'S UP?" Bart motioned for one of his teen workers to take his place bagging groceries as he answered his phone.

"Thank you." Trina waited for the response she knew was coming.

"Thank me for what?" Bart figured she knew about the donation but decided to play along.

"For your donation. Deb and Kerry are thrilled." She swallowed, clearing her throat. "Thank you for Fare."

"Ahh. You're welcome. I knew you wouldn't let me return the amount you paid for Fare's bail. I thought a donation was a good idea."

"A very good idea. It came at a very good time. They needed the money."

"Good. I'm glad it was needed." Bart thought maybe more was needed. He didn't think he would ever be able to help Deb and Kerry enough.

Trina thought it was time to change the subject. "We're meeting Jeremy and Jennie at Jennie's farm on Tuesday and following them to the Millers' farm—if that's ok."

"Sounds like a good plan." Bart watched a line form at the store's second checkout but didn't want to rush his sister.

"We're meeting early; don't eat breakfast. We're stopping at a Cracker Barrel or somewhere."

241

"I like the sound of that, too." He waited.

"I'll let you go. I know you're at the store. I can hear some-one saying, "Mr. Shaw, Mr. Shaw."

Bart laughed. "I hear that a lot."

"I bet you do. And Bart—"

"Yes."

"I love you." Trina said it quickly and ended the call even quicker.

Bart lowered his phone and took a deep breath. *I love you, too, Squirt.*

Chapter Twenty-Two

ERE THEY ARE! Jennie picked up her purse and the pasta salad she made with just a few peas added. The perfect compromise.

"Jeremy!"

"I'm coming!" Jeremy locked the back door and followed Jennie.

Bart turned his truck around and stopped behind Jeremy's SUV.

Trina rolled down the window. "I know we're a little early. This way we'll have more time for breakfast."

Bart opened his truck door and stepped around to shake hands with Jeremy. "She's excited."

Jeremy laughed at Bart's expression. The perfect *she's my sister—what can I do* expression.

"I'm excited and hungry. Let's go, gang." Jennie the planner was ready for the day. "We'll pick up Grandpa and Mrs. Williams on our way out of town.

GRANDPA CHARLIE stood on the curb waiting for his ride. Jeremy smoothly pulled to the curb and opened his door as Jennie opened her door.

"Grandpa, I'll get in the back. You take the front." Jennie gave her grandpa a hug.

"No, I'm getting in the back with you. Lizzie gets car sick if she rides in the back."

Grandpa walked around the car, shook hands with Jeremy, then slowly lowered himself into the back seat. "Good morning. Right on time." He waved at Trina and a young man waiting in a truck behind Jeremy's car. "Does Trina have a beau?"

"No, Gramps, that's Bart, her brother." Jennie didn't say more. Someday she would probably share the entire story but today wasn't the day.

"And now we'll pick up Mrs. Williams." Jeremy pulled onto the road. Bart followed.

JEREMY OPENED THE CAR door and walked up the sidewalk to escort Mrs. Williams from her little house to the car.

"He's a fine young man, Jennie girl."

"He is, Grandpa. He really is. I'm one lucky girl."

"Oh, I wouldn't say lucky. I'd say you're one smart young lady."

Mrs. Williams settled into the front seat and turned to look behind at Jennie and Grandpa in the back seat. "Good morning, Charlie. Good morning, Jennie. What a beautiful day for our little adventure!"

Jennie beat her grandpa to a response. "It truly is."

"Lizzie, you're looking very nice today. As usual." Grandpa was never one to ignore a pretty lady.

"Now Charlie, you're making me blush."

Jennie grinned. Such a sweet couple.

JENNIE SENT a text to Trina. *Is the Cracker Barrel at the next exit ok for breakfast?*

244

Trina's quick reply: *Perfect.*

MR. GANTZLER, Mrs. Williams, this is my brother, Barton. I call him Bart. Bart, Mr. Gantzler is Jennie's grandpa and Mrs. Williams is his—um—"

"I'm his lady friend." She noticed Bart's confusion. "I'm a widow. We went to school together a few years ago."

Grandpa laughed. "Just a few years ago."

BACK ON THE ROAD after their breakfast, Jeremy looked in his rearview mirror at Jennie. "I like Bart. He seems like a nice guy."

"I'm so happy for Trina. She loves having her family back in her life again."

"And all because of a little horse named Fare," Jeremy added.

"I believe there must be a story behind that comment." Grandpa loved stories.

"Oh, there is but it'll need to wait." Jennie added, "Right now we're going to an Amish barn raising—all because of two little horses named Oscar and Melody." Jennie lifted her phone to snap a picture. "Look at all those horses and buggies!"

Jeremy slowed the car. "I think I'll park along the road instead of pulling into the drive." He remembered his passengers. "Will you be able to walk up to the house?"

Grandpa answered quickly. "Good idea. I'll have a good excuse to hold this sweet lady's arm on the walk."

"Oh, Charlie. You don't need an excuse to hold my hand." Mrs. Williams's cheeks bloomed a rosy glow.

Jeremy put on his blinker and slowed to a crawl before parking along the road. Bart followed.

"What do you need me to carry?" Jennie reached for the small cooler holding the pasta salad and a few bottles of water.

"You get the salad and I'll get my tools." They both slung a folding camp chair over their shoulder.

Trina and Bart joined them, Bart carrying his toolbox, Trina a warm dish, both carrying chairs.

As they reached the Miller farm drive, a young Amish man stopped his buggy and spoke to the elderly couple. "If you please, I will take you up to the house."

Mrs. Williams didn't hesitate. "Well, thank you, young man. I would love a ride. Charlie?"

"Yes, of course." Grandpa turned, winked at Jennie and whispered, "When have I ever turned down a buggy ride?"

"Not in my recent memory," she whispered.

They waited for the buggy carrying the seniors to move, and continued their walk.

"What did you make?" Jennie was curious.

"I made a corn casserole." Trina carried an insulated bag. "I think this will keep it hot until lunch."

"Yum! Is that the one with corn bread mix and sour cream?" Jennie loved that recipe.

"One of my favorites," Trina answered and motioned to Jeremy and Bart walking ahead. "I think they bonded over grill duty last week."

"I think so. I'm so happy for you and Bart."

"Thanks. I'm enjoying being close to my family again. Mom calls almost every day and Bart every couple of days. I'm going to help out at the store once in a while. You know, on those busy days around the holidays."

"Don't you even dare think about moving!" Jennie would miss her friend.

"Don't worry. I don't want to give up my farm. I think a bit of space is good no matter how much you love your family."

BY THE TIME they finished their walk, Elizabeth Miller already had Grandpa and Lizzie seated in chairs under the shade of a large oak tree.

"It's so good to see you." Elizabeth looked at Bart with a welcoming smile.

"Elizabeth, this is my brother, Bart." Trina motioned for Bart to step forward.

He put down his tools, wiped his hands on his jeans, and held out his hand. "It's nice to meet you."

Jeremy stepped forward. "It's nice to see you again, Elizabeth. How's our boys, Oscar and Charlie?"

Elizabeth laughed, covering her mouth with one hand. "They are both doing well. Charlie is excited about the barn and I'm sure Oscar will enjoy his new abode."

"Mr. Jeremy!" Charlie Miller ran up to the group. Wait 'til you see what Oscar and I can do!"

"Now, Charlie, there might not be time today. We have a barn to build." Elizabeth lovingly placed her hand on her son's shoulder. "Why don't you take Mr. Jeremy and Mr. Bart over to the crew and introduce them? I see they've brought their work gloves and tools."

"Come with me!" Charlie proudly led the way.

"He's very excited. Daed is letting him help."

Trina noticed a foundation for the barn, made of large field rock, seemed to be in place. "I love the foundation. It looks old."

"We used rocks salvaged from the original barn. A small crew built the foundation last week." Elizbeth gazed toward the stacked rocks. "It will seem like part of Isaiah is still here. As a young boy, he helped gather some of the rock when they built the addition to the barn."

"That's really nice." Trina asked, "Are you building the same type of barn today?"

"We don't need a big barn so we're building a small four-stall barn for horses and buggies, and then another building to store hay and tools."

"Will they build both today?" Jennie asked.

"They'll try. It looks like we have a nice large crew ready to work. I think most of the actual building will be done today. Some men will return tomorrow for the small finishing jobs, I think." Elizabeth watched her father share the building plans with the crew. "Charlie designed the horse barn."

"That's impressive." Jennie would ask Jeremy all about it later. She picked up the cooler. "I brought a salad. Should I take it to the kitchen? I could leave it in the cooler."

"Ja, let's walk up to the house. We may keep it in the cooler. The kitchen refrigerator is full."

"I brought a corn casserole. It'll stay hot in this carrier," Trina shared.

"Thank you. We'll have plenty of food. That is good. The men get hungry after working so hard."

Elizabeth introduced Jennie and Trina to the gathering of Amish ladies busy in the kitchen. "These are my friends. Jennie is the one who has our mare, Melody."

The ladies looked at one another and nodded. Jennie was sure they all probably heard the story of Oscar coming back home. Their smiles were warm. They didn't seem concerned about these strangers being invited to spend the day at an Amish barn raising.

Jennie and Trina followed Elizabeth outside.

"Oh, my, look!" Jennie pointed to the Amish men gathered in the empty spot soon to become a major construction zone. Jeremy and Bart stood with the Amish men, apparently getting instructions.

"Looks like they've been hired." Trina wished woman could help with the construction. She knew how to swing a hammer and handle a saw.

"I guess we'll just sit and watch." Jennie glanced at the house. "They don't seem to need more help in the house at the moment. Maybe we can help when it comes to bringing everything outside for lunch."

"And cleaning up. You always need extra hands for cleanup," Trina added.

Although Jennie wasn't a sit-back-and-watch sort of girl, she didn't want to intrude or bother Elizabeth, so she sat.

Elizabeth must have read her mind. She appeared out of nowhere. "Once they get started, we'll be busy carrying drinks and things out to the crew. Would you like to help?"

"Yes!" Trina and Jennie said together.

"I thought so. We could also use some help making sand-wiches."

"We're ready!" Jennie and Trina followed Elizabeth back to the kitchen and joined a sandwich-making assembly line.

The ladies joked and laughed as they worked. Jennie and Trina caught some of the Amish phrases. Elizabeth handed them each a white apron.

"Thanks!" Jennie put the apron over her head and turned her back to Trina. "You tie mine; I'll tie yours."

Trina tied the apron and then turned for Jennie to recipro-cate. Elizabeth motioned for them to grab a knife and a large jar of peanut butter. Various jars of homemade jellies were lined up on the counter.

"Now this I can do. I'm pretty good at peanut butter and jelly sandwiches." Jennie picked up a loaf of homemade bread and looked for a long knife. A young girl handed her a serrated knife attached to a wooden piece that was used to measure the size of the slices.

"I like this. What a great invention." Jennie thanked the girl. She giggled and scooted away from the Englisher who had never seen a proper bread knife.

Jennie thought the hardest part of the job was not licking her peanut butter-and-jelly-sticky fingers. She searched for a paper towel.

Trina scraped out the last of the peanut butter. "That's it, unless they have more." Somehow, Trina thought they proba-bly had a lot more.

An older Amish lady carried over another huge jar of pea-nut butter. "Here you go." She chuckled.

"Here we go!" Jennie agreed.

After making what seemed like a thousand sandwiches, Jennie was ready to sit down and enjoy a cold drink. She noticed the turkey and ham sandwich makers were cleaning up. "I think it's time for us to clean up."

Trina agreed. They wiped off the remaining jelly lids and jars with a wet dish cloth, wiped the counter, and took their knives to the kitchen sink where two Amish teens washed dishes standing in their stocking feet.

Elizabeth motioned to several jugs of tea. "Do you mind taking these jugs to the drink table? And grab a nice drink for yourselves. We have a bit of time before the crew will break for the noon meal."

"Look at that!" Jennie pointed. The framed walls were being lifted into place. She saw Jeremy and Bart on the framing crew. "It looks like they'll place the trusses soon."

"Ja, and then the wall framing crew will start framing the walls for the storage barn." This wasn't Elizabeth's first barn raising. She could probably direct the crew if needed.

After Elizabeth walked away, Jennie grabbed a glass of cold tea. "I'm glad Jeremy and Bart are on the wall crew. They can frame a wall with both feet on the ground."

"Me, too! I know Bart doesn't care much for heights." Trina remembered making fun of her brother for refusing to get on a Ferris wheel at the county fair.

Jennie noticed Amos and Agnes Stoltz, and several other older Amish men and ladies, sitting with Grandpa and Mrs. Williams. "I don't think we need to worry about Grandpa and Mrs. Williams. They seem to be part of a nice group chat."

Trina unfolded one of their chairs and sat. "Sit down while we have a few minutes."

Jennie sat. "It does feel good to sit."

Sipping their tea, Jennie and Trina watched the barn take shape. It wasn't long before the first group of men walked toward the house.

Jennie motioned to several picnic tables full of food. "They work fast. I didn't notice anyone carrying out the food. Should we help?"

"Let's sit. We'll do clean up."

Jennie watched the men gather in a circle for a silent prayer. Jeremy was in the first group. While he prayed silently, she was very sure he wanted to pray out loud. He loved praying in a group, hearing each person add a petition.

THE AFTERNOON proceeded in the same fashion as the morning. At day's end, the walls were up, the roof plywood in place, and the shingles started. All the dishes were back in the kitchen, washed and stacked. Grandpa and Mrs. Williams sat quietly; relaxed, possibly napping.

"I'm pooped." Trina pushed her damp hair off her face and sat down. "These Amish women look like they're good for a few more hours and they worked harder than us."

"I know. I guess we're lightweights. And here I thought my farm work kept me in shape, although most of my time is spent sitting in front of a computer screen." Jennie was beginning to rethink her fitness plan.

"Me, too! My farm work isn't enough to balance out my computer time." Trina added, "Or sitting on a mower."

"Here come the guys. They look beat." Jennie poured two glasses of water. "Here, drink up."

"Thanks." Jeremy drank the glass of water in what seemed like one gulp and held it out for more.

"Do you want me to drive home?" Jennie offered.

"I'm tired but you look tired, too." He looked at Grandpa. "He also looks tired."

"I guess us non-Amish can't even keep up with our Amish friends for one day," Trina joked.

Bart added, "Nope. And here I thought I worked hard at the store."

"Mr. Jeremy, Miss Jennie, when can I come to your house?" Charlie bounced as he talked, glancing around to make sure his mom hadn't heard him ask. She wouldn't be happy to know he invited himself.

"When are you out of school for the summer? You don't want to miss school." Jeremy really thought Charlie wouldn't mind missing school for a few days.

"In two weeks. We get out early to help with the first cutting of hay."

"But if you help with haying, when can you visit?" Jeremy waited for the answer.

"Mom will let me help with haying for a few days and then let me visit a few days." That's what he hoped, anyway. "Can I bring Oscar? I want to show you what we can do."

"Maybe that can be arranged. We'll need ask Miss Marcy about picking him up with her horse trailer."

Jeremy looked at the young, eager face. "I'll tell you what, we'll talk to your mom later. She's sort of busy today."

Charlie wasn't about to be put off. "Could you just tell her I'm invited? And maybe set a date? Then we can plan."

Jennie couldn't resist the sweet teen. "Yes, we can." She moved toward Elizabeth saying goodbye to a group of her friends. Jeremy followed with a huge grin.

Jennie waited quietly. Charlie rushed to his mom's side but remained silent. He knew better than to interrupt. Elizabeth smiled and silently acknowledged her son by placing her arm over his shoulder. She finished her goodbyes and turned toward Jennie.

"Thank you for joining us today. The help was good." Elizabeth smoothed her apron and glanced at the aprons Jennie and Trina still wore.

Jennie noticed and quickly took off her apron; Trina followed. "We almost forgot we were wearing these. I hate to give it back to you dirty."

"That's fine. I have a few loads of dish towels and aprons to do tomorrow." Jennie thought *a few* was probably an understatement.

Charlie ran out of patience. "Mama, I'm invited to visit Miss Jennie's farm. In May. When school is out for haying. I will help with haying and then go?"

Elizabeth looked at Jennie who explained, "He is welcome to stay in my extra room."

Jeremy spoke up. "Or with me at my house, if you prefer. And if Marcy agrees, he may bring Oscar." Jeremy looked at Charlie, "Remember, we need to ask Miss Marcy if she's willing to pick him up with her trailer."

Elizabeth thought for a moment. "May we visit your area one day? I would like to see where Charlie will be staying." She didn't want to offend Jeremy and Jennie. Even though she trusted them, she couldn't send him off to the English world without knowing the situation. "I hope you understand."

"Of course. Any mom would want to know where her child would be staying." Jennie looked at Jeremy. "Are you free on Saturday, Jeremy?"

"I am. Is that a good day to visit? Don't schedule a car. We'll pick you up." He thought a moment and then asked, "How many will visit? We may need to bring two cars."

"No need. I will ask Daed. He would like to visit Mr. Gantzler's farm and will hire our driver. I will bring Micah. I'm sure Mom will be happy to care for the baby for one day. I think there will be four of us."

"We'll see you Saturday." Jeremy teased Charlie, "Don't worry, you won't have to spend a day without horses. We have three horses and Marcy's ponies."

"And Melody!" Charlie remembered.

THE CAR WAS QUIET on the trip home. They were what Grandpa called, *talked out*. It was hard to imagine Grandpa being *talked out*. Jennie smiled at him dozing, his head against the door, his mouth open. Mrs. Williams remained awake, making an occasional comment.

"Grandpa, we're almost home and are dropping Mrs. Williams off first."

"That's fine." He leaned forward as Lizzie looked back. "Do you mind if I go home without coming in for a bit?"

"I don't mind, Charlie." She gave him an affectionate smile. "Thank you for inviting me to meet your Amish friends. I enjoyed the day very much."

Jeremy parked the car and walked Mrs. Williams to her door. "Do you need anything before we leave?" Mrs. Williams's large dog, Moose, came bounding to the door. "Do you need me to take this fellow out for a bit?"

"No, I have a fenced back yard for some potty time. He's getting older and doesn't seem to want to leave the house as much anymore."

Satisfied that Grandpa's lady friend was fine, Jeremy returned to the car and drove to the Appleridge senior apartments.

"No need to escort me to my door, young fellow." Grandpa climbed stiffly out of the back seat.

Jeremy waited until he saw Grandpa wave from his apartment window before driving away.

"In the wise words of your grandfather, do you mind if I go home without coming in for a bit?" Jeremy waited for Jennie's answer from the back seat.

"I don't mind, but only if I get a kiss, or two, first."

"I'm happy to oblige, ma'am."

And he did!

Chapter Twenty-Three

HEY, YOU TWO! Jennie waved at Megan and Cassy on their horses in Lainie's arena.

"Hi, Jennie!" they both yelled.

Megan added, "What are you doing here?"

"She came to see us, of course." Cassy answered for Jennie.

"Well, yes, to see you, and, of course, Lainie." Jennie walked over to the fence.

"Lainie's in the barn getting Shadow saddled." Megan got off Starlight to check her girth. "Yup, I thought so." She tightened it one more notch, then climbed on the fence to mount instead of placing her foot in the stirrup.

"I heard you're going to Trina's for a bit of practice on Saturday." Jennie held her hand, palm down, out for Starlight to touch. Treasure stepped forward.

"I think Treasure wants attention, too." Cassy leaned forward in the saddle to stroke her mare's neck as Jennie stepped over to acknowledge the horse.

"We're going to have Amish visitors on Saturday. Charlie, along with his mom, brother, and grandfather. Charlie is going to spend a few days with us in May." Jennie left off the part about Elizabeth vetting the situation.

Cassy read between the lines quickly. "And his mom needs to make sure we're not crazy, heathen people."

"Yes, that." Jennie agreed chuckling, as Lainie led Shadow toward the group.

"What are my star students telling you now?" Lainie teased.

"I haven't been here long enough for much. I was telling them about Charlie and family coming for a little visit on Saturday, and if you're holding a team practice at Trina's, I may bring them to watch." Jennie quickly added, "If that's ok?"

"It's perfectly fine." She looked at Cassy and Megan. "I guess we better dream up something fantastic."

Megan's eyes widened in fear; Cassy's eyes widened with excitement.

"Nothing crazy; I already have a few fun ideas." She led Shadow through the gate and then returned to where the group waited.

"How was the barn raising?" She added quickly, "It was a good decision for me to stay home. We had a good day and accomplished a lot." Lainie looked at her students.

"We finished our drill pattern," Megan added.

"It's neat and Treasure and I get to do a little solo jump at the end." Cassy loved being the most senior rider. But then, she was also the oldest on the team and the only college student.

"I can't wait to watch. The barn raising was neat. They almost finished a four-stall barn and a hay storage barn. Amazing."

"Did Jeremy and Bart help?" Lainie asked.

"They did. Trina and I made sandwiches, served food, and cleaned up." Jennie let out a little breath. "The Amish work really hard at everything. We were pooped."

"Tell us more about Charlie." Cassy was interested. "Is there anything we should know? I mean, any dos and don'ts?"

Jennie thought a moment. "No, I can't think of anything except modest attire. You'll all be in riding clothes and I've never seen you wear skimpy halter tops and short shorts while riding."

Megan laughed, "Not hardly. I wouldn't be allowed out of the house with much skin showing, riding or not. Dad's a bit old-fashioned that way."

Lainie put both hands on her hips. "Good for your dad. Fashion has gone crazy and most of it's not only suggestive, but also unattractive."

"Lainie, how old are you?" Cassy couldn't resist. "Are you turning into a prude?"

"I'm not old and I'm not a prude and I don't need to let it all hang out to feel good about myself."

Cassy looked hurt. "I was only kidding. Sorry, Lainie."

"I'm not mad. I just want young girls to find their self-worth from thinking as individuals and not from following the crowd. Don't let the world decide your worth."

Jennie agreed. "Think about the people who dictate fashion or the ones who follow the trends. Are they the sort of people you would want to emulate? And, if they are, ask yourself why?"

"No, I guess not, but when you say *the world*, what do you mean?" Megan thought she knew, because Pastor Shearer talked about what *the world* values occasionally, but she wanted Cassy to hear it.

Lainie waited. That was a question for Jennie to answer.

"It means valuing material things or things and ideas that don't honor Christ. It's a question of who you want to follow. Do you want to follow Christ or the world?"

Cassy asked, "But what does it mean to follow Christ?"

"It means we want to live a life of faith and trust in our Savior because he already loves us. You don't need people or things to prove your value because we're already cherished and valued by a loving God." Jennie wished Jeremy was here to answer. He always had a nice way of sharing his faith without sounding judgmental.

"But why wouldn't God like fashion?" Cassy didn't understand why God would care.

Jennie leaned against the fence and ran her hand through Starlight's mane. "I don't think God is against fashion, if you mean looking nice. If you mean wearing something to be noticed, or wearing something because you're afraid of being teased for not having the most current style, or, well, I'll say it, or laughed at because you aren't sexy, that's pressure to conform to what the world says is cool, and it steals your self-esteem. Don't look to others to feel valued. God already values you more than you can imagine."

Cassy thought for a moment, "It kind of depends on why you're wearing or doing something?"

Smart girl, thought Jennie. "Yes, I suppose so." *Oh boy, now I'm in way over my head. God, please help me and give me the right words.*

Lainie spoke up. "When I was traveling around teaching for the Follow the Leader program, I did a few things I'm embarrassed to share." She shook her head. "That's funny, really.

The program was called Follow the Leader and I was following friends and people who turned out to be the wrong leaders to follow. I saw what everyone else was doing and followed without really thinking. It didn't seem wrong, but it felt wrong. I wouldn't have been able to answer why it felt wrong; it just did. Now I know it felt wrong because I was looking for happiness in things that made God sad."

Megan asked, "Why sad?" She sometimes felt sad.

Lainie continued, "Sad because I didn't know how much God loved me. I was trying to find happiness in things that took me further and further away from him.

Jennie looked at Lainie and smiled. "That's a nice testimony." She looked at Cassy. "The Amish believe wearing modest clothing will help their lives stay focused on God."

Megan brightened. "I get it. It's like wearing school uniforms. When you wear a uniform, you don't worry about friends wearing clothes more trendy or expensive than you."

Jennie nodded. "Yeah, you're right. I guess the Amish do have a dress code of sorts. They all wear the same type of clothing."

"But let's get back to what kind of clothing is bad. I mean, we don't wear long skirts and dress like Amish girls. I don't think how we dress is bad." Cassy loved a good debate and she wasn't ready to let this conversation end—even if Treasure was getting a bit impatient.

"Maybe it's not so much *how* we dress as it is *why* we dress a certain way, like Cassy said." Megan looked at Jennie.

"I agree. Why we dress a certain way would definitely dictate how we dress and act." Jennie loved these talks.

Lainie thought so, too. "The why is very important. Since our team wears riding attire, it's modest attire necessary for our rides. Even so, we wear pants and I don't think Amish girls wear pants. We also cut our hair and they don't. So, we wonder, will they find us offensive?"

Jennie wasn't worried. "I don't think they'll find us offensive. Like you said, our girls wear riding attire. Of course, maybe that's what Elizabeth Miller wants to check out before she sends her fourteen-year-old son into our world."

Cassy laughed. "You mean into the lion's den?"

Megan couldn't resist. "You mean into the lioness den, don't you?"

"Yes, and we do have a few fourteen-year-old girls who may think Charlie is pretty cute." Lainie thought so, anyway. Even with his bowl haircut.

"I'm keeping you from your ride." Jennie stepped back from the fence and looked at Lainie. "Let me know what time it would be good to bring Charlie and his family to Trina's farm."

"I need to confirm with Trina. As it stands now, we're riding at two." She laughed and added, "In modest riding attire."

Jennie nodded and turned to walk to her truck. Still thinking. *I wasn't expecting that conversation. Wait until I share it with Jeremy.*

Chapter Twenty-Four

arcy put down Riley's grooming brush. "They're here!"

Jennie hurried out of the tack room, wiping her hands on her jeans. "Oh, my. A bit early." She waited for Marcy to tie Riley in the aisle so he wouldn't follow, and they walked up the drive together.

Charlie was the first one to climb out of the van. "Hello, Miss Marcy and Miss Jennie! Where's Mr. Jeremy and Melody?"

Elizabeth climbed out next and helped Micah down the big step to the ground. "Now Charlie, just wait a minute."

Amos climbed down from the front seat and leaned in to talk to the driver.

Jennie stepped up, "Mr. Stoltz, does your driver need anything? I could recommend a few places for lunch or he is welcome to stay parked here."

Amos closed the van door. "Thank you. He has family nearby and is going to spend the day with them. It is gut." Amos used the Amish word for good.

"Ok." She smiled at Charlie. "Jeremy will be here in a few minutes. Should we go in the house?" She teased Charlie because she knew he wanted to run to the barn.

Seeing the pain on the youngster's face, Marcy spoke up. "Why don't I take Charlie to the barn?"

Elizabeth nodded and then asked shyly, "May we use your bathroom?" Micah was wiggling by her side.

"Of course. Would anyone like a water or something cold to drink?"

They went in the house to use the facilities. Jennie offered ice tea, root beer, or water.

"Just give me a nice glass of water, Jennie. I don't need bottled water." Amos walked over to the sink as Jennie handed him a glass.

"Ice?" She opened the freezer compartment.

"Not needed; thank you." Amos sat at the table. "I like this table in this little nook. You can see almost everything from here."

Micah whispered something to his mom. "I'll ask." She brushed hair from his eyes, thinking it was time for a haircut. "Micah would like a glass of root beer, if you please."

"I have it in a bottle. Grandpa's favorite." She reached into the refrigerator.

"Since we're going to the barn, do you mind if I pour it into this container?" Jennie held up one of her stainless metal bottles. "I can make one for Charlie, too."

"I think that is a very good idea," Elizabeth agreed.

With thirst quenched for now, Jennie led her guests outside just as Jeremy pulled into the driveway.

"Welcome, welcome!" Jeremy greeted the friends. "Where's Charlie?"

"Marcy took him to the barn. He couldn't wait for you," Jennie teased Jeremy. He hated being late for anything, and because their friends were early, it almost seemed like he was late.

Jeremy walked over and shook Amos's hand. "Very good to see you again, sir."

Amos chuckled. "I believe I feel a callous or two on your hands from all that heavy labor on Tuesday."

Jeremy played along. "You Amish sure do like to make us English folk do your work."

Amos cackled, "You Englishers are too easy to sway. We are like Tom Sawyer, yes?"

Jeremy patted Amos on the back. "Yes."

Elizabeth giggled, "Well, I bet when we get to the barn Marcy will have Charlie busy doing her work. He probably begged her to help."

"Me, too, Mama?" Micah asked.

"Yes, Micah, you, too."

Three adults and one eager little boy strolled to the barn. The eager little boy tugged on his mom's arm.

"This is a nice barn!" Elizabeth walked down the clean aisle, greeting each horse. "Do you keep them inside?"

Jennie answered, "Not much. We bring them in to eat or to wait for something special, like meeting our friends. This is Julep, and Sadie, and —"

"Mama, there's our Melody!" Micah reached up to pet the mare's nose.

"Micah, Melody isn't ours anymore," Charlie simply stated as he groomed Stuffin.

Jennie looked at the little boy's sad face and squatted to be eye level. "Micah, Melody will always be your Melody because your dad raised her. We're just keeping her here to enjoy. Is that ok?"

The little boy nodded. "It's ok."

Marcy walked over to greet the guests. "I usually offer a carriage ride to our guests, but I don't suppose that would be much of a treat for you folks."

Amos cackled again. "Well, I don't suppose. I've never ridden on one of those fancy marathon carriages, so I would be open to taking a turn on yours."

"Feeling the need for speed?" Marcy teased. "My ponies would be happy to oblige."

"I did in my younger years. We Amish aren't opposed to a little race down a country road now and then again."

"Do you want me to get the carriage?" Jeremy offered.

"Sure, let's give Mr. Stoltz a ride to remember." Marcy winked.

"Well, then, I guess you better call me Amos. We should be on a first-name basis before you scare me to death."

Hearing Amos's voice, Melody nickered. "Hello, mare. You remember me, eh?"

"She remembered me, too, Granddad." Charlie switched brushes, ready to put the finishing touch on the gray pony.

Amos looked at Jennie. "Have you hitched this sweet girl, yet?"

"No, not yet. We don't have the right-sized vehicle. We're keeping our eyes and ears open to find one. Cassy and Megan, whom you'll meet later, have been on her back. She was great."

"I'll keep my eyes open for a nice vehicle; maybe a two-wheel cart?"

"Thank you; that would be awesome." Jennie motioned for Elizabeth to join her on the barn bench. "Charlie, you're welcome to ride Melody while Marcy drives the ponies."

Jennie didn't have to say it twice. Charlie reached for Melody's halter and led her into the aisle for grooming. Jennie got up from her seat on the bench to walk to the tack room for her grooming box.

"You sure have some nice horse brushes. I like this one." Charlie held up a nice, soft, short-bristled finishing brush.

Jennie noticed a funny look on Elizabeth's face. If Charlie mentioned too many *materialistic likes*, he probably wouldn't be allowed to visit again.

"Thanks, Charlie; Jeremy gave me that one in honor of Melody."

"I think she likes it. It's almost like the one we use at our home."

Jennie relaxed. So did Elizabeth. Charlie wasn't being envious; he was just being friendly. There was a big difference.

STUFFIN AND RILEY stood patiently as Marcy took up the reins and climbed onto the carriage. Amos sat on her left side and Jeremy stood on the hind step. All wore helmets. Amos didn't object, although the Amish never worried about such things.

"Grandpa, you look different in that helmet." Even as young as he was, Micah knew better than to say Grandpa looked silly.

"I think Miss Marcy is going to go very fast if she wants me to wear this helmet."

Marcy didn't want the child to worry. "Don't worry; I'm a good driver. It's just a rule I have—everyone riding in my carriage wears a helmet."

Amos secretly wondered why the nonAmish didn't also wear helmets when driving cars. That seemed much more dangerous.

Marcy clucked to the ponies and they walked out to the mowed path. She warmed them up slowly—first at a walk, then trotted a lap.

"Hang on, here we go!" She asked the ponies to canter and they were happy to oblige. She couldn't resist a few tight corners without slowing, causing Jeremy, who stood on the back step, to grab the bar for balance. Amos hung on while grinning.

They cantered along the twisty paths, the carriage bouncing a bit, the passengers laughing and hanging onto the seat sides and back. Marcy slowed the ponies to a trot for one more lap, then a walk.

Amos spoke first. "This is a very nice team of ponies and you know how to handle the lines."

Marcy beamed. "Thank you. I love this pair and I love getting them out on a challenging marathon course."

Amos turned slightly to look at Jeremy. "And this is what you will do with Melody?"

"Hopefully, yes. But we'll start out slow."

Amos settled back into his seat, crossing his arms. "Yes, I think she will be a good mare for this. She has a bit of spunk. But she is also very careful about where she puts her feet."

"Both of those things are good." Marcy turned the ponies into the barn paddock. "And look at him!" Marcy pointed to

Charlie as he swung up onto Melody's bare back. She was only wearing a rope halter—no bridle, no saddle.

Marcy halted the ponies. "Do you want me to turn around and go back out with you?"

"Yes, Miss Marcy." He added, "Micah wants a ride on the carriage." Charlie usually looked out for his little brother.

"I'll get down and we can put Micah here in my seat. Yes?" Amos already had his two feet on the ground and was motioning for Micah who was already wearing the child's helmet Marcy handed to Elizabeth earlier.

With her passengers seated, Marcy asked her ponies to *come around* to the left, turning the carriage.

"Here we go!" Marcy asked the ponies to trot down the mowed path. She kept the pace slower. The carriage barely bounced. The little boy giggled.

"Hang on tight." Marcy asked the ponies to canter slowly on a straight path; she didn't take any quick turns.

Charlie cantered Melody alongside the carriage. Jeremy noticed how securely he sat on the horse and how nicely the mare responded to everything Charlie asked. The boy certainly had talent. Melody looked pretty good, too.

Marcy slowed to a trot, then a walk. Charlie waved and continued cantering around Jennie's pasture. He headed for a tree log jump on the edge of the path.

"Look at that little stinker!" Jeremy watched Charlie jump Melody over the log and head for another.

"He's quite the rider." Marcy slowed the ponies to a walk and then asked for a halt. She wanted to see the Charlie and Melody show.

"Little stinker." Micah giggled.

Uh-oh, I need to remember little ears, thought Jeremy.

Charlie slowed Melody to a trot before riding over to his fan club in the carriage.

"That was pretty awesome." Jeremy added, "You sure can ride."

Charlie blushed and reached over to pet Melody's neck. "She's fun."

"Well, you make it look easy." Marcy clucked to the ponies and headed for the barn.

At the barn, Jeremy jumped off the back of the carriage. Micah hopped down before Jeremy could help. Marcy walked the ponies into the aisle and asked them to *whoa stand.* Jeremy stood by, ready to grab a rein, but it was never needed. Stuffin and Riley knew their jobs.

Marcy and Jeremy quickly unhitched and unharnessed the ponies, tying them in the barn aisle before rolling the carriage to the side.

Amos studied the carriage. "So, this is what you call a marathon carriage; it's built to travel off road."

Marcy lifted one of the shafts and moved it side to side and up and down. "It's made for rough territory and tight turns. But it looks really nice on the road, too."

"Not too comfortable for passengers, though." In Amos's world, a carriage needed to accommodate several people and sometimes a family.

"No, not made for passengers unless they want to hang off the back step," Jeremy added as he was usually hanging off the back step.

The aisle was full, with three horses being groomed. Charlie gave Melody a nice rub down while Jeremy groomed Riley and Marcy groomed Stuffin.

"Will we see Mrs. Williams and Charlie Gantzler? Amos asked.

"We'll pick them up on the way to Trina's farm. We want to show you our town of Appleridge," Jennie answered, then added, "I wish we would've picked them up earlier. Grandpa would've really enjoyed watching Charlie ride Melody."

"When Charlie returns, maybe Mr. Gantzler will see him then?" Elizabeth asked.

Jennie thought so. She also thought Elizabeth's comment meant they passed the audition and Charlie would return to Appleridge in the near future. "Let's finish up here and we'll turn the horses out to spend the rest of the day in the pasture. Trina has invited all of us to her farm for a cookout and to watch Lainie's team practice."

Chapter Twenty-Five

everal vehicles were required to move the party to Trina's. Jeremy picked up Mrs. Williams and Grandpa in his car. Jennie drove Elizabeth and Micah in her truck. Amos and Charlie rode with Marcy.

There were several trucks and cars parked near Trina's arena, and two trucks with horse trailers in Trina's pasture.

Grandpa and Amos Stoltz greeted each other as old friends do. Elizabeth hung back shyly. Jennie vowed to stick by her side until she seemed comfortable. Charlie grabbed his brother's hand and raced to the pasture fence.

Jennie's parents, Ellen and Ed McKenzie, joined the group and also Susan and Dr. Adrian Peterson as well as several of Trina's boarders and their families.

Bart offered his hand to Jeremy. "How's my grilling buddy?"

"Ahh, we won that job again?" Jeremy didn't mind.

"Yup, and I brought nice juicy burgers from the store." He looked at the boys. "I brought plenty. I saw how that youngster could eat at the barn raising."

"You should see how he can ride!" Jeremy exclaimed.

"I saw him harness and hitch some of the buggies after the barn raising. I don't know much about horses, but he seems to have a nice way with them." Bart shook hands with Amos and nodded at Elizabeth. "Trina's up at the house. She's setting up the food tables on the front porch. I think we're going to eat first and then watch the riders after." Bart led the way to the house.

"Welcome! Welcome!" Trina called out as the group made their way up the stone walk. "I think we all know one another." Heads nodded in affirmative. "Our chefs today are Bart and Jeremy." She looked at the guys. "And as soon as they grill the burgers we'll eat. Drinks are in this cooler." Trina pointed to a large cooler sitting against the wall of the house. "Help yourself to a drink, find a place to sit. Sorry I don't have enough chairs, but I have porch steps."

"We brought chairs." Jennie noticed Elizabeth was sitting on the porch steps with her mom. "I'm just going to get a few chairs out of the truck."

Jennie's dad joined her. "Let me help. Did you see the chairs I made for Trina?"

"I saw those nice chairs. You do know, I'm still waiting for some to make their way to my house, too." She waited for her dad to comment.

"Ahh, so you've mentioned. I'll get right on that." He chuckled because he had several just waiting to join Jennie on her farm; maybe in time for her birthday.

CHARLIE SAT ON THE FENCE and watched the horses. Especially the chestnut horse with the white mane and tail. He had to be a Morgan. He sure looked like one, anyway. He looked just like his horse, Stormy. He missed Stormy. He quickly thought of Oscar. *Thank you, God, for Oscar.*

Fare lifted his head and nickered. It was time to leave the sweet grass and greet the young human. He walked to the fence and lifted his nose to the boy's face, blowing grass-sweetened breath. Charlie blew out his own breath in a greeting. They remained nostril to nostril for a few seconds. "Hey, fellow. You sure are a nice-looking fellow." Charlie was tempted to slip onto the horse's back.

"He's a nice horse, isn't he?"

Charlie startled, jumped off the fence, and grabbed Micah's hand.

"I'm sorry to scare you. I thought you heard me pull up. I'm Adrian Peterson. The local vet."

"Nice to meet you, sir." Charlie didn't offer his hand. "Are you a horse doctor?"

"I am. And dog and cat and just-about-any-animal doctor. And you must be the young man who has Oscar."

"You know Oscar?"

"I met Oscar when he was at Jennie's place. A perfectly healthy and very nice horse." Adrian turned to look at his car. "Say hello to my wife, Susan." Susan waved as she lifted a basket from the back seat of the car. "I think you'll meet my daughter, Megan. She's riding today."

Charlie looked at the people walking up the path to the house. "I guess we better go up now." He turned to stroke Fare's neck. "Do you know his name?"

"His name is Fare. Actually, I think is full name is My Fare Thee Well, or something like that and he's a—"

"He's a Lambert Morgan." Charlie was sure.

"I can see you know horses. I think you're correct." Dr. Peterson looked at Micah. "Do you know horses, too?"

"I have a pony. I know my ponies." Micah answered, then hid behind his brother's leg.

Dr. Peterson laughed. "I bet you do!"

The boys and the vet walked to the party. "Do you know who owns the Morgan?"

Dr. Peterson answered. "I sure do. Fare belongs to Trina. Or I guess you could say, Trina belongs to Fare."

"How can a person belong to a horse?" Charlie was puzzled.

"Well—when a horse comes into your life and brings a lot of happiness, I think you belong to them."

Charlie thought for a moment. "Then I've belonged to a lot of horses and now I belong to Oscar."

"I'm sure you do and my daughter, Megan, belongs to her horse, Starlight."

"Did Starlight bring happiness?"

Adrian thought this was a very intuitive young teen. "Yes, she did. She brought happiness and confidence to Megan at a time when she had lost both."

"MR. GANTZLER, would you please say a prayer?" Although Trina knew the Amish preferred silent prayer, she didn't think a spoken prayer would be offensive. Prayer was prayer—spoken or silent.

"Father, we thank you for this day together with friends. It's a beautiful day. We thank you for this food to nourish our bodies. Bless the hands that prepared the food and grant our friends safe travel when they return to their homes. In your precious name."

Everyone said, "Amen."

Hands quickly filled plates. People perched on porch steps, on folding chairs under a tree, some found a few chairs on the back deck, a few on the front porch, and on the bench brought up from the barn. Megan and Cassy arrived before the food was gone and quickly filled plates. Conversation flowed as freely as the food.

"Megan, come and meet my new friend." Adrian motioned for his daughter and Cassy to join him under a tree.

"Hi, I'm Megan."

"I'm Cassy."

"I'm Charlie and over there's my mama and my brother, Micah." Micah was sitting beside Elizabeth on a porch step. The girls turned to look at the Amish family.

"After we eat, do you want to go with us down to the barn? The rest of the team will be here soon." Megan took a huge bite of her cheeseburger. "Our horses are tied to the trailer, eating hay."

Cassy asked. "Are you the one with Oscar?"

"Yup. Oscar owns me." He looked at Dr. Peterson.

Both girls wore puzzled looks on their faces.

"I was just telling Charlie that when a horse brings happiness, instead of us owning them, they own us," Dr. Peterson explained.

"Wow, Dad, that's really nice. I didn't know you thought of it that way." Megan didn't know her dad was so intuitive, although since her disaster last summer, he seemed more sensitive to her feelings.

Dr. Peterson decided to change the subject. No use in getting too sentimental. "Charlie and Fare have become buddies."

"Hey, maybe Trina would let you ride Fare. Do you want us to ask?" Cassy wasn't sure, but she wasn't afraid to ask the question.

"That would be great." Charlie stuffed the last bite into his mouth, ready to go.

"Megan, I think Charlie likes your favorite word." Megan's dad couldn't resist teasing her about the use of the word *great*—Megan's favorite word.

"Charlie, he's teasing because I say *great* a lot." Megan pretended to be offended, but she wasn't.

"I'm finished; let's go to the barn." Cassy was ready.

"Let me tell Mama I'm going with you." Charlie walked over to his mother.

Dr. Peterson couldn't resist. "You girls take good care of him, you hear?"

"Dad! You know we will," Megan answered.

Adrian lowered his voice. "Just remember, he's a young Amish boy who may or may not understand how to interact with young ladies."

"Dad, I don't think most fourteen-year-old boys know how to interact with girls." Megan gave her dad a look that said more than she shared.

Adrian chuckled as he walked away. Charlie jogged to catch up with the girls.

"Charlie, do you ride much or only drive horses?" Cassy asked.

"I do both. I'm riding Oscar now." Charlie placed his straw hat back on his head after losing it as he ran.

Cassy pointed to his hat. "I like your hat. Do you wear a helmet when you ride?"

"No, I don't have a helmet at home. Miss Marcy asked Granddad to wear a helmet when he rode on her carriage and Jennie gave me a helmet to wear when I rode Melody."

"And you didn't mind wearing one?" Megan asked.

"I didn't mind. It wasn't too bad."

"So, if Trina or Lainie asks you to wear a helmet when you ride here, that would be ok?"

"It's ok. Why?"

"We have all these rules to protect farms and instructors from liability in the event of an accident. Wearing a helmet is required." Cassy thought a moment. "The Amish probably don't worry about liability or sue one another."

"No, we don't. It would not be pleasing to God to blame someone for an accident."

Cassy didn't know how to respond. She pointed to the pasture. "Looks like more of our team have arrived. Let's saddle up." She looked at Charlie. "I wonder if Lainie could borrow a horse for you to ride?"

"I think I would like to watch first." Charlie wasn't too sure what to expect from something called a performance drill team. He saw Miss Lainie setting up several jumps in the arena.

Megan noticed Charlie's expression. "We ride patterns to music. It's fun!"

"Hey, girls. Hi Charlie." Lainie was rounding up her team. "Let's get started. Saddle up and warm up your horses."

Lainie heard about Charlie's riding ability from Marcy. "I hear you're quite a good rider."

"I do like to ride. Oscar and I are a team." Charlie didn't think he sounded like he was bragging. Mama always reminding him to be humble in all things.

"If you would like to stick with me, I'll answer any questions you may have. I may recruit you for help."

"Just tell me what you need done." Charlie hoped it involved something with the horses. Eyeing the manure bucket and fork near the arena gate, he thought maybe he would help with clean up. Picking up manure sure wasn't as much fun as riding horses.

Lainie motioned for her riders to gather around. "Good afternoon, ladies. Thank you for getting saddled and warmed up on time. Make sure you thank Miss Trina for allowing us to practice at her farm. Please clean up the area around your horse trailer. Trina has provided muck buckets to use. Leave the filled buckets near the arena gate and she'll take care of them."

Lainie looked at Charlie, sitting on the top rail of the arena fence in his black trousers, blue shirt, suspenders, and straw hat. What a cute kid!

"And team, this is Charlie Miller, he's our guest today. Charlie knows quite a bit about horses—riding and driving horses. Please help him to feel welcome."

A multitude of greetings followed. "Hi, Charlie!" "Welcome!" "Hello!"

Charlie waved with a smile on his face. Lainie had to turn away from the group for a moment to hide her own smile. The young girls seemed very enamored with the Amish teen.

"Ok. Positions please. We'll walk the pattern without music first. The poles are on the ground so you can walk over them instead of jumping."

The riders moved to the end of the arena and lined up by the gate. "Ready. Go!"

Lainie spotted a few little problems but nothing major. A couple of horses hesitated before walking thru the jump and over the poles. Funny, she thought, although the horses easily jumped the poles, trotting over the poles wasn't quite the same, and different always caused a horse to think.

"Very good. Any questions?" Lainie waited.

"Miss Lainie."

"Yes, Cassy."

"There was a little confusion when we crossed the arena. We should pass right arm to right arm in that section?" Cassy knew that was correct. She just wanted Lainie to help clear up the confusion without singling out several girls.

"That's correct. We did have a slight bobble. Are we ok now?"

Everyone nodded.

"Ok, good. Now let's do it again, at the trot, no music."

The riders moved at a trot to the arena gate.

"Positions, please. Ready. Go!" The horses trotted the pattern smoothly.

"What do you think, Charlie?" Lainie looked at the youngster balancing on the fence beside her.

"I think it looks fun and they look good. Are they having fun? They don't look like they're having fun."

"Good observation. They look very serious. We need smiles." Lainie agreed.

The team finished and Lainie asked them to gather around. "That was good. Are you having fun? Because I couldn't tell."

"I'm having fun!" Tera, the youngest member of the team, shouted.

A chorus of "Me, too!" followed.

"Good!" Lainie turned to Charlie. "What do we need to see?"

"Smiles!" Charlie shouted and then shyly lowered his head. The brim of his straw hat hid his face.

"That's right. Smiles would tell me you're having fun. A smile also relaxes the body. Some of you are a bit tense. Relax. Smile."

Lainie turned to see what caught the attention of a few of her riders. "I see our audience has arrived."

Lainie spoke to those gathering to watch the team. "Welcome to our practice. It is a practice and not a performance; however, it is the first time the riders have had an audience."

She looked at her riders. "Ok, this time we'll trot to the music. Charlie and I will put the poles on the jumps. Ask your horses to jump over the poles. Any questions?"

Tera had a question. She obviously wasn't shy. "What if my pony trots over the pole but doesn't really jump?"

"That's fine. It will change the timing a little. Make sure you find your partner and stay on the pattern. But, Tera, I'm pretty sure your pony will jump. His legs are shorter; it's harder for him to trot over the poles at that height. He'll probably think jumping is easier."

Lainie jumped off her perch on the fence and motioned to Charlie to follow. "This time I'll turn on the music. Do you remember the introduction and when to start?"

She could tell by their glances at one another that they weren't sure. Lainie took out her phone and set it and a small speaker on the top of a barrel outside the fence. She found the music and made sure the phone was connected to the speaker via blue tooth. It wouldn't be as loud as they needed for the riders to hear from the far side of the arena. Of course, those gathered to watch would hear.

"Let me play a bit and see if you remember." She started the music. The introduction played. She indicated with her arms when the drill routine would start.

"Do you want me to play it again?"

Cassy spoke up. "Maybe again."

The girls looked more confident after hearing the music the second time.

"Ride over to the gate while Charlie and I set the poles."

Charlie and Lainie finished and then climbed over the fence. Lainie turned to the group. "Ladies and gentlemen, may I present the Appleridge Performance Horsemanship Team!"

The group of friends and family applauded. Lainie started the music.

The team looked confident, the horses relaxed, and the smiles were contagious. Lainie was very pleased and very proud.

The drill ended with all riders lined up in the center of the arena to a round of applause by the spectators.

"Great job, Team! Come on over and meet your fans."

The riders rode to the fence to soak up the congratulations.

Charlie found his mom. "I want to do that, Mama!"

"Well, maybe you could practice with the team. I'll check with our Bishop. We don't dance to music and riding to music may be like dancing." She saw her son's face fall and quickly added, "Maybe we'll get permission for when you visit. One time. Ok?"

He nodded. "I understand." Charlie felt a hand on his shoulder. His grandfather.

"That looked like fun for the girls. I think it is fine for you to visit their world, and maybe ride with them, but it isn't something that you'll be doing in our world."

"But what makes it wrong?" Charlie didn't think it looked wrong to ride listening to music. He liked music.

"We believe you should not call attention to yourself." Amos spoke softly. "We will talk more at home. Yes?"

"Yes, sir." Charlie motioned to the riders getting off their horses. "I promised to help."

"Go, son. Help is gut." Amos looked at Elizabeth as Charlie jogged to the girls, most of them already unmounted and leading their horses to the horse trailers. "He is a gut boy. He will be fine."

Elizabeth watched her oldest son walk among the girls. "Yes, he will be fine. We are among good people, and it is good to expose him to a different world, especially among good people."

Amos agreed. "Our friends won't lead him astray. They respect our faith and will watch over him."

Jennie realized Elizabeth and Amos were discussing something quietly—something probably private. She waited until they finished before approaching.

"Did Charlie enjoy watching the team performance?" Jennie asked.

"Performance is a challenging concept. We Amish do not perform or draw attention to ourselves." Elizabeth was comfortable sharing her thoughts with Jennie.

"Oh, I'm so sorry. I didn't mean to expose Charlie to anything you find offensive." Jennie realized her mistake.

"Please don't worry. We'll explain to Charlie and he will understand." Elizabeth looked at her daed with a silent plead for help.

"We are not offended. Charlie, and Micah here, will be exposed to a different world before they commit to the Amish way of life. I'm very thankful we have you to help." Amos was sincere.

"Help?"

"I believe you and Jeremy, and the others, respect our faith and will do nothing to lead Charlie astray. His exposure to a different, and what he thinks is a pretty exciting, world is guided by non-Amish friends we trust. It's not always that way, you know."

Jennie felt a little better. "I understand. Please give me guidance so I don't unknowingly do anything to violate your faith."

"It's been a good day, Jennie; thank you for inviting us." Elizabeth adjusted her bonnet. "I'm comfortable for Charlie to spend a few days with you and Jeremy. He will sleep at Jeremy's house?"

"Yes, of course. Jeremy leaves for a mission trip on Monday and he'll be home in two weeks. Just in time for Charlie's visit." Jennie decided to ask, "Does he have permission to ride Melody with Lainie's team?"

"We will explain this to our bishop. I think he will agree for this special visit." Elizabeth was thankful their district had an understanding and somewhat flexible Bishop.

"Do you need me to drive you back to my house?" Jennie added, "To be picked up by your driver?"

Amos answered, "If you please, call my driver and give him directions. He'll pick us up here."

"Are you ready now?" Jennie could see Charlie at the trailers helping to load horses and equipment. "I think Charlie is being a big help."

"Please call now and tell our driver we are ready. By the time he arrives, Charlie should have everything under control," Amos answered.

Jennie smiled. She loved Amos's understated humor. "Yes, sir!"

BART ENJOYED helping Trina with her gathering and meeting more of her friends, although he was tired of cooking hamburgers. He arrived with forty quarter-pound hamburgers in a cooler, and fortunately, now he could hang up his apron. There wasn't a single hamburger left.

"I don't know about you, but I don't want to cook another hamburger for a while. Thanks for sticking with me."

Jeremy patted Bart on the back. "No problem. At least we were able to grab a burger for ourselves before they were all gone."

Bart was still trying to know the ins and outs of the group. "So, have you and Jennie known each other long?"

"We competed against each other in 4-H as kids. And just so you know, she took great delight in besting me as much as possible."

"Ahh, I can see that doesn't bother you much. You won the prize." Bart thought so, anyway.

"Very observant. Yes, I won the prize. We want a future together. We're going to wait a while to make it official." From the height of Trina's deck, Jeremy searched for the person of his affection. There she was, down by the barn talking to their Amish friends.

"Help me out. Give me a little tutorial on everyone here at the party. I need to put names to faces."

"Let's see. I need to fill you in on a couple of people not here first. As you already know, Jennie's best friend, Belinda Peterson, is a vet student at the University of Florida. She's also the sister of Megan Peterson." Jeremy pointed to the barn. "Down there by the white trailer."

Jeremy continued, "Belinda and Sam are a couple. Sam boards his horse at Jennie's place. He's a farrier. Me, Jennie, Sam, and Belinda have been friends for a long time. Ok so far?"

Bart nodded. "It seems like you're all old friends."

"New friends are welcome. Marcy, Lainie, and Trina are new friends. You already know about Marcy keeping her ponies at Jennie's barn. She moved here last year and is a nurse at the hospital. Lainie moved here last fall after teaching a clinic here at Trina's place. She liked the area and stayed. There's more to that story. That's Lainie's story to share—or not."

Bart nodded to tell Jeremy he understood. "She and Trina seem pretty close."

"Yes. Trina, Lainie, Marcy, and Jennie are really good friends. Up to now, other than Sam, who works all the time, I'm usually the lone male. Welcome to the group, new friend! You make the odds a little better!" Jeremy picked up a wire brush to scrape the grill as he talked.

"Cassy is a college freshman and probably the senior member of Lainie's team. She and Megan have become best friends. You know our new Amish friends, and you met Grandpa Charlie and Mrs. Williams."

"I enjoyed talking with them at the barn raising." Bart pointed to two older couples sitting in folding chairs under the oak tree.

"That's Ed and Ellen McKenzie, Jennie's parents, and Dr. and Susan Peterson, Megan and Belinda's parents. Dr. Peterson is a vet. He comes out here when needed."

Jeremy scanned the property for others.

Bart spoke up, "I know Trina's boarders—all very nice women."

"I think that's it." Jeremy put the brush down and lowered the top of the grill. "And we're off duty."

"I heard you talking to Trina about Charlie. So, you think he's pretty good with horses?" Bart had an idea rolling around in his head.

"I think he's VERY good with horses. Amos told me Charlie's dad, Isaiah, was well-known for breeding and training outstanding Morgan horses. Charlie seems to have learned a lot from his dad at a very young age."

"He seems very attracted to Fare." Bart always made it his mission to keep a close eye on Trina's Fare.

Jeremy chuckled. "I think it's easy to be very attracted to Fare. When I look into his kind eyes and touch him, I feel like all is well with the world."

"I know what you mean." And Bart did. Since finding Fare, his life had definitely changed for the better. Much better.

Chapter Twenty-Six

eremy carried a basket of clean clothes to his car. "Thanks for doing my laundry."

"I didn't mind. I hated to see you spend the afternoon at the laundry mat when we could spend time together doing laundry." Jennie laughed but was also serious.

Jeremy and his sister, Sarah, were slowly selling and distributing things from their parents' house. They sold the washer and dryer to a young family. They both were willing to give the washer and dryer set to the family. Instead, they took the fifty dollars offered by young father when Jeremy realized the father found great joy in being able to pay for something his family badly needed. Sometimes *free* could steal self-respect.

"Will you be in the same area for this mission trip?" Jennie glanced in the back of Jeremy's small SUV and saw what seemed like survival supplies.

"Yes, the same area. The need is great. I think we'll be sleeping in tents again. I brought my own this time. At least I know it's waterproof. I have my own cot, too."

"Be safe."

Jeremy pulled Jennie into his arms for a long hug. "I will. Keep me in your prayers."

"I will; always." She sighed.

"This is the last of my three trips this spring. When I get home, we'll talk." Still holding Jennie, he spoke while balancing his chin on her head.

"Ok. When you're ready, we'll talk." Jennie had a million thoughts on the subject; however, at the moment, she didn't know what else to say.

"I'm glad you have good friends." Jeremy's voice cracked. "Sam said to call him if you need anything."

"Ok."

"Bart said the same. He's willing to help if needed."

"Ok."

Jeremy stepped back to look into Jennie's face. "Please don't cry."

"I'm ok, really. It's just that goodbyes are hard. If you choose to make mission trips your career, we'll need to work on our goodbyes. Maybe turn them into 'see ya laters.'"

Jeremy loved Jennie's willingness to make things better. "Or maybe, 'work hard but have fun.'"

"Or, 'don't come back until you save the world.'"

"That one is too much pressure," Jeremy kidded.

"Yeah. No one can save the world in two measly weeks." Jennie played along.

"See, the trip suddenly seems shorter already. It's only two measly weeks."

"That it is." Jennie reached up and offered Jeremy a kiss. "You'll always be my hero. Go then and save the world. Or at least make it a lot better for a few people."

"I'll do my best." Jeremy climbed into the car and drove down the driveway, tooting his horn when he turned onto the road.

Go do what God has called you to do, because that's the person I love. Jennie climbed the deck steps to the quiet house.

BART SAT in the Cracker Barrel, studying his proposal, waiting for Kerry and Deb from Save a Morgan Rescue. He stood up when the hostess led two women to his table.

"Barton?" Deb held out her hand when he nodded. "I'm Deb."

Kerry held out her hand, "I'm Kerry. It's so very nice to meet you in person."

"Please, sit down." Bart waited, then seated himself.

"Thank you for accepting my invitation." Before Bart could continue, the waitress came to the table to take drink orders.

"Thank you for your much-appreciated donation." Kerry couldn't wait one moment longer to show her appreciation. "The donation helped us to rescue one more horse last week. He's at my house. I'm afraid we won't be able to rescue more until we find another foster home."

"Well, that's what I've been working on." He took a moment to study the menu quickly so he was prepared when the waitress returned.

Kerry leaned forward, ready to hear more from Barton.

"I did a bit of research on the needs of horse rescues. Correct me if I'm wrong, but the three largest needs are money, places to foster horses, and preparing the rescue horses to be placed in good homes."

Deb put her menu down. "I would agree with all three."

"Is this a full-time job for you both? I mean, do you get paid?" Barton asked.

Deb looked at Kerry. "You can answer for us both."

"It does turn into a full-time job; however, we don't get paid." Kerry continued, "We have other jobs to pay the bills."

"I took the liberty of speaking to Elizabeth Miller and her father, Amos. We met at the barn raising."

Conversation paused as the waitress approached their table with drinks and paused to take their lunch orders.

Bart glanced at his notes as they ordered.

"I leased five acres of Elizabeth's land. A parcel separating her farm from her parents' farm."

Kerry was surprised Elizabeth leased land to a nonAmish. She was eager to hear more.

"I plan to build a barn. Or, I should say, I will pay the Amish to build a barn on the acreage. I'll need your help designing the barn."

Kerry asked, "Ok, but why our help?" She looked at Deb who remained silent, listening.

"Because you'll know what you need." Bart waited for his words to make sense.

"Why?" Kerry gasped, "Oh, my! For us?"

Bart nodded. "For the Save a Morgan Rescue."

Stunned silence. Bart savored the joy of his announcement.

"I will sublease the barn to the rescue for $1 a month. Make sure you put that in your budget. I have several conditions."

Kerry finally squeaked, "I'm listening. Oh, my!"

"If for any reason the rescue stops operating, the barn will be given to the Millers."

Deb couldn't stop nodding her head. She grabbed Kerry's hand and squeezed.

"The facility is in honor of Isaiah Miller and I would like to call it Fare Thee Well."

"That's neat. I can understand the Amish wouldn't want Isaiah's name used for promotion or advertising." Kerry knew the Amish shunned attention.

Deb asked, "So we'll call it the Fare Thee Well Farm for Rescued Morgans?"

Bart answered, "The Fare Thee Well Farm for Save a Morgan Rescue."

"Thank you so much. Does Trina know yet?" Deb didn't think so or she would have called. Unless Bart asked her not to call.

"No, you're the first. I wanted to make sure this idea was acceptable."

"Yes, yes, yes!" Kerry was very excited.

"Wait, I have one more condition." Bart hesitated. "Charlie will be your trainer. He will work with the rescued horses and prepare them for new homes."

"Even with this wonderful endowment, I'm not sure we will be able to pay for a trainer—and he should be paid." Deb was doing quick math in her head.

Bart agreed. "Yes, he should be paid. Especially, since he will be making it his career. I would like to join your Board and help raise funds."

Kerry looked at Deb. "We don't have anyone who is actively fundraising and that's been a huge problem. We certainly welcome your help."

Bart didn't want to be too pushy; however, if this venture was going to succeed, he thought they needed a little more organization. "Are you interested in adding to the organization?"

Kerry was the first to respond. "Yes, of course. With your help."

Deb was puzzled. "This is a huge and expensive undertaking. Why are you doing this, Barton?"

Bart waited for the waitress to place their food on the table before answering.

"I was what I call a *taker*. I took anything and everything to supply my drug habit. I didn't care who I hurt. I caused my parents pain, I took something very precious away from my sister, I destroyed our family." His voice quivered. "I finally cleaned myself up and became a *giver*. The joy of giving heals the pain of taking. I spent years looking for Fare. I was heartbroken when I thought he was shipped for slaughter. You saved him. Your hard work and dedication saved Fare. Then Fare gave me back my sister—my family."

Kerry wanted to give Bart a moment. "Hey, let's eat before our food gets cold. Do you want me to say a prayer?"

Deb and Barton nodded.

"Father, thank you for this generous gift from Barton and the meal we share. Help us to always use this gift wisely. Amen."

Bart nodded his thanks to Kerry for giving him a moment to gain control of his emotions and for the prayer.

"I can't think of a better way to honor my sister and to thank you."

Deb was caught mid-chew, somehow managed to swallow, and added, "We can't, either!"

Bart laughed. The air seemed lighter. His chicken and dumplings were delicious.

"Does Charlie know yet? What if he isn't interested?" Kerry laughed. "Never mind—that's a stupid question."

"Not a stupid question at all. I've spoken to his mother and grandfather, of course. I explained everything when I asked to lease the land. They spoke to their bishop and asked for his blessing. Charlie doesn't know yet, and, of course, it's all contingent on Charlie wanting the job."

"I can't imagine him not wanting the job." Deb wiped her mouth with a paper napkin.

"I think he'll want the job. He's only fourteen, but he isn't too young, considering the Amish leave formal school after eighth grade. Mrs. Miller said he wants to work with horses." Bart held out his glass when the waitress arrived for refills. "There are still a lot of details to cover—legalities. It's best for everyone to be on the same page and I want to keep it as simple as possible."

"I agree. We have an attorney who is on the Board and volunteers her time for the rescue." Kerry took out her phone to give Barton a name and number.

Chapter Twenty-Seven

harlie waved goodbye to his family from the passenger side of Marcy's truck with the horse trailer
attached and Oscar riding in back.

"Are you excited?" Jennie asked from the back seat.

"Yes, ma'am. Will Mr. Jeremy be at your farm when we get there?"

"He may not be there when we get there, but he'll be there later this afternoon. He's been on a mission trip for two weeks. They've been building a library and a meeting place for kids in Appalachia. He's been teaching a bible study, too."

"I like Mr. Jeremy." Charlie looked at Jennie in the back seat.

"Well, I like him, too." She laughed.

"Are you going to marry Mr. Jeremy?" Charlie wondered why they weren't married.

"I am, but we aren't planning a wedding." Jennie was surprised at the question.

Marcy teased. "I think they're taking too long to get married. Don't you, Charlie?"

"Marcy!" Jennie pretended she was mad, but she wasn't. She also didn't expect this Amish youngster to be so forward with his questions. "Don't gang up on me, you two!"

Charlie turned around to face the front, his face red.

"I'm only pretending to be mad. Let's talk about Oscar and what you've been doing together." Jennie changed the subject quickly.

"We've been jumping. Like the performance team." Charlie welcomed the opportunity to talk about Oscar.

"Do you want to do something with the team while you're here?" Marcy took her eyes off the road for a second to look at the teen in black pants, suspenders, and a straw hat.

"Yup. Maybe they'll let me ride in a practice?" Charlie hoped so—he would follow the promise he made to his mama and not show off.

Jennie leaned forward. "I think that can be arranged. Miss Lainie already invited you and Oscar to the fun day she's having at her place this week. You'll be busy."

With Oscar in back, they didn't stop for lunch and arrived at the farm before noon. Oscar backed down the ramp and sniffed the air, his ears pricked forward. Jennie heard a nicker from the pasture.

"I think your friend, Melody, knows you're here, Oscar." Jennie motioned for Charlie to bring Oscar into the barn and then out the back door to the pasture. "Since he's been here before, I think he'll be fine in the pasture. What do you think?"

"Oscar will be fine." Julep rushed toward the fence, ears flattened back. "But will this mare?"

"Ahh, you're right, she's saying, 'not yet.' Let's keep Oscar in this paddock for now."

Julep's strong response surprised Jennie, especially since Oscar was part of her herd and in the same pasture only a few weeks ago. "I think Julep wants to make sure Oscar remembers she's in charge around here.

"Is anyone hungry? I'll treat at the Bake & Shake," Jennie offered.

"Just let me unhook the trailer." Marcy wasn't scheduled to work until later in the afternoon.

Jennie followed Marcy to her truck and held out her hand with two twenty-dollar bills. "Jeremy asked me to give you this for hauling Oscar. And I'll top off your tank after lunch. Thanks for driving."

Marcy didn't reach for the money. "No need. I'll appreciate the tank top off and lunch. That's more than enough. I think I'm going to enjoy having that youngster around for a while. I plan on getting some free driving tips from him!" She planned on letting him drive her ponies and watching and learning as much as possible.

JENNIE DROVE with Charlie. Marcy followed in her truck. The Bake & Shake was a favorite early morning hangout for Grandpa and his friends. Locals called the retired men the B & S club after the place they gathered to sample fresh-baked muffins, while drinking gallons of freshly brewed coffee, and offering a commentary on just about every subject being discussed in the Appleridge community. The Bake & Shake was well-known for fresh-out-of-the-oven muffins and donuts in the morning. The lunch ladies crowded into the bakery at lunchtime to enjoy homemade tuna salad, egg salad, and chicken salad sandwiches on freshly baked buns. The after-school crowd ordered ice cream sundaes and shakes. The bakery was also well-known for their all-the-way chili dogs—enjoyed by all ages.

Looking at the time, Jennie thought they would sneak in between the lunch crowd and the afterschool crowd. She proved to be correct as they easily snagged a high-top table.

Charlie looked around, checking the place out. "It smells good in here."

"They're usually baking something." Jennie retrieved a small tablet from her purse, pen poised to their orders. "Charlie, everything's written on the chalk board."

Charlie perused the board. "I think I'll take the chili dog with chips and a chocolate milkshake." He looked at Jennie and added, "If that's not too much."

"It's not too much. Marcy?"

"Tuna salad on whole wheat with lettuce and tomato and a diet Pepsi, please. Ask them to throw a few cherries in the glass along with crushed ice."

Jennie placed the order and returned to the table with their drinks. She noticed Charlie eyeing the bakery case. "We'll get a dozen cookies to take home for later. What's your favorite?

"Peanut butter!" Charlie didn't need to think for a second.

"You and my grandpa; that's his favorite, too." Jennie got up to pick up their order when the counter girl waved.

Marcy added, "Must be because you share the same name."

Charlie cackled, sounding just like his grandpa Amos.

"Charlie, how about we hitch up the ponies tomorrow?" Marcy reached for a napkin to wipe her hands.

"Can I drive the ponies?"

"That's what I was counting on. I'm thinking you may have a few things to teach me." Marcy looked at the youngster who looked like a normal teen with his hat on the seat instead of perched on his head. He had a cowlick that kept his blond hair to the side of his face instead of obedient bangs of the Amish bowl haircut.

"Oh, I don't know about that, Miss Marcy. Grandpa said you handle the lines really well." Charlie thought so, too.

"Well, thank you." Marcy took a sip of her drink, looking very pleased.

JEREMY PLACED both feet firmly on the deck to stop the movement of Jennie's back porch swing, standing up as she pulled into the driveway with Charlie in the passenger seat. Charlie climbed out of the truck and bounced to Jeremy.

"I'm here, Mr. Jeremy, and we went to the—" He looked at Jennie.

She helped him out with the name. "The Bake & Shake."

"The Bake & Shake for lunch. I had a chocolate milkshake."

Jeremy pointed to Charlie's lip. "I believe I can see a bit of that chocolate milkshake!"

Charlie rubbed his face on his shirt sleeve, then pulled Jeremy's arm. "Come on; come see Oscar."

Jeremy presented his sad face. "I think I'm going to the barn to see Oscar."

She laughed at Jeremy's sad face message. He would get a proper welcome home from her later. "I'm going into the house for a minute. I'll be out soon." She wondered if Charlie would keep them hopping all week.

Linda Amick Algire

"I put a load of laundry in the washer. Hope that was ok."

"Good idea. All your stinky laundry needs to be done before it adds an interesting fragrance to the house!"

"And just so you know. I added a bit of vinegar to the load and I brought a whole gallon with me." His voice became a shout as Charlie pulled him toward the barn.

"Good job!" Jennie turned so he couldn't see the smile on her face.

But he knew it was there.

LAINIE PARKED beside Trina's truck at The Café and waved to her friend through the window.

The waitress, Angie, nodded when Lainie motioned to Trina waiting in the booth.

"Thanks for coming." Trina smiled at her friend.

"You didn't have to twist my arm." Lainie looked around the full room. "It looks like a lot of people had the same idea."

"That's why I got here early. I know you have lessons later on this afternoon."

"Thanks. What's up? You said we needed to talk about something in person. I hope nothing happened while the girls practiced at your farm."

Trina shook her head no. "Everything was good, and everyone enjoyed watching."

"Good to hear."

"Sorry to worry you. I just have a lot to share and thought it would be good to share in person."

Lainie looked at her friend. "Spill it. You look like you're about to burst."

"Let's order first." One glance at the specials board and Trina was ready.

Bernice, a much older and another loved waitress, came for their order.

"I'll take the spinach quiche special." Trina nodded at the board. "It comes with a side salad?"

"It does." Bernice waited.

"With ranch dressing on the side, please."

"You got it." She looked at Lainie.

"Hmmm, this is a hard decision." She closed the menu. "But I'll have the same, only with a bit of salad with my ranch dressing."

Bernice was back with two salads before Trina could share her news. She placed the salad, dripping with ranch dressing, in front of Lainie.

"You live dangerously, young lady!" She laughed. "I gave you extra!"

"Thank you, ma'am!" Lainie dug into the salad. "What?"

Trina pretended to look pious. "Maybe we'll say a prayer?"

Lainie pretended to look chastened. "I'm hungry!" They both laughed.

"Let's say Grandpa Charlie's favorite prayer. Together they said, "Good food, good meat, good God, let's eat!"

Then Lainie added, "And thank you so much for fun lunches with friends. Amen."

The quiche arrived, and after a few bites, Trina was ready to share. She gave the short version.

"Bart has leased a few acres between the Miller and Stoltz farms. He's paying the Amish to build a barn for Save a Morgan

Rescue, and he wants Charlie to prepare the horses for adoptions and new homes."

Lainie was unusually speechless, her fork frozen between plate and mouth.

Finally, a quiet, "Wow."

"Charlie is with Jennie. He'll be here all week."

"I know; he's invited to ride with the team. The girls are excited."

"Bart says that after the barn is built, they'll need money to pay Charlie to prepare the horses for new homes. He wants to hold a fundraiser at my farm and—and—"

"Spill it, Trina." Lainie waited.

"Um—he wants to know if your team would perform and allow Charlie to ride, too."

Lainie sat back—thinking. "You know, that's a good idea. We won't call it a performance. We'll call it a demonstration. Charlie can't perform."

Trina agreed. "He is allowed to help raise money for a good cause. We've checked with Elizabeth and Amos."

"Several of the girls have rescue horses. The little wonder pony that Tera rides is a rescue, my horse is a rescue, Megan considers Starlight a rescue, and I think there are others."

"There are also some horses that have rescued their owners." Trina thought so, anyway. "I know I was. Fare kept me out of a lot of trouble when I was a teenager."

"And now he has rescued your family." Lainie added, "Let me talk to the team and their families. When did he want to hold the fundraiser?"

"He wants to hold it on Saturday. You were planning on practicing at my place Saturday, right?"

"How can he pull it all together by then?"

"It's not going to be a huge public event. He's lined up several potential sponsors and wants to invite them to the farm to show them the *bang for the buck,* so to speak. They'll be able to see for themselves—teens with their horses and Charlie's skill as a trainer. He thinks if they see, they'll be willing to donate."

"Sounds good. The girls had a blast last time."

"Having fun is the best advertisement for future sponsors."

"That's what I think, too. They want to compete and that can be fun if the focus is on learning, making our horsemanship better, helping friends—it could be called a lot of things. It's the focus that counts."

Trina smiled at her friend. "I so agree."

MEGAN EXPERTLY backed her horse trailer, using a three-point turn to head in the opposite direction. They were on a mission to pick up Charlie and Oscar for a fun day at Lainie's barn.

Climbing out of the truck, Cassy spoke first. "Remember, Lainie said not to scare this poor kid."

"What? Me?" Megan was offended.

"Not just you; both of us."

"She must think we can get a little crazy sometimes." Megan pretended an evil laugh.

Charlie walked out of the barn, his straw hat crooked on his head. "Hey."

"Hey, remember me? I'm Megan."

"I'm Cassy. Are you ready?"

"I remember. Thanks for picking up me and Oscar."

Megan answered, "No problem."

Silence. None of the three knew what to add to the conversation.

"I'll get Oscar." Charlie turned and almost ran back to the barn.

"I wonder where Jennie is?" Cassy thought it was odd Charlie greeted them by himself.

"There she is now." Megan pointed toward the house at Jennie walking toward the barn with her phone held to the side of her face. They waited at the front barn door.

"Yes, I understand. Ok, thanks. Bye." Jennie ended the call.

"Thanks for picking up Charlie and Oscar. I really need to buy a horse trailer." Jennie hugged each of her young friends.

"No problem." Megan didn't mind.

"I've been asked to write up a little narration about the team and Charlie for Saturday. I thought I would just go along with you and observe today."

Cassy breathed a sigh of relief. "That's good. Charlie seemed a little wary of us."

Jennie laughed. "Isn't everyone?"

"Jennie!" Cassy relaxed. "You're so funny."

Charlie led Oscar into the barn and stood quietly.

"Just so you know, these two are trouble with a capital T. You should be very careful." Jennie had to clamp her lips together to keep from laughing at Charlie's wide eyes.

When Jennie snorted, Charlie knew she was joking. "The same has been said about me." He looked at the girls. They were now compatriots—in a sense. He relaxed. "Miss Jennie, are you going with us?" Charlie hoped so.

"I am. Someone needs to make sure these two don't lead you astray."

Charlie nodded. But now he couldn't tell if Miss Jennie was being funny or not. He led Oscar to the trailer and up the ramp.

Megan lifted and latched the ramp. "He loads like a champ."

Charlie laughed. "He loads like he does it every day!"

"He's traveled more lately than my horse, that's for sure," Cassy acknowledged.

They climbed into Megan's truck, Jennie in front holding a riding helmet, Cassy and Charlie in back.

"Don't you have a saddle or anything?" Megan looked at Charlie in the rearview mirror.

"Nope."

"Charlie rides bareback most of the time. Julep's saddle doesn't fit Oscar." Jennie answered. "We haven't found one for Melody, either."

"Maybe Lainie has an extra saddle?" Cassy tried to remember.

"I like bareback. It's ok." Charlie didn't want to ride in one of those strange English saddles the girls used.

"I have a nice suede bareback pad you could use." Megan loved riding bareback. "It's great for keeping all the sweat and dirt off your pants."

"I'll give that a try." Charlie thought it would be a good idea to keep sweat and dirt off his pants. He only brought two older pairs for the entire week and one new pair in case they went to

church or out for dinner. The Amish didn't have large ward-
robes.

At Lainie's, Oscar backed out of the horse trailer and
looked around. This place was new. His human Charlie was
with him. He was fine.

Chapter Twenty-Eight

Wilson Mark pulled up to the empty sale barn. The office looked open. Good.

"Hey, Wilson, long time no see!" Edison Mark stepped forward to greet his cousin. "What brings you out this way?"

"I need to gather some facts before my reporter prints her own." Wilson sat down on a metal folding chair by Edison's desk.

"This sounds serious. Hey, do you need anything? Coffee?" Edison held up an empty stained coffee mug and pointed to the office pot.

"Sure, I'll take some." Wilson reached for the mug, got up, and walked to the well-used coffee machine on the back wall of the office.

"Ok, cousin, first, how's the family?" Edison always envied Wilson having a family.

"Good. Both girls are out of college and Martha is retiring from teaching this year."

"Good for her. I bet her students will miss her. How about you? That paper keeping you busy?" Edison refilled his mug and then dumped a large spoonful of sugar in and stirred.

"I've hired a young writer. She's taken the load off and has really spiced up the CC. Circulation numbers are up. That brings me to this visit. My writer has written a nice informative article on a horse rescued from this sale."

"What do you mean rescued? We run a clean sale." Edison stiffened.

Wilson thought his cousin seemed a bit defensive. "She hasn't written anything damaging to your reputation—yet."

"What do you mean, yet? Come on; what's going on?" Edison thought maybe he did know.

"Apparently, this horse, a little Morgan horse, was sold in a backdoor deal. He never went through the sale."

"Yeah, we know that happens and it's not good for our business. It cheats us out of our commission."

"Why don't you stop it?" Wilson sat back down and relaxed after his second sip of coffee.

"Why?" Edison thought for a moment. "I guess because we've been so busy and some of the backdoor buyers also buy through the sale."

"You don't care they're cheating you?"

Edison put his mug on the cluttered desk. "We care, but like I said, business is good and those same buyers buy legitimately."

Wilson decided to head in another direction. "This particular horse was sold to a kill buyer. A well-known kill buyer who lied to the woman selling the horse. He told her he was looking for a nice horse for his children. He recommended saving the commission fee by selling the horse to him before the sale."

Edison said nothing. But his face revealed this wasn't news.

Wilson continued. "I see a lot wrong with this myself. Word gets out, cousin. Actually, the story is being printed in the next CC. I sure wish I could print something about how you're working on a solution."

Edison slapped the desk. "A solution? In case you haven't noticed, we sell horses here. I can't guarantee every horse will find a good home after the sale and I'm not going to try."

"Calm down." Wilson himself stayed calm. "I'm not here to accuse you of anything."

Edison sat down again. "I don't like those kill buyers any more than anyone else. What am I supposed to do about all the unwanted horses? I can't save the world."

Wilson didn't agree. "You can do something. You can make sellers aware about backdoor deals. They are unacceptable and tell them why. I don't think you'll lose all that much business if you ban the buyers who are cheating you, anyway. They're making money and tarnishing your reputation in the process."

"It's not that easy. Some horses will still end up with a kill buyer, even if they do go through the sale.

Wilson stood up. "If they go through the sale, they at least have a chance, and you're not dealing in the kill trade. Like it or not, that's what you're doing by allowing kill buyers to tell their little stories to unsuspecting sellers."

Edison was just fine pretending he didn't know what was happening. But now, Wilson was making sure he could no longer pretend.

"I like horses. We sell some real nice horses."

Wilson looked at his cousin. "This is a good sale. It has a good reputation. If you allow more kill buyers, and there will be more if you allow them to continue, you'll be known as a kill sale. I'm sure you'll make good money as a kill sale, but you'll also lose quality sellers and buyers."

"You know that's not what I want." Edison crossed his arms. "So, about that article—"

"I debated about pulling the story, then decided to let it run. It's well-written and doesn't blame your sale barn for the situation. Jennie, my reporter, wrote about the lies being told to get horses cheap."

"If the article's going to run anyway, why come out here?" Edison asked. "It doesn't sound so bad."

"I wanted to give you a chance to make some changes— changes I'm sure Jennie will agree to add to her article.

"The way I see it, and tell me if I'm wrong, if you make sellers aware of the danger, you've done your duty. You already advise sellers to set a minimum bid. Right?"

"We do. A reserve bid will usually keep a horse out of kill buyer range and—." Edison realized what he was saying. "We've had the right approach all along."

Wilson smiled at his cousin. "You have. That's why I was surprised to read Jennie's article. She doesn't name this particular sale, but I knew it was here, based on the location."

"I'll come up with a flyer to post. Maybe I should advertise in the old CC?" Business was usually so good, Edison never thought about advertising. "It won't hurt to list our sale requirements in an ad. Who knows, maybe it'll bring in more good sellers and buyers. I think your readership spills over into our area."

"I'll tell you what: You come up with a flyer and I'll give you ad space for the cousin discount. Let's say—free."

"You got a deal." The men shook hands. Wilson handed his empty mug to Edison. "Email me the information when you put something together. I'll need it quick; say by Tuesday. We go to press next week."

"Wilson. Thanks." Edison walked his cousin out to his car.

EDISON GOT to work as soon as Wilson drove away. He wouldn't call Wilson's visit a wake-up call of sorts. Well, maybe it was. Was he guilty of fraud? Was he guilty of helping the kill buyers?

I guess when I allowed things to happen, things I knew were wrong, but chose to take the easy route and ignore, well then, yeah, I guess I'm guilty. Darn that Wilson, he always could make me see what I never want to see. Edison chuckled. *But I like him. He's a good guy.*

ATTENTION!

15% Sale Commission must be paid on all sales. Fraudulent sales (backdoor deals) will cause sellers and buyers to be banned from all future sales.

SELLERS BEWARE!

Backdoor deals are almost always perpetrated by kill buyers. All horses, regardless of breeding and training, are in danger. Don't fall for a promise of a good home. Kill buyers tell convincing stories to make a quick profit. Horses are shipped to Canada and Mexico for slaughter. Horse slaughter is illegal in the USA.

All horses going through the sale must have a set reserve. The reserve should be higher than the price per pound offered by the slaughter industry. Our office staff will help you set the best price.

In the event your horse does not sell, and you need to rehome the horse as quickly as possible, please contact a reputable rescue from the list below. They will do their best to assist. Many breed organizations also offer breed-specific rescue assistance.

Edison Mark

Equine Sale Barn of Pennsylvania

Wilson printed the notice found in his email. They could turn this into a nice ad. Jennie may even want to add the information to her article.

He must have started to write as soon as I left today. And, he took it a step further by sharing a list of horse rescues. Good for you, Edison.

Wilson printed a copy for Charles and marked the ad as free with a note—*Do your magic; make it look nice.*

He forwarded a copy of the email to Jennie with a note— *Let's discuss.* Jennie would be out on interviews and working from home; he wanted to make sure they connected.

"OK, CHARLIE, your turn." Lainie motioned for Charlie to ride Oscar forward. "Any questions?"

Charlie, wearing a helmet instead of his usual straw hat, could pass for almost any young teen. "I'm ready!"

Lainie nodded and held up her stopwatch, ready to time Charlie and Oscar on the obstacle course.

Charlie trotted Oscar in a circle, then zeroed in on the first obstacle: a rope gate. He asked Oscar to line up beside the gate and lifted the rope from the post, asked Oscar to go through the gate, turn, and line up again, backing a little so Charlie could place the rope loop on the post again.

"Real slick, Charlie!" Lainie encouraged. The girls cheered.

They proceeded through the remaining nine obstacles: crossed a small wooden bridge, jumped a small jump, backed between poles, retrieved a letter from a mailbox, deposited the letter in another mailbox, weaved through a cone pattern at a trot, cantered a figure eight changing leads, asked Oscar to move sideways over a pole, and ended with Charlie dismounting in the center of the arena and running to the gate with Oscar following.

"Picture perfect." Lainie clapped. "And I think you are our fastest time!"

Lots of cheering followed. Charlie stroked Oscar's neck with a huge smile.

"Did everyone get a turn?" Lainie scanned the group.

"Can we go again, Miss Lainie?" Tera yelled.

"We've had a big morning. Let's break for lunch. Take care of your horses. Make sure they're cooled down, give them hay and water, then meet me at the barn."

Lainie turned to hide her smile as the entire group of girls surrounded Charlie. She walked to the barn to check on lunch. Several mothers already had a small buffet set up on a table in the barn aisle.

"Thanks so much!" Lainie eyed the potato salad, deviled eggs, buns, cheese and sliced meat platter, vegetable tray, and cookies. "This looks perfect."

Susan Peterson placed a large stack of paper plates on the table. "We have water and soft drinks in the cooler."

"Susan, don't forget to leave me your receipts. I'll reimburse you for lunch." Lainie looked at Susan who was also her landlord."

"No receipt. It's a potluck! All the families contributed." Susan hesitated. "Ok, maybe a small reimbursement for the drinks and ice—those are the only things I purchased."

"Thanks so much! I can certainly reimburse you for the drinks—at the very least."

315

The chattering group of riders moved as one into the barn. Lainie thought Charlie looked right in place, laughing and talking with the girls. They quickly filled plates and found places to sit—on tack trunks, upside-down buckets, and folding camp chairs. Chatter stopped temporarily as the riders stuffed food into their mouths. It seemed the morning's games aroused a few appetites.

Charlie, wearing his straw hat instead of a helmet, chatted with the girls and didn't seem self-conscious, although he was probably the only one not sporting a cell phone in his back pocket. Conversation seemed to entertain most of the group. A few girls snuck a peek at their cell phones.

"I love Oscar." Tera sat beside Charlie on a tack trunk.

"Thanks. He's a good horse." Charlie answered, but didn't look at Tera. "He looked at Lainie. "Miss Lainie, that horse at Miss Trina's house. Do you know him?"

"He's a horse Miss Trina lost, and then was found at a sale and rescued by the Morgan group. Why?"

"I like him. He looks like Stormy." Charlie got up to grab another cookie.

"He's a Morgan and your family raised Morgan horses. Do you think maybe he looks like one from your area?"

"He looks like my Stormy." He bit his lip, sniffed, looked away. "How old is Miss Trina's horse? Do you know?"

"I think he's somewhere around eighteen or twenty. I could ask Trina, or you could ask when we're there on Saturday." Lainie added, "I hope you ride with us Saturday."

"We'll teach you our drill pattern," Cassy offered.

"Yes, ma'am, I would like to ride on Saturday." He looked at Cassy as she dug in the cooler for a canned drink. "And I would like to learn the drill pattern."

Lainie stepped up onto a small stool. "If I could have your attention for a moment." The riders looked at their teacher and waited. "Before we clear the arena, you may play with the obstacles for one hour, then, Cassy, you'll be in charge of practicing the drill pattern."

Cassy nodded her approval. "And Megan, will you help?" She looked at her friend.

"Sure, I'll help even though I don't think you'll need much help."

Oscar, tied in at the end of the barn aisle, whinnied. "I think my Oscar is ready to have more fun." Charlie looked around for the trash barrel after he stuffed one more cookie in his pocket.

Megan noticed. "Charlie, I need to introduce you to my dad. He's a cookie monster, too."

Charlie's face reddened. "I think I met your dad. I liked him. Now I know why." He quickly escaped the conversation by walking toward Oscar.

Cassy whispered, "You embarrassed him."

"I didn't mean to, but I guess I did." Megan frowned. "I'll go and apologize." She picked up two cookies.

"I'm sorry." She held out a cookie as she took a bite out of the other. "I was just trying to be funny. I guess I wasn't."

Charlie reached for the cookie hesitantly.

"Go ahead. It's my apology."

Charlie smiled and took the peanut butter cookie. "Mama says to always accept an apology when it's offered, and I always try to listen to Mama." The cookie disappeared in two bites.

LAINIE ENJOYED watching the horses and riders from her seat on Shadow's back. "Come on, Shadow, time for us to get moving." Trotting around the perimeter of the arena, she kept her eyes on the group. After three laps, she slowed to a walk and looked at her phone to check the time.

"Ok, everyone, let's clear the arena. It's time to work on our drill pattern. Here's your challenge. Tie your reins so they won't fall or drag on the ground. Ask your horse to follow you as we move the obstacles."

The group hopped off their horses, secured reins, and got to work. The horses stuck to their humans like glue.

"I'm impressed. Good job!" Lainie climbed on the fence to mount Shadow. Some riders did the same, others mounted from the ground, Charlie swung up in one leap. He wasn't showing off. It was just his usual style of mounting Oscar.

The drill practice went well and Charlie followed easily. Cassy was in her element as the leader.

Lainie didn't like turning a pattern into a drill. She made a note to stop calling it a drill pattern. She needed to come up with better words to describe their group and what they did.

"Ok, everyone. Enough practice. We don't want to actually drill our horses or ourselves into boredom with a pattern. It looks great. You are free to ride in groups out in the pasture. No racing, please."

She rode out into the pasture to keep an eye on things. A large, open field could be challenging for some riders and horses. As she rode, she watched, pondered, and talked to her horse.

"What do you think, Shadow? Should we call this group something other than a performance drill team? We want to have fun and do other things beside perform and drill."

Megan rode up beside Lainie. "How about we change the focus of our group?"

"You must have been reading my mind!" Lainie acknowledged.

Megan laughed. "No, I heard you talking to Shadow."

"What do you think?" Lainie scanned the pasture. All was well.

"I think we can come up with a better name. Something more fun."

"Such as?" Lainie wasn't feeling very creative.

"Hmmm, not sure right now. I'll think on it." Megan turned Starlight and cantered to Cassy and Treasure on the other side of the pasture.

Lainie watched her with a smile. She was sure those two girls would put their creative minds together and come up with a catchy name. She rode over to where Jennie sat on the fence watching the fun.

"I should have told you to bring Julep or Melody." Lainie chastised herself for not thinking of it earlier.

"I didn't think of it, either. Besides, this was a special fun day for your team."

"I guess we'll need to have a Fare Friends day. Remember our promise to do something fun together every month?" Lainie hinted. She knew Jennie was the organizer of their group.

"I remember. It seems like forever ago. It's been a busy time for us all."

Lainie wasn't going to be deterred. "Which is exactly why we need to be intentional."

Jennie jumped off the fence. "I'm on it!" She thought for a moment. "I heard you talking to Megan about a name for your team. I have a few suggestions."

"I'm listening." Lainie knew Jennie could be witty at times.

"Ok, how about—Horses in Time, Hands & Hooves, Pattern Partners, Hay Play, Horse Play Partners, Heart of Horsemanship, Hearts & Horses—"

"Whoa! How do you do that?"

"Do what?" Jennie was puzzled.

"Come up with that stuff so quick." Lainie added, "I like several. Maybe I'll gather the group and we'll take a quick vote."

OSCAR STOOD IN THE TRAILER, waiting for his ride back to Jennie's farm. "This sure was fun. Thanks for inviting me, Miss Lainie."

"Thanks for joining us. Are you coming to Trina's on Saturday?" Lainie didn't think Charlie would miss it. It didn't hurt to ask.

"Yes, ma'am. Mama and Granddad are coming. They want to watch, and then I'm going home."

"What are you going to do tomorrow? It's going to be a nice day."

"Miss Marcy and I are driving ponies," Charlie shared.

"That sounds fun. But isn't that something you get to do all the time?" Lainie was just trying to get the teen to talk and talking about horses always seemed to do the trick.

"Miss Marcy drives fast!"

Lainie chuckled. "Yes, she does!"

Chapter Twenty-Nine

*B*art and Margaret arrived at Trina's farm early on Saturday, fully prepared with a large cooler packed with all sorts of cheese and salami from the store deli, another cooler with drinks, and a large selection of crackers and snacks. He didn't want his sister to worry about playing hostess today.

Trina rushed from the barn, arms open, reaching for a hug.

"It looks like you've been busy." Bart gave Trina a one-armed hug and pointed to a long row of chairs beside the arena.

"I asked my friends to drop off chairs during the week. It's quite an interesting collection." Trina thought it was colorful, too. "Thanks for ordering the port-a-john." She motioned to the bright pink hut sitting under a tree.

"I didn't want our guests running up to the house. I think we should keep everything down here." Bart scanned the area. "Where should we set up the tables?"

"I thought the barn aisle would be best. My boarders helped me clean up the barn yesterday. It looks good and it's near what I call the barn kitchen."

"I'll unload everything and then move my truck." Bart started to lug a cooler from the truck bed.

"Let me help." Trina grabbed one handle. Margaret relaxed on the barn bench, willing to let the younger folk fetch and carry.

"Did you hear from Amos Stoltz and Elizabeth?" Trina asked.

"Yes, they'll be here. They want to meet potential sponsors and watch Charlie perform—well, not perform. You know what I mean." Bart stretched his back. "Where's a pallet jack when you need one?"

"Only a grocery man would think that!" Trina declared.

"That's me! And Squirt, just so you know, I really like working in the store. I only wish I could go back and tell Dad when he was alive. I could have been a huge help instead of a big headache."

"Hey, we aren't going to rehash the past. That isn't you anymore. You are a hard-working, generous, good son, good brother, and horse saver of sorts, and don't you forget it." Trina punched his arm.

"Ok, Squirt!" Bart teased and jumped to avoid another hit. For a little thing, his sister could really pack a punch.

FARE NICKERED at Oscar as Charlie led the gelding beside the pasture.

Oscar nickered back.

"I guess they know they're from the same tribe." Cassy laughed.

Charlie led Oscar over to the fence. The two horses greeted each other like old friends.

"That's funny. It really is like they know each other," Jennie observed. "But how could that be?"

Charlie said nothing. It would come to him eventually. He was sure.

TRUCKS AND CARS lined the drive leading to Trina's barn. Bart said a silent a prayer of thanks for the beautiful spring day; not too hot, not too sunny, very pleasant. He greeted people as they arrived—potential sponsors, Trina's boarders, friends, and family.

He turned on a wireless microphone to test the rented sound system. "Welcome, everyone." Heads turned in his direction. It worked! "Thank you for coming today. Please find snacks and drinks in the barn. There are plenty of chairs by the arena. We'll get started in about fifteen minutes."

Bart found Jennie talking to Amos Stoltz and Elizabeth Miller. "It's nice to see you again. This is an exciting day." He looked at Jennie. "Are you ready?"

Jennie smiled. "I'm ready. Jeremy is talking to Charlie. He looked a bit nervous. Either that or he needed to be rescued from Cassy and Megan." She looked at Amos and Elizabeth. "I'm just kidding. He actually held his own quite well this week. He is a wonderful young man."

"We're fond of him, too," Amos teased.

"I missed him. It's the first time he's been away from home." It had been a very long week for Elizabeth.

Jennie pointed to a gathering of chairs under a maple tree. "Grandpa and Mrs. Williams are saving seats for you over there."

Once they were alone, Bart scanned the group. "Let's get this party started."

Jennie agreed.

"Again, welcome to Loving Life Farm, owned by my sister, Trina Shaw. Thank you for sharing your Saturday with us. At this time, I would like to introduce Jennie McKenzie. Jennie will tell you a little about our purpose here today."

Jennie took the microphone.

"Thank you, Bart." Jennie hesitated. Surprised. Her boss, Wilson Mark, and another gentleman were taking a seat near the barn. She took a moment to breathe deeply.

"Thank you for sharing this day with fellow horse lovers. You may not have been a horse lover upon arrival today, but I'm sure you'll be enchanted by the time you leave.

"Barton Shaw has a mission—a mission to save horses. Barton's search for a lost horse is his testimony. In the grips of drugs and grief, he unfairly sold his sister's horse without her permission. This led to a ten-year estrangement and a time of deep sorrow for the Shaw family. It's a sad story and one he willingly shares. The lost horse was a Morgan horse named My Fare Thee Well."

Elizabeth opened the well-worn journal on her lap and scanned the entries. Looking at the horse, then at the journal again, she nudged her father and pointed to an entry. He lifted his eyebrows but didn't say a word.

"Fare was sold to a kill buyer in a backdoor deal at an auction. A week later, Barton tracked Fare to the auction. After years of searching, he despaired, thinking he was one week too late to save Fare."

Jennie paused, allowing time for Trina to lead Fare into the arena.

"Unknown to Barton, Fare was rescued with only minutes to spare. Please welcome My Fare Thee Well. Fare is owned by

Trina Shaw. Many would say, Fare really owns Trina, and perhaps, Barton, too—he holds a piece of their hearts."

Fare's chestnut coat gleamed. He tossed his white mane and pranced. Trina laughed, those gathered clapped, and Elizabeth Miller's eyes followed the beautiful horse.

"Fare's story has a happy ending. He was rescued from the kill buyer, and then Fare rescued his family. That's the short version of this story, anyway." Jennie stopped, made eye contact with the group, and smiled before continuing.

"Barton Shaw is partnering with Save a Morgan Rescue—a registered nonprofit organization. Many of you have been asked here today to support Save a Morgan with a one-time donation or a reoccurring donation. At this time, I would like to introduce the founders and dedicated ladies behind Save a Morgan Rescue and the ladies who rescued Fare. Please welcome Kerry Casin and Deb Thompkins."

Jennie motioned for Kerry and Deb to come forward. Kerry reached for the microphone.

"Save a Morgan has a mission to save Morgan horses in trouble. Our resources and foster homes are limited. Sometimes, we only have a few hours to raise funds and to locate a foster home. When we fail, the horses are loaded into cramped trailers for the cruel trip to Canada for slaughter. When we fail to raise funds quickly enough, we're forced to look into those sad eyes and say we're sorry." Kerry's voice quivered and Deb took the mic.

"Many Morgan breeders and former owners are willing to help. Unfortunately, we usually only have a few hours from the time we find a horse until they are scheduled to ship the evening of the sale. It's always been our dream to have a safe barn, a place to move the horses to quickly. A place to evaluate and prepare the horses for their new homes.

"Barton Shaw certainly doesn't call himself a horseman, but it's his mission to honor one little horse that healed his family. Barton has leased five acres in the Sugar Creek area to establish the Fare Thee Well Farm, where a young Amish trainer will heal, train, and prepare the horses for new homes."

Charlie, sitting on Oscar near the arena gate, heard Deb talk about an Amish trainer and wondered who would be hired. *Maybe I could apply for the job. Oscar, we could work together as a team.*

Deb handed the mic back to Jennie. "Thank you, Deb. Both Kerry and Deb will be available for questions following our presentation." Jennie motioned for Kerry and Deb to remain with her.

"Ladies and gentlemen, please enjoy the amazing horses and riders of Hearts & Horses led by Lainie Anderson."

Jennie cued the music. The group started from the ground, leading their horses into the arena full of fun obstacles. Those gathered cheered as each horse navigated a particularly big challenge. After two songs played, the group mounted and began riding and playing with the obstacles from the saddle. Then, they went single file to the rail and circled the arena at a trot as Jeremy, Bart, Jennie, and Trina moved the obstacles and cleared the arena.

Cassy blew a whistle signaling the start of their riding pattern. It was an intricate pattern of horses and humans, riding single and in pairs, and ending with all the horses trotting on the rail around the arena as Lainie set up a few jumps. The group then played follow the leader at a canter, with Charlie as the leader, jumping jumps and just having fun.

Jennie heard several comments from those watching. "That boy can sure ride!" "They look like they're having fun!" "I love that little girl on her pony!" "Mom, can I join Hearts & Horses? Please!"

At the end of the presentation, the group lined up, side by side, across the length of the arena.

"Thank you for coming today. Remember, Kerry and Deb are here to answer questions, as is Barton Shaw. We would like to thank Trina Shaw for her hospitality and Lainie Anderson for sharing her talented group."

Lainie motioned for the group to ride over to the fence and whispered to Jennie. Jennie quickly added, "Please come on up and meet Hearts & Horses."

Jennie turned off the microphone and took a deep breath as the spectators showed their appreciation with a few minutes of applause.

Elizabeth walked to the fence. "Thank you both. This is a good day."

Trina was the first to answer, "You're very welcome."

Jennie looked at the group of smiling faces. "Charlie and Oscar were wonderful. We've really enjoyed having him this week."

Elizabeth opened the ledger she held against her chest. "I brought Isaiah's breeding and training ledger. I want to show it to Deb and Kerry. Charlie is creating a special fund of his own. If any of Isaiah's horses are in trouble, we want to act quickly."

She looked at Trina. "Did I hear correctly? Your horse's name is My Fare Thee Well?"

"It is. He's a Lambert Morgan. I understand that's what Isaiah bred."

"Is that his registered name?" Elizabeth asked.

"Yes, it was his registered name when Dad bought him, and I liked it."

Elizabeth smiled. "Have you ever noticed anything interesting on his papers?"

"Um, I guess not. He had his current papers with him at the sale; that's how Kerry and Deb found me. No one must have recorded the transfers. I don't know how many people owned him after me." Trina looked at a smiling Elizabeth still clutching the ledger. "Why?"

Elizabeth scanned the group for her son. She walked over to the fence and called him. "I want Charlie to hear this, also."

"You know, Charlie mentioned that Fare seemed familiar." Jennie looked at Elizabeth and now Amos who joined them at the fence. "Do you know Fare?"

"When Isaiah and I were courting, he started breeding Morgans. The first foal was his favorite. He was a chestnut with a white mane and tail. I remember Isaiah was so excited because the white mane and tail is classic for a Lambert Morgan." Elizabeth paused. "He decided to keep the foal. About three years later, a gentleman who visited our community to purchase produce asked about purchasing the young horse for his twelve-year-old daughter. I remember Isaiah saying the horse, the horse he named My Fare Thee Well, would be perfect for a child."

"Wait! You think Fare is that horse?" Trina was quickly starting to understand and doing the math. "How old would this horse be now? Fare was three when Dad bought him, I was twelve and I'm twenty-eight now. I lost him when I was eighteen and he's been gone for ten years. Yikes! I'm confusing myself!"

Jeremy stepped up. "That would make Fare nineteen."

Trina, Jennie, Amos, Elizabeth, Lainie, Barton, and even Charlie looked at Jeremy and stared.

"What?" Jeremy asked. "Am I wrong or something?"

Trina giggled. "No, you're correct. Fare is nineteen."

"I think we're all just amazed you ran those numbers in your head so quickly," Jennie added.

"What can I say, I'm good with numbers."

Amos chuckled. "You certainly are!" He looked at those gathered in a circle. "I remember that foal. Our Charlie here wouldn't remember. He wasn't born yet, and the Amish don't have photos."

The group of young riders were dispersing and busy greeting friends, but Charlie remained on Oscar's back, in the arena, near enough to listen to the conversation. Oscar lifted his head and nickered at Fare as Trina walked him toward the group.

"Trina, how did you sneak away while I was explaining my amazing math skills?" Jeremy teased.

"I thought maybe Fare needed to be here for the rest of this conversation."

Fare nickered at Oscar and tossed his head. Then he posed, ears forward, eyes alert.

Charlie looked at Fare and then at his grandfather. "Grandpa, if Daed loved Fare, and Fare loved Daed, then Fare owned a piece of Daed's heart."

"Well, that's true." Amos's face revealed the love he had for his grandson.

"And if Fare held a piece of my daed's heart, I think it's still in there somewhere because when I see Fare, I feel my daed's love."

No one said a word. They all stared at Charlie and then at Fare.

Jeremy spoke softly. "Charlie, I think you're right. I believe we can sometimes feel things we can't see."

"And sometimes it takes a very special horse to heal a broken family," Bart added.

"And sometimes, it takes a very special horse to heal a bitter heart," Trina shared.

Elizabeth wiped a tear and added, "And sometimes it takes a very special son and a very special horse to feel the goodness of God."

Epilogue

A small group celebrated the opening of Fare Thee Well Farm. There were no pictures taken. Barton Shaw and Mark's Market provided the groceries for refreshments the Amish ladies cooked and baked.

Charlie humbly accepted the opportunity to follow in his father's footsteps—preparing horses for a better future—as his mother and grandparents fought to hide the pride that couldn't help but seep into their hearts.

The bishop blessed both the barn and Charlie's future as Appleridge friends and the Amish community joined together to welcome two recently rescued horses on opening day—an old, lame mare and a young gelding. The gelding would be trained and prepared for his new home. The mare would experience gentle care and love, and if her condition proved to be untreatable, she would be humanely euthanized.

That is the reality of horse rescue. Healthy horses have a future. Some are simply saved to end their lives with dignity and kindness, kindness being most important for both humans and God's special creatures.

ABOUT THE AUTHOR

Linda Amick Algire loves to write inspirational stories with entertaining characters—always including horses. Her stories turn a messy world into a place of love and friendship.

Linda invites you to stop in and visit for a while at www.fawnsongfarm.com where you may also find a bit of Appleridge news. Please leave Linda a note when you visit—she loves hearing from readers!

Enjoy A Sneak Peek!

The Next Book in the
Faith, Family, Friends & Horses Series

Kasey's Kindness

Kasey was up early on Saturday to make breakfast. Drew loved a nice Saturday morning breakfast when he wasn't on duty. She enjoyed a bacon-and-eggs kind of Saturday morning, too. When Drew was at the fire station, she usually had peanut butter and jelly toast. She was discovering that Drew's new job meant there were plenty of groceries in the fridge.

She was dressed in jeans and a t-shirt, wielding a spatula when Drew walked into the kitchen. "Oh, are you going somewhere?" He smiled because he knew, darn well, she wouldn't be able to stay away from Lainie's barn. "I'll give you a ride out to the farm and we can throw your bike in the bed of the truck for you to ride home later."

Kasey had the decency to look sheepish. "Thanks."

Drew opened his wallet and found a five-dollar bill. "Here's a bit of money in case the girls go out for a bite of lunch. It should be enough for something."

"Thanks. I already packed a peanut butter and jelly sandwich and some cheese and crackers—just in case that's what they do."

"What time do you want to get there?" Drew hoped not too soon as he eyed the eggs and bacon on his plate.

"Don't worry, you have time for breakfast; however, you're on dish duty," Kasey teased.

"Yes, ma'am. I'll have you know, as the new guy on the crew, I've been getting some clean-up practice at the station."

"It will serve you well." Kasey laughed. She did most of the chores around the house because she wanted to, not because Drew assigned her the jobs. After living in places full of trash and dirty dishes when she was a child, Kasey had developed into a bit of a neat freak. She enjoyed scrubbing floors. Yes, most people would think her strange, but Drew seemed to appreciate her efforts. He was a pretty neat guy himself, most of the time, and neither one liked clutter. Of course, there was never enough money to collect much clutter.

They finished breakfast and Kasey rinsed the dishes to leave in the sink to soak while Drew drove her to Lainie's barn. "What do you have planned for today?"

"I'm going grocery shopping and then I may clean up this yard a bit. I think it will look a lot better with a bit of clean up. I may also wash the truck."

Kasey felt a twinge of guilt. "Do you want me to stay here and help?"

"No, I don't. I want you to enjoy a Saturday with horses. You do enough around here already."

"Ok, thanks." She looked fondly at her uncle. When he decided to follow his dream of becoming a fire fighter, he began to take physical conditioning seriously and worked out diligently. He was in great shape and Kasey suspected working in the yard was just another way for him to keep physically active on a quiet Saturday at home.

LAINIE SPOTTED THE TRUCK pulling into the drive and breathed a little prayer. *Father, I hope I can offer this girl something good. I know you can, so I'll turn it all over to you and I'll just follow your lead.*

Drew and Kasey climbed out of the truck and looked toward the barn. Lainie motioned for them to come on in.

"Hey. I'm glad you came, Kasey." She smiled at them both. "The girls should start arriving soon."

She glanced at Megan and Cassy tacking up their horses in the barn aisle and motioned for them to join her. "You met Megan, and this is Cassy. Cassy, this is Kasey. She and her uncle just moved to Appleridge."

Always courteous, Cassy held out her hand. "It's nice to meet you both."

Drew stepped forward to shake Cassy's hand. Kasey nodded.

"Kasey, why don't you come with us and meet Treasure and Starlight?" Cassy led the way and Drew was relieved to watch Kasey follow.

"Thanks for inviting Kasey. We had a long talk. I didn't realize how much teasing she endured at her last school. That's made her a little cautious about making new friends." Drew spoke to Lainie but kept his eyes on his niece until he saw her shoulders relax as soon as she ran her hand down the neck of the smallest horse.

"You're welcome. She'll be fine here. I don't put up with that sort of thing." She chuckled. "And the horses don't, either."

"Well, thanks, I'm going to leave and get some work done at home before my next shift. Kasey doesn't need her uncle watching like she's a two-year-old." Lainie wanted to keep him talking. He didn't look quite ready to leave his niece in her hands yet, in spite of what he just said.

"What brought you to Appleridge? I've only been here about a year myself."

"I'm the newest hire in the Appleridge Fire Department. A dream come true for me; I'm not so sure about Kasey."

"Well, welcome. It's a great community. I came here needing a new life and some good friends and I found them both."

"That's good to hear. Very encouraging." Drew waited for the next question he was sure would come, but it didn't.

"You look like you expected me to say something." Lainie was usually very perceptive.

"I guess. The next question usually is, 'Are you raising your niece?'"

"Oh, ok, I'll play along." She crossed her arms. "Why are you raising your niece?"

"You upped the ante a bit by skipping ahead." Drew laughed and then sadness flashed across his face. "I can answer in one word—drugs."

Lainie responded kindly. "That's all you need to say. It's a word that has ruined more lives than I care to count. I don't think there is a family anywhere that hasn't been touched by that word—somehow."

Drew nodded. "Thanks. But, you know, that word doesn't always end badly. I feel so blessed to have Kasey in my life. She is as precious as any daughter. I've never married because a lot of my dates couldn't understand my first responsibility was to Kasey."

"Then I say you are the lucky one to escape any relationship that didn't understand."

Drew smiled. "I think so, too."

LAINIE USUALLY RODE her horse, Shadow, during team practice, but today she decided to stay on the ground to be near Kasey.

She motioned for Kasey to follow her to the arena fence as Megan and Cassy mounted and rode toward a group of their teammates.

"We have a team of ten riders. Everyone trailers their horse to lessons and practice. Only Megan and Cassy keep their horses here." She noticed Kasey's puzzled face. "I'll explain later."

Lainie climbed up and found a seat on the top rail of the fence; she motioned for Kasey to do the same. "Ok, gather around!"

Kasey almost fell off her perch. For a little person, Lainie could sure yell.

"Welcome, everyone. I want to introduce you to Kasey Jones. She just moved here with her uncle and she'll be a Junior at Appleridge High."

A chorus of, "Welcome! Hi, Kasey!" followed.

Kasey smiled shyly and gave a little wave.

"I'll give you a few minutes to warm up your horses and then we'll do a few exercises, a few jumps, and end with our latest pattern."

The girls rode away in pairs—talking, smiling.

A few parents stuck around to watch. Others unhitched their trucks and took off for a quick trip to town.

"Do you have riding experience?" Lainie looked at Kasey. She noticed the cowboy boots right away.

"Yes. I worked at a barn and was paid in lessons. I loved taking lessons because I rode a lot of different horses."

"English or Western?" Lainie wanted to keep conversation flowing. She was also interested.

"Both. I wanted to learn everything. I don't think there really is much difference. Is there?" She glanced sideways at Lainie.

"You are absolutely correct. Good horsemanship is good horsemanship regardless of the saddle."

"I noticed your team rides in both, so I wondered."

"We also have a young Amish boy who rides with us occasionally and he rides on a bareback pad."

"Wow." Kasey liked Lainie's easygoing nature.

"So, do you want to help out here?"

Kasey didn't answer right away. At the last barn, she was the hired labor instead of being a part of the group of girls boarding their horses at the farm. They never became friends. She hoped for more at Lainie's, but, apparently, she was just potential labor.

Lainie noticed the disappointment. "I'm not looking for a hired hand. I require all the girls to do their own work; I just thought you wanted to be around horses."

"Oh, I do. I really do." Kasey felt a twinge of regret.

"Well, as you know, being around horses requires a lot of work."

"I do. I'm sorry, Miss Lainie. I'm not afraid of work. But—"

"But you also want to be part of our group, of course." Lainie added, "Let's get this practice started."

Lainie hopped off the fence and motioned for Kasey to follow her into the middle of the arena. She directed the girls in a few exercises and then a game of follow the leader. Kasey helped her set up a few jumps and other obstacles. Finally, they were ready to practice their pattern to music and Lainie and Kasey removed the obstacles and found seats on the fence again.

"Wow, they're really good." Kasey couldn't stop herself from feeling excited. "It looks like fun!"

"Now, those two comments are music to my ears. Thanks!" Lanie turned off the music and motioned for the riders to ride toward the fence.

"That's all for today. You're welcome to ride in the pasture and jump a few of the log jumps. Be careful, and remember, no racing. If you need to leave, take plenty of time to cool down your horse. I have water in the barn for both humans and horses. Stay hydrated, please."

She looked at Kasey. "You're welcome to stick around and meet some of the girls. I'm sorry I don't have an extra horse for you to ride. I've been on the lookout for a nice lesson horse."

"Thanks, I may walk around. I'd like to meet everyone but maybe not all of them today."

As Kasey walked to the barn for a drink of water, Megan rode up on Starlight. "It's good to see you. I'm glad you came." Megan dismounted.

"Thanks. Your horse is nice. Is she a Quarter Horse?"

"She is."

Kasey lifted her hand and looked at Megan for permission. When Megan nodded, Kasey stroked Starlight's neck. "Lainie said you keep your horse here."

Megan motioned to an older farmhouse up the drive from the barn. "I live here. Lainie leases the barn from my parents."

Kasey sighed. Another rich girl. They never seemed to have much use for her.

Megan continued, "My sister is in vet school, and after her horse died, I couldn't keep Starlight here by herself and Dad didn't want to buy another horse and get into what he calls the horse business again." Megan laughed and decided to continue. "Cassy and I boarded our horses at Jennie's place. You probably haven't met her yet, but then I moved Starlight here because it was easier since I live here and Cassy and Treasure came with us."

Kasey couldn't quite follow Megan's explanation and Megan noticed. "We have plenty of time to catch up. Right now, just know you're welcome."

Kasey relaxed and continued to walk with Megan and Starlight to the barn.

"Do you need any help?" Kasey was eager to do something— anything.

"I'm good; thanks." Megan took off Starlight's bridle and handed it to Kasey, then she put on Starlight's halter and tied her in the aisle. "She stroked the mare's neck affectionately before continuing. She then unfastened the back cinch and then the front cinch, and slid the heavy saddle and blanket off the mare's back. "Follow me; I'll show you the tack room."

Kasey noticed how easily Megan carried the Western saddle. She followed Megan to a neat tack room, carrying the bridle.

Megan gave a little grunt and swung the saddle up onto an empty saddle rack. She noticed Kasey scanning the little room. "Lainie likes to keep everything neat and organized—as you can see." Bridles hung neatly hanging from special hooks. One wall had several shelves for supplies.

"Do you want me to wipe off Starlight's bit?" Kasey walked over to a small sink and reached for a paper towel.

"Yeah, thanks! Then it goes here." Megan pointed to an empty rack.

Megan hung the saddle pad on a bar under the saddle.

Kasey's stomach growled. Embarrassed, she wrapped one arm around her middle as she held the bridle with the other hand.

"I'm hungry, too!" Megan laughed.

Cassy walked into the tack room carrying Treasure's small English jumping saddle across one arm.

Megan couldn't resist teasing. "Showoff. That's it—I'm getting myself an English saddle."

Cassy grinned, "You don't want to be Megan the cowgirl anymore?"

They both took off their riding helmets and placed them on the top shelf.

"Do you ride?" Cassy looked at Kasey. Her smile was friendly.

"I've taken a few lessons—both English and Western."

Megan couldn't resist. "Which do you like better—English or Western?"

Kasey hesitated. "I guess it depends on what I'm doing. I think I would like an English saddle to take a few jumps like the team did today but a Western saddle if I was going on a long trail ride."

Cassy put two thumbs up. "She's a smart girl, Megan. That was a very savvy answer."

Kasey started to relax when she realized she wasn't being tested; they were just being friendly.

"Next week we're all staying and having a picnic, but today, Lainie, Megan, and I are going to the Bake & Shake for lunch. Do you want to come with us?" Cassy looked at Kasey.

Megan searched her jean pockets looking for money. "All I have is a five but that should be enough for a hot dog and Coke."

Cassy didn't have pockets in her riding tights. "I think that's probably what I have. I need to look in my car. And why are you laughing?" She pretended to glare at Megan.

"I'm laughing because I have pockets and you in your fancy English tights don't. I think being a cowgirl has its advantages."

Kasey was enjoying the banter between the two friends. "She pulled a five from her jeans. Drew gave me a five this morning. I really need to find a job."

Lainie caught Kasey's comment as she walked into the tack room. "What kind of job are you looking for?"

"Oh, it would be great to do something with horses, but I also clean houses and babysit." Kasey realized she was sharing more information than she planned on sharing. Somehow, she trusted these new friends. *Please, God, don't let them hurt me.*

"I'll keep my ears open. You probably don't want anything with too many hours. Right?"

"No, not during school. Every time we move, it takes me a while to—" She was definitely sharing too much information.

"It's hard to find your place in a new school with new teachers." Megan added, "But I think you'll like Appleridge High, and besides, my mom is a teacher if you ever need a little help."

"Thanks. I don't want anything to happen to my grade point average. I'll need scholarships for college."

"What do you want to study?" Cassy was interested.

Lainie interrupted before Kasey could answer. "Hey, let's go, we can talk while we eat."

They turned Starlight, Treasure, and Shadow out into the pasture and climbed into Lainie's cherry red truck.

"Wow, nice truck." Kasey settled into the leather back seat of the two-door Silverado.

"Lainie will need to share the story of how she happened to get this truck. It's quite a story." Megan climbed in beside Kasey and gave Cassy the front passenger seat.

"Don't worry, Kasey, we'll bore you with all our stories sooner or later," Lainie commented as she started the engine.

THE BAKE & SHAKE buzzed with the Saturday lunch crowd. The barn girls waited a few minutes before snagging a small high-top table with four tall stools.

"Have you been in here yet?" Cassy looked at Kasey.

"Only once when I stopped for an ice cream cone. It's a neat place."

Megan pulled out a stool. "And one of our favorites."

Lainie nodded to the menu board. "It looks like a Coney dog, chips, and a drink is the special. All for five bucks."

"That's almost always the special and I'm glad." Megan waved her wrinkled five-dollar bill.

Kasey joined in, waving her money.

Cassy got up. "I'll place our order. Do we want our dogs all the way?"

Three heads nodded.

"Regular or BBQ chips?" Cassy waited.

BBQ was the reply from everyone.

"Drinks?"

This time the response was varied with one Pepsi, two Mountain Dews, and one diet Pepsi with cherries added.

Kasey laughed as Cassy recited the order, pretending she was English paid staff. "And for Miss Lainie, we will be most happy to add cherries to the diet soft drink."

Lainie enjoyed the banter and especially enjoyed seeing Kasey relaxed and having fun.

"Kasey, since I interrupted you before you told us what you wanted to study, I'll ask now." Lainie paused for effect. "What do you want to be when you grow up?"

Cassy quickly place their order and hopped on a stool ready to join in the discussion. "I just finished my first year of college and I'm still asking myself that question!"

Kasey took a deep breath. "I want to be a veterinarian." There! She said it out loud and it was the very first time she shared that dream with anyone.

"Good for you!" Lainie encouraged. "There you go, Megan; if your dad is looking for some help, tell him about Kasey."

Kasey looked at Megan. "Your dad is a vet?"

"Yup, and my sister, Belinda, is in vet school at the University of Florida. She's coming home to spend a few weeks this summer. She hasn't been home since last summer. I'm anxious to see her."

Kasey suddenly felt inadequate. "Wow. Is that what you're going to do, too?"

"Nope, definitely not! I want to go into graphic arts or teach like my mom. Or maybe, teach graphic arts." Megan thought that was funny.

Lainie observed Kasey's expression as she listened to the conversation. Kasey seemed jealous—or something.

"Hey, there's our order." Cassy popped off her stool.

"I'll help." Megan followed.

Kasey watched them go. Lainie spoke. "Someday, ask Megan to tell you about her experience last summer. She followed a dream and it didn't work out very well and now she's trying to find her way again. Everyone has their own struggles. I'll tell you about mine someday."

Kasey didn't know how to respond. She chose honesty. "Sometimes I'm so envious I can hardly stand myself. I guess I shouldn't be. You're right; I don't know."

"We never know. We also never consider the many things in our lives to be thankful for until we start being thankful." She smiled. "I didn't know about being thankful until I moved to Appleridge. The next thing I knew, I was going to church, something I never thought I would do, and making friends. Real friends."

"I've learned not to trust people who are called friends. I guess I've never had real friends."

Lainie watched as Cassy and Megan carefully balanced trays of food and drinks as they walked to the table. "You do now."

Made in the USA
Columbia, SC
22 September 2021

45124666R00217